HELP WANTED

"Sam, we've got a job for you."

"Outdoor job?"

"Outdoor job," Herrington confirmed. "Up north on the reservation."

Sam scowled as he asked, "Doing what?"

Now Brayton took over. "Sam, I got me a trouble-making Indian up there name of Joe Potatoes. I want you to hunt him up and take him up in the mountains with about six quarts of whiskey. Don't bother feeding him because he'll be so drunk he won't eat. When he's passed out for the tenth time or so, just take his clothes, blankets and his flint and steel. Pneumonia will do the rest, I reckon."

"With what kind of money, Con?" Sam asked calmly.

"Would a couple of hundred dollars do it, Sam?"

"Yes, a couple of hundred would do. It sounds like pretty small potatoes."

LUKE SHORT
THE PRIMROSE TRY

BANTAM BOOKS

TORONTO • NEW YORK • LONDON • SYDNEY • AUCKLAND

THE PRIMROSE TRY
A Bantam Book / February 1967
2nd printing . . . June 1984

ISBN 0-553-24125-7

Published simultaneously in the United States
and Canada

Bantam Books are published by Bantam Books, Inc.
Its trademark, consisting of the words "Bantam
Books" and the portrayal of a rooster, is Registered
in U.S. Patent and Trademark Office and in other
countries. Marca Registrada. Bantam Books, Inc.,
666 Fifth Avenue, New York, New York 10103.

PRINTED IN THE UNITED STATES OF AMERICA

H   11 10 9 8 7 6 5 4 3 2

Chapter 1

REGULAR passengers on the lone coach of the Primrose & Northern mixed train knew that the water stop at the Long Reach tank was always a short one, so they did not bother this night to get out and stretch their legs.

To make sure that no one else did, the brakeman came through the half-filled coach where a third of the passengers were asleep, intoning quietly, "Just a water stop, folks."

The two men seated beside each other both looked at the brakeman, and then when he was past them the small dark man next to the window said, "He's new."

The other man, older and also dressed in clean range clothes, said dryly, "He's the only thing new on this wreck of a railroad."

This was to be the last conversation they were destined to have with each other.

Outside the car, now quiet, they could hear the sound of a horse walking slowly down the length of the car in the chill September night. Morton Schaeffer, the man by the window, turned his head to look out, but of course could see nothing because of the reflection on the window of the coach's overhead lamps. Deputy Marshal Newford did not look out, but lazily eyed the retreating figure of the brakeman. Then the horse stopped walking.

A second later the roar of a shotgun erupted out in the night. Simultaneously came the sound of shattering glass. Mort Schaeffer caught the shot full in the face. He was dead before the sound reached his brain. The force of the shot drove him into Marshal Newford, who, with a strangled cry, raised his left hand to his left eye.

A lone man in the seat ahead of the pair, jumped to his feet, turned, saw Schaeffer's mangled face, and fainted. By the time the brakeman had run back down the aisle, Schaeffer had rolled to the floor and Newford was trying to staunch the flow of blood from his own left eye. It was only then that the passengers, some talking, some shouting, were becoming aware of what had happened.

Three weeks later the same train and the same coach brought Deputy U.S. Marshal Sam Kennery into the big brick station at Junction City, this new state's capital. Kennery was not aware that his seat on the night train from the north was only one removed from the seat where Schaeffer had been ambushed. Kennery was a stranger to this country and he did not even know that Morton Schaeffer had been killed.

As the train ground to a halt beside the station platform, four women, talked out after a long journey, came down the aisle, eager to be greeted on the dark platform by their menfolk and children. Sam Kennery remained seated until they were past, then rose, yawned, and stretched his more than six feet of hard-muscled frame. Afterwards he reached down, brushed the newspaper off his dust-colored Stetson and restored its proper center crease with big, long-fingered hands.

He was a man of thirty, dressed in a duck jacket over a calico shirt, and the commoner's boots he wore held a dull polish which in itself was a mild deception, since they were seldom polished. His face, however, held no deception; it was lean, weather-burned a few shades darker than his pale, thick, short-cut hair. His very blue eyes held a veiled alertness above a thin nose that a ham-handed Army surgeon had reset imperfectly after it was broken. Its ridge had a slight jog near the bridge, and Kennery, who looked in a mirror only to shave, had seen it often enough to forget it. His mouth was wide above a deeply cleft chin which had a suggestion of stubbornness about it.

He reached up now and lifted down the lashed blanket roll from the overhead rack, picked up his saddle from the floor, and then moved down the now deserted car to step onto a poorly lighted platform. A hack, whose legend "Prairie Hotel" painted on its side was lit by the carriage lamps, was drawn up to the edge of the platform. When Kennery moved toward it, the driver moved toward him to take his blanket roll and saddle. As Kennery handed them to him, he said, "Leave them behind the desk. I'll walk."

"We'll have them in your room for you, sir."

Kennery waited until the hack had pulled out before he stepped off the platform and headed toward the town.

The newly finished State House, some fifteen blocks away and perched high on a river bluff, was impossible to mistake in the light of the night's half moon, and now Sam headed for it. Instead of traveling the main street, he cut off to the west, picked up the residential section, and in turn was picked up by a dog that, after barking, passed him on to a dog in the next block.

He was remembering now the letter from Marshal Wilbarth: "Come to the State House when you get in, and on your way keep out of sight." It had been a strange letter, a communication—or rather, lack of communication—that baffled and irritated him. His own boss, Marshal Tom Freed, had been almost as uncommunicative. "We're loaning you to Wilbarth. He'll be in touch with you," Freed had said. When Kennery had protested that Junction City was not in their judicial district, Freed had said, "What do you care? Wilbarth wants a new face, one that isn't known." Further than that, Freed refused to discuss why Wilbarth wanted him. He would say only that the commissioner approved the loan of a deputy to Wilbarth.

The capitol building, as Kennery saw it from the curving drive through the capitol grounds, was a massive and imposing three-story stone affair, topped by a gilded dome. Lamps were burning in a few of the second-story offices, and only then did Kennery remember that the legislature was in session with its night committee meetings. Only four years ago Junction City was the territorial capital, and the first act of the legislature had been to appropriate money for the new capitol building. It was, Sam thought, as he mounted the steps, a place that would impress the millionaire mine owner as much as the lowliest line rider of this newest state.

Once inside the building, Sam tramped down the marble-floored corridor in search of the basement stairs, according to Freed's instruction. So far, he reflected, he had been seen only by the hack driver and five over-protective dogs.

He went down the stairs and walked along the lower corridor to the room under the governor's office, with a closed door bearing the legend, "U.S. Marshal." He could see a pencil of light beneath the door, and when he knocked he was told to enter.

Kennery stepped into a long narrow room and halted abruptly at the sight of two men seated across from each other at a long table that held a tall lamp. They were both in shirt sleeves and a white drift of paper between them told Kennery he had interrupted a conference. Even their expressions told him that. The younger of the two men had a faintly truculent look on his narrow face and Sam noted that he wore a black patch over his left eye held in place by a ribbon that circled his head of dark hair. This would not be Wilbarth, or else Freed would have mentioned he was blind in one eye. Kennery's attention shifted to the bigger and older man and he said quietly, "Evening, Marshal. You wrote me. Name's Kennery."

Marshal Wilbarth rose and pushed his chair back. When he was erect Sam saw that he was a huge man, wide and tall. His hair was as white as his full mustaches, capping a face that could have been carved out of the same marble that floored the corridors. It was a pale face, stern as a deacon's, and would not, Sam guessed, smile easily. His eyes were gray and chill, but when he moved towards Sam and extended a huge hand, his voice was friendly, almost gentle. "Glad you're here, Kennery. The train must have been late."

"It was on time. I walked." They shook hands, and with his free hand the marshal gestured towards his companion, saying, "Meet Anse Newford. He's one of my deputies." Newford rose now and he and Sam shook hands across the table.

"Notice anyone hanging around the depot?" the marshal asked.

"Didn't look. Was I supposed to?"

Wilbarth sighed and said, "I don't reckon. Sit down. Take off your coat if you want."

"If you mean was I followed, I wasn't," Sam said.

"That's what I wanted to know." Wilbarth said dryly.

Keeping his coat on, Sam sat down in the barrel chair half facing Wilbarth, who was still standing. Then the marshal said with quiet bluntness, "I expected an older man."

Sam said just as quietly and bluntly, "That's one department where I can't accommodate you, Marshal."

Wilbarth accepted this unsmilingly, but the hint of a grin touched Newford's shadowed face.

Now Wilbarth seated himself. "Did Freed tell you why you're loaned to us?"

Sam shook his head. "Your letter didn't tell me anything, so Freed didn't. He probably figured that was the way you wanted it."

Wilbarth seemed not to have heard, for his expression of resigned disappointment did not change. He only said to Newford, "Tell him, Anse."

In an unemotional tone of voice, Newford told of bringing in a witness by train, and of the ambush at the water tank in which Schaeffer lost his life and he himself lost his eye.

"Witness to what?" Kennery asked when Newford had finished.

A glint of appreciation came and went in Newford's good eye, and then his glance shifted to the marshal as if he were deferring to the older man.

Wilbarth cleared his throat. "For the past six years a Texas drover by the name of Big Dad Herrington has had the beef contract for the Indians on the reservation up north. The Indian agent's name up there is Con Brayton. Between the two of them they've milked the government out of tens of thousands of dollars. Herrington would drive up there and deliver, say fifteen hundred head. Brayton would pay him for three thousand. Herrington would return him half the difference. In six years that came to a pretty wide chunk of money."

"Schaeffer knew this, and that's why he was killed?" Sam asked.

Wilbarth nodded. "Schaeffer always received the herds and kept the tally. He was an agency employee—a white man married to an Indian."

"Was Schaeffer in on it?" Sam asked.

Wilbarth pointed a finger at Newford, and at this signal his deputy took up the story. "No, he wasn't, but he got suspicious towards the end. Brayton would order the herd split up into a dozen small herds to be scattered all over the reservation. He'd appoint Indian herders, and even if they could count they wouldn't bother to. Brayton claimed that the grass for miles around the agency was grazed out. What he really wanted was to scatter the herds so no accurate count could be made, and Schaeffer suspicioned this. He still wouldn't have talked if it hadn't been for one thing. Brayton had a taste for Indian women, and he made the mistake of trying for Schaeffer's wife."

Wilbarth interrupted. "That's when Schaeffer wrote us. I sent Anse up there and he pieced together what he just told you. Herrington and Brayton were indicted for criminal fraud. Their trial was scheduled for two and a half weeks ago. Schaeffer, of course, was the star witness, and Anse was bringing him down for the trial. Everything looked fine until they stopped to take on water at the Long Reach tank. Since then we've had no case against them. The judge granted us a delay, but Brayton's and Herrington's lawyers are howling for the indictment to be quashed, and the judge can't hold out forever."

Sam shifted in his chair. "Where are Brayton and Herrington now?"

Anse Newford said sourly, "Out on bond. The judge ordered them not to leave the district."

"They're here then?"

"Oh, no," Newford said bitterly. "They're down in Primrose. That's about as far away from this office as they could get and still stay in the district."

Sam frowned in puzzlement. "You want me to go up to the reservation and get more evidence for you?"

"I do not," Wilbarth said flatly, almost angrily. "Why hunt up evidence of fraud when you can turn up evidence of murder? I want that pair hanged."

Sam only nodded and Anse Newford said softly, "That's a large order, Mr. Sam Kennery. Both Brayton and Herrington have solid gold alibis. They were in a Primrose bar about nine hours by train from where Schaeffer was killed."

Sam grimaced in sympathy and looked at Wilbarth. "What's my move, Marshal?"

"I wish I knew, but I don't," Wilbarth said wearily. He leaned forward and continued. "All I can tell you is that both men know all my regular deputies and special deputies. Brayton's and Herrington's attorneys are in the judge's chambers every other day complaining that their clients are being persecuted by my office. The judge warns me so often that I'm helpless. You're not."

Anse spoke up. "One thing might help you, Kennery. Brayton and Herrington are prime boozers and wenchers."

Sam had already gathered that, and now he asked, "I'm to use my own name?"

The marshal nodded. "They won't have heard of you."

"Who am I? What do I do?"

The marshal looked at Newford, who only shrugged, and Wilbarth's chill glance shuttled back to Sam. "This is the best we could come up with, Kennery. You won't talk about yourself, so that means you've got something in your past that's bad. You're in Primrose waiting for a friend to join you. If you can do it safely, hint that this friend is serving time in the pen, say for a bullion robbery."

"And why did I pick Primrose as the place to meet him?"

"They'll figure that out for themselves. Consolidated at Primrose is the biggest mine in the state. There are three or four others in the Raft River Range behind Primrose. That means gold and payrolls. Make out that you've come to where the money is."

Newford snapped his fingers then as if remembering something. He rose, moved over to one of the two roll-top desks at the rear of the room, opened the drawer to get something from it, and returned to the table. Still standing, he dropped a buckskin pouch on the table in front of Kennery, and by the sound of the muted clink of coins Sam knew this was money for expenses.

Wilbarth said, "When you run out of that get in touch with us."

"How?"

"Write me," Wilbarth said. "Never show up here unless you've arranged a night appointment with me."

Kennery nodded. "What else should I know?"

"Just one more thing," the marshal said. "Sheriff Morehead in Primrose knows you're coming. He'll get in touch with you. Trust him, he's a good man." Wilbarth rose. "The Primrose train leaves at six-thirty every morning. Be on it tomorrow." He extended his hand and Kennery rose and took it.

"I don't have to tell you that we won't be there to see you off," Wilbarth said.

Across the table, Newford got up and watched Sam pocket the buckskin sack. Newford said, "When things look rough, just remember there's a new grave in the cemetery north of town. It holds a man with no face."

"I'll remember a man with one eye too."

Newford gave him a faint twisted smile. "Yes, there's that too," he said quietly.

Outside in the night Kennery passed the last of the newly planted trees on the capitol grounds and took the dirt street that slanted down toward the center of town. No wonder Freed had waited to let Wilbarth explain his reason for requesting a special deputy, Kennery thought. It was the kind of situation that anyone connected with a marshal's office hated. No evidence and iron-clad alibis and a wicked pres-

sure of time. Once the judge was forced to set a trial date
and Brayton and Herrington were freed for lack of evidence,
the two men would disappear, he was sure. How much time
did that leave him? That, too, was an unknown, he thought.

He moved into the business district, passed dark stores
and lighted noisy saloons until he came to the Prairie House,
a big brick hotel that was the town's best. He resisted the
impulse to stop at the saloon off the entry lobby. If the
watchers Wilbarth had mentioned were not wild imaginings,
the first place they would watch would be the hotels' saloons.

He registered under the incurious gaze of the night clerk,
took his key, climbed to his room, found his bag and saddle
already there, and went to bed.

Chapter 2

IT was a sunny morning with a hint of October bite in the
air when Kennery stepped out onto the platform of Primrose's frame depot. He moved out of the slow traffic of passengers and slacked his blanket roll and saddle onto the
platform. Looking around him, he saw that the town was
built at the very base of the foothills of the towering Raft
River range. Against the foothills and within easy sight were
the hoist frames and mill stacks of the mines and mills that
had made Primrose one of the richest mining areas in the
state.

Kennery spotted the hotel hack at the far end of the platform and, lifting his saddle and blanket roll, he headed for
it. To the hack driver of the Primrose House, who took his
gear and stored it, he was just another cattleman dressed in
range clothes and half-boots with a worn duck jacket over
his cotton shirt. A worn holster sagged below the bottom of
the jacket and worn leather gloves were stuffed in the right-
hand pocket.

As he had done last night, Kennery instructed the driver
to take his gear into the lobby because he wanted to walk.
The train pulled ahead toward the mill yards, and now,

because he had been seated on the mountain side of the car, he got his first close look at the Raft River, which they had roughly paralleled on the way up from the capital. Kennery could see that the rushing river bisected the town and this side of the river seemed to belong to the mines and miners. A dingy saloon whose sign read "Miners Rest" was the largest building in a block of shabby saloons, cafés, and dance halls. Walking down toward the bridge that spanned the boiling Raft River, Kennery passed many of the miners in rough clothes, big boots, and round-crowned wool hats that seemed to be their working uniform. Big, high-wheeled ore wagons empty and full made up most of the street's traffic.

Crossing the wooden bridge that put him on the south bank of the river, Kennery knew immediately that he was in a different kind of town. Grant Street, the main thoroughfare, was wide and was lined by tie rails. Many of the buildings were brick or stone, and had wooden canopies over the plank walk. Buggies, wagons, and saddle horses were clustered at the tie rail while the lazy midmorning wagon and horse traffic moved along the street.

It was, Kennery thought, a substantial-seeming cowtown. Tall cottonwoods shaded the residential part of town, and as he moved up the street he saw that the two-story white painted Primrose House with its wide veranda running the length of the building was the most impressive structure on the street. As he approached the steps he saw that a couple of dozen barrel chairs, some occupied by idlers, were scattered the length of the veranda. Up the street he could see the livery stable with its wide arched doorway. This part of the town was his kind of town, he thought, as he mounted the steps and entered the lobby.

The big carpeted lobby held a scattering of horsehair and leather-covered sofas and easy chairs, and as Kennery crossed to the desk he glanced through the closed glass-paned doors into the dining room and saw waitresses preparing the tables for the noon meal. A gray-faced, middle-aged man stood behind the counter, his back to the key rack, and gave Kennery a civil "Good morning." Sam returned his greeting and then said, "You have weekly rates here?"

"Certainly," the clerk replied. "Going to stay with us a while?"

Sam wished he could really answer that question, but he only said, "A week anyway." As he was registering he heard

men's laughter behind him and when he had signed his name
he turned to find its source. At the far end of the lobby on
the up-street side were open double doors that showed a
portion of the long mahogany bar and its glistening back
mirror.

The clerk spoke to his back then. "This saddle and blanket
roll would be yours, wouldn't they, Mr. Kennery?"

Sam turned and nodded. The clerk had walked out from
behind the counter, and now he picked up the blanket roll
with one hand and the saddle, held by its horn, with the
other. He was headed for the stairs beside the dining-room
door and Sam spoke quickly. "I can find my room if you'll
give me my key."

The clerk halted, put down the saddle and blanket roll,
reached in his pocket, and held out the key. Sam took it,
lifted his saddle by the horn and slung it over his shoulder,
then stooped down for the blanket roll.

"Thank you," the clerk said quietly. Sam nodded. The
clerk understood that Sam was deferring to his age, and
was grateful.

As Sam climbed the stairs he wondered if he might get
another look at the register, for Herrington's and Brayton's
names had not been on the page he signed. But it would be
foolish to try for that second look and arouse curiosity, he
thought, for hadn't Wilbarth said both men were staying at
the Primrose House?

Once in his spare, clean corner room, he washed up and
then returned to the lobby and went into the bar. He saw
immediately that affectionate attention had gone into the
planning of this room. The bar itself was long and solid and
the brass of its rails and the spittoons were shining. On
either side of the lobby entrance were two round baize-
covered tables, and the chairs pulled up to them were barrel
chairs like those on the veranda; these were polished by the
pants' seats of hundreds of gamblers. The walls were paneled
with a dark wood and held many photographs, some of horses,
some of mines and mills.

At the table near the rear Sam could see in the bar mirror,
four men were seated, playing cards. Three other cowmen
were bellied up to the bar down the room and they interrupted their conversation long enough to regard him with
a friendly curiosity. The bartender moved away from them
and came up to ask Sam's pleasure. He was a red-faced, red-

haired man past middle age, and when he spoke Sam guessed that he was English or Irish.

Sam ordered his drink, and while the bartender was pouring it, Sam said, "Nice place you have here."

"Thank you. It's the closest thing to a club we've got."

Sam pointed to the bar mirror and remarked, "With that chunk of glass you can't have many fights in here."

"They are not allowed here, sir. We move them out into the street." He turned then and went back down the bar.

Sam drank his whiskey and was surprised at its golden smoothness. A boom of laughter came from one of the card players. Sam seemed to be looking at his glass, but he covertly studied the four men in the mirror. The man with his back to the wall had a face that, to Sam, was a type. It was a thin, still, bleach-eyed face, the face of a touchy, mean Texan in his middle thirties. He was the type that raised hell in every northern trail town. Certainly the laugh hadn't come from him.

It was the man seated facing the bar that interested Sam. He was the only hatless man in the room, with pale hair so closely clipped that he looked bald. In contrast, his bushy eyebrows were almost the size of small mustaches and they seemed to hood his eyes. From what Sam could see of him from the waist up, he was a big man with wide shoulders and meaty arms under a checked shirt, over which he wore an open vest. The face was a puzzle. It was heavy, but the nose was small and aquiline, the shape of a parrot's beak, with a knife-like ridge. The mouth was wide and loose-lipped, but was now pursed in concentration. As Sam watched, the man played a card, and again came a bellow of laughter that was beginning to get on Sam's nerves. Big Dad Herrington? Sam wondered.

Now men began coming in from the street entrance for their before-dinner drink. The card game broke up, and now Sam caught a glimpse of the big man as he moved toward the bar with the others. He had a vast belly topping short, stubby legs, yet the length of his mammoth torso gave him a height well over six feet. The card players each had a quick shot of whiskey, then moved past Sam and disappeared through the door to the lobby. In the bar mirror Sam saw them cut across the lobby toward the dining room.

Could the first man, the Texan, be Con Brayton? If so, he and Herrington made a formidable-looking pair. Sam had his second drink, paid, and then moved out into the lobby, his hunger whetted by the liquor.

The dining-room doors were open now and a pretty Junoesque girl with her blond hair banded on top of her head was in frowning conversation with a younger girl in the white uniform of a waitress. As Sam moved toward the doors, heading for the hat rack beside them, he heard the younger girl say vehemently, "I don't care, Louise! I won't serve that disgusting beast any more."

"All right, Tenney," Louise said with a sigh. "Trade with Mary." Then Louise looked up at Sam approaching and smiled. "How are you, Mr. Kennery? Are you alone?"

At Sam's nod, Louise gestured, "Just follow her."

Sam did so, eyeing the trim figure of the girl ahead of him. As she drew out a chair and turned to face him, Sam saw the single ring on her left hand. Dregs of anger were still in her eyes. She gave him a practiced smile which wrinkled her small nose in an engaging way and it brought a smile from him. He sat down, and while she poured a glass of water for him he studied the menu chalked in large letters on the blackboard by the kitchen door.

"The liver is very good today."

Sam glanced up at her. "Liver is never good. Why do you say that?"

"Because my mother cooked it," the girl said tartly, flushing a little.

"That's family loyalty for you," Sam observed.

Tenney looked at him carefully, sizing him up with eyes of so dark a violet they seemed almost black. A fleeting smile started to form on her lips and she suppressed it.

"I'll make a deal with you," she said. "I'll bring the liver. If you don't like it, don't eat it and I'll bring you the stew."

Sam hesitated, pretending to ponder this. "What if I eat it all and don't like it? Will you bring me the stew?"

"More than you can eat." She turned then and headed for the kitchen. "Tenney," Louise had called her. Strange name, and one Sam had never heard before, but oddly attractive.

He looked about the room now and saw that a scattering of diners—all men—had moved into the room while he was talking with Tenney. His attention, however, rested again on the four men who had first come in. He could hear the big man's periodic laugh over the murmur of talk in the room, and he decided that it rang as false as an old maid's giggle. An easy laugh was always suspect in his book.

Tenney returned almost immediately with the liver and rings of onion, with a side dish of sweet potatoes half drowned in a brown sugar syrup. Sam was appalled at the combination and he looked from the plate to Tenney. "Don't watch me. Go get me some coffee, please."

When she left, Sam picked up knife and fork and slashed at the liver, expecting the usual boot-sole texture. Instead, it cut like butter and he took the first bite. It was something new for him. It had been cooked with some herb that had diminished the liver flavor, blending with it and dominating it.

When Tenney returned with his coffee she approached his table with a faint smile on her face. Halting beside the table, she put down the coffee and said, "Do I take it back?"

"Try it and I'll hit you," Sam said. "Is there more?"

She gave a low throaty chuckle. "All you can eat."

Sam pushed his now empty plate toward her and said, "Your name's Tenney and there's a disgusting beast in this room, isn't there?"

Surprise washed over the girl's face and she said, "Yes to both your questions, but how did you know?"

"I overheard you talking with Louise. Can you point out the beast to me?"

"Why should I?" Tenney asked cautiously.

"Because the daughter of anyone who can cook like this deserves protection."

Tenney laughed shortly. "And needs it."

Sam said nothing, waiting for her to decide whether or not she would tell him. Finally, as she reached down for his plate, she said, "Don't look, but you see those four men over at the wall table behind me?"

"I've already looked."

"The fat one."

"I call him laughing Johnnie," Sam said dryly. "Who is he?"

Tenney said grimly, "Big Dad Herrington from big, big Texas."

"What's he doing here?" Sam asked casually, hiding the satisfaction of his right guess.

"Out on bail for cheating the government out of a lot of money."

"Why is he a beast, Tenney? Oh, my name is Sam Kennery. Yours is Tenney. All right, Tenney, why is he a beast?"

Tenney shook his head as she tried to dismiss a memory, then she said with quiet anger, "My mother and I live in this building. I have to lock my room when she isn't with me. Does that give you some idea?"

"Who owns this place, and why isn't Big Dad thrown out?"

"Louise's father owns it—Mr. Selby. And he doesn't know. You won't tell him, will you?" she asked quickly.

"What's against it?" Sam challenged. "No girl should have to put up with that."

"Promise you won't tell him. He's got a heart that's barely ticking. He'd try to kill Herrington, and Herrington would only kill him. He—"

Her head swiveled, and Sam glanced from her to see Louise Selby halting beside the table.

"Everything all right, Tenney?" she asked.

It was Sam who answered her. "I'm new here, miss. I was just asking my way around."

"I'll tell you anything you'd like to know, Mr. Kennery, but Tenney has customers to wait on."

Tenney fled before Sam could tell her that he really didn't want the second helping. Louise Selby looked at him and smiled. "She is pretty, isn't she?"

"I didn't notice," Sam said with a straight face.

Louise Selby chuckled. "Of course not," she said. "Nobody ever does." And she left.

Sam finished his pie and coffee, and while he was drinking the last of the coffee, Herrington and his companions got up and moved towards the door, stopping at the high desk beside the door to pay Louise Selby for their meal. Sam finished his coffee and followed them to the desk. Halting in front of it, he put down a coin. "That was a good meal, Miss Louise," he volunteered.

"Thank you. I'll tell the cook."

"You know those men that just went out the door?"

"Two of them," Louise said. "They're staying with us."

"That thin fellow with the light eyes that always looks mad—I think I've seen him somewhere."

"That would be Seeley Carnes. He's the trail boss for the big man, Mr. Herrington."

Sam shook his head. "Doesn't ring a bell, but thanks."

Out in the lobby, Sam got his hat and started for the stairs. He heard a woman's voice call softly, "Mr. Kennery."

He turned to see Tenney, a small tray in her hand, coming

toward him. She halted before him and said, "You won't say anything to Mr. Selby?"

"Nothing but hello," Sam reassured her.

She smiled her thanks and headed for the bar to fill a drink order for one of the diners inside.

Sam started for the stairs, now feeling some puzzlement over what Louise Selby had told him. Where was Con Brayton? he wondered. Seeley Carnes had undoubtedly been called as a witness for the defense at the trial and that explained his presence. For the present he had Herrington to work on, and that meant Seeley too, although he had no notion of how he could meet them. It could be simple enough to invite himself into a poker game with them when the game was open. Still, that would be only the beginning, for a poker-game acquaintance was one of the most fleeting of associations, and anything but friendly in an open game. He would simply have to watch for an opening to meet them.

In his room he went over to the corner where his saddle was stowed, lifted it, and slung it over his shoulder, then headed back downstairs. He had no notion if he would need a horse or not, but simple caution told him a mount should be available.

At the livery stable he spent a pleasant hour looking over the horses that were for hire and trying them, and finally he chose a big bay gelding that looked like a stayer. Before he paid for the week's hire of the bay, he made sure that it was to be his horse, available to him at any and all times. Afterwards, he returned to the Primrose House, crossed the lobby, and went to the desk. The clerk, who would be Mr. Selby, was doing some paper work in a cubbyhole beside the key rack where he could keep an eye on the desk. At Sam's approach he left his work and came up behind the desk.

Sam said, "I'm just guessing, but would you be Mr. Selby, the owner?"

"I am," the gray-faced owner replied. "Anything wrong, Mr. Kennery?"

"Nothing wrong. I'm after information. Where's the newspaper office?"

"Primrose hasn't got a newspaper, Mr. Kennery. We're too close to the *Capital Times* in Junction City."

"What do you do for local news? Pick it up at the barber shop?"

Mr. Selby smiled and said, "Partly, but the *Capital Times* prints the Primrose news. It gives us a whole page about three times a week."

"They have a correspondent here?"

Selby nodded. "Yes. He's a bright young fellow that clerks at Pollock's Emporium down the street. Name's Ben Harness."

Sam thanked him and went out. This was a chore he should have done in Junction City; but Wilbarth, understandably in a hurry to beat the trial date, had not given him time. He wanted to read the account of Schaeffer's murder and of the indictment of Brayton and Herrington. Maybe it would answer some questions that he hadn't had the time or the sense to ask Wilbarth.

Chapter 3

POLLOCK'S Emporium was a huge store that sold dry goods, hardware, and groceries. The hardware section was closest to the door Sam entered, and he inquired of the clerk there where he could find Bill Harness.

The clerk pointed to a red-haired young man behind the dry-goods counter adjoining and Sam moved over there and halted before him.

"Something for you?" Harness asked. He had a bright, friendly face, and couldn't have been over twenty.

"I'm Sam Kennery. Don't want to buy anything, but maybe you can help me. You're Primrose's correspondent for the *Capital Times*, I'm told."

The young man nodded and at the same time grimaced. "Yes, sir. The worst newspaper in the West, and I guess I help make it bad."

Sam grinned and the young man smiled too. "Do you keep a file of the *Times?*"

"I surely do," Harness answered wryly. "Why? Well, Red Macandy—he's the editor—is not only the crookedest newspaper man in the state, but the cheapest and the drunkenest. He pays me by the line for what I send him. Every month his check is short, so I keep a file to check against his swindling."

"Could I have a look at that file?"

"Help yourself," young Harness said. "It's in my room at Mrs. Blake's boarding house." He jerked his thumb over his shoulder. "That's a white-painted house on the right in the middle of the next block, right behind the store. Tell her I sent you." He hesitated. "Or maybe I could remember what it is you want to look up?"

"Won't bother you with it. I'm much obliged for the look at your files."

The redhead nodded, then said, "They're stacked in my closet, the latest on top."

Out on the street Sam followed Ben Harness' direction, found the house, and, as predicted, the door was opened by a buxom, gray-haired Mrs. Blake. After Sam stated his business, she directed him to Harness' room, the last on the left of the upstairs corridor.

Harness' room was small, and book-filled shelves almost covered one wall. The single easy chair and the bed plus a littered desk and a straight chair jammed the room.

Sam threw his hat on the desk, and opened the closet door. With both hands he lifted a third of the two-foot pile of newspapers, placed them beside the easy chair, and settled down for some reading.

The account of Brayton's and Herrington's arraignment was reported with bias, malice, and relish in the series of signed articles by Red Macandy. The bare facts were stated plainly enough. The charge against Brayton and Herrington was a dual one—collusive embezzlement and defrauding the United States Government of an excess of twenty thousand dollars.

However, Macandy had not been content with the bare facts. Brayton, according to him, had been a failure in three businesses in the old territorial days before Senator Wagenknect had paid off a debt by wangling him a job as Indian agent. Macandy hinted that Brayton used blackmail on the Senator, who was a wenching and drinking companion of Brayton when they were both territorial legislators in the capital city. Brayton's wife had left him because of his fondness for the company of women other than herself. Macandy went into as much detail as he dared about the failure of Brayton's three businesses. His article barely skirted libel, and Sam guessed that Macandy could probably prove everything he wrote about Brayton. It was a cruel piece of writing, Sam reflected. After all, Ulysses S. Grant had failed in business and was overfond of the bottle, but he was quite a general.

In the following issue of the *Times,* Macandy took Herrington apart in a similar article. He had less to work on here, for Herrington was neither a native of the state, nor a government official. Macandy managed, however, to dredge up half a dozen arrests of Herrington for disturbing the peace in a succession of trail towns. He hinted that the embezzlement of twenty thousand dollars was laughable, pointing out that the charge covered only three of the six years that Brayton had associations with Herrington. The true amount of the embezzlement was probably triple the sum the government named.

Herrington, Macandy said, had got his nickname "Big Dad" not because of his size, but because of the astounding number of progeny he had fathered in Texas while remaining a bachelor. Macandy was careful to say this was only one of the many rumors that seemed to follow Herrington, such as his infinite capacity for alcohol, his friendly spending, and his maniac rages.

Attorneys for the two men were Amos Thurston and Lee Phelan of the firm of Thurston, Phelan & Russell, who were also the attorneys for the giant Consolidated Mining & Milling Company of Primrose.

Sam now hunted down the issue of the *Times* that announced the ambushing of Morton Schaeffer. The only thing new that he learned from the account was Macandy's speculation that there had to be two ambushers, for how could one man alone, prowling around the Long Reach water tank in the darkness, be certain which side of the passenger car Morton would be seated on? If he had chosen the wrong side, Macandy reasoned, he would have had to ride either around the locomotive and thus risk being seen by the engine crew, or around the entire train. The shot had come too soon after the train stopped for him to have done that; therefore, Macandy argued, there must have been two assassins, one for each side of the train.

Macandy had pointed out, of course, that Schaeffer was the prosecution's star witness in the upcoming trial of Herrington and Brayton. By adding that Schaeffer had no other known enemies, he implied that Herrington and Brayton

were the only ones who could profit by Schaeffer's death.
He was, in fact, pointing the finger of suspicion at them
while stating that both men had unimpeachable alibis at
the time of Schaeffer's murder. He was right, Sam thought.
Wilbarth and Newford had probably gone over the details
of the ambush so many times that they had forgotten to tell
him of the probability of two men staging the ambush.

The delays of the trial which the court granted were duly
noted in subsequent issues of the *Times*.

When Sam had finished reading, he wondered what he had
learned. Thanks to Red Macandy's poison pen, he had a
pretty fair character assessment of the two conspirators. He
knew he could never like this Red Macandy, but his guess
was that Macandy's hints, innuendoes, and reports of rumors
held a measure of truth. Another thing he had learned was
that two men were involved in the murder of Morton Schaeffer.

Dusk was beginning to fall when Sam returned the papers
to their pile and scribbled a note of thanks to Harness which
he propped against the pillow and then left the house.

Somehow, and tonight if possible, he had to meet Herrington
and be accepted by him. If Herrington accepted him,
Brayton would too. Lacking any other way of meeting Big
Dad, there remained only the chance of an open poker game.

When he entered the Primrose House and turned toward
the bar he saw that it was beginning to fill up. Even before
he reached the door he heard, with an irritability rare in
him, the bray of Herrington's laugh. Sam thought: *The
rope'll choke that off, my fat friend*.

The bar was fairly crowded, and all the chairs at the
tables were taken up by card players. Glancing at the rear
table on his way to an empty place at the bar, Sam saw
that Herrington had the same seat he had occupied at noon,
and Seeley Carnes, as before, sat on his right. With the
chairs all filled, Sam would have to wait until one of the
players cashed in his chips.

The bartender recognized him and said, "Good evening,
Mr. Kennery. What's your pleasure?"

"That same whiskey," Sam told him. He wondered if Mr.
Selby, the proprietor, made a point of instructing all his
help, including his daughter, to learn the names of the hotel's
guests. Though a stranger, in town only some seven hours,
he had already been called by his name several times by several
people. Could it be that they knew of him and knew

the purpose of his visit? That, he decided, was impossible.

He poured his drink just as Herrington's bellowing laughter overrode the noisy talk of the room, and again Sam winced.

His drink down, he was thinking about having another when he felt a hand grasp his elbow. He half turned to confront a stocky bulldog of a man wearing the badge of a law officer on his open vest. He had a square, tough face that was unsmiling now. This would be Sheriff Morehead, and Sam had a dismal feeling of approaching disaster. *The damned idiot*, he thought. Wilbarth had said Morehead would get in touch with him, and Morehead had chosen to greet him in front of thirty or more men, including the man they were both after.

"Mister, I've had my eye on you," the sheriff said in a hoarse, gravelly voice.

Looking at him, Sam saw the wink of one eye.

"Will you please come along with me to my office?"

Did the wink mean the sheriff wasn't serious? Sam didn't know, and he thought he might as well play this as any stranger would.

"What for? I like it here."

"I won't ask you again," the sheriff said. His voice seemed to override other voices in the room and talk trailed off.

Sam said quietly, "I said I like it here."

"Come along. I don't want trouble."

This time Sam spoke loud enough for the whole room to hear it. "Go away."

The sheriff took one step backwards and his hand went to his gun.

Swiftly, Sam's hand streaked to his holster and came up with his six-gun cocked and pointed.

A look of disbelief came over the sheriff's face, but his right hand moved outward away from his gun.

"That'll get you dead, Sheriff."

The men closest to the two began to back off, crowding into each other.

The sheriff stared at him for a long moment and then said, "You might as well come now. If I go away, I'll come back with three more men. They'll have shotguns."

Sam pretended a sullen indecision. "What do you want of me?"

"Nothing, but I think another sheriff does. Now, what'll it be? Shotguns?"

"I should have shot you," Sam said, and began to holster his gun.

Before his gun reached its holster Morehead extended his hand. "I'll take that."

Grudgingly Sam held out the gun and Morehead took it. "Now walk out ahead of me through the lobby."

Sam moved past Morehead as talk began to swell. He wanted to look over to see if Herrington had watched this, but that was too risky. With a surly look on his face, eyes straight ahead, he tramped past the standing card players into the lobby and out the veranda door. He could hear the excited talk well up behind him. On the boardwalk Morehead caught up with him and they took a few strides side by side in silence.

"Pretty good for no rehearsal," Morehead said dryly. He looked sideways at Sam. "For a minute I thought I had the wrong man and I was dead."

"What's it get us?"

"We hate each other, for one thing."

"That was for Herrington then?"

"Mostly."

Two men were approaching, and by the light of the veranda lamps Sam saw them looking curiously at the sheriff and himself. Just as they were passing, Sam said, "You couldn't be dumber or wronger if you were drunk, Sheriff."

The sheriff waited until the two men were out of earshot, then said quietly, "Keep it up. That's what we want."

At the sheriff's rear corner office in the big stone courthouse a block behind Primrose House, Morehead turned up the lamp on his desk and closed the door. Then he gestured to a chair beside the desk. His office, Sam thought, could be duplicated in every county seat in the state—the littered desk, the gun rack on the wall, the ancient horsehair sofa for the wounded or the weary, the foul cuspidor for the chewers, and the reward dodgers tacked to the wall.

Morehead sat down in the swivel chair and regarded Sam carefully. Sam said nothing, realizing that this was the first real look Morehead had had of him.

"Thought you'd be older," Morehead said.

Sam smiled faintly. "I'm beginning to think I've got a baby face."

Morehead shook his head. "It's not that, it's— Doesn't matter." He tilted his chair back, cleared his throat, and said, "Met Herrington yet?" When Sam shook his head Morehead said, "You will tonight."

"You sound pretty sure."

"I am," Morehead said flatly. "Any man that hates the law is Herrington's friend. He's been riding me, and now he'll ride me more."

"Where's Brayton?"

"Due in tomorrow. He had to go back to the agency on some government business. I've got a deputy with him."

"Anything I should know about him?"

"I'll answer that question by asking you one," Morehead said, and he almost smiled. "You got a good head for drink?"

"Average, I reckon. Why?"

"Brayton's never really sober, but don't let that fool you. He never makes a slip, so don't count on his booze helping you."

Sam nodded. Booze and women, Wilbarth had said. "What else can you tell me about either of them?"

Morehead sighed and shook his head. "Nothing. When they aren't drinking at the Primrose bar, they're drinking at one of the sporting houses across the river. They spend a lot of time with their lawyers. That's all I can tell you after watching them for ten days."

"Do they ever talk about their trial?"

"Yes. They claim there won't be one," Morehead said sourly.

He stood up, and Sam got up and faced him. "I think you better go back now, Kennery. I've told you all I know, which is nothing. Your story is that I got a reward dodger today that fitted your description. One of the aliases of the wanted man was Kennedy. Kennery is close enough to that, plus the description, to make me pull you in for questioning. Your alibi is that you were in prison when Kennedy committed the crime. You showed me your prison release, which I'll keep until you leave town."

Sam grinned. "What was I in prison for?"

"Take your choice," the sheriff said with a grim humor.

"You're not telling me to move along?"

"No, you're a free man, but bad, and I'll be watching you, tell them."

"But will they ask?" Sam asked wryly.

"If they don't I'll turn in my badge," Morehead said in his gravelly voice. He extended his hand. "Good luck, and if I can help let me know."

On his way back to the Primrose House Sam thought about Morehead's move tonight. It was a clever one, and if Morehead was right it was the best of all possible ways to gain an introduction to Herrington. But once he'd met him, where did he go from there? He didn't know, and the only thing he could do was wait for the mistake that Herrington or Brayton was bound to make.

As he mounted the veranda steps he considered his next move. Should he go into the bar and brag; or should he do what the average hardcase, familiar with trouble, would do— not make himself too conspicuous? The latter course seemed the most sensible, and when he entered the lobby he headed for the dining room.

Louise Selby, standing by the door, gave him a cool nod of recognition, but no more than that. There was no smile, no small talk.

The dining room was not even half full and Sam went to the table where he had been seated this noon. Herrington and Carnes were not in the room, and he supposed they were still drinking.

Tenney must have been in the kitchen, for Sam didn't see her. The menu blackboard told him, take it or leave it, that he was having steak for supper. Tenney came out of the kitchen then, saw him, hesitated only a second, and came up to his table. Her dark eyes were chilly, and the smile was absent from her usually cheerful face. She halted beside him and said in an expressionless voice, "Good evening, sir."

Sam looked up at her, feeling a faint surprise. "The name is Sam Kennery."

"Yes, sir, Mr. Kennery."

"Make it Sam."

"No, Mr. Kennery."

Sam was silent for a moment, regarding her, and then he knew what was wrong. It was the same thing that made Louise Selby greet him with the barest civility. He watched Tenney as she filled his glass.

"How would you like your steak, sir?"

"If I said rare you'd bring me charcoal. What's wrong, Tenney?"

"Who said anything was? And don't call me Tenney."

"That business with the sheriff?" Sam asked.

"Oh, that's nothing," Tenney said bitingly. "Somebody threatens to kill Sheriff Morehead every day. Mr. Selby encourages all our customers to do it."

"Nobody leans on me, Tenney. Not even if he wears a star."

"Why did he try to?"

"He thought I fitted the description on a reward dodger."

"And did you?"

Let's get it over with, Sam thought. "No, I was in prison when the crime the dodger named was committed."

A momentary shock showed on Tenney's face. She looked swiftly at him, and then her glance slid away. "How would you like your steak, sir?"

"Rare, and don't bother putting arsenic in the gravy. I can tell."

"Rare, no arsenic," Tenney said evenly. She turned and headed for the kitchen.

This is one thing you hadn't counted on, my friend, was Sam's thought. You can't be a hardcase in the eyes of the town and be a jolly good fellow to Tenney. She was the town, and saw what the town saw and heard what the town said. To her, then, he was a hardcase—too fast with a gun, bad-tempered, insanely rash, and a rebel with a prison record to boot. That was the character he had assumed for Herrington, and the one he must wear for Tenney.

When she returned with his supper she placed his plate before him and said, "Would you like coffee, Mr. J.B.?"

Sam looked up at her and saw that her face was cold. "J.B. standing for what?" he asked.

"Jailbird, sir," Tenney said, and she moved off, heading for the kitchen again.

Sam's perception told him that she cared enough about their day-old relationship that she was disappointed, angry, and contemptuous because of his revelation. If he had been just another man to her she wouldn't have bothered to get angry, and that thought comforted him a little. Neither of them spoke when she returned with his coffee.

Finished with his supper, Sam paid at the desk and Louise Selby unsmilingly gave him his change and thanked him. Like Tenney, she did not want to look at him, and she spoke her civil good night with eyes averted.

Chapter 4

AS Sam stepped into the lobby he heard Herrington's bray of laughter coming from the saloon. He halted, rehearsing his next move. The thing to do was to act as if nothing out of the ordinary had happened, which in itself would suggest that he had done this before and that he regarded the sheriff as a bumbling fool who just happened to wear a star.

Sam turned and saw Mr. Selby approaching across the lobby. He waited until the gray-faced little man halted before him.

"I'm told you drew a gun on Sheriff Morehead, Mr. Kennery. Is that correct?"

"It is." Sam paused, watching him. "Do you want me to leave?"

"I've been thinking of asking you to, but I decided against it. I just want you to understand that shooting or fighting in my saloon won't be tolerated. Alec has a shotgun under the bar that he's not afraid to use."

"Has there been any shooting or fighting, Mr. Selby?"

"No, and there'd better not be."

"Who went for his gun first?" Sam asked quietly.

"The sheriff, and he has a right to."

"You're wrong there, but I won't make trouble for you, Mr. Selby."

Sam saw the look of righteous contempt in the hotel owner's eyes before he turned and moved toward the saloon.

The bar was fairly crowded, and Sam, after a casual glance around the room, had to make his way toward the rear before he could find a place for himself. In his look around the room he had seen Herrington and Carnes seated at their usual table.

Alec, the bartender, came up to him, but this time there was no greeting. Wordlessly, he placed a bottle of Sam's favorite whiskey and a glass on the bar and retreated. So he was in Alec's bad books too.

He poured a drink he really didn't want and looked up into the back bar mirror. He could see only the bar drinkers toward the front of the room reflected in it. He was suddenly aware that the talk had muted and he saw that he was being watched by several of the saloon patrons.

He was reaching for his glass when a deep voice behind him said, "My friend, I'd like to introduce myself." Sam turned slowly and saw Herrington, a smile under his beak of a nose, standing there, hand extended.

"I'd like to shake your hand, Kennery. My name's Herrington."

Sam held out his hand, a feigned look of puzzlement on his face.

"Mr. Herrington, how are you, sir?"

"Like to join us for a drink? It's a pleasure to meet the man that made Morehead take water."

The corner of Sam's mouth lifted in a faint smile. "That's an easy way to earn a drink, Mr. Herrington."

"If you have the nerve," Herrington conceded. "Come along."

Seeley Carnes, wearing his hat, as usual, stood up at their approach and Herrington introduced them to each other. Sam sat down across from Carnes and put his hat on an empty chair next to him. Herrington eased his vast bulk into his chair and looked with approval at Sam while Carnes poured the drinks.

"That showdown made my day, my week, my month," Herrington said, then opened his mouth and brayed his booming laugh.

Sam shrugged. "Somebody had to teach him some manners."

"What was graveling him? I saw it, but didn't hear anything."

"He wanted me to come with him and wouldn't tell me why. When I told him to go away he started for his gun and I was ahead of him."

"By a Texas mile," Carnes said. He had a thin nasal drawl that Sam knew was going to bother him as much as Herrington's laugh did.

"You went, though?" Herrington said.

Sam nodded. "He promised me three men with shotguns if I didn't."

Herrington looked at him shrewdly. "That means you want

to stay here. If you didn't want to, you'd have shot him and run."

Sam nodded. "That's right. A man is going to meet me here."

"So you promised the sheriff you'd be a good boy, is that it?"

Sam grinned crookedly and nodded.

Seeley Carnes said then, "Why'd he want you in the first place? You only come this morning."

Sam said almost indifferently, "That's a standard play with some of these whistle-stop sheriffs. They spot a stranger they think means trouble, so they pull him in and question him. Sort of puts a man on notice that he's being watched, I reckon. Like a warning."

"What was his excuse, though, for pulling you in? Like I said, I couldn't hear."

Sam grimaced in disgust. "The oldest one of all. He had a reward dodger that fitted my description." He paused, and then he laughed. "The smart law men never figure this, but a man can change his looks at the nearest barber shop and change his name when he walks out."

Herrington's bray of laughter exploded, but Seeley Carnes regarded Sam unsmilingly.

"Was it you?" he asked.

"Not this time," Sam said idly, and added, "The wanted man was left-handed, the dodger said. All the sheriff had to do was look at where I wore my gun. Besides that, I was in jail when the crime was committed. No, the sheriff just wanted to warn me. I don't reckon he'd even read the dodger."

Carnes made no comment, and it occurred to Sam that Carnes was the shrewder of the two, even though he worked for Herrington. He had picked up the fact that Sam had been here only one day, and his questions, though seeming casual, were to the point.

"Well, I invited you over for a drink. Pour 'em, Seeley," Herrington said.

Carnes almost filled three big water glasses with whiskey and distributed the drinks. Sam picked up his glass, dipped his head to Herrington in a careless gesture of thanks, and the three of them drank. From his vest Harrington took out two cigars, tossed one to Sam, put the other in his mouth, and lighted it.

Sam was wondering why Carnes hadn't been offered a cigar when Carnes reached in his pocket and drew out a doeskin pouch. He lifted out a book of cigarette papers and took out one. Opening the pouch, he lifted out the coarsest, blackest shreds of tobacco Sam had ever seen, rolled a cigarette, and lighted it. The first whiff of smoke from the cigarette that Sam caught came almost as a physical shock. It had the rawest, rankest reek of tobacco he had ever smelled, and it somehow reminded him of burning rope.

Sam lighted his cigar now and surprised Herrington regarding him carefully. Sam thought it was time for him to show a proper but polite curiosity about them. "You must be from around here?"

Herrington shook his head. "How do you figure that?"

Sam shrugged. "You know the sheriff good enough to cuss him out."

Herrington looked at Seeley, and Seeley said, "Tell him, Dad."

Herrington regarded Sam with a look of pride and benevolence. "Kennery, if I had any hair, Sheriff Morehead would be in it. He greets us in the morning, checks on us at noon, and sees us to bed. You see, I'm waiting a court trial and Seeley's been subpoenaed as a witness."

Sam raised his eyebrows in feigned surprise but he kept silent.

Herrington continued, "I'm a drover, Kennery, and Seeley here is my trail boss. We've been delivering contract beef to the agency up north for half a dozen years. Never had a complaint from the agent, but one of the agency's hired hands got a notion I was being paid for more cattle than I delivered." He took a gulp of whiskey and continued. "He said I split the overpayment with the agent, so me and the agent are charged with fraud. Trial's coming up in a week or so unless we can haze the judge into making it sooner."

Sam held up his cigar, studied it a moment, then looked over it at Herrington. "I'd heard of a lot of long counts on Indian beef, but I never heard of a man going to jail for it." He scowled. "Your trial here?"

"Junction City," Herrington said, then added, "But there won't be any trial. The government's chief witness is dead, and they can't prove a thing without him. We're down here because the marshal in Junction City wouldn't let us alone. We got a court order restraining him from—they call it 'harassment,' don't they?"

"I wouldn't know," Sam said. "They got the agent locked up?"

"We're both out on bond," Herrington said sourly. "He had to go back to the agency with the guard Morehead put on him. He'll be in tomorrow."

Sam said philosophically, "They never let a man alone, do they?"

"It's a damned nuisance," Herrington growled. "Pour up, Seeley, then we better go eat before they lock the dining room on us."

Seeley poured another big drink for each of them and Herrington downed his in two huge gulps. Seeley did the same, but Sam only took a sip of his.

Now Herrington stood up. "Come and eat with us, Kennery."

"I've had supper, thanks."

"Well, come and sit with us."

"That fellow I was supposed to meet, remember?" Sam said. "He might come in."

"Hell, he'll check at the desk."

Sam said quietly, "He won't know me by that name," and grinned.

Herrington smiled knowingly. "See you later, then."

Seeley Carnes gave him only a curt nod before he picked up their bottle and they made their way out of the bar.

Well, Morehead had known his men, Sam thought. Herrington had made the move the sheriff anticipated. Sam's story had seemed to convince both Herrington and Seeley, although Sam wondered about Seeley. Was he really convinced that Sam was what he pretended to be? Behind that cold face and chilly eyes, was there a suspicion of him? Hadn't it been Seeley, though, who urged Herrington to tell of the fraud? Was there a purpose behind his urging, or was it his stiff way of acknowledging that they, too, were crooked and proud of it?

Sam looked at the glass of whiskey before him with distaste. It wouldn't do to leave it here for them to find on their return; that was bad saloon manners, yet he didn't want the drink. He reached out for the glass now, cupped it in his hands for a moment, then unobtrusively poured the contents in the cuspidor beside his chair.

Afterwards he went up to his room.

Chapter 5

HERRINGTON and Carnes were greeted at the dining-room door by a distant and resigned Louise Selby. She gave them a cool good evening, and did not escort them to their table. They had got in just as she was about to close the doors, which meant that one of the girls and probably Mrs. Payne would have to stay late to take care of their suppers.

Big Dad led the way to their table where Seeley took off his hat, put the bottle on the table, and sat down across from his boss. Mary, the plump waitress, came up to the table, filled their glasses with water, and took their orders. The first thing both men did was to drink half the water in their glasses and refill them with whiskey. It was a practice Louise Selby loathed, but her father had told her to ignore this dining-room drinking since they were good spenders and so far had caused no trouble.

"What do you think of this Kennery?" Big Dad asked.

"Well, he's got a nerve all right," Carnes conceded.

Herrington looked at him shrewdly. "What's there about him you don't like, Seeley?"

Carnes's thin lips curled up at the corners. "Well, for one thing, he ain't from Texas."

"Besides that, though?"

"He speaks too good."

"Like me, you mean?" Big Dad said. "Hell, if they taught you to read you can't help but talk different."

"I reckon," Carnes said indifferently.

"You think he's a real hardcase, Seeley?"

"Gamblin' type, maybe." Seeley frowned. "He ain't duded up like a dealer. Still, he's got money and he don't ask about jobs. He can unload with a gun too. Yeah, I'd say he's a hardcase, but only medium hard."

Herrington took a swig of his drink and looked reflectively over Carnes's head. "He's what I was fifteen years ago before

I got me this belly. You didn't know me then, did you, Seeley?"

"No, but sure as hell I heard of you."

"Wonder if he'll be around after the trial?" Herrington asked.

Seeley drank then, wiped his mouth with the back of his hand, and said, "Dunno. Why do you care?"

"I'd like to have him around," Herrington said. "He makes me laugh, and I figure he'll fight for money, marbles, or chalk, just for the hell of it."

"What would he do?"

Herrington shrugged his massive shoulders. "*Segundo* to you during the winter. Buy cattle, trade for horses, but mostly take on any Y.S. rider he meets, even hunt 'em."

Mary brought their food then, and while they ate in silence Seeley reflected on what his boss had said. Kennery would work under him in the winter and probably take a trail herd north next summer. True, he might be of help in Big Dad's long-standing and continuing feud with Yancey Slater and his crew. For the past five years Big Dad had hired every one of his Chain Link hands with the utmost care. First, they must know how to handle a gun and when to use it. Their willingness and ability to work, he left up to Seeley to develop. What Big Dad wanted was a mean, tough, fighting, hair-trigger crew that could steal far more beef than was stolen from them. Kennery was of the required pattern, but was there something beyond that? To put Kennery in as *segundo* meant that Dad would have to demote Harry Olds, who would quit, and jump Kennery over four or five fight-hardened and trail-hardened hands who wouldn't take kindly to the move. It'd mean that Big Dad wanted to groom Kennery for Carnes's own job of foreman and trail boss.

It could happen, Carnes thought cynically, remembering how he himself had been hired ten years ago when he was twenty. He and a colored cowboy were driving a remuda south and stopped off at Tascosa for a drink and some sleep, and the Chain Link bunch was passing through too. Typically, they were cocky, quarrelsome, and mean. Seeley and his colored partner were in no mood for the hazing the Chain Link crew tried to give them. Gunplay broke out in the saloon, and Seeley, quick with a gun, killed the chief tormenter and wounded two others before he made it across

the street to the shelter of a feed barn. About eight of them
came after him, surrounded the barn, and started moving
in on him. He was alone, for his partner lay dead on the
saloon floor. His chances of surviving this one were next to
nothing, he had reckoned there in the feed barn. They would
get him in the end, but he would take a couple more with
him.

It was then that Big Dad Herrington, known all over the
Panhandle and below it for his fighting, feuding, and hell
raising, stepped through the saloon doors onto the boardwalk. Seeley knew who he was, and had already decided to
go for the chief and forget the Indians when Herrington
bellowed to his men. He called them to him, and singly and
in pairs under a blasting sun they came over to him. Seeley
remembered thinking, *Well, I can't be this lucky.* He waited,
and after a short parley the Chain Link crew moved back
into the saloon, leaving Herrington standing alone. Then
Herrington started toward the feed barn. Even in those days
he was a bear of a man, short-legged, yet tall, without the
belly that he toted around now. He stopped in the door of the
feed barn and called, "Come out, you. The shootin's over."

Seeley, covering Herrington, came out from behind a feed
box. Herrington moved into the shade and the two men
halted, regarding each other.

"Who you working for?" Herrington asked.

"Myself. Trading horses."

"Stealing them, too?" Herrington continued, still agree-
able.

"When I can," Seeley answered calmly.

Herrington laughed then. It was the first of ten thousand
of those braying laughs that Seeley was to hear, and he
didn't like it any better then than he liked it now.

"Well, I'll buy your horses and you'll work for me," Herrington had said.

"How do you know I want to?"

"Well, figure it out," Herrington said. "I can call those
boys back, and more with 'em."

"And I can shoot you before you even start across the
street."

Herrington laughed again. "I like that. Sure you could,
but you won't. You'll take my offer."

"Hell, your crew would shoot me the first time I turned
my back."

"Not if I say no, and I've already said no. They started

that trouble and they paid for it. There'll be no grudges, and you better not carry one either. Now come along."

This was the way Big Dad had hired him, and it was because he was outnumbered and had chosen to fight rather than take water. And this could be the way he would hire Kennery, who had made Sheriff Morehead take water. Seeley liked Big Dad and was loyal to him, but he had no illusions. Over these ten years Seeley had learned that when caution took the place of daring, when thought replaced action in a man, he was useless to Big Dad. Well, Herrington couldn't fault him on that score, and Seeley intended that he never could.

Seeley said aloud now, "Yes, he could give Yancey's boys some trouble, but can you get him?"

"I'll find a way," Big Dad said quietly and reached for his whiskey glass.

Next morning Herrington and Carnes were in the small group that waited on the depot platform as the train from Junction City pulled in. It was a crisp morning, sunny but chilly. As the passengers filed off, a tall emaciated man in a dark townsman's suit cut away from the other passengers and moved over toward Herrington and Carnes in a long, ungainly stride. When Con Brayton halted before the other two he did not offer to shake hands and neither did they, nor did he put down his carpet-covered valise.

"Well, Con, where's nursie?" Herrington asked.

"I left him asleep in the seat," Brayton said contemptuously. "He couldn't guard a ten-day-old baby."

Herrington's bray of a laugh came then and Brayton eyed him almost balefully, as if he had learned to live with Herrington's laugh but didn't like it. His white shirt and string tie, along with his black stetson, gave him a vague look of authority, as if he might be a preacher or a doctor. In spite of his height, he was a stoop-shouldered man, with a long, creased, drink-ravaged face. Full black mustaches managed to hide a weak mouth, but only emphasized a receding chin above a huge Adam's apple. His gray, red-rimmed eyes were arrogant with meanness. He said impatiently, "If we want a seat in the hack, we'd better move."

The three men turned and moved toward the hack at the edge of the platform.

"How's your Injuns, Con?"

"Stinking. As usual."

Because of the presence of other passengers in the hack, they did not speak on their short ride to the Primrose House. Once in its lobby, Herrington said, "Dump your bag and we'll meet you in the saloon."

"No, come up to the room," Brayton said flatly. "We've got to talk. I got a bottle."

"Full?" Herrington asked.

"No. Seeley, pick up a bottle and some glasses in the bar and then come up."

Brayton went over to the desk, picked up his key from Mr. Selby, and then led the way up the stairs. Once in his room, he shucked off his coat, loosened his tie, and then took a bottle from his bag.

Herrington had crossed the room and was looking out the window. Without turning, he said, "What's bothering you, Con?"

"Wait for Seeley," Brayton said curtly.

Herrington turned around, and was thoughtful as he watched Brayton, bottle in hand, go to the washstand, pour a couple of inches of whiskey in a tumbler, and toss it down. Then the door opened and Seeley came in carrying a tray with a bottle and three glasses.

Brayton said, "Make your own," and he moved over to the bed and sat on the edge of it. Herrington came away from the window, and on his way to the bottle he handed Brayton a cigar, which was accepted with a grunt. While Seeley made the two drinks Brayton lighted the cigar, and Herrington, as if it were his prerogative, went to the lone easy chair and sat down. Seeley, still wearing his hat, put his shoulder against the wall by the washstand, rolled one of his stinking cigarettes, and waited for Brayton to begin.

Brayton looked at Herrington now and said, "Dad, I think we got trouble."

"Up there? What kind?"

"Indian trouble. Specifically, Joe Potatoes."

"Hell, if he wants money, give it to him," Herrington said.

Brayton gave him a humorless smile, revealing big yellow-stained teeth below his mustaches. "That I've already done," he said dryly.

"Then what does he want?"

"More money. Lots more. It's what he's apt to do if he don't get it that scares me," Brayton said. "He and Lil— that's his wife—drank up what we paid him. It was more money than they'd had in all their lives, and Lil likes it."

"I thought she was one of your girls, Con," Herrington said.

Brayton scowled. "What's that got to do with it? She still is, but she and Joe want money. They've got a taste for high living now."

Herrington's bray of laughter was predictable. "High living," he said. "A stinking sod hut with a couple of elk hides on a dirt floor—that's what they've got now. What do they want us to do? Build them a frame house?"

Brayton said wearily, "You don't get me, Dad. Up to now they've been too poor to buy booze steady. Now they've got a taste for it."

Seeley put in then, "Is Joe talking?"

Brayton shook his head. "Not yet, but he says he will."

"Does Lil know about Schaeffer?" Seeley asked.

"Joe says no. These bucks tell their women only what they want to. All Lil knows is that Joe came up with booze money once, so why doesn't he do it again."

"Why doesn't he throw her out?"

"Why, Joe feels like she does. He got money once, so he wants more."

The three men were quiet for a moment and then Seeley Carnes broke the silence. "Kill him."

Brayton swiveled his head to look at him. "Who does it, Seeley? You, with one of Morehead's guards watching? Or me? Or Dad here?"

Seeley's lean face flushed. "No, I don't reckon."

"When the court frees me I go back to the agency," Brayton said angrily. "You two go back to Texas. I got to live alongside of Joe and pay and pay and pay."

Seeley smiled thinly. "Wait until the court frees us all and Morehead's guards are pulled off. I'll take care of Joe."

"It won't wait, Seeley," Brayton said flatly. "Joe gave me until the half moon. That's a week."

Seeley swore viciously and came away from the wall. Looking at Herrington, he said, "That ain't enough time to send for anyone, Dad."

Herrington said one word: "Kennery."

Brayton looked at him and then at Seeley. Both men were looking at each other, ignoring him.

"What's going on here?" Brayton demanded. "Who's Kennery?"

"Sam Kennery," Herrington said quietly. "A hardcase that drifted in here on yesterday's train. Morehead tried to hooraw him, and Kennery put a gun on him so fast you couldn't see his hand move. He's tough and mean, and he's known jail. Known it a lot of times, I'd reckon."

"*He* says," Seeley said thinly.

Herrington scowled. "You don't trust him?"

Seeley shook his head. "I never said that. We just don't know him that good."

"Tell me more about him," Con said with sudden interest.

"All right, here's everything I know. Seeley, if I miss anything, tell me."

Herrington went on to recount their entire conversation with Kennery the evening before, and Seeley listened carefully, occasionally nodding confirmation of one of Dad's points. Brayton was listening intently, and his face seemed to reflect a faint skepticism.

Herrington finished his account of the meeting by saying, "He's no tinhorn, Con. A tinhorn would have come back from the sheriff's office and bragged for a while in the saloon as if he was saying, 'Look what I done. I'm a tough enough *hombre* that I backed down the sheriff.' Instead, you know what Kennery did after he left the sheriff's office?"

"Tell me."

"Went in and had supper alone, just like he figured nothing had happened—or if it did happen it wasn't important. Like I told you, he even down-talked it to us." He looked at Carnes now. "I figure him for a cool head. What about you, Seeley?"

"If he didn't like you he could be trouble, all right," Seeley said, half grudgingly.

"If he's what you say he is, he'll likely come high," Brayton observed.

Herrington said impatiently, "What if he does? This way you only pay once, not every time Joe and Lil feel like getting drunk."

"How do you know he'll do it?"

"Damn it, man, I don't, but I'll bet my bottom dollar on one thing—if he turns us down he won't run to the law with our proposition." He looked at Seeley. "Am I wrong?"

"I reckon you're right on that," Seeley drawled.

Herrington heaved his bulk out of the chair, went to the bottle, and poured himself a drink. Then he moved over to Brayton, who had seated himself on the bed again. He replenished Brayton's drink, and handed the bottle to Seeley, who poured his own.

Brayton drank, then wiped his lips with a swipe of his shirt sleeve. When he could breathe evenly he said, "Dad, you're asking me to trust a man I've never even seen."

Herrington was standing by his chair, about to sit down. Now he said, "Tell you what. Let's go down to the bar. My guess is Kennery will be there, or will come there. Let's ask him to eat with us. You can see for yourself, Con. Look him over. Don't sound him out, just look him over."

"Fair enough," Brayton said. "Let's go."

Chapter 6

SAM, in his room, heard the three men in the corridor as they went towards the stairs. He waited a few minutes and then went out into the corridor himself and descended to the lobby. He cut across it and entered the barroom, which held a scattering of men dedicated to their noon drink.

As he approached the bar he looked casually about and saw Herrington and Seeley with a third man whose back was to him. None of them looked at him, and he moved up to the bar. Alec's greeting was civil but cool as he put a bottle and glass before Kennery. Since there was no change in Alec's attitude toward him, it was reasonable to suppose that he had gained no status in Alec's eyes by drinking with Herrington and Carnes. A good man, this Alec, Sam thought. If you associate with crooks then you're a crook too in Alec's book.

Sam poured a drink and had downed it when he saw Herrington's reflection in the bar mirror. Herrington was coming toward him, and Sam, not pretending surprise, turned to greet him. "Morning."

"And a good morning to you," Herrington said, extending his hand. Sam shook it and Herrington cupped Sam's elbow in his left hand in a friendly gesture. "Come on over to the table, Kennery. Want you to meet a fellow."

Sam picked up his glass and bottle, and followed Herrington to the rear table. Herrington gave Sam time to put his bottle and glass down on the table and Brayton time to stand up before he introduced them. "Kennery, this is Con Brayton. He's the Indian agent I was telling you about last night."

Sam shook hands with Brayton, murmuring the amenities, while thinking that here was a scoundrel who really looked the part. As Sam and Brayton seated themselves, Herrington said, "What's the bottle for, Kennery?"

"It's my turn," Sam said easily. "Have a drink, gentlemen."

Although there was already a bottle on the table, Herrington politely accepted Sam's offer and was followed by the others.

Brayton said pleasantly, "Dad was telling me about your run-in with Morehead yesterday."

"Wouldn't call it a run-in," Sam said carelessly. Then he smiled. "It was more like a run-out by Morehead."

This brought a hoot of laughter from Herrington, and Sam reminded himself to make no more jokes, however sorry they might be.

When Herrington's laughter ceased Seeley Carnes asked, "Your friend show up, Kennery?"

"Not yet, but he's a fiddlefoot. Might even've met a girl. Still, he's bound to run out of money sometime."

"It's tough to find work around here now," Herrington said. "Roundup's over and the beef is shipped. There's a lot of men riding the grub line already. You can ask around, though."

"Not interested," Sam said. "He won't be either."

Sam was aware that Brayton was covertly studying him, and now he looked at the agent, surprising him into speech.

"You don't look like a miner, Mr. Kennery. Cattle and mining is all Primrose has to offer."

"We'll make out," Sam said carelessly, even smugly.

"You can always rob a bank," Herrington said, and laughed at his own joke.

Sam nodded and said quietly, unsmilingly, "If we have to, yes." He saw Herrington's quick glance at Brayton, and he finished his drink.

"Dad, I'm hungry," Brayton said. "Let's eat."

"On your money or government money?" Herrington asked, and winked at Sam.

Brayton gave his humorless, yellow-toothed smile. "They're the same thing, ain't they, Dad?"

They had finished their drinks, and Herrington said, "Come along Kennery. You can't eat alone."

Sam nodded and got up. He picked up his bottle, moved over to the bar, and silently paid Alec for the drinks. Remembering Brayton's close scrutiny of him, he wondered if there was any chance the agent might have heard of him and identified him. It was a remote chance, but if it was so he'd know soon. He wasted a few moments selecting some cigars in order to give Brayton an opportunity to tell Herrington of his possible identification. Afterwards, he went out into the lobby, joined the three, and they moved into the dining room. They got a forced smile from Louise Selby and went over to Herrington's usual table.

Tenney, on her way with a tray to a diner near the door, saw them and took a course around a table to avoid them. Sam, who was in the rear, tried to catch her eye, but she looked straight ahead, ignoring him. To his encounter with Morehead and his confessed prison record, he was adding his association with Herrington, whom Tenney loathed. There was really no reason why she should speak, Sam thought grimly.

The noon meal turned out to be a kind of chess game for Sam, and a puzzling one. Brayton was trying, in a seemingly casual way, to find out his background and as much of his history as he could. Obviously, Sam couldn't hide the fact that he'd had some schooling, so he didn't try. His story was that he was the runaway son of a revivalist preacher and had dedicated most of his short life so far to breaking every moral rule his father believed in. He'd been a trail hand, a bodyguard for a Mexican politician, a prospector, and a drifter. Without seeming to care much what he was revealing about himself, he managed a series of wry anecdotes of the scrapes he'd been in, shooting and non-shooting, that planted the information he wanted them to believe. Seeley Carnes, taciturn as usual, listened and watched and occasionally nodded, but took no part in the conversation.

It was a long meal, so long that they were the last ones out of the dining room and had to have the door unlocked for them by Louise Selby.

They halted in the lobby and Brayton went over to where he could get a look at the clock behind the desk. Coming back to them he said, "We were due in the lawyer's office five minutes ago, Dad."

Herrington groaned. "Another two-hour session?"

"Longer, I reckon."

"Well, let's go by way of the bar." To Sam he said, "We'll see you around drinking time, Sam."

This was the first time Sam had been called anything but Kennery, and he was certain now that if Brayton had had any suspicions and related them to Herrington before dinner, the friendly use of "Sam" wouldn't have happened. "Drinking time it is, Dad," Sam said carelessly.

The three of them headed for the bar, and Sam, remaining in the lobby, went over to the desk where a stack of the *Capital Times* were for sale. He bought a paper and then took a lobby chair where he could see through the glass doors into the dining room. Louise Selby, Tenney, and Mary, their own dumpy little waitress, were setting places for supper. Over his opened paper Sam watched them. Presently Louise Selby appeared at the dining-room door with Mary, who was carrying a coat. Louise let Mary and herself out, said good-bye and Mary crossed the lobby, heading for the veranda and the street. Louise disappeared down the corridor toward the Selby apartment beyond the desk. All the help was accounted for except Tenney, who must be in the kitchen.

Sam got up, and under the gaze of Mr. Selby, back of the desk, he went over to the stairs and climbed them. The second-floor corridor was empty and Sam turned left toward his own room. When he came to number eight he halted, tried the door, found it locked, and reached in his pocket for his key ring. He found the blank key of the same type as his own room key and isolated it. Then he drew a match from his pocket, lighted it, and held the blank over the lighted match until it was smoke-blackened. After that he inserted the blank key in the keyhole and twisted it firmly several times.

Withdrawing the key, he noted where the lock tumbler had marked the smoke-blackened metal of the key. The key on the ring to the blank was not really a key, but a heavy piece of wire. Putting this wire key against the blank he drew out his pocket knife. Opening the longest blade, he scored the wire at the place opposite the mark on the blank. Then, isolating the wire from the other key, he slipped it into the blade slot of the knife and, using the knife as pliers, he bent the wire at the mark he had scored. He pocketed the knife and inserted the wire into the keyhole, turned the wire, and heard the lock click open.

Stepping inside the room, he withdrew the wire key, closed the door behind him, and looked around. Although the two beds in Herrington's and Carnes's room had been made up that morning, it was in a disarray that no chambermaid could do much about. A couple of saddles and saddle blankets were stacked in the corner behind the one easy chair. Beside them were piled a couple of dozen issues of the daily *Capital Times*. Herrington and Carnes apparently kept close track of what the newspapers had to say of them. In the corner by the bed nearest the window was a bulky blanket roll, a carbine leaning against it.

First, he moved to the closet and saw that it held several suits, all of them the size that would fit Big Dad. Several pairs of boots were lined up against the wall, and a small trunk was at the rear.

Going next to the dresser, he pulled open the top drawer, which held nothing but clean shirts and socks. He was lifting these when the door opened so silently he did not hear it. Then a voice said, "Well, jailbird, working your way back to prison?"

Before he turned he knew it was Tenney speaking. When he glanced at her he saw her standing, hand still on the doorknob, a look of anger mingled with contempt on her face.

He said levelly, "Come in and shut the door, Tenney."

"When I come in, I'll come with Mr. Selby. I watched you pick that lock from down the hall, and now you're caught."

"That's right," Sam said. He moved over to her, took her by the wrist, and firmly drew her into the room, saying, "Be quiet, Tenney." Then he shut the door.

When he turned he saw the fright in her face and saw her throat muscles begin to tighten for a scream. Swiftly he clamped his hand over her mouth and in as gentle a voice as he could summon, he said, "Tenney! Tenney! Believe in me, will you?" He took one hand from her mouth and the other from her shoulder.

"Believe in you!" Tenney said hotly. "You're nothing but a thief!"

"Tenney, we can't argue here." He pointed to the easy chair. "Sit down in that chair and see if I steal anything."

"I will not."

"All right, stand there and watch me."

"You can't keep me here!" Tenney said fiercely.

"I don't want to keep you here," Sam said. "All I want to do is search this room. Watch me do it."

He went back to the dresser, checked the other drawers, and noted the *Stockman's Journal* on which shaving gear was laid out. Moving past the beds then, he went over to Carnes's blanket roll. He threw the carbine on the bed and tossed the blanket roll beside it, then untied the throngs that held it. All the while Tenney was watching him with mingled suspicion and anger. When Sam glanced at her he was not sure whether she would make a break for the door or not, but he was gambling on her curiosity.

When he unrolled the blanket roll, he saw the couple of shirts and two pairs of socks that seemed to make up the contents, except for two foot-long twists of Carnes's favorite Mexican tobacco. When he went to lift the clothing, though, to look under it, he felt the weight it held. Parting the shirts, he saw that they had wrapped the two parts of a disassembled shotgun. Excitement stirred him now, but he did not let it show in his voice as he looked across the room. "Come here, Tenney."

Slowly Tenney came over to him, and Sam gestured toward the bared gun parts. Tenney looked at them and then at him.

"It's a shotgun," Tenney said and then added tartly, "If he had that rifle too, he had to carry it somewhere."

"That's right," Sam said quietly. He replaced the gun parts and the shirts, rolled up the blankets, tied them as they had been tied, stacked the blanket roll in the corner and leaned the carbine against it just as he had found it.

"Let's go, Tenney."

"Yes. Right down to Mr. Selby."

"All right," Sam said agreeably. "But first we'll see your mother. Is she still in the kitchen?"

The strangeness of his question held Tenney silent for a moment, and then she said, "Yes. Why do you want to see her?"

"Is there a back stairs?" Sam asked. At Tenney's nod, he said, "Let's take that. Come along."

Once in the corridor, Sam took out his wire key, relocked the door, and fell in beside Tenney. They walked the length of the corridor in silence. At its end Tenney opened the last door on the right and led the way down a dark stairwell faintly lighted by a single window. The door at the bottom of the stairs opened into the kitchen, and Tenney opened it without so much as looking back at him.

It was a big kitchen, with a long serving table in the center of the room. An iron range stood alongside a big sink with a pump. The serving table was flanked by several chairs, and in one of these sat a fine-looking woman so young-appearing she could have been Tenney's older sister. She wore a full apron over her short-sleeved blue cotton dress. She had been peeling potatoes, but when she saw Tenney followed by a man strange to her, she stopped her work. She looked at Tenney with puzzlement, then at him. In the level glance she gave him there was no friendliness, but neither was there fear. She had the look of a durable, patient woman who knew her worth.

Tenney moved around the table, and Sam, following, took off his hat. Halting by her mother, Tenney said, "Mother, this is Mr. Kennery. I was counting linen in the closet and heard him come upstairs. I watched him pick the lock of Mr. Herrington's room and I watched him search it."

Mrs. Payne looked at Sam again, this time more carefully, before she said, "Then go tell Mr. Selby."

"He wanted to see you first, Mother." Tenney looked at him and added, "I don't know what for. Maybe he wants to buy me off and thinks you'll let me take the money."

Mrs. Payne looked at Sam. "What do you want of me, Mr. Kennery?"

"Well, I wanted to meet the best cook I've ever known and I wanted to set a few things straight."

Mrs. Payne said unsmilingly, "What's there to set straight?"

"Plenty," Sam answered. "To begin with, Tenney started out liking me, but in two days she won't speak to me except when she caught me picking a lock."

"Maybe she doesn't think you have much character, Mr. Kennery. If you admit to picking a lock she must be right."

"Is that what you think, Tenney?"

"That's too kind for you!" Tenney said fiercely. "You pulled a gun on Sheriff Morehead and you admit you've been in jail. You're even proud of it. You've cozied up to those three rotten men, and now I've caught you breaking into their room to see what you could steal!"

Sam nodded, and then he did a strange thing. He was

standing beside an empty chair, and now he raised his right foot, put it on the chair, and reached inside his boot. He drew from a pocket sewn inside the boot something which he kept hidden in his fist. Straightening up, he walked around the table and extended his fisted hand to Mrs. Payne. "Will you keep this for me, Mrs. Payne?"

Tenney's mother looked at him in bewilderment, but then she held out her hand. Sam deposited the badge of a deputy U.S. marshal in her palm. Both Tenney and her mother looked at it, and then in common surprise raised their glances to him.

"I'm a deputy U.S. marshal, Mrs. Payne. I'm on loan to the marshal's office at Junction City. You can confirm that by asking Sheriff Morehead."

"Be sure I will."

"I'm trying to hunt down the murderer of Morton Schaeffer. Does that name mean anything to you?"

"Nothing."

"He was to be the key government witness at the trial of Herrington and Brayton for criminal fraud. Do you recall a man being ambushed on a train at a water stop north of Junction City about a month ago?"

"I do, Mother," Tenney put in.

Sam didn't look at her. He was watching Mrs. Payne, who in turn was carefully regarding him.

"I'm here to find and arrest the man who used that shotgun."

"Then why did you hold a gun on Sheriff Morehead?"

"That was a fake, Mrs. Payne. It was Morehead's idea, and a clever one. I needed to meet Herrington and Brayton, because certainly Schaeffer's murder could profit only that pair. I had to prove I wasn't afraid of the law or impressed by it, and prove it in front of them. It's worked up to now, Mrs. Payne."

"Why are you telling me this?" Mrs. Payne asked then.

"Because if you believe me, Tenney will believe me; and if Tenney believes me, she can help me."

Now he looked at Tenney, into whose face had come a flush of color.

"Are you saying I haven't a mind of my own?" she asked angrily.

"No. I'm saying I think you respect your mother's judgment. Am I wrong?"

Tenney's face softened. "No," she said quietly.

"Will you keep that badge for me, Mrs. Payne?"

"Why do you want me to?"

"I'll be traveling in some rough company," Sam said. "If they found that on me it would buy me a shot in the back." He paused. "Now do you believe me, Mrs. Payne?"

"I do," Tenney put in before her mother could speak. "Sam, was that shotgun I saw the one that killed Morton Schaeffer?"

"It could be, Tenney, but I'm not sure. Possession of a shotgun doesn't prove anything. We have to put Carnes with that shotgun at the Long Reach water tank on the night of June the thirteenth.

"How will you do that?" Mrs. Payne asked.

"That's where Tenney comes in, Mrs. Payne." To Tenney he said, "Can you get a look at the register in the lobby without making Mr. Selby suspicious?"

"Of course," Tenney said. "Mary and I look at it a lot. Mr. Selby wants us to learn and memorize the names of all the guests. So we're looking at it all the time."

"Can you find out what date Carnes signed in? Or maybe you remember?"

Tenney frowned and thought a minute. "He came after Herrington and Brayton, but I really didn't notice. There was usually one or two men with them at every meal. It wasn't until several days after he got here that I realized he was a regular." She stood up now. "I'll go look."

Tenney went through the swing doors into the dining room. Sam and Mrs. Payne regarded each other now and, oddly, neither of them was ill at ease.

Sam said, "I've given Tenney a rough time, I'm afraid."

"She enjoyed your teasing, but the business with the sheriff frightened her."

Sam nodded. "It was meant to. I had a story to set up, and Tenney had to believe it and spread it."

Mrs. Payne smiled faintly. "Well, she believed it and spread it to me."

"Where it stopped, I'll bet."

"Yes. You see, I couldn't gossip if I wanted to. The Selbys and the girls are the only people I see."

"You take Sundays off, don't you?"

She nodded. "Tenney takes over here and I ride all day, mostly to get the kitchen smell out of my head."

"If I'm here next Sunday, can I ride with you?"

Surprise came into Mrs. Payne's face. "Why, of course, but why would you want to?"

"I'm just guessing, but I think you need a man around you some of the time. I think you need to hear him cuss, and scold him, or tell him how different things were when you were a girl."

Mrs. Payne's smile was a sad one, somehow acknowledging the truth of what Sam said. "It is lonely sometimes." She nodded toward the door in the rear of the rooms. "We have two rooms back there. Counting them and the kitchen, it makes up our world."

"Tenney's too?"

"No. Tenney has her good times. She goes to dances and church doings."

"With anyone special?" Sam asked carelessly.

Suddenly Mrs. Payne laughed, and Sam thought it was pure delight to hear her.

He smiled and said, "Did I say something funny?"

"No, but you're making your point about my need to be around men."

Sam said, "You've lost me, Mrs. Payne."

"No, I haven't. You like Tenney. You want to know if she likes you, or if she likes some other man. You've noticed the ring on her finger and you're wondering if she's engaged. I can tell you right now her ring is only insurance against the attentions of drummers and cowboys. You'd be surprised how often it works." She paused. "How am I doing in my study of man?"

"You're doing all right in your study of this one," Sam said.

Tenney came in then from the dining room and found them laughing. She was so surprised that she halted, looking from one to the other, and asked, "What are you two laughing at?"

Sam looked at Mrs. Payne and said quietly, "I think your mother will tell you sometime, Tenney. What did you find out?"

Tenney came over and sat down in the chair she had vacated. "Seeley Carnes registered on September fifteenth, Sam. Does that mean anything?"

Sam was silent a long moment, feeling a stir of excitement. "It could, Tenney. The trial was set for the fifteenth. Schaeffer was killed on the thirteenth. It's a long two day's ride from the Long Reach water tank to Primrose, but it could be done." He shook his head. "Still, suspicion isn't proof."

He stood up. "Tenney, how has Carnes treated you?"

"Why, not at all. When I had their table he never spoke to me except to order. I'd guess he hasn't even noticed that Mary's waiting on him and I'm not."

Remembering Mary's dumpy figure, Sam said dryly, "Your guess is wrong. Still, keep it that way, Tenney. You don't like Herrington, so you don't like Carnes. Treat him the way you've been treating me, and keep on treating me the same way." He reached for his hat and said quietly, "Thank you both."

The two women watched him cross the kitchen and take the back stairs, closing the door behind him.

Tenney picked up her apron, tied it, and sat down. Mrs. Payne was already at her task of finishing peeling the potatoes. When Tenney picked up her knife and reached for a potato, Mrs. Payne said quietly, "Say something, Tenney."

"All right. I'm numb."

"You're not alone," her mother said.

Sam climbed to the second floor, his mind still turning over the information Tenney had gotten for him. Of the three men, Seeley Carnes would be the hardest to get close to. Beyond that, there were still things that Sam couldn't answer. How did Seeley know the Primrose & Midland would stop at the Long Reach water tank, and that it would be dark? Brayton would know that, but Brayton was in Primrose when Schaeffer was killed. Had Brayton made a previous trip to the agency—one Sam didn't know about? If he had, he could have met Carnes and briefed him; or the second killer could have known the train time, but who was he?

It was important that he see Morehead tonight and try to sort out the bits in this puzzle. He would also have to tell him of the Payne women's knowledge of his identity. Had he been foolish in trusting Tenney and her mother? He didn't think he was that bad a judge of character. Tenney, for all her acquaintance with men at the Primrose House, wouldn't gossip about him, he was certain.

Chapter 7

HERRINGTON, Brayton, and Carnes, as Big Dad promised, were free of their lawyers by drinking time. They had saved a seat for Sam at what was turning out to be their table in the crowded bar. Both Big Dad and Brayton seemed in low spirits, while Carnes was his usual taciturn self. Over whiskey, Sam learned that their lawyers had failed again to win a dismissal of their case by the court. The prosecution had been granted another week's postponement of the trial, and while Herrington and Brayton cursed the judge for a biased fool, Sam silently blessed him.

Both Brayton and Herrington drank heavily before and during the meal, and Sam looked forward with dread to a long and alcoholic evening in their company. During supper he kept galncing covertly at Tenney who, as far as he could tell, never once looked at him. He had a mounting feeling that this situation with his three companions was becoming intolerable. True, he had a tenuous link between Seeley Carnes and Schaeffer's murder, but the proof of it must come from one of the three. The initiative was in their hands; all he could do was to listen passively, hoping that an incautious word, a slip of the tongue, would betray them.

Sam heard his name spoken and looked up to find all three regarding him.

"The whiskey gettin' to you, Sam?" Herrington asked from across the table. "I've been talkin' to you and you never heard. You comin' down drunk?"

Sam grinned faintly and shook his head. "No, I was just thinking, Dad. This fellow I was to meet was due here ahead of me. I've been here two days now, and no sign of him and no word from him. I was studying on what might have happened to him, is all. What were you saying to me?"

"I said why don't we all go up to my room where we can talk private?"

"Suits me," Sam said indifferently.

They rose, paid at the door, and then mounted the stairs to Herrington's and Carnes's room. Sam entered the room after Big Dad and he looked about it casually, as any man does when he enters a strange room. There were new papers on the dresser top which they had probably brought back from their lawyer. While Seeley got Brayton's key and went next door for an extra chair, Herrington busied himself with fresh drinks.

When Seeley returned with the chair he indicated to Sam that it was for him. Herrington took the easy chair, while Brayton and Seeley sat on separate beds. Herrington and Brayton lighted cigars; Carnes built a cigarette and lighted the foul Mexican tobacco. Sam had declined a cigar by saying, "No, I've had too many, Dad. A few more, and the first fresh air I breathe will knock me cold."

Herrington's bray of laughter sawed at Sam's nerves and he saw Herrington and Brayton exchange glances.

"You want some fresh air, Sam?" Herrington asked quietly. Sam grinned. "You got any, Dad?"

Herrington for once smiled instead of laughed. "Not here, but I can send you where there is some."

Sam came alert, and a feigned puzzlement showed on his face. He looked at the other two, who were watching him, and then his glance returned to Herrington. "You trying to tell me something, Dad?"

Herrington nodded. "Kind of roundabout, Sam. We've got a job for you if you'll take it."

"Outdoor job?"

"Outdoor job," Herrington confirmed. "Up north on the reservation."

Sam scowled as he asked, "Doing what?"

Now Brayton took over. "Sam, I got me a trouble-making Indian up there. I want you to hunt him up and take him up in the mountains with about six quarts of whiskey. Don't bother feeding him, because he'll be so drunk he won't eat. When he's passed out for the tenth time or so, just take his clothes and blankets, and his flint and steel. Pneumonia will do the rest, I reckon."

Sam studied the drink cradled in his lap, hiding his face so that the elation he felt might not be betrayed by his expression. When he looked up he saw the three men watching him intently.

"With what kind of money, Con?" Sam asked calmly. Herrington and Brayton exchanged glances again, and then

Herrington said, "Would a couple of hundred dollars do it, Sam?"

"You don't like this Indian either, Dad?"

"That's right."

"Yes, a couple of hundred would do," Sam said. "I've killed Indians for nothing."

Once more Herrington's laugh exploded and Sam waited until it died out before asking Brayton, "Why this business with six quarts of whiskey, Con? Why not a bottle to toll him out of camp and then shoot him?"

"Yes, you can do that, but only if the other don't work."

"You just want him dead, is that it?"

Con nodded slowly.

Sam got up and went over to the bottle of whiskey on the desk. This Indian they wanted dead had to be either the ambusher or his partner. He must try to confirm this without seeming too curious. Picking up the bottle, he made the rounds, pouring each of them a drink and finally one for himself. All the time he kept silent, and when he returned to his chair and sat down, Herrington said, "Something troubling you, Sam?"

"A few things, Dad," Sam said. "Like who do I pull down on my head when I've killed him? Fifty Indians? The whole damn reservation? The U.S. army, or the U.S. marshal? Just so I know."

Brayton snorted. "Nobody, Sam. Oh, his wife will yell some, but she'll never know why he was killed—or died."

"Can I be the judge of that, Con? Why am I killing him?"

Con and Herrington looked at each other, and Sam thought, *Here it is.*

Seeley Carnes spoke for the first time. "No." He was answering Sam's question.

Both men looked at Seeley Carnes, and Sam tried to read their expressions. Brayton looked annoyed and Herrington almost angry.

Herrington said impatiently, "We'll all be in this together after he's dead. What's the harm, Seeley? We got to have it done, don't we?"

"There's other men that'll do it," Seeley said.

Brayton grimaced. "You find one before the time's up, Seeley."

Seeley shrugged and said nothing.

Sam put in quietly, "Maybe you better get yourselves a

new boy. If you won't tell me what this will drag down on me, then it must be plenty."

Brayton stood up, fury in his ravaged face. "God damn it, Seeley! You gone crazy?" He paused. "Come out in the hall." He headed for the door, and Seeley, after getting Herrington's nod, followed him.

He closed the door behind him and moved across the hall to where Brayton had halted.

"What the hell's the matter with you, Seeley? Kennery's already agreed to kill him. What's the matter with telling him why? Would you take money to kill a man when you didn't know what it would pull down on you?"

Carnes said in a flinty voice, "If I asked that question I reckon the answer would be a lie. You better make your answer to Kennery a lie, Con."

"You make up the lie then," Con countered.

Seeley started to speak, but he didn't, and his face remained set in stubborn disapproval.

When Seeley didn't respond, Brayton went on, "What's the harm in the truth? He already knows we're up for trial, he already knows we want Joe dead, and he's willing to kill him for us. If he hasn't already guessed that Joe is tied in with Schaeffer's killing, he's pretty dumb."

"All right," Seeley said. "Tell 'im, but hold out the one thing, Con." He paused, and then asked with seeming irrelevance, "Con, you think I'd stop at killing you if you put my neck in a noose?"

Brayton stood silent, but after a moment he answered truthfully, "No, I think you'd kill me."

"You better believe I would. Now, here's what you tell Kennery. You tell him why you and Dad had Schaeffer killed. You tell him why Joe Potatoes has to be put away; but just remember, never bring in my name. Schaeffer's killing—Joe done it alone. You got that, Con? Joe done it alone."

"You don't care then if we tell him the true story?"

"Not one damn bit—just so I'm left out of it. Do it that way, Con, and I'm happy. Don't do it, and you're dead."

"What a hell of an uproar over something so simple," Brayton said. He moved away from the wall, brushed past Seeley, and went back into the room. Seeley trailed him in.

Sam had heard through the door the sound of their low conversation but not the words, and he sipped thoughtfully at his drink. He surprised Herrington watching him with an

expression of quiet approval on his heavy face. Sam kept his
own face expressionless, but he was reviewing what had just
passed. Had he pushed them too far too soon? No, he
didn't think he had. Any prudent killer would first assess
the consequences before taking on a job of that sort, and that
was exactly what he was doing.

The murmur of talk in the hall had ceased and Brayton
and Seeley were back.

"Dad, Seeley's agreed," Brayton said. "Let me talk, will
you?" He returned to the bed. "Here's the way it is, Sam.
There was a key witness for the government on his way to
testify against us in our trial. He was a lying, double-crossing
crook that worked for me at the agency, and I should have
fired him years ago. We couldn't let him testify. We paid
this Indian—Joe Potatoes we called him—to get Schaeffer
and he did. Maybe you read about it, or heard about it?"

"No."

"Well, like a lot of Indians, Joe loves his booze. He's
blackmailing us now, and there'll be no end to it. After he's
dead nothing will happen. You got to take my word for
that, Sam. If he was a chief or a member of the Council,
that would be different, but Joe's nothing. Nobody likes him,
and nobody trusts him. If they find him dead of pneumonia,
nobody'll be surprised. If they find him shot they'll figure
somebody got even with him and, believe me, a lot of people
had reason to. His wife is a whore and her family's dis-
owned her." He paused. "That satisfy you, Sam?"

For answer Sam looked at Seeley. "That's pretty small
potatoes, Seeley."

Carnes actually flushed. "Now I hear it spoke, I reckon it
is."

Sam turned to Brayton. "Half down now, and half when
I get him—that all right?"

Both men reached for their wallets at the same time. Both
were smiling. Between them, they rounded enough eagles
to make Sam's hundred, then had another drink in celebra-
tion.

Afterwards, Brayton took over the chore of instructing
Sam. He got only as far as telling him to take tomorrow
afternoon's train north as far as the stop called Boundary
when Seeley interrupted. "Con, why don't you take Sam down
to the bar and finish that? Me and Dad got some Texas talk
to chew over. We'll be down when we're through."

Brayton looked surprised, and his glance went to

Herrington. Herrington looked a little surprised too, but he seemed to acquiesce.

Brayton got up. "Come along, Sam," he said.

When they had left the room, closing the door behind them, Herrington asked, "What Texas talk, Seeley?"

Carnes crossed over to the bed and sat down, facing his boss. He began quietly, "Dad, we're makin' a mistake hirin' Kennery."

"Prove it."

"I can't. It's just a feelin' I've got."

Herrington scowled, and his glance at Seeley was at once searching and skeptical. "Funny. The feeling I've got is that we've found the right man. What's there about him that spooks you?"

"Nothin' spooks me. Nothin' ever spooks me," Carnes said flatly.

"The hell it don't," Herrington replied roughly. "I noticed when Con came back from talking with you out in the hall he never told Kennery you were with Joe."

"Damn right he didn't. I told him he'd better not tie me in."

"So you're not spooked," Herrington said dryly.

Carnes came to his feet and Herrington saw that he had scored. Seeley was white around the mouth and his bleached eyes held a wicked glint. "Careful, Dad."

"All right, all right," Herrington said placatingly. "I'm just trying to understand you. Here we got this whole thing set up and paid for, and now you're backin' off. Why?"

"I'm not backin' off," Carnes said sullenly. "I'm only tryin' to warn you."

"Damn it, Seeley, be reasonable!" Herrington exploded. "What else could we do? There ain't time to send for someone we know. And you can't stand out in front of the hotel and say to everybody that comes along, 'Want two hundred dollars for killin' an Indian?' Me, I think we're blind lucky."

"What if he takes the money and runs?"

"That's a risk," Herrington conceded. "One we got to take."

"What if he goes to the law?" Carnes persisted.

"Why, if he does, we call him a liar. There's the word of the three of us that we made him no such a proposition."

"Aah," Seeley said in disgust. Turning, he put one hand under the back of his belt and began to circle the room slowly.

Herrington leaned forward, elbows on knees, forearms crossed. "This ain't like you, Seeley. Name me one thing about him that looks wrong."

Seeley halted and looked at his boss. "All right. Where's this friend he's been expecting? If he's so damn set on meetin' him, why would he take four or five days off to earn two hundred dollars?"

Big Dad snorted. "Why, this friend's kept him waitin'—Why shouldn't *he* keep *him* waitin'?"

"If there is a friend," Carnes said cynically.

"We can't know that, and why does it matter a damn if there's no friend? If Kennery runs out on us, we've lost one hundred dollars. If he delivers, we're safe. He can't talk, and we won't talk. Can you shoot that down, Seeley?"

Carnes resumed his pacing, shaking his head from side to side. "It's just a feelin' I got, Dad. This is no good."

Big Dad stood up. "Well, you're out of it and safe, Seeley. It's me and Con that takes the risk, not you."

"Well, I'm goin' to watch him," Carnes said flatly.

"Go ahead, but you got damn good eyes if you can see as far as that Indian reservation."

His bray of laughter followed, and Carnes looked at him with malevolence in his pale eyes.

"Let's go drink up, Seeley," Herrington said. "They'll be wondering what's keeping us."

He moved past Carnes toward the door; then, as if something had just occurred to him, he halted and turned. "Don't pick a fight with him, Seeley," Dad said quietly. "Let him get this job done. Afterwards I don't care." He smiled. "Yes, I do care. I like you, Seeley. I'd hate to have to bury you."

Chapter 8

AROUND midnight, Sam parted from Brayton, Herrington, and Carnes in the second-floor corridor. Their good nights were alcoholically cordial, and Sam went the short distance to his own room and let himself in. After lighting the lamp on the dresser, he moved over to the bed, propped up the pillow, and leaned back against it. From his jacket pocket he took the letter of introduction that Con Brayton had given him. It was addressed to Roy McCook, who, Brayton said, was a friend who ran the trading post at Boundary and who would supply him with whiskey and a horse. The envelope was unsealed and Sam read the contents. It was simply a request that McCook should supply Sam with everything he asked for.

He tossed the letter on the bed and reviewed this incredible day. He had been hired almost casually to kill the Indian who had killed Schaeffer. It was an unbelievable piece of luck for him, but when he analyzed it, he was not much farther toward getting evidence on Carnes than he had been this morning. True, he had the name of the Indian implicated in Schaeffer's killing, and he had evidence, unprovable in court, that Herrington and Brayton had paid him to kill the Indian. What, he wondered, had Carnes said to Brayton out in the hall this afternoon, and what had Carnes said to Herrington under the guise of "Texas business." So far, neither by words or actions of the three, did he have anything to tie Carnes in with Schaeffer's killing? There was Carnes's shotgun and his date of arrival in Primrose. In sum, nothing.

Sheriff Morehead, Sam knew, should be told of what had happened today and of his pending visit to the reservation. He realized then that he did not know where Morehead lived, and even if he did, he couldn't talk to him without risking being seen. It would be insanely risky to go to the courthouse to see the sheriff. Even if he saw him on the street or at the depot, the risk of being seen talking with him was still there. Yet Morehead should know what had passed and what was coming up.

It came to Sam that there was a way to communicate with Morehead without having to speak with him. He got up, blew out the lamp, and crossed to the door. He fumbled for the knob, found it, and opened the door. The second floor was quiet; the only sounds he could hear were the distant muted talk and laughter that came up the stairwell from the barroom. Stepping out into the hall, he quietly closed the door behind him, and slowly moved down to Brayton's room. Here he halted and listened, and presently he picked up the sound of deep rhythmical breathing.

Moving on to the room next door which Herrington and

Carnes occupied, he halted again. The sound of raucous snoring reached him through the door. He listened carefully but failed to pick up the sound of a second person's breathing, which the snoring probably drowned out. It didn't matter really, for the snoring would cover any small sound he would make on his way to the stairwell.

Achieving it, he went down the steps, crossed the dimly lit lobby, and went down the veranda steps to the plank walk. Here he moved on past the street entrance to the saloon and turned right at the corner. Passing the blank back of the saloon, he made out the bay of the loading dock for the kitchen.

The small one-story wing off the kitchen would be Tenney's and her mother's room. He halted, letting his eyes adjust to the darkness, and presently he made out the shape of a rain barrel at the corner of the wing, and then the door that was the outside entrance to their room. Approaching it, he knocked firmly on the door, and then put his back against the wall. The door opened, casting a shaft of lamplight on the ground.

"Who is it?" Tenney asked.

"It's me. Sam. Douse the lamp, Tenney, and let me in."

He waited until the light was blown out and then stepped into a room whose furnishings he could not even see. Halting a step inside the door, he felt Tenney brushing his sleeve as she closed the door.

"What is it, Sam?" Tenney whispered. Before he could answer, Mrs. Payne's voice came from the doorway of the other room.

"I'm awake, Tenney."

"I'm sorry I had to do this, Mrs. Payne, but it's the only way I can talk with you."

"That's all right," Mrs. Payne said.

Unable to see either woman, Sam felt their friendly presence. "Tenney, can you see Sheriff Morehead tomorrow morning and give him a message?"

"Of course I can," Tenney answered from almost beside him.

He continued, "Tell him I'm heading for the reservation tomorrow. I don't know how long I'll be gone. Tell him I was paid tonight by Herrington and Brayton to kill the Indian they say shot Schaeffer."

"They paid you?" Tenney asked incredulously.

"A hundred dollars now. A hundred dollars when he's dead."

Mrs. Payne's voice came from closer by.

"Can't they be arrested for that?"

"Yes, but not yet. Tell Morehead to stay away from them. Also, if he plans to see the train off tomorrow, tell him not to. Tell him if he sees me on the street before train time not to stop me or talk to me. You might tell him, too, that if I knew where he lived I wouldn't have bothered you tonight."

"Important things aren't bothers," Mrs. Payne said quietly.

"One more thing, Mrs. Payne. I told you to keep my badge until I called for it. I'd like it now." He heard the rustle of her nightdress as she left the room.

When Tenney spoke she seemed very close to him; he even caught a pleasant smell of newly washed, sun-dried hair.

"Sam, if you don't kill this man, won't they know and turn on you?"

"I wish they'd try, Tenney. It would make things a lot easier, but no to your question. I think I'll have the goods on Carnes before they know we have the Indian."

He felt a touch on his arm and then Mrs. Payne spoke to him. "Here's the badge, Sam."

Sam thanked her quietly and said, "I don't know when I'll see you two again, but I will. Good-bye for now."

They said good night, and Sam stepped out into the darkness. The night was so quiet that he could pick up the distant sound of the thudding of the Consolidated Stamp Mill working night shift across the river. From the livery up the street he could hear the quiet bickering of a couple of horses back in the corral.

He was almost past the loading dock when he caught the faint scent of burnt tobacco. It took him only the time of two quick steps that put him past the loading dock before his memory told him this was the smell of Seeley Carnes's raw Mexican tobacco with which he had become familiar these last few days.

He didn't break stride as he headed for the corner. If that smoke had come from Seeley Carnes's cigarette, it meant that Carnes had perhaps seen him go into Tenney's place and certainly had seen him come out. Dismay touched him for a moment. Was Carnes following him? If he was, it meant his actions were suspect to Brayton and Herrington.

Rounding the corner, Sam flattened himself against the front of the saloon. How would they interpret his visit to Tenney? A tryst? Hardly, not with Mrs. Payne there.

Sam poked his head around the corner then and looked down the dark alley. He thought he saw something moving in the darkness but he couldn't be sure. Deciding to take the chance, he moved back around the corner, flattening himself against the saloon wall. He had taken less than a dozen cautious steps when he heard the sound of a door down the alley being hammered on. Swiftly then, he moved as quietly as he could against the wall toward the loading dock. He had barely reached its bay when a shaft of lamplight appeared from Tenney's door. It revealed Carnes standing in the alley, facing the door.

Sam heard Carnes say, "Miss, I was coming down the alley and I saw a man go in your place."

Tenney's voice came to him faintly as she said, "Surely you're mistaken."

"No, I'm not. Look around in there."

"But the door was locked," Tenney said.

Carnes said flatly, "I seen what I seen. Look around in there. I'll help you." Swiftly Carnes stepped up to the door.

By the diminution of the lamplight, Sam knew that Tenney was trying to shut the door on Carnes, but suddenly the lamplight increased and Carnes disappeared inside.

Sam ran then, heading for the door. Even as he ran, the lamplight faded. Did it mean that Tenney had fled to her mother's room? He could hear nothing except the pounding of his own feet as he reached the door and lunged through it. Tenney was standing in a back corner of the tiny living room holding her wrapper across her nightgown with one hand and holding the lamp with the other. When she turned her head towards the doorway, Sam could see the fright in her face. He hauled up just as Seeley Carnes stepped out of the bedroom.

At the sight of Sam he halted, and the two men looked at each other.

"What are you doing in this house?" Sam asked.

"I saw a man come in here and they won't believe it. But he's hid here all right."

Sam moved toward him. "If you saw him come in here, you saw him go out. It was me."

"Then what were you doin' here?" Carnes demanded.

Behind Carnes Sam could see the dim figure of Mrs. Payne standing back in the room.

"Not that it's any of your damn business, Seeley, but I came to tell Tenney and her mother good-bye."

"You could have told them in the morning," Carnes said coldly.

Sam moved toward him. He saw the fingers of Seeley's right hand unclench and he saw beyond it the form of Mrs. Payne move out of the way into the darkness.

"Again it's none of your business, Seeley, but I'll be long gone by daylight."

"You're goin' to Junction City on the train," Seeley said flatly.

"And I'll catch it ten miles out of town at the Calico Flats switch-off."

"Why?"

Sam said contemptuously, "So a certain Mr. Morehead won't telegraph ahead and have me watched." He added then, with quiet menace in his voice, "You have a long nose, Seeley. I aim to change the shape of it."

Carnes's hand streaked for his gun and he had grasped the butt of it as Sam finished his lunge. His left hand clamped down on the wrist of Seeley's gun hand, sealing the gun in its holster. At the same time, with his right arm bent, Sam rammed his elbow in Carnes's face with a savage full-bodied swing.

Carnes stumbled back against the door frame, instinctively raising his left hand to his face. Sam felt Carnes's right hand tug and he lifted Seeley's wrist. The gun came out of the holster and was barely clear of it when Sam swept down his right hand and batted the gun out of Carnes's hand. It clattered to the floor at Tenney's feet.

Carnes, with his back against the door frame, now had a position that could anchor his weight. He moved his foot against the wall, lowered his head, and drove at Sam, trying to butt him with his head. It caught Sam on the shoulder and spun him around off balance, but he still held Carnes's wrist with his left hand and, falling, he pulled Carnes two steps forward; then, using his falling weight as a lever, Sam yanked on Carnes's arm. The Texan was propelled past him in a staggering off-balance lunge. Sam hit the floor with a crash that drove the breath from him in an anguished grunt. He rolled over in time to see Carnes, far off balance and running, trip on the door sill and sprawl out, face down, in the alley. He had regained his knees when Sam came hurtling through the doorway and smashed him flat in the alley's dust.

Moaning softly, Tenney came to the doorway, still holding the lamp. She saw both men, hatless now, come to their feet facing each other, and she noticed that Seeley Carnes was bleeding from a torn lip that Sam's elbow had mashed.

Now the real fight began, with the whole alley to maneuver in. On the first move Sam was the quicker. He came at Carnes, accepting a clout on the side of his head as the price of closing in. He drove a solid ramming blow into Carnes's midriff, and Tenney could hear the great explosion of Carnes's breath that followed. He instinctively wrapped his arms around his middle and bent over. Sam moved a half-step to his right, then drove his fist into the side of Carnes's face. The force of the blow spun Carnes half around and off balance, so that he stumbled across the alley, head down, and rammed head-first into the door of the sturdy shed that stored the hotel hack at night. Sam caught him on the rebound, putting both hands on Carnes's shoulders and yanking him around. Carnes spun and, coming out of the spin, he kicked out with his right leg.

The blow caught Sam behind the knee, pulling that leg out from under him so that he pitched on his side. Rolling over to come to his knees, he caught another kick that knifed into his side. As he rose he heard the great shuddering inhalations as Carnes fought to get his breath back. Sam tested his numb left leg, found it would hold him, and moved in again, this time with a determined fury that frightened Tenney and her mother, watching from the door. Carnes fought viciously, fiercely trying to stop Sam's slugging advance. He was trying desperately to reverse their roles, to take the fight to Sam, instead of being relentlessly pushed back. He was fighting equally hard to regain his breath.

With a kind of dogged, killer stubbornness, Sam moved Carnes back. The blows of Carnes that he couldn't check or parry, he took silently, always moving forward, always punishing Carnes's body, never his head.

Slowly Carnes was backed toward the corner of the house, where a great rain barrel stood against the house in the loading dock's bay and out of the alley.

Carnes backed around the house and into the barrel and tried to step around it, but Sam, his quarry cornered now,

Enjoy the best of Louis L'Amour in special volumes made to last as long as your pleasure

As a reader of Louis L'Amour's tough and gritty tales of the Old West, you'll be delighted by <u>The Louis L'Amour</u> Collection— a series of hardcover editions of Louis L'Amour's exciting Western adventures.

The feel of rich leathers. Like a good saddle, these volumes are made to last—to be read, re-read and passed along to family and friends for years to come. Bound in rugged sierra-brown simulated leather with gold lettering, <u>The Louis L'Amour Collection</u> will be a handsome addition to your home library.

<u>Silver Canyon</u> opens the series. It's the memorable tale of Matt Brennan, gunfighter, and his lone battle against duelling ranchers in one of the bloodiest range wars the West had ever seen. After <u>Silver Canyon</u> you'll set out on a new adventure every month, as succeeding volumes in the Collection are conveniently mailed to your home.

Receive the full-color Louis L'Amour Western Calendar FREE—just for looking at <u>Silver Canyon</u>. Like every volume in <u>The Louis L'Amour Collection</u>, <u>Silver Canyon</u> is yours to examine without risk or obligation. If you're not satisfied, return it within 10 days and owe nothing. The calendar is yours to keep.

Send no money now. Simply complete the coupon opposite to enter your subscription to <u>The Louis L'Amour Collection</u> and receive your free calendar.

The newest volume...

The newest volume I placed on the shelf of my 8000-volume home research library was very special to me—the first copy of _Silver Canyon_ in the hardcover Collector's Edition put together by the folks at Bantam Books.

I'm very proud of this new collection of my books. They're handsome, permanent and what I like best of all, affordable.

I hope you'll take this opportunity to examine the books in the Collection and see their fine quality for yourself. I think you'll be as pleased as I am!

Louis L'Amour

Send no money now–but mail today!

☐ **YES!** Please send me _Silver Canyon_ for a 10-day free examination, along with my free Louis L'Amour Calendar, and enter my subscription to <u>The Louis L'Amour Collection</u>. If I decide to keep _Silver Canyon_, I will pay $7.95 plus shipping and handling and receive one additional volume per month on a fully returnable, 10-day free-examination basis. There is no minimum number of books to buy, and I may cancel my subscription at any time. The Calendar is mine whether or not I keep _Silver Canyon_.   85019

☐ I prefer the deluxe edition, bound in genuine leather, at only $24.95 each plus shipping and handling.   87015

Name _____ _(please print)_

Address _____

City _____ State _____ Zip _____

In Canada, mail to:
Bantam Books Canada, Inc.
60 St. Clair Avenue East, Suite 601
Toronto, Ontario M4T 1N5

had no intention of letting him escape. This was where the fight would finish. He drove Carnes back into the wedge and against the wall, then slugged blow after blow into the Texan's lean body. Again Carnes made the mistake of lowering his arms to protect his midriff. Instantly then Sam went for Carnes's head. He drove a blow into the Texan's jaw that smashed his head back against the building. Finally, with a blow that caught Carnes's head on the edge of the jaw, the fight ended. Carnes's knees buckled and he fell forward into Sam's arms. Sam pushed him back into the wedge of rain barrel and wall, and then, holding Carnes erect, he reached down into the big barrel. It was half full.

Then he knelt, took his hand away from Carnes's chest and let his body slack over his shoulder. Lifting him, Sam dropped him, jack-knifed, into the rain barrel. The water geysered up, and when it had settled, Sam saw that its level was just under Carnes's chin. The Texan's legs, unable to bend at the knees because of the confining barrel, pointed straight into the air.

Sam stumbled around the barrel, reached the loading dock, folded his arms on it, and put his head on his arms. Only then was he aware that Tenney and her mother had come out into the alley with the lamp to watch the fight's finish. He heard them come up behind him, but for the moment he could only fight for more air to breathe.

When his wild panting lessened, he straightened up, wincing at the pain the smallest movement brought. Turning his head, he saw Tenney, lamp in hand, and her mother standing close beside him.

Mrs. Payne held his hat out to him and said quietly, "He'll never get out of that barrel without help, Sam."

"You feel like helpin' him, Mrs. Payne?" Sam asked dryly.

"No, but if I call myself a Christian, I ought to."

Sam nodded and went slowly back to the barrel. He put both hands on its rim and pulled the barrel toward him. It tipped on its side with a thud, and a cascade of water swirled around Carnes's body. Grabbing Carnes by the collar of his jacket, Sam dragged him out of the barrel and let him fall on his back in the mud.

Then he looked at Mrs. Payne and said, "That's a comfortable place to rest, Mrs. Payne. I've used it a couple of times myself."

Mrs. Payne smiled. "All right, let's leave him there."

"Are you hurt, Sam?" Tenney asked.

"All over," Sam said. "I can make it to bed though."

He looked at Tenney's mother and said, "Mrs. Payne, he may be at you again. Stick to my story. I came to you yesterday afternoon while Herrington and Brayton were with their lawyer. I asked your permission to see Tenney. You didn't like me much, but left it up to Tenney. I was going to take her to your church social tomorrow night. The reason I came to your house was to tell Tenney I'd be out of town for a few days. I didn't tell you where I was going, or how. That's absolutely all you know."

"I'll remember," Mrs. Payne said. She looked down at Carnes. "Why did he come to our place?"

"He doesn't trust me, Mrs. Payne. He followed me here and waited until I left. I think he thought that I might be meeting Sheriff Morehead in your rooms. I believe he thought he'd find Morehead there if he searched the place."

Now Sam looked at Tenney. "Tenney, tell Morehead about this too. You can forget about warning him to stay away from me. I've got to leave before daylight to back up my story to Carnes."

"What will Brayton and Herrington do about your beating up their friend?"

"Laugh, I would judge," Sam said. "I'll say good night now."

Tenney, a coat over her uniform against the morning chill, was at the courthouse by seven-thirty next morning. As she turned down the corridor she saw Sheriff Morehead unlocking the door of his office at the rear corner of the building. She was congratulating herself on her timing when Morehead turned and started for the side door. He wasn't unlocking his office, he was locking it, Tenney saw, and she called, "Oh, Sheriff."

Morehead turned and halted, and Tenney hurried down to meet him. As she stopped before him, Morehead said in his gravelly voice, "Why, hello, Tenney."

"Can I talk with you, please?"

"Can you make it later on, Tenney? I was headed for the depot."

"That can wait. You've got to hear what I have to tell."

Morehead looked at her strangely and then moved past her, reaching in his pocket for his key. Unlocking the door, he stood aside and Tenney moved into his office. Morehead gestured to the chair beside the desk and Tenney seated herself; then he took off his hat and sat down in the swivel chair. "What is it, Tenney?" Morehead asked.

"It's about Sam Kennery," Tenney said. She told him of Kennery's midnight visit to them.

As she talked, a look first of bewilderment and then of incredulity came over Morehead's square face.

Tenney stopped speaking, halted by his expression, and said, "What did I say?"

"You mean you know Kennery's a deputy U.S. marshal?"

Suddenly Tenney realized that events had moved so rapidly for Sam Kennery that he had not even had time to let the sheriff know about this.

She began at the beginning then, telling how she had surprised Kennery picking the lock of Herrington's room, of his visit to the kitchen, of his identifying himself and asking her and her mother for help. She told of watching Sam's search of Herrington's and Carnes's room and of his finding a shotgun in Carnes's blanket roll. As she progressed to the events of the late evening when Kennery was offered and accepted money for killing the Indian who was implicated in Schaeffer's murder, Morehead could only look at her with undisguised amazement and embarrassment. When she paused, Morehead shook his head.

He said, "I feel like a man with an unfaithful wife. He's always the last to know. I'm the sheriff here, but you're the one who tells me what my marshal friend has been doing."

"I haven't told all of it yet, Sheriff." She told him then of Seeley Carnes's visit after Sam had left, and of Sam's return and the subsequent fight.

Morehead listened to this with pure pleasure. When she finished, he said, "Won't that beating change Herrington's and Brayton's mind about Sam?"

"I don't think so," Tenney answered. "The reason I don't is that first thing this morning I went up to Sam's room. It was empty and his blanket roll was gone. If they had called it off last night, Sam wouldn't have gone, would he?"

"Certainly he would," Morehead said. "Fired or not, he'd be off to get that Indian, wouldn't he?"

"But he'd have taken the train instead of pretending he didn't want you to see him."

"That's true," Morehead agreed. "Now go back, Tenney. Does Kennery think Carnes was with the Indian when Schaeffer was shot?"

"I think he does. I think he hopes the Indian will give

him proof." She leaned forward in her chair then and asked, "Who is Kennery, Sheriff? I know he's a deputy U.S. marshal, but who is he?"

"That's what I asked in my letter to Marshal Wilbarth. He quoted me a letter from Kennery's boss. Kennery was a rancher up north. He was going to marry a girl. It seems she was a teacher in a tough cattle town that was the center of a range war. She got caught in the cross fire of cowboys shooting it out on the street."

Tenney asked the inevitable, "Was she killed?"

Morehead's slow nod answered her. "The sheriff there was a coward and afraid to take sides. Kennery went to the U.S. marshal and asked to be deputized so he'd have the law behind him when he hunted down her killers. He did just that. Afterwards, he wanted to resign and did, but his marshal kept reappointing him and assigning him to jobs. Kennery finally gave in because, as he put it to his marshal, he was making a career out of mourning for the dead girl."

Morehead spread his hands and shrugged. "That's about all I know of him, Tenney, except that his marshal said he was far and away the best man ever to wear the badge in his district."

Tenney was silent a moment. "How sad," she said quietly.

Sheriff Morehead looked at her a long moment and then said gently, "Any sadder than your mother losing a young husband? Any sadder than you not even remembering your father?"

Tenney stood up. "I guess not, but nobody should feel sorry for me. You don't miss what you can't remember."

Morehead rose too. "Well, Tenney, you've earned a deputy's badge over these last few days. Still, I don't think a person should wear one who's never shaved, do you?"

Tenney laughed and Morehead gave his small smile. "Keep in touch with me, Tenney," he said. "That's the only way I'll know what's going on around here."

Chapter 9

SAM caught the Primrose & Midland train at the Calico Flats spur where it halted to pick up a couple of cattle cars. He turned his horse loose to find its way back to town and boarded the car with his saddle and blanket roll. He had the whole afternoon to speculate on how Herrington and Brayton would react to his beating of Seeley Carnes.

His exhausted sleep last night after the fight had been uninterrupted. If they had been angry with him or if they had changed their minds about hiring him to kill Joe Potatoes, they would have wakened him and told him the deal was off. Since they hadn't, then he must assume that they still wanted him to go through with the murder. A corollary was that they had believed what Carnes undoubtedly told them of events leading to the fight. Carnes would have had to tell them that he broke into the house of Kennery's girl and got beat up for his pains. As far as Sam could see, nothing was changed. No, there was one change—an unimportant one. Seeley Carnes's dislike of him was changed into hatred now.

The train from the south arrived at Junction City after dark, as the one from the north had, but later. As he had done before, Sam gave his bedroll and saddle to the driver of the Prairie House hack and made his way again by back streets to the capitol on the hill. Sam had no doubt that the dogs that had barked at him before were the same ones that barked at him tonight. The State House had fewer lighted windows than on his previous visit and Sam wondered, tramping the bricks up to the marble steps, if Marshal Wilbarth and Newford had already called it a day.

The marble corridors of the building held a few lighted lamps; the basement corridor was lighted too, and, again the pencil of light showed under the door of the Marshal's office.

Sam knocked and entered, and saw Marshal Wilbarth

in shirt sleeves seated at his roll-top desk. Wilbarth rose at Sam's entrance, picked up the lamp, and came toward him. Holding the lamp in his left hand, Wilbarth unsmilingly extended his hand, saying, "Back so soon, Kennery?"

"You can thank Sheriff Morehead for that," Sam said.

Wilbarth put the lamp on the big table and gestured to the chair opposite him and Sam sank into it and took off his hat. As Wilbarth seated himself, Sam noted the dark circles under his eyes. His face was astonishingly pale and Sam wondered if the man had been in the sunshine an hour in the past two weeks.

Wilbarth regarded him closely and then observed, "You've been in a fight."

Sam started to raise his hand to his bruised cheekbone, then let it drop. "That's right."

"Well, what have you got for me?" Wilbarth asked patiently.

Sam reviewed the fake saloon quarrel with Morehead that led to his introduction and acceptance by Herrington, Brayton, and Carnes. He told of his efforts to establish himself as a thoroughly undesirable character, as proven by Tenney's disgust with him. "The real break came," Sam said, "when I was caught picking the lock of Herrington's room by Tenney Payne. I talked her into taking me down to the kitchen to meet her mother before turning me in to the owner. I told the two that I was a deputy U.S. marshal, and something about the case I'm working on."

"You told the girl and her mother that?" Wilbarth asked incredulously.

"How else could I explain the lock-picking and the search of the room? How else could I find out from the hotel register when Seeley Carnes arrived at Primrose?"

"Then you're known all over Primrose by now."

"Is that a fact or a guess?" Sam asked.

"Well, a guess, but a good one, I think," Wilbarth said grimly. "A woman will keep a secret about herself, but damned if she'll keep anybody else's secret." He sighed. "Well, go on."

Sam recounted finding the shotgun in Carnes's room and of establishing his date of arrival, which was two days after Schaeffer had been ambushed.

"You think there's any connection?"

"Tell me your guess when I've finished," Sam said. Then

he told of the meeting last night in Herrington's room when he was hired to do the murder, and as he progressed Wilbarth's face came alive and he leaned forward, his gray eyes bright with excitement. When Sam reached in his pocket and put down on the table the hundred dollars in gold eagles, earnest for killing Joe Potatoes, Wilbarth stared at them almost with disbelief.

Sam went on to repeat in detail the curious reluctance of Seeley Carnes to have Brayton reveal the reason for the three of them wanting the Indian killed. Sam finished by saying, "What did Con Brayton say to Carnes out in the hall that made him change his mind?"

Wilbarth thought a moment. "Likely he promised to keep him out of it, wouldn't you judge?"

"So you think there were two men assigned to kill Schaeffer?"

"Why, that's obvious," Wilbarth said.

"It's so obvious that you didn't bother to tell me you suspected there were two men. I had to go through the files of the *Capital Times* to have Red Macandy point it out in print."

Wilbarth looked at him unbelievingly. "My God, you mean neither of us told you?" He watched Sam shake his head, and then he raised his hand and rubbed his closed eyes with his thumb and index finger. "I *am* sorry, Kennery. Anse and I have been short on sleep for too long." He let his hand drop. "Yes, there had to be two men, and after what you've told me I think Carnes is the other one. And to answer your way-back question, I think Brayton promised to keep Carnes out of it and let Joe Potatoes take the whole blame."

"Joe Potatoes," Sam mused. "What kind of a name is that, Marshal?"

"The name Brayton gave him, I reckon," Wilbarth said contemptuously. "Brayton won't learn their language and he can't remember or pronounce their names, so he names them himself. They learn to answer to it, and that's all he cares about."

Wilbarth got up, moved over to his desk, and from one of the drawers drew out an envelope. Returning to the table, he picked up the eagles and put them in the envelope and sealed it. When he had sat down again he said in his soft voice, "Now, about the fight?"

Sam told him of last night's events that led up to his

brawl with Carnes. He added his own opinion that since neither Brayton nor Herrington had demanded an accounting from him, the situation was unchanged.

Wilbarth nodded in agreement. "You've done a fine job so far, Kennery."

"Thanks, but it's a girl who did most of it."

"Well, a girl can't do the rest of it," the marshal said. "Tomorrow you take the train north. Anse will be on the same train, but you won't be traveling together and you won't talk to each other. Do just what Brayton told you to do: look up McCook and give him Brayton's letter. By the way, is it sealed?"

Sam shook his head, reached in the pocket of his duck jacket, brought out the letter, and laid it in front of Wilbarth. "Just the usual, Marshal. 'This is a friend of mine; give him what he asks for' type of letter."

Wilbarth read the scribbled note, returned it to its envelope, and without comment tossed it to Sam. "Anse will take the stage from Boundary to the agency. I'll give him some harmless job that will keep him hanging around the agency post. I doubt if this Joe Potatoes will recognize him, but it doesn't matter if he does. He'll keep you in sight at all times. Try to pick up Joe at night. Take him down to the stock pens south of the agency before you give him Brayton's message. What was that message?"

"That I'm carrying money and whiskey for him from Brayton."

The marshal nodded. "Anse will see you pick up Joe and he'll be down at the pens waiting for you. After you've taken Joe you'll both head for Crater. That's the county seat of Summit County and it's a two-day ride from the agency. I'll be waiting for you at the county courthouse there. Anse will have the warrant."

"Suspicion of murder?"

Wilbarth nodded. "The sheriff up there is an old friend of mine. I was his deputy once. I'll tell him the public story, if anyone is interested—that Joe has been smuggling whiskey into the reservation. You'll have the evidence with you."

"You think Joe will talk right away, Marshal?"

"I doubt it. You said Brayton told you Joe understood English?"

At Sam's nod, the marshal said grimly, "Well, we'll let him overhear enough to scare hell out of him."

"Will I stay with you there for the questioning?"

"Not long. You'll have taken time enough as it is. If Joe talks enough later to implicate Carnes, I'll get word to you through Morehead."

The marshal yawned, and Sam, taking the hint, rose and was reaching for his hat when a sharp, almost arrogant knock come at the door.

Sam looked at Wilbarth, who stabbed a pointing finger toward a door in the wall behind Sam. Sam grabbed his hat and moved swiftly to the door, opened it, stepped inside a small storeroom, and closed the door.

The knock came again, and Sam heard Wilbarth call irritably, "Who is it? Come in." He heard the corridor door open and then Wilbarth said sourly, "Oh, hello, Red."

"Who were you talking to, Marshal?" a surly voice asked.

"If I was talking, I was talking in my sleep," the marshal said. "What are you doing here, Red?"

"Covering a late committee meeting upstairs. The *Times* never sleeps, you know. I was headed home when I saw the light in your office, so I came back. You got anything for me, Marshal?"

"Nothing but contempt. For you and your damned newspaper," Wilbarth said calmly.

This, then, was Red Macandy, the *Capital Times* editor, Sam thought. He was surprised at Wilbarth's open rudeness.

"Come, come, Marshal, it's men like me that make you boys at the trough earn your swill." His voice was taunting, and now Sam leaned down and peered through the keyhole.

Wilbarth was out of his line of vision, but Red Macandy was squarely in it. He was a dumpy, jowly, middle-aged man, dressed in a rumpled townsman's suit. A half-chewed, unlit cigar was wedged in the corner of his mouth. As Sam watched, he removed the cigar, which, exposed now, was merely a great wet wad of chewed tobacco. He pointed it at Wilbarth.

"The government got another week's postponement on the Brayton trial yesterday. What are you"—he stabbed the cigar at Wilbarth again—"you, yourself, doing to earn that postponement?"

Wilbarth's usually mild voice had altered into hardness when he spoke. "You want me to name witnesses so they can be shot too?"

"Come on, I know your witnesses. That's public information."

"Go home, Red," Wilbarth said wearily.

Through the keyhole, Sam saw the light diminish, and he
guessed that Wilbarth had removed the lamp from the table
to his desk.

He saw Red Macandy look toward the door of the storeroom, and then he moved swiftly out of Sam's vision. When
he appeared again, he was on the near side of the table and
close. Straightening up, Sam clamped his hand on the doorknob, and only seconds later he felt the knob tried. He held
it immovable, and then he heard Wilbarth's sharp command:
"Get away from there, Red."

"There's somebody inside holding that knob!" Red snarled.

"Then you better give up and get out," Wilbarth said
stonily. "I'm locking up."

"But there's somebody in there," Red insisted.

"If there is, she can spend the night there," Wilbarth said.
"There's a cot inside—a dusty one, but still a cot."

"*She?*" Red said.

Wilbarth spoke tiredly. "You snooping fool. That lock has
been jammed for a month. Why do you think I've got all
that junk on top of my desk? Anse's desk too? Get out, Red.
I'm blowing out the light."

"Very funny," Red said sourly, and Sam heard him move
away.

He heard Wilbarth's footsteps as he moved the length
of the room, then the sound of a door being locked came to
him. Cautiously, he opened the door and entered the light-
less room. In the darkness he went over to the corridor door
and tried it. Sure enough, Wilbarth had locked him in.

Sam moved back then to the storeroom, took out a match,
and struck it alight on his boot sole. There was the cot with
blankets on it that Wilbarth had mentioned. As the match
died, Sam smiled. Like him or not, Wilbarth was a tough
one, Sam thought. It didn't matter that Red Macandy probably didn't believe Wilbarth's story about the jammed door
and did believe that someone was in this storeroom. What
did matter was that Red didn't know who it was.

Sam was undressing when he heard the corridor door being
rattled. He moved quietly across the room, guessing that
Red Macandy had returned on the off chance that Wilbarth
had returned to free whoever was in the closet. There was a
long silence, and then he heard Red Macandy's growling
voice. "Bastards!"

Long before daylight Wilbarth let himself into his office

and Sam roused. "Get any sleep, Kennery?" The marshal spoke from the doorway into the darkness.

"All I want."

"Better move out now while it's dark. Red might be here early. For all I know, he may have somebody watching outside now, so don't strike a light."

As Sam pulled on his boots and felt around for his jacket, he told Wilbarth of Red's return after the marshal had left, and of the door rattling and the cursing.

They both laughed, but afterwards Wilbarth said soberly, "That was a close one, Kennery, and could have meant real trouble. If he'd seen you he'd have asked around and found someone who saw you on the Primrose train. He'd have checked in Primrose, tied you in with Herrington and Carnes, and then he'd have dragged me into it. He probably would have accused me of making a deal with that pair, with you as the go-between. Whatever he wrote, though, would have tipped off our three blackbirds."

Sam had put on his jacket. "I sent my saddle and blanket roll to the Prairie House in the hack," he said. "How do I get them without showing myself?"

"Anything in your blanket roll that would identify you?"

Sam thought a moment, and said, "No."

"Then leave them. McCook will outfit you."

They went out in the dimly lighted corridor, but instead of going up the stairs to the lobby, Wilbarth continued down the hall and they exited by way of an outside basement stairway. They parted at its head, and Wilbarth said, "See you in Crater, Kennery. Good luck."

Chapter 10

THE *Capital Times* office, a block off Main Street, was wedged between a saddle and harness shop and a hardware store. It was a narrow building whose wide front window was painted white up half its height. This morning both the printer and Billy Foster, Red's reporter and ad salesman, were there ahead of him. Red gave them a surly good morning, peeled off his coat, and took out from his side pocket the notes of last night's committee meeting. He went to the desk placed midway between the window and the railing that separated the press from the office. As he sat down he said to Billy Foster, a handsome, curly-haired young man dressed in a suit that would have graced a whiskey drummer, "Get out of here, Billy. Get us some money."

"You want me to hit Governor Halsey's office this morning?"

"No, the marshal's. Ask him who he was hiding from me last night."

Billy got up and headed for the coat rack. "Will he tell me?" he asked.

"Of course not. Ask him anyway. Get him mad."

Billy took his hat and left, and Red began to scribble out his story of the Senate Finance Committee meeting last night.

Finished with the story, he went back and gave it to the printer, and then returned to his desk. Taking a cigar from one of the desk drawers, he lit it and tilted back in his swivel chair.

He had a game that he often played in idle moments, which consisted of trying to identify his fellow townsmen by their headgear, the only part of them visible above the painted lower half of the window. This morning, however, the game had lost its savor. He was thinking without any charity of his meeting last night with Marshal Wilbarth. He was positive that he'd heard Wilbarth talking to someone when he knocked on the door, and that whoever it was had hidden in the closet and had held the knob to prevent the door from being opened.

Who was it? And why the secrecy?

Red was certain that Wilbarth knew he was in deep trouble, and on two counts. The marshal's office had allowed a key witness in the Brayton-Herrington fraud case to be murdered in the presence of a deputy marshal, thus destroying the government's case. The other count was that Wilbarth, his deputy, and his special deputies had failed to unearth even a clue as to who the killer or killers were. Which count, Red wondered, related to the man hiding in the closet? Had Wilbarth turned up a secret witness, such as some drover who, like Herrington, had been given a long count by Brayton and split the overpayment with the agent? Or had Wilbarth turned up one of the passengers on that fateful trip who recognized

Schaeffer's assassin? Red doubted if the latter were true. He himself had talked to the brakeman and to the handful of passengers who were on the car that night. They were unanimous in saying that from the lamplit coach they could see nothing out in the darkness.

Did the fact that Wilbarth hid the person in his closet mean that he knew Red would recognize him if he saw him? Possibly. On the other hand, it might be a stranger whose identity and description had to be kept a secret for his own safety.

Well, there was only one thing to do, Red decided. It involved the leg work which he both hated and loved: hated because it took effort, and loved because there were always surprises in store.

He got up, took his hat, and went out, and in the chilly morning headed for Main Street. Once there, he turned and headed for the Prairie House, silently cursing the trouble Wilbarth was putting him to. He knew Wilbarth was only getting even with him for the editorial riding that Red had given him ever since Schaeffer's death. Red had a deep distrust of all politicians, no matter of what party, and since Wilbarth was a political appointee, he was fair game.

On the two blocks between the Grandview and the brick and stone Prairie House, Red spoke to a dozen people. Half of them returned his greeting coldly, and the rest managed to be looking in store windows or across the street when he passed them. At least two men he knew found a break in the long tie-rail where they could cross the street to avoid him. He knew this, was used to it, and didn't care.

The Prairie House hack was neither at the front entrance of the hotel nor at the side entrance, and Red wondered at this. The morning trains to Primrose and to the north had both pulled out some time ago, and the familiar green hotel hack should have been pulled up at one of the entrances.

Red crossed the big empty lobby, circled a huge potted plant in front of the desk, and spoke to the elderly clerk.

"Morning, Russ. Where's the hack?"

The clerk looked at him with dislike. "The hack is for hotel patrons only, Red."

"Hell, I know that. I want to talk with Steve."

"When he's done taking passengers to the train, he always washes down the hack, if it's a nice day. You'll find him out in back."

Red didn't bother to thank him and left by the side entrance. He found Steve Lister, the hack driver, where the clerk had told him he would. Coatless, sleeves rolled up, Steve was sponging the spokes of a rear wheel when Red halted beside him.

"What're you doing that for, Steve? It ain't rained for a week."

"Dust," the hack driver said curtly.

Steve was past middle age, a burly man who had been with the hotel since it was built while the region was still a territory.

"Got a minute, Steve?" Red asked. Steve reluctantly tossed the sponge in the bucket and even more reluctantly came erect.

"I'm trying to find out the name of a man. Don't know what he looks like, how old he is, or where he comes from. You met both trains last night, didn't you?"

"Always do," Lister said coldly. He had a rough, squarish face that was not good at masking his feelings, and now they reflected not only dislike but irritability.

"Who'd you bring in from the early train?"

"Four strangers. Their names are on the register."

"How many did you bring here from the Primrose train?"

"Five. Two of them I know and so do you. The names of the others will be on the register, like I said."

"Then the last seven names on the register that I don't know will be everyone you brought in last night?"

Steve was momentarily puzzled, but when he followed Red's reasoning he nodded. "Unless somebody come in after them. Ask Russ. And you better make that the last eight names."

"How's that?" Red asked.

"Fella give me his saddle and blanket roll and told me he'd walk."

Red came alert now. "What'd he look like, Steve?"

Steve said promptly, "About thirty, cowboy, but clean, over six feet tall, wore a brown duck jacket."

Red eyed him thoughtfully, and said, "Sure you aren't making that up, Steve? It was night, the platform was dark, and unless he came close to your carriage lantern you couldn't see him that good."

"That's right," Steve said. "But I seen him again at the depot this morning at the first train."

"With a saddle and blanket roll?"

"Come to think of it, no," Steve said, a momentary puzzlement in his face. "Still, he could have throwed his stuff on the seat to hold it, then come outside again. You see, I never took him in the hack. He must have walked again."

Still suspicious, Red said, "Funny you'd notice him that much, Steve. Why did you?"

Steve frowned. "I dunno rightly. He just had a 'go to hell' look in his eyes."

"He was mean-looking—is that it?"

"No, that ain't it," Steve said flatly. "He just looked like he owned as much of the world as he wanted."

"Arrogant?"

Steve shook his head. "I don't know that word, Red."

Red pulled a cigar from the breast pocket of his coat and extended it to Steve, who shook his head, saying, "I don't smoke and you shouldn't either."

"Don't preach to me," Red snarled. "Save it for your Sunday School boys."

Red back-tracked to the lobby and again faced the clerk. "Russ, give me a look at your register, will you?"

"Ain't supposed to." Russ's voice was firm.

Red folded his arms and leaned them on the counter and regarded Russ almost with pity. "Think a minute, Russ. Do I have to get the sheriff, bring him down here, and have him watch me while I look at the register? He won't thank you for that. He'll think you're an idiot."

"You looking for a criminal?"

"I am. Now let's look at the register."

Reluctantly the clerk shoved the big register toward him.

"Anybody check in this morning?" Red asked, as he scanned the register.

"Nope."

Steve had been right. Red knew two of the last eight names.

"Who checked out for the morning trains?"

Russ turned the register so he could read the names. "That one and that one," and he put his finger on two of the signatures.

"Which train?" Russ asked.

"Primrose."

"None of them for the last train?" Red asked.

Russ shook his head. Now Red straightened up and asked mildly, "You wouldn't have a saddle and blanket roll that Steve brought in last night, would you?"

Russ pointed under the desk. "Right here."

Red felt a leap of excitement as he walked around the end of the counter. Beneath it were a worn saddle and a blanket roll. Kneeling, Red dragged out the blanket roll.

"Watch me, Russ. Make sure I don't take anything."

He untied the thongs that held the blankets and unrolled them on the floor. Two calico shirts, a neckerchief, a pair of spurs, and some clean socks were all the blanket roll held, and Red restored them in the shape he had found them. The blanket rerolled, Red rose. This surely had to be the gear of the man who hid in Wilbarth's closet last night. If it wasn't, then why had it been left unclaimed? There was only one reason for the saddle and blanket roll still being there—the man hadn't wanted to be seen claiming them.

"All right, Russ. Thanks."

As Red walked around the counter, Russ said, "What did this fellow do?"

"Killed his wife," Red said carelessly, and headed through the lobby for the street. Once there, he turned toward the station some ten blocks away. The morning was warming a little, but Red didn't notice it. He didn't even notice the people he met, nor did he speak to them. Once out of the few blocks of business district, Red ran off the plank walk and took to the road.

The depot platform was empty, and Red headed directly for the ticket office inside. The agent had heard him approach, Red knew, but in the fashion of all railroaders, took his time in getting up to the window.

"Hi, Perry."

"Going some place, Red?"

"No. How good's your memory, Perry?"

"Not good."

"I'll describe a man that bought a ticket for the early train this morning. See if you can remember where he bought a ticket to."

He went on to give Steve's excellent description of the man and Perry frowned thoughtfully behind his steel-rimmed glasses as he listened. When Red was finished, Perry nodded.

"I remember. He bought a ticket to Boundary."

"You wouldn't know his name, would you?"

"How could I?" Perry asked.

"That's the trouble with you railroads," Red said in happy malice. "You just don't care who travels with you."

"No"— But Red had already turned away.

Red went over to one of the empty benches and sat down.

He pulled out a cigar, which he clamped in his mouth but did not bother to light. What had he learned this morning? That a young man Wilbarth considered worth hiding last night was now on his way to Boundary, which in all probability meant to the agency. Was Wilbarth trying to shore up the government's case against Con Brayton, hunting new evidence to be used in the government's case against him—new evidence to be used in the trial? But why the secrecy? Maybe Wilbarth last night had been speaking the truth when he implied that if the man was identified in the *Times*, he might be killed, as Schaeffer had been.

More important, was it worth a story in the *Times*? It would have to be one of those stories that began with "Rumor has it." He could say that an unidentified man had a secret night conference with the marshal, and the following morning entrained for Boundary and the reservation. The story might go on to ask if new evidence had been unearthed or was in the process of being unearthed for use in the trial of Brayton and Herrington.

Red knew the value of such rumor stories. They invariably infuriated the office holder mentioned, and sometimes their angry denials could be revealing. Predictably, such a story would anger Wilbarth, but he doubted if the marshal could be taunted into any damning revelations.

Or he could print a story headlined "Who Is This Man?" and give Steve's description, plus the destination of the mystery man's train trip. He could make a kind of contest out of it, offering a small reward for anyone who could identify him.

Reluctantly Red rejected both ideas. Any such move now would be premature. And when it came right down to it, whose side was he on—the government's or Brayton and Herrington's? Red instinctively loathed all authority and those who held it, but he conceded that some form of authority was necessary. Contrariwise, he had a secret admiration for the swindle by Brayton and Herrington of government property. It took the kind of large-scale gall that he wished he himself possessed.

Not that he condoned murder to cover the swindle, mind you. It was just that two smart men had deceived a stupid government. Well, then, whose side should he be on? Burley Hammond, who owned Consolidated Mining & Milling, and also Red, had told him he wasn't interested in the case. It was a federal matter and not a state one. If it had been just the opposite and Governor Halsey were involved, Hammond would have ordered Red to go all out against the state government. Therefore, there was no urgency about identifying the mystery man.

Still, Red wasn't going to let it drop. The mystery man had come in from Primrose, the end of the line for passenger travel. He'd write Bill Harness today giving him the man's description and asking him to try to identify the stranger. If he wrote Bill, the letter would have to be accompanied by an overdue check, and Red sighed.

He got up and headed back for the office.

Chapter 11

WHEN Steve Lister finished washing down the hack, he drove the team around to the Main Street entrance of the Prairie House and went inside. Red had been gone only minutes when Steve suddenly remembered that he had seen the man Red wanted to identify some days ago. It was last Sunday, in fact, when a man alighting from the train from the north had told him to take his saddle and blanket roll in the hack, and that he would walk. He remembered it very well because the hack was so crowded that Jimmy Barth, the State Senator and a resident guest of the hotel during the legislature session, had sat in the front seat next to him. He could place the day because Jimmy spent each weekend with his family upstate, returning on the Sunday night train to be in time for the Monday session of the legislature.

More out of curiosity than interest, Steve now strolled up to the desk under the indifferent regard of Russ. Steve disliked Russ, who loved to bang the bell and order him to take out a guest's luggage in the tone of voice a plantation owner might have used in speaking to his slave in the days before the war. Steve halted before the register and leafed back to last Sunday night's registrations. The man's name would probably be the last on the Sunday list, for at nine o'clock when Steve had gone off work the saddle and blanket roll were still behind the desk. Looking at the register, he saw that the name Sam Kennery was the last registration for Sunday night.

Afterwards Steve went over to his customary chair against the wall near the front of the lobby and sat down. Should he tell Red Macandy he knew the man's name? He disliked Red, as did most people who knew him, and there was no reason to do him a favor. Besides, Red had offered him a cigar when everybody in town knew that Steve hated tobacco as he hated the devil. Indeed, he was famous for his lay sermons at his church against the Wicked Weed. This morning he judged that Red's offer of a cigar was an insulting gesture of contempt toward him and his beliefs. No, he was going to keep the name Sam Kennery to himself.

Following Marshal Wilbarth's instructions to the letter, Anse Newford went aboard the train first and took a front seat, while Sam, boarding last, took a rear seat. The ride across the sere October prairie was a dull one. In late morning they stopped at the drab coal-mining town of River Valley for a half-hour layover while the passengers flocked into a grimy café across from the depot for a quick meal. Here again Anse sat with several stools between himself and Sam.

It was early afternoon when they pulled in for the water stop at Long Reach and the brakeman came through the car with his customary chant that this was only a water stop. When he was gone, Sam got up went out on the car's platform, and descended to the lower step and looked at the bleak prairie that ended against the near mountains. This was the spot where Schaeffer was killed and Newford lost an eye. Sam wondered what Newford was thinking right now, and it was not difficult to guess. When he went back to his seat, the brakeman ahead of him was discussing the shooting in the prideful tones of a man who had witnessed murder. Either the brakeman was an unthinking clod of a man, or he hadn't recognized Newford, because his description was graphic and bloody. Newford, Sam noticed, did not turn around like the other passengers forward in the car to hear the brakeman's description of that fateful night.

Once through the timbered pass, they were soon on the prairie again. It was late afternoon when the train screeched to a halt as the brakeman intoned, "Boundary, Boundary. All Boundary passengers off."

Sam was the first one off and he looked about him. Fifty yards from the track and across a dusty road was a low adobe building. Its badly painted sign above the entrance proclaimed it "McCook's Trading Post." A smaller sign below it said "Liquor." Set apart from the trading post was a small log house backed by a large corral. A team and buckboard with tandem seats were alongside two Indian ponies at the hitch rack; Sam supposed this was the stage to the agency.

He moved off toward the trading post, and he could hear footsteps behind him. That would be Anse, he thought, but he did not look back to confirm it.

The interior of the trading post was dark and cool, and smelled of untanned hides and coal oil. It was a shabby room whose shelves held bolts of dress goods, denim pants, socks, and a good supply of navy blue blankets. A couple dozen axe handle were in a nail keg, and above them a line of shiny new lanterns hung from nails on the wall. Three barrels against the left wall held dried apples, beans, and black jerky. The right wall was taken up by a stained and grimy plank bar on sawhorses. Beyond it, toward the rear, were the stinking hides. A fat squaw, her blanket loose around her shoulders, was studying the bolts of dress goods, not touching them. An Indian, probably her husband, was squatting alongside the barrel of jerky, his back against the wall. He wore buckskin leggings and moccasins, and a cotton shirt, tails out. Neither he nor the woman even glanced at Sam.

Behind the bar a middle-aged man was pouring whiskey from a gallon jug into a row of pint bottles. As Sam moved over towards him he heard Newford enter the post.

At the bar Sam halted and said, "Mr. McCook?" The man nodded without taking his eyes off his pouring. Under a buttonless vest he wore a dirty blue striped shirt that was collarless, and Sam noted that the brass collar button of the shirt had made a faint green stain on his neck. The man had needed a shave for the past month. Sam reached in his jacket pocket for Brayton's letter, and then out of the corner of his eye he saw Newford come up to the bar. Sam turned and looked at him. "Go ahead," he said. "This can wait."

Newford nodded his thanks and said to McCook, "When does the stage leave?"

McCook set down the jug and, without looking at either of them, turned his head toward the rear of the room and yelled, "Barney." Only then did he look at Newford, and

Sam noticed that his pale eyes were red-rimmed and blood-shot.

"That'll be five dollars," McCook said to Newford.

"For a five-mile ride?" Newford asked in disbelief.

McCook shrugged. "It's a hot walk, but go ahead."

Wordlessly, Newford reached in his pocket for the money. As he did so a young Indian dressed in cotton shirt and Levi's came out of the back room and passed him on his way to the door.

Lazily McCook moved up to Newford, who tossed a gold coin on the bar. "You got a good thing going for you in that stage," Newford said.

"Yup, but it's almost always government expense money. They can afford it."

Newford got his change and walked out, and then McCook turned his attention to Sam.

"Got a letter for you," Sam said, and held out Brayton's letter in its envelope. McCook read it and said, "Yup. What can I do for you?"

"I need a horse, saddle, blankets, and a couple quarts of whiskey."

McCook nodded. "Take the gray out in the corral. Saddle's in the shed. I'd do it myself but these damned Injuns would steal the store if I went outside. I'll have your blankets and whiskey ready for you."

Sam went out through the back door and headed for the open-faced shed behind the house. He found the saddle in the corner of the shed and lugged it over to the corral, which held three horses. Taking the rope from the saddle, he moved into the corral. The gray eyed him curiously but stood perfectly still as Sam put the loop around his neck and led him out to be saddled. Afterwards, Sam lengthened the stirrups and led the horse to the rear door of the post. In his absence McCook had wrapped the two quarts of whiskey in the two new navy blue blankets. Both ends of the blanket roll were tied. He waited in the doorway as Sam came up.

"I might have to keep this horse a while," Sam said.

"Don't matter. Con will pay." He frowned. "Can I ask where you're going?"

"No."

"Well, I hope you get there," McCook said. He turned and disappeared inside the post.

As he picked up the agency road Sam noticed that the buckboard was already gone. Headed north on the dusty road, he realized he was entering Brayton's domain. Nothing marked its boundary, but when he saw the first cluster of tepees he knew he was on the reservation. The faraway children playing among the tepees stopped their game long enough to watch him, and Sam knew from long experience that the news of his presence here would precede him by moccasin telegraph. It might even reach Joe Potatoes, who, though not expecting him, might want to have a look at him out of simple curiosity. As he rode through the bleak country he could not suppress a feeling of expectancy. If Joe Potatoes could be persuaded to talk, then his trip back to Primrose would be the purest pleasure. He wondered idly how Brayton and Herrington would receive the news of Joe's betrayal and their own arrest. He thought he knew how Carnes would receive his—not with protest, but with violence.

In the lowering dusk he saw two mounted Indians coming down the road toward him, but they immediately pulled off it to skirt him. Then, topping a rise, he saw a mass of yellow-leaved cottonwoods far ahead of him and he guessed that this was the site of the agency. The next rain, he was thinking, would wipe out all the color and winter would soon clamp down on this barren land. Between him and the cottonwoods he saw a huge corral and the stock pens where the monthly beef issue took place. This was the place where, with luck, he would take Joe Potatoes so that he and Newford could seize him.

Brayton had never bothered to describe Joe's appearance, nor had he said whether he was young or old. That was carelessness on his own part, Sam thought wryly—he should have asked. Beyond the agency trading post were a couple of log warehouses off to the north and they made up the remainder of the agency buildings. The lamps inside the post had already been lighted against the lowering dusk.

As Sam rode up to the tie-rail he wondered at the number of ponies, and then he remembered the Indian sense of timelessness. Where a white family man would come home at the end of his work day for supper and rest, the Indian ate when he was hungry and kept his own hours. The pattern of Indian life, Sam thought, was to have no pattern at all. Dismounting, Sam tied his horse, then went up the two steps and across the veranda to the open door, and halted just inside it.

The post was one huge room, its rafters supported by spaced log pillars. There was a counter running the depth of

the room on the right and a similar one on his left, and behind
these counters on shelves were stacked the trading goods,
clothing and hardware. From the pillars hung tangles of
harness and rope. A few new saddles were in evidence and
Sam guessed these were a hard item to move in a land whose
people rode bareback. It was a room filled with many
varied items, from the black Stetsons coming into favor with
the Indians to moccasins made by the Indians to be sold to
those of them who had no women to make them. Three
Indians who had come in to escape the evening chill had
seated themselves on the counter to the left. Behind the right
counter to the rear was a tow-headed young man talking with
an Indian man in his own language. When the Indian moved
off to join his friends at the counter the young man looked
up, saw Sam, and came toward him behind the counter.

Sam went up to the counter and halted under an overhead
kerosene lamp.

"If you're looking for Dad, he's back eating supper," the
young man said pleasantly. He might have been nineteen,
and he had the unweathered and worried-looking face of
a person who spent his time indoors concerning himself with
money.

"Don't need him," Sam said cheerfully. "You can likely
tell me. Where could a man put up here and get something
to eat?"

"At the agency, sir. The agent's not here now, but his
housekeeper will feed you. There's a sleeping room up in the
attic." He added with a faint smile, "I heard you were on
your way."

Sam nodded and smiled too. "I figured you would."

"You can put McCook's horse in the corral behind the
agency," the young man said, and then added almost with
embarrassment, "If you're broke, you can sleep here on the
floor tonight after I shoo the Indians out."

"What time would that be?" Sam asked.

"Nine o'clock."

"And how did you know I'm riding McCook's horse?"

The young man used a wholly Indian gesture. He literally
pointed with his lifted chin to the group of Indians across
the store. "One of them told me."

"No secrets around here," Sam observed.

"No, sir."

"Give me five pounds of jerky and five pounds of flour
and some matches, will you?"

The young man left to fill the order and Sam strolled back
to the door. If they knew he was coming and they knew
he was riding McCook's horse, they might know he also had
two quarts of whiskey in his blanket roll. It was not quite
full dark, but he saw that lamps were now lighted in the
agency building. When the young man brought him the supplies in a muslin flour sack, Sam paid him and thanked him.

He rode over to the agency barn and turned his horse out
into the corral adjoining the barn, where it joined two others.
By matchlight he found a feed bag and the oats in the
barn and fed his horse. He loosened the saddle cinch, but
left the gray saddled.

It was full dark when he rounded the house with his
blanket roll and supply sack, skirted the dark office, and
mounted the steps to the small porch. The door was opened
by a gaunt Indian woman wearing a prim long-sleeved cotton
dress.

"Can I put up here for the night?" Sam asked. As he spoke,
he saw beyond her shoulder Anse Newford and a half-breed
Indian eating at the big dining table in the room.

She said, "Come in," and Sam stepped past her. Newford
and the breed regarded him curiously and Sam gave them a
civil "good evening." The Indian woman skirted the table,
drew out a chair alongside Newford, and vanished into
the kitchen.

"There's a wash bench out by the back door," Newford
said.

"Does the woman speak English?" Sam asked of the breed.

"Not speak good but she understand good," the half-breed
said. He was, Sam supposed, an agency employee of Brayton's.

Sam slacked his blanket roll in a corner but kept the sack
of supplies; he threw his hat on his blanket roll and went
out into the kitchen. The Indian woman was at the stove,
and when she heard Sam approach she turned.

"Can you make me up some bannock tonight? I'll be
leaving very early." He extended the sack and the woman
opened it and looked and felt inside. Withdrawing her hand,
she held up one finger and said, "Hour."

Sam went outside, found the wash bench, and washed up.
He came back through the kitchen, followed by the woman
with a platter of steaks.

The supper was good, and so was the company. The breed
was bursting with curiosity to know Sam's business on the

reservation, but all Sam would say was that he was passing through.

"You buy McCook's horse?" the breed asked craftily.

"I'll be back," Sam said. Then he and Newford matched lies for the breed's benefit. Newford said he was a deputy marshal requested to come here by Brayton to investigate whiskey smuggling; there had been some trouble with drunken Indians on the reservation. The breed said there was always trouble with drunken Indians. Newford said he'd hired a horse from Buckhalter, the post trader, and was heading out tomorrow. Sam said he himself was a horse buyer short-cutting the reservation to pick up a herd at Lansing. He'd drive the horses back south, dropping off McCook's gray.

Finished with his supper, the breed rose and said he would see Newford in the morning, but Newford said he would be gone long before daylight. The breed went out, and Newford, hearing the Indian cook clattering pans in the kitchen, judged it was safe to talk.

"I found our man, Sam," he said quietly.

"How?"

"Easy. I asked the trader who the worst drunks were and he pointed out Joe Potatoes as one of 'em. He was still at the post when I left."

"Then it's tonight?"

Newford nodded. "No sense waiting if we find him. You leave here first and tie your horse behind the post, then go inside and buy a bandanna or something. If Joe is still there, I'll go up and talk to him. When I leave, pick him up any way you can. I'll head for the corrals. Did you notice that cedar-stake branding corral when you came by?" At Sam's nod, Newford said, "That'll be the place. Talk loud enough so I can pick up your voice. He's big and—"

"Watch it," Sam cut in.

On the heels of his warning the Indian cook came into the room and placed Sam's flour sack with the still warm soda bread in it on the table. Sam got up, held out his hand, and said to Newford, "If I don't see you again, good luck."

Newford, still seated, extended his hand and said, "Luck to you."

Sam turned to the Indian woman. "How much do I owe you?"

"You want bed?"

When Sam shook his head, she said, "Half dollar supper, quarter dollar cook."

Sam paid her and went over to his blanket roll with the sack. He picked up the blanket roll, put on his hat, paused at the door, and said, "So long." Then he stepped out into the night.

At the corral he stored his provisions in the saddle bag, tied on his blanket roll, but not before undoing a thong and removing a bottle which he placed in the other saddle bag. Afterwards he cinched up and rode up toward the post. Circling it in the darkness, he tied his horse at a grindstone which his mount had swerved to avoid, and afterwards went back to the front veranda and entered the store.

There were still a few Indians around, but they had all moved off the veranda to escape the chilling night. The same young man was behind the counter, and for all Sam knew the same Indians were seated on the other counter.

Sam asked the young clerk for a bandanna and was trying on gloves when Newford entered. Newford cut to the counter where the Indians were seated. Sam watched him halt before them and say something to them, after which the Indian in the middle slid off the counter. Newford moved a few paces to the rear of the store and the Indian followed. He was, Sam saw, a big and burly young man with a blanket tucked into the waistband of his filthy Levi's. His hair was braided tightly and fell below each shoulder in front. Newford, with a scowl on his face, talked with him a few minutes and then shook his head, left him, and went out the front door.

Sam found a pair of gloves he liked, rammed them in his hip pocket, and paid his bill. Afterwards he moved over to the other counter where Joe, standing now, was evidently recounting his conversation with Newford. The Indians laughed at something he said, but as Sam approached they fell silent. Joe turned to look at the reason for their silence and Sam halted beside him.

"Come outside, Joe," Sam said pleasantly.

For a moment Sam thought he was going to pretend ignorance of English, but either his curiosity or the realization that Sam had seen him talking with Newford seemed to change his mind. Sam headed for the door, hearing the whispering of Joe's moccasins on the floor behind him.

Sam stepped out onto the veranda and halted in the dim light cast by the overhead lamps inside. Joe Potatoes halted too and Sam studied the sullen, suspicious, and sick-looking face.

"Brayton sent me," Sam said finally.

"You got money?"

Sam nodded. "Whiskey too."

"Where?"

"You got a horse?" Joe looked puzzled, then slowly turned his head and pointed with his chin to one of the horses at the tie-rail.

"Wait there." Sam turned to head for the steps.

"You pay," Joe said.

Sam halted. "Not here," he said flatly and went down the steps.

When he had retrieved his horse and circled back, Joe was already mounted on his Indian pony and Sam reined in beside him. "We'll ride down to the issue corral, Joe."

"No. Too far."

"That's where the rest of the whiskey is, Joe. I hid it."

Sam reached back and opened the flap of the saddle bag and took out a bottle of whiskey. He held it out to Joe, saying, "Here's a start, Joe." Joe reached for the bottle and Sam heard him swiftly wrench out the cork. He heard a gurgle of the whiskey and then an explosion of breath after the whiskey went down.

"Now, let's go, Joe." Dutifully Joe fell in with him, and as Sam's eyes became accustomed to the darkness he could see Joe riding beside him, the bottle held on his thigh.

They had not even passed the agency before Joe took his second drink. On the half-mile ride between his third and fourth drink Joe asked, "How much money?"

"Brayton didn't say, Joe."

"How much whiskey?"

"Ten bottles," Sam lied. He heard Joe's grunt of satisfaction

When they came to the issue corrals Joe halted his pony. "Where?" he asked.

"At the branding corral," Sam said. They skirted the bigger holding corral in silence and approached the branding corral. Remembering Anse Newford's admonition to make himself heard, Sam said loudly, "How you going to pack all this booze, Joe?"

"I hide it again," Joe said.

"You mean you don't trust me, Joe?" Sam said, loud and clear.

"No take chances," Joe said flatly.

Sam picked a spot at random, dismounted, and then he struck a match.

"What you lost?" Joe asked.

Sam held the match high in the still night and said, "I marked it by a rock against the posts, Joe. Help me look." The match died.

Joe slipped off his pony, bottle still in hand, and began walking in the opposite direction to that Sam had taken. Sam reversed his direction then so that he put himself between Joe and his pony. As quietly as he could he moved up behind Joe, wondering whether he should wait for Anse or take Joe alone.

The decision was made for him, for Joe, hearing Sam behind him, turned. Sam lifted his gun now and said quietly, "All right, Joe, you're under arrest. I've got a gun on you. Drop that bottle."

Joe lunged toward him, raising the bottle as he would a club. Without even thinking it, Sam knew that this Indian dead would do them no good. Instinctively, he raised his right arm, gun in fist, to ward off Joe's blow. When it came slashing down, the bottle hit his six-gun and smashed, showering him with broken glass and blinding him with raw whiskey. Sam pivoted aside. Through tears flushed into his eyes by the raw whiskey, he saw that Joe still had the jagged half of the bottle in his hand. Joe's lunge turned into a run as he raced for his horse only a few yards away, and Sam exploded into motion, aiming to put himself between Joe and the horse.

Then, out of the deep darkness of the close-set corral poles a figure hurtled into Joe, sending him reeling in Sam's direction. In mid-stride, Sam raised his gun and brought it down on Joe's skull. It was a hard blow, audible in spite of the cushioning of Joe's black Stetson. Joe never caught his balance. He simply folded to the ground and lay on his back. Sam put a foot on Joe's right arm, and with his other foot he kicked the jagged glass out of Joe's limp hand.

Newford loomed out of the night, leading Joe's Indian pony, and halted by Sam, who was now wiping his wet face with his jacket sleeve. Kneeling by Joe, Anse said, "There should be a knife." Presently he came up with it. "Man, you smell like a saloon," he observed.

"I'd rather have that stuff on me than in me," Sam said. Then he added, "Let's get him loaded while he's still out. Where's your horse?"

"With yours."

Sam moved off into the night, found the horses, and re-

turned with them. Anse had rolled Joe over on his face and
had handcuffed his hands behind his back. Now he and Sam
picked up Joe's slack body and wrestled it astride the pony.
With Anse's rope, they tied Joe's feet together under the
horse's belly, and Sam's rope they looped over the pony's
head for a lead rope.

Only then did Sam draw out his newly bought bandanna
and really wipe the whiskey well from his eyes and face.

"You lead or do I, Anse?"

"I better. We head northeast for a low pass. The boss drew
a map for me."

Sam said grimly, "Then let's move. Nothing happens in daylight these Injuns don't know about. Let's see if we can get
out of their way tonight."

Suddenly, Joe's Indian pony snorted and reared, and at the
same time tried to wheel. Anse, holding the lead rope, tight-
ened his hold on it, and Sam, knowing the horse would run
when all four feet were on the ground again, lunged in behind Anse and seized the tail of the rope. Predictably, then,
the horse's forequarters came down as Joe shouted a command
in Indian.

Both Anse and Sam dug in their heels as the pony lunged
against the rope. They had to give a little before the horse
was choked down; it turned and came toward them to slack
the rope.

"That was close, but not good enough, Joe," Sam called.

Joe, now that his trick of feigning unconsciousness had
failed, straightened up but he did not speak. Anse took the
lead rope, moved over to his horse, dallied the rope around
the horn, and then swung into the saddle. Sam mounted his
gray, and the three men moved off into the chilly night,
heading northeast for the mountains that blacked out the
stars on the jagged horizon.

Chapter 12

THEY traveled through the foothills, and at dawn were in the
timber. When they picked up a creek they followed it until

it cut through a grassy park. Here Joe was unloaded and seated against a tree, where his legs were tied and his arms were freed. While Anse picketed the three horses Sam brought out a bannock and the jerky. Joe watched all this with a stolid indifference. When Anse returned to the camp, his boots were glistening with dew; he knelt at the stream, had his drink, and then came up to Joe.

Sam had already divided the bannock and jerky and put Joe's portion within reach of him. Anse looked at it and then at Joe. "Better eat it, Joe," he said. "It won't taste so good when I tell you why you're under arrest." He paused. "Remember Schaeffer? You worked for him."

Joe might have been deaf, for all the expression on his face.

"I can't promise you this, Joe, but I think they'll hang you for his murder."

He indicated Sam. "This is Deputy U.S. Marshal Sam Kennery, Joe. Maybe he wants to say something to you."

Anse glanced at Sam, who was watching the Indian.

"Only this, Joe," Sam said quietly. "Try to escape and one or both of us will shoot you in the legs. It won't be so bad if we don't break a bone. Still, they'll hang a man even with a broken leg. It's just a little uncomfortable waiting."

Joe didn't bother to look at him.

Anse took a paper from his jacket pocket, unfolded it, and held it down for Joe to look at. "Let's make it legal, Joe. This is a warrant for your arrest on suspicion of murder and complicity in murder. Now you've seen it, and I'll so testify at your trial."

Joe didn't even look at the warrant.

They ate and rested while their horses grazed, and afterwards they rode on, using game trails through the timber when they could, and staying far away from the stage road that crossed the mountains.

That night they camped by a stream in the timber. They built a fire this time and had the same things to eat they had had that morning. Sam's extra blankets were used for Joe, who slept with wrists handcuffed and feet bound. Sam took the guard till midnight, then Anse till dawn.

At mid-morning of the following day they crossed the pass, which held a foot of snow between the shouldering peaks on either side. They met no one and, as far as Sam could tell after circling their back trail twice that morning, were not followed. Maybe Brayton was right when he said nobody knew or cared enough about Joe to be concerned by his disappearance.

It was close to dark when they came out of timber where a broad valley lay below them. A cluster of distant lights told Sam by their number that this was not a ranch but a sizable settlement. It would, of course, be Crater, named for its location in the vast bed of a long extinct volcano. Minutes later they picked up the road they had avoided so carefully for the past two days, and now the three rode abreast in the chilly night.

It was full dark when they picked up Crater's main street. As far as Sam could tell, most of the buildings were made of logs from the surrounding mountains, although an occasional frame building testified to the presence of a nearby sawmill. It was a gloomy-looking town in the dark night, with only the saloons and a big frame hotel at the main four corners lighted.

As they passed the hotel Sam said, "Shall I check here for Wilbarth?"

"He said he'd be at the courthouse," Anse said. And he added, "We got him this far; let's get him behind jail bars."

Sam saw Joe studying the town. It was almost the first time in two days that he had really paid attention to anything. The livery stable with its lanterns flanking the archway marked the end of the business district. Beyond this there were lamps lighted in the houses and cabins along the way now and then. Sam saw a big building looming up on the left ahead of them. That would be the courthouse, he judged, and as they approached it he saw the lamps burning in a front corner office. At the tie-rail closest to the door they halted, dismounted, and freed Joe's legs. Joe was so stiff that Sam had to heave his leg over the pony's back, and when he hit the ground his legs wouldn't hold him. Anse caught him before he fell and held him erect while Joe kicked out one leg and then the other to free himself from the stiffness. When he could stand erect alone, Anse touched his arm and they went toward the faintly lighted steps of the courthouse. Joe had set some kind of a record for silence even for a Indian, Sam thought. He hadn't spoken since his capture two nights ago.

They picked up the cross corridor, turned left, and saw Wilbarth standing in the doorway of the sheriff's office, in the light from the lamp inside. He was wearing a dark suit, his only concession to the amenities expected of a public official. Newford spoke first.

"Here's your man, Wes. You wouldn't know it from him, though."

"Cold ride?"

"Cold enough," Anse said.

Wilbarth stepped up, touched Joe's arm, and said, "Come inside."

Joe moved into the room, Wilbarth behind him, Sam and Anse following. An elderly man rose from the chair facing the desk that a younger man was leaning against. Both men were dressed in denim pants and wool shirts, and Wilbarth introduced them as Sheriff Ritter and his deputy, Byron Packer. Sam and Anse shook hands with the two men and then Packer moved over toward Joe. "Who's got the handcuff key?" he asked.

Anse gave it to him and Packer paused by Joe and pointed to a railed-off staircase at the side of the big room.

"Downstairs, Joe."

Without a look at any of them, Joe went across the room and vanished down the steps, Packer behind him.

Wilbarth looked at Sam and Anse. "A quiet one?" he asked.

"He hasn't said a word, Wes. I mean that literally. Not a word in two days."

"Kennery, how'd you get him?"

Sam told him how Anse had pointed Joe out to him, and of their capture of him and his attempt to break away. As he was finishing, Packer came up the stairs, took his jacket and hat from a nail on the wall, and waited until Sam was finished. Then he said to Sheriff Ritter, "I'll get some grub for him."

Wilbarth said to Anse and Sam, "That's what you two better do for yourselves."

The three men moved out of the office and Ritter observed to Wilbarth, "I'll trade you one of my deputies for one of yours."

Wilbarth smiled faintly and went over to the chair by the desk. "He after your job, Al?" he asked, sitting down.

"Of course," Ritter said. "Behind my back he's saying I ought to be put out to pasture."

They began reminiscing about their long-ago association, and were still at it when Packer came in with the tray holding Joe's supper.

Wilbarth gave Joe fifteen minutes to eat it, and then they broke off their yarning. Rising, he said, "Let's go see him, Al."

In the three-cell jail below they found Packer taking out the tray from Joe's cell, which contained two cots. Finished with his meal, Joe was lying down and he didn't even look at them. Sheriff Ritter picked up Packer's chair and carried it to the cell, indicating the cot was for Wilbarth.

The marshal began matter-of-factly. "Joe, Brayton told us you understand English and speak it, so don't pretend you don't know what I'm talking about. First, I'll repeat the charges filed against you and tell you what your rights are."

He proceeded to do just that, telling Joe that he could be legally held for forty-eight hours on each charge, of which there were two. He was entitled to legal counsel, and there were two lawyers here in the county seat. If his lawyer so demanded, he could be freed on bond after ninety-six hours had passed. The court would undoubtedly place a bond on him of an amount that he could not possibly raise; therefore, to all intents and purposes he was a prisoner from now on, with no hope of being freed until trial. Unless he wanted to spend the winter here he had better talk. Specifically, he had better answer the questions Wilbarth was about to put to him. Joe listened as would a deaf man, who, hearing nothing, showed no reaction to words spoken to him.

Wilbarth continued, "Joe, one of those men who brought you in—the tall one—was paid a hundred dollars by Brayton to go up to the reservation and kill you. Brayton even told him why he wanted you killed. On the night of June the twelfth you and another man waited for the train to stop at the Long Reach water tank. You rode alongside the passenger car until you found Mort Schaeffer, then you shotgunned him through a window."

There was a racket on the stairs and Wilbarth waited till he saw Packer step into sight and halt in the doorway almost under the overhead lamp.

Wilbarth continued, "We have proof Brayton paid you and the other man to kill Schaeffer. We also know you've been blackmailing Brayton. Do you know what blackmail is, Joe?" Joe was looking at the ceiling and didn't answer. "You're asking Brayton for whiskey money, Joe, or else you'll turn him over to the law. That's why he wanted you killed. Now we don't think you killed Schaeffer, Joe. We think the other man did. What was his name?"

Suddenly Wilbarth got up and went over to Joe's cot. Joe was asleep.

Again there was the sound of footsteps on the stairs and Sam and Anse emerged from the stairwell and halted under the lamp. Wilbarth glowered at them and said to Packer, "Wake him up and keep him awake."

Packer came into the cell and went over to Joe and shook him. Joe opened his eyes and looked past Packer at the ceiling. Wilbarth, to Sam's surprise, was not angry. He was studying the wall of the cell, in which there was a window, and then his glance shifted to the other two cells, which also had windows. Packer and Sheriff Ritter watched him, puzzled.

Wilbarth turned to Ritter and said, "Will those two windows open?"

"Yes. It gets pretty hot here in the summer, Wes."

"Packer, open them now. But first take the blankets from his cot." Wilbarth looked past Ritter. "Anse, can you stay awake until midnight, when Sam can spell you?"

"Sure. Spell me to do what?"

"Joe likes to sleep, so we'll see how he does without any," Wilbarth said. "I want one man in the cell without a gun. That'll be you for tonight, Packer. You got any warm clothes here?"

"A sheepskin up in the office."

"Go get it," Wilbarth said. "A second man—that'll be you until midnight, Anse, and Sam till dawn—will sit in the corridor riding shotgun. I've got a mackinaw you can wear. Whoever's in the cell with Joe will keep him awake if the cold doesn't. Now, gentlemen, we'll ventilate this place."

Packer took both of Joe's blankets, which were folded on the foot of the cot, deposited them in the corridor, then opened the cell window, after which he opened the windows in the other two cells. The chill night air, close to freezing, blew into the cell block. Anse borrowed Sam's duck jacket and Packer went upstairs and returned with a sheepskin.

Once Anse had locked Packer in with Joe, he took up his vigil in the corridor. Sam and Wilbarth parted with Sheriff Ritter at the courthouse steps and headed for the hotel in the frosty night.

Chapter 13

WHEN Billy Foster came into the *Capital Times* office in mid-morning he found Red Macandy in shirt sleeves seated at the square desk. Billy shrugged out of his coat, hung it on the coat rack, and moved over to his slot in the desk facing Red. He was seating himself when Red said, "How's Wilbarth this morning? Still on the boil?"

"He's out of town."

Red leaned back in his chair, removed the half-chewed cigar from his mouth, and coldly regarded Billy. His thin saddle of red hair was uncombed this morning, and Billy, catching the reek of stale liquor, guessed that Red just possibly hadn't even been to bed last night.

"Where?" Red asked.

"Bailey wouldn't tell me."

"Who's Bailey?"

"Special deputy. He takes messages when they're both out of town."

"Newford gone too?"

Billy nodded. "That's right."

"Where?" Red asked again, bitingly.

"I don't know," Billy said flatly, a show of anger in his voice. "You told me to keep track of Wilbarth, and Bailey wouldn't talk. What am I supposed to do? Read Bailey's mind?"

Red tossed his cigar butt in the ash tray, making it a gesture of disgust. "Oh, nothing like that. You're only supposed to earn your wages. You're told that both the marshal and his deputy are out of town. You aren't even curious as to why."

"What good would curiosity do me?" Billy asked hotly. "What do you expect me to do? Throw Bailey down, grab him by the ears, and beat his head on the floor until he talks?"

Red leaned forward and said in quiet fury, "That's

enough of your lip, Sonny. I'll spell out what you should do, because you're too damned stupid to think of it yourself. Go to Bales's livery. That's on Main Street. Get a stranger to show you where Main Street is. At Bales's see if the marshal's horse is there. A horse is a four-legged domesticated animal that people ride. If the horse is there, then ask if Wilbarth has rented a rig. A rig is something a horse pulls and a man rides in. If Wilbarth didn't hire a rig, you go to the choo-choo depot, Sonny. Ask Perry when Newford left and when Wilbarth left. Ask him where they bought tickets to. Write it down, because you're not bright enough to remember. Then ask someone at the depot how to get back to this office. Now get the hell out of here!"

Billy stood up, his face white with anger, and crossed over to the coat rack under Red's baleful regard. His coat on, Billy moved to the door and went out, slamming the door behind him with a violence that shook the building.

Red opened the right-hand drawer of his desk, took out a cigar, and jammed it into the corner of his mouth. He was quiet. That damned kid would kill him yet, he thought bleakly. It was a mistake to allow him to do anything except sweet-talk a bunch of local pants-sellers into advertising their wares in the paper.

His choler now under control, Red thought about the disappearance of both Wilbarth and Newford. Something was up. Was it connected with the visit of the man in the closet? That thought caused him to glance over at the clock above the file shelf on the right wall. The mail would be up by now, and with any luck there would be a letter from Ben Harness saying either that he could or couldn't identify the man in the closet.

His cigar still unlighted, Red got up, put on his coat and hat, and stepped out into the overcast day. There was some weather coming, Red thought, and the prospect of it heralding the coming winter depressed him.

Junction City's post office had originally been in a rear corner of Cleveland's hardware store on Main Street. As the capital city grew and its mail load increased, it was moved to one of the back storerooms, into which a door was cut that let on to an alley that was often clogged by freight wagons, drays, and tethered horses.

Red threaded his way through the alley traffic and entered the dark post office, where a dozen people, half of them women, were waiting in line before the window. Red took his place at the end of the line, and it was then that he remembered he hadn't lighted his cigar. He proceeded to do so now, puffing furiously to get the half-wet cigar to burn. The cloud of smoke erupting around him caused two of the women in the line to look back at him and cough ostentatiously. Red ignored them.

When he received his mail he didn't examine it, knowing by experience that the room was too dark to read it. Leaving the alley, he walked the block to the Prairie House and entered the saloon off the lobby. At the bar he ordered whiskey, took his glass and bottle to the nearest of the three tables, and sat down.

After one drink, which was purely medicinal this morning, he looked through his mail. Sure enough, there was an envelope addressed in Ben Harness' impatient handwriting. The letter inside read:

> Red, your check was two dollars short and I can prove it.
> Yes, I think I know the man you described. He's been hanging around drinking with Brayton and Herrington. As soon as you pay me the money owed, I will telegraph his name to you.
>
> Y'r Disob'nt Serv't
Ben

Red swore so furiously that the bartender's attention was attracted to him. Morosely, Red had another drink, paid up, and headed for his office.

When he entered it he saw that Billy Foster had returned. He, too, had stopped at the post office, probably on his way to the depot, for he was reading a letter which he quickly folded and rammed in his hip pocket. Red put his hat on the top of the rack and came over to his desk.

"Well, Buster, what have you got for me?" he asked as he sat down.

Billy looked at him with hatred, but said tonelessly, "Wilbarth left yesterday for Crater. Newford left two days before that for Boundary."

Red thought about this a moment. Then, remembering his talk with Steve Lister, Newford was on the train with the man who had been in the closet. Any connection there? Surely if they'd been together Steve would have mentioned it. Still, both of them were headed for Boundary, and presumably for the agency.

But what was Wilbarth doing in Crater, which was north

of the agency and the reservation? There must be some connection between the reservation and Crater, but Red couldn't guess what. And how could the man in the closet be a drinking companion of Brayton and Herrington and still be friends with Wilbarth, the man who was going to help prosecute them? There was something funny going on here, Red's instinct told him, but the sum of the parts didn't add up to a recognizable whole. Something was missing, and he intended to find out what it was. Reaching in his desk drawer, he drew out an envelope and addressed it to Ben Harness in Primrose. He put inside it three dollars, two of which were owed to Ben and the third was to pay for the telegram.

Afterwards he reached in the bottom drawer and drew out the well-thumbed notebook that contained the names and addresses of perhaps five hundred people in the state, ranging from politicians to madams of sporting houses. In the back of the book was a list of the paper's correspondents. Since the *Capital Times* was the only daily newspaper in the state, and therefore widely read, Red had long ago arranged to have a stringer in the county seat of every county in the state. Usually it was the editor of the weekly newspaper if the county seat had one. Crater, he remembered, didn't. The name of his stringer in Crater was listed as Martin Flagg. A notation beside the name identified him as the station agent and telegraph operator.

Red reached for a sheet of copy paper and scribbled the following message:

FIND OUT U.S. MARSHALL WES WILBARTH'S BUSINESS IN CRATER. TELEGRAPH IN DETAIL. RED MACANDY.

Red folded the paper and tossed it and the envelope across the desk to Billy. "Send that telegram, Billy, and mail this letter."

Billy stood up. "They both cost money," he said coldly.

Red swore at him as he reached again for his wallet.

It was almost noon when Martin Flagg, station agent at Crater, heard his call on the telegraph sounder. Picking up a pencil, he pulled a pad toward him and translated the clacking of the sounder into Red Macandy's message to him. Flagg was a heavy, soft, pale man of fifty with curly, almost kinky, graying hair who relished the dirty stories exchanged in Morse code between agents down the line. By nature a gregarious man, he had a termagent wife who saw to it that after working hours he was never out of her sight. Accordingly, he welcomed any diversion, and Red's telegram promised him one. He knew, of course, that Wilbarth had come in on yesterday's train, but he had no notion of the marshal's business. He acknowledged receipt of the message and signed off.

Leaning back in his chair, he pondered his next move. After the noon meal he would forego his customary nap and go down to the courthouse. Chances were that old fogey of a Ritter would be out having his dinner, leaving Byron Packer alone in the office, which was just what he wanted.

Ritter, Flagg reflected, had been sheriff for so long that he acted like the emperor of a tiny kingdom; he was dictatorial, secretive, and senile, and only kept in office by a flock of relatives spotted through the county. Packer, on the other hand, was a young go-getter who would probably become the county's sheriff at next month's election. He would, Flagg judged, be very cooperative with a voter, and Flagg was certainly that.

Flagg put on his coat, overcoat, and hat, threw some wood in the pot-bellied stove in the waiting room, locked up the station, and tramped through the chilly noon to his modest home. At twelve-thirty, almost to the minute, he climbed the courthouse steps and went into the sheriff's office. Sure enough, Packer was seated at the sheriff's desk writing. He looked up as Flagg entered and gave the agent the easy smile of an ambitious politician. "Well, Martin, the train's quit runnin'?"

"Of course," Martin said. "You know they can't run without me."

They both laughed and Flagg moved over, unbuttoned his coat, and took a chair beside the desk.

"What can I do for you?" Packer asked.

"Nothing really. I'm just curious. I saw Marshal Wilbarth at the depot yesterday, but I only had time to say hello. What's he doing up here?"

Elbows on the arms of his chair, Packer raised big meaty hands and steepled his fingers. Martin's question started a train of thought which was really a list of resentments. Wilbarth and his two deputies had not only taken over the office and jail, but the marshal had treated him as a not-very-bright hired hand. Packer had them to thank for a chilly evening and a short night's sleep. He could look forward to the same thing tonight if the Indian didn't talk today. Moreover, Wilbarth was an old friend of Ritter's, and therefore was in the opposition camp. All three federal men had left him out of their confidence so emphatically that, while he knew the Indian was being held until he named his partner in committing the murder, he did not know the special status of Kennery nor the nature of his special assignment. What finally decided him to answer Martin, however, was that Ritter, who should have taken him into his complete confidence, hadn't thought it necessary to do so.

"Why, Wilbarth is up here to question an Indian that Kennery and Newford brought up from the reservation. They think the Indian and another fellow killed Mort Schaeffer. You remember that shotgunning of a passenger car at the Long Reach tank?"

"Yes. Pretty bloody."

"Well, the Indian's not talking," Packer said smugly. "If he was my prisoner I'd go down to the store and get me an axe handle. He'd talk, or there'd be a dead Injun. All they're doing is keeping him awake until he trades some talk for some sleep. They were at him all night and all of today."

"What's this Indian's name?"

Packer shrugged. "They call him Joe."

"Why'd they bring him here? Junction City's got a jail."

"You got me there, Martin. Maybe Wilbarth just wanted to chew the rag with his old friend Ritter."

Martin frowned in thought, and then spread his hands and shrugged. "Doesn't make sense. They could have got the train at Boundary and been in Wilbarth's office that night. Instead, Wilbarth travels all day and the other two cross a mountain range to get here."

That reminded him of his job. "What did you say the names of his deputies are? I'd better write them down."

Packer waited until Flagg drew pencil and paper from his inside pocket and then told him the names.

"How do you spell Kennery?"

"Ain't seen it spelled, Martin, and he ain't the kind of a man you'd ask."

Flagg made his guess and wrote it down. Afterwards he got up, saying, "Thanks, By. I better get the railroad runnin' again."

"This for the *Capital Times*, Martin?" When Flagg nodded, Packer said, "Mention me, will you, Martin? Say I was the inter— How do you pronounce that damn word? It means questioning."

"Deputy Byron Packer was one of the interrogators, I'll say. That all right?"

Byron smiled. "Fine, Martin. Now if you could just not mention Ritter, it would be even better."

Martin smiled. "I never intended to mention him. Thanks again, By."

Chapter 14

From the *Capital Times:*

SCHAEFFER MURDER SUSPECT
SEIZED BY U.S. MARSHAL

A reservation Indian known only as Joe was captured by two Deputy U.S. Marshals Monday and is being held in the county jail of Summit County at Crater for questioning in the shotgun death of Agency employee Morton Schaeffer last June. U.S. Marshal Wes Wilbarth is in Crater today interrogating the suspect with the aid of Deputy Sheriff Byron Packer. U.S. Deputy Marshals Sam Kennery and Anson Newford are credited with capturing the Indian and removing him from the reservation to a safe jail.

While Wilbarth was unavailable for comment, it is presumed that he chose the Summit county jail to protect the Indian from the same fate that befell Mort Schaeffer, who was killed en route to testify in the criminal fraud trial of Big Dad Herrington and Indian Agent Con Brayton.

The Times has learned through its Primrose correspondent that Deputy Marshal Kennery was in Primrose last week and was seen in the constant company of Herrington and Brayton. There is considerable speculation in the capital today as to the significance of this association. It is even rumored that the District Attorney's office is negotiating with Brayton and Herrington before their upcoming trial, using Marshal Kennery as go-between.

"Mother!" Tenney cried.

When Mrs. Payne, startled by the anguish in Tenney's

voice behind her turned from the stove she saw that her daughter's face was deathly pale, her lips trembling. Tenney thrust out a newspaper to her and said, "Someone left this in the dining room. Here." She pointed to the headline, and Mrs. Payne, spreading the paper, read the news story. She looked at her daughter then and the two women stared at each other, wordless for the moment.

"Dreadful!" Mrs. Payne said softly. "That ruins Sam's plans."

"What if Sam hasn't seen this? What if he comes back with the story that he killed the Indian? Brayton and Herrington and Carnes will kill him!"

"Surely the Indian has talked, or they wouldn't have told of his capture."

"Then why was Carnes having dinner with the other two? Why hasn't he been arrested? Or why hasn't he run?"

"Yes, why hasn't he?"

The two women eyed each other helplessly.

"Maybe Sheriff Morehead is watching them. Surely, if Carnes is guilty they'll ask Morehead to arrest him," Mrs. Payne said.

"But what if Sam doesn't see this issue of the *Times*? What if none of them in Crater sees it? What if Sam is on his way back? Who knows him to tell him?"

"Did he tell you when he was coming back?"

Tenney shook her head. "He's told you everything he's told me. Only that he'll take the train back. Somebody's got to get word to him, Mother."

"Morehead?"

"Won't he be needed here to arrest Carnes?"

The entrance of Mary, the other waitress, ended the conversation, but when Tenney returned to the dining room with a tray of desserts, her heart was still pounding wildly. She told herself that Sam was bound to know of the *Times* story. But was he? What if he had changed his plans and was riding back across the reservation, out of touch with all news of the outside world? Or if he took the train back, as he had said, nobody would recognize him to tell him. The very fact that Brayton, Herrington, and Carnes had unconcernedly eaten their dinner in this room earlier meant that up until this very moment Wilbarth and the others had failed to get information from the Indian. Or could it mean that the Indian had talked—implicating someone other than Carnes? She could only answer that by falling back on Sam Kennery's judgment that it was probably Carnes who killed Schaeffer.

She distributed the desserts and refilled water glasses almost unaware of what she was doing. Why hadn't Brayton and Herrington been arrested for paying a man, namely Sam Kennery, to kill the Indian? She thought she knew the answer to that one. Herrington and Brayton, along with Carnes, would deny the whole story and doubtless would accuse Sam of making it up to shore up the government's case against him. After all, it was one man's word against the word of three. That must be so, or Marshal Wilbarth would have ordered Morehead to arrest Carnes. All of it, Tenney thought, added up to the fact that Sam must be told before he reached Primrose that the three men knew he had betrayed them.

On her way back to the kitchen Tenney made up her mind. She found her mother at the chore of scraping plates. Coming up beside her, Tenney said, "Mother, stop a minute and let me talk to you."

While Mrs. Payne was washing her hands at the big sink, Mary brought out a tray of dishes and went out again. Tenney waited until she was out of the room and then said, "Mother, shouldn't I go to Junction City and head Sam off?"

Mrs. Payne gave Tenney a look of incomprehension. "How would you find him, Tenney?"

"There's only one train a day from Crater that carries passengers. If Sam had come in on that last night he would have taken a train here this morning, wouldn't he?"

Mrs. Payne nodded and Tenney went on. "I have time to change my clothes and take the train to Junction City. It gets in before the train from the north. I can wait at the depot and find out if Sam's on tonight's train. If he isn't, I'll wait for tomorrow night's train, and the next night's if I have to. If I miss him and he slips by me, I'll be at the depot watching the train to here every morning. How can I miss him?"

"Tenney, surely he'll have heard." It was a half-hearted protest, a mother's protective urge.

"Do you read the paper every day, Mother? Do I? Then why should Sam?"

"I know," Mrs. Payne said quietly.

"I'm going, Mother. I have some time off coming. We've got enough money for the train fare. Mary's sister can take my place while I'm gone."

"Then go, Tenney. Hurry now and change your clothes. I'll ask Mary about her sister."

Tenney hugged her mother, and then ran across the kitchen to the door that led to their rooms.

Sam waited for the early morning train at Crater, watching through the depot's dirty windows a swirling snowstorm that had started around midnight. The night telegrapher sold him his ticket, and Sam paced the overheated waiting room as the train was made up for the journey south. He reviewed last night's maddening, almost farcical questioning of Joe.

Last evening Wilbarth had given up his plan to starve Joe of sleep. When Wilbarth ordered the windows closed and Joe covered with blankets, it was less a humanitarian move than a necessary one. Joe, shivering, was literally asleep on his feet, sustained between Packer and Anse. Joe was a heavy man, and the weight of his slack body had exhausted the two supporting him. Wilbarth and Sam had spelled them, but it soon became apparent that Joe would exhaust them too. They made a ridiculous picture, two men dragging a snoring burden around a narrow cell, and Wilbarth, realizing that Joe had won, ordered him to be put on the cot and covered. Afterwards, leaving Packer as the corridor guard, Wilbarth left the courthouse with Sam and Anse.

Two days and three nights of questioning had brought not a word from Joe. He couldn't, or wouldn't, understand that Brayton had not only betrayed him, but had paid for his death. Tomorrow a court-appointed lawyer would take over for Joe. Wilbarth and Anse would wait over another day to see Joe arraigned and indicted, but Sam had been ordered back to Primrose.

When the train pulled alongside the depot platform Sam saw that he was the only passenger from Crater. He passed the time of day with the bundled-up brakeman and then stepped up into the empty passenger car. He chose a seat in the middle of the car where drafts from both doors would be the least chilling, threw his blanket roll on the overhead rack, and slacked into the seat. He was surprised to find that these past nights when his ration of sleep had been short and uncomfortable, sometimes non-existent, had not tired him out. Though his body was weary, his mind wasn't; the frustration of Joe's silence was riding him. He and Wilbarth had relied so heavily on Joe's eventual cooperation that they had not planned beyond that, in case Joe kept his silence.

The original plan was for Sam, equpped with Joe's confession and a murder warrant for Carnes's arrest, to return to Primrose and take Carnes into custody. Now they had no plan, or rather they had a half-plan that seemed unlikely of success. Sam was to return to Primrose, tell the trio that they were rid of Joe, whose body would be hidden by the winter snows that were already here in the high country, and claim his hundred dollars. He did have in his blanket roll Joe's stinking buckskin shirt bloodied by a butcher-shop steak. If this was not proof enough he was not to argue, but instead to accept good-humoredly their verdict on the payment. It was hoped by both Wilbarth and Sam that this would further ingratiate Sam with them, and that in continued association with them they would let fall information that would solidly implicate Carnes. *Pretty creaky,* Sam thought wryly.

Sam took off his jacket and rolled it up to use as a pillow, and closed his eyes. Drowsily he thought of Wilbarth's frustration too. Wilbarth was a good man, Sam reflected. The average law man had fought Indians at one time or another and considered them sub-human. At the hands of an officer other than Wilbarth, Joe would have been beaten within an inch of his life, or tortured in the same way that Indians had tortured white men. Wilbarth, however, had treated Joe's rights as he would have treated a white man's, even though the solution of a heartless murder lay in Joe's dark, secretive mind. Finally, in spite of the rattling, jolting train, welcome sleep overtook him.

He slept fitfully most of the day, and was sleeping when the brakeman came through the half-filled car, its overhead lamps lighted against the outside dark. He called out, "Junction City. End of the line. Junction City."

The other passengers filed past Sam as the train ground to a halt. He stood up, put on his jacket, and lifted down his blanket roll, and then he noticed that the car was swaying slightly. What Sam had thought was the natural roll and sway of the car on the trip down had been exaggerated by driving wind that was now buffeting the car. When he moved out onto the car platform, the full force of the wind hit him and he knew that this was the prelude to the snowstorm they had run out of in the early afternoon. Stepping down onto the platform, he shouldered his blanket roll and was heading for the row of hacks when he heard a woman's voice call out behind him, "Sam! Sam Kennery!"

Sam turned and saw Tenney running toward him. She was bundled up in a heavy ponyskin coat and was holding onto her tiny hat as she came up to him.

"Why, Tenney. What are you doing here?"

"Waiting for you, that's all. Just waiting for you, and thank the Lord you're here."

"What's happened?"

The wind almost whipped the words out of his mouth, and Tenney said, "Let's go inside where we can talk, Sam. I've got something to show you."

Sam took her arm and they moved toward the big depot and into the high-ceilinged waiting room. It was almost deserted, and was warm and quiet.

Sam turned Tenney to face him, hands on her arms, and he looked closely at her face. She did not look troubled; on the contrary, her dark eyes held a strange excitement. Her dark hair piled on the top of her head was wind-blown and looked attractive.

"What have you got to show me, Tenney?" he asked.

She shrugged Sam's hands away, then reached in her handbag and drew out a newspaper, which she unfolded. She was watching him as she did so. "Have you seen the *Capital Times?"* she asked.

Sam shook his head, and Tenney gave him a strange smile that seemed to hold beyond its sweetness a kind of relief.

"It's on the front page, Sam. Go over by the lamp."

Sam went over by one of the lamps on a wall bracket and Tenney trailed after him. Halting by the light, Sam unfolded the newspaper. Tenney had circled the story with ink and his attention went to it immediately. As he read Macandy's story, despair washed over him, and on its heels came a wild anger. This, then, was the dead end of their plan, its aims revealed to Herrington, Brayton, and Carnes. There was a hard bitterness in the set of his mouth as he folded the paper and turned to regard Tenney. Slowly the reason for Tenney's being here came to him.

"You came to warn me, Tenney," Sam said simply.

She nodded. "I couldn't let you meet them again thinking you had them fooled. They could have trapped you and killed you."

"And would have," Sam said grimly.

"What are you going to do, Sam?"

He shook his head. "That's too quick, Tenney." He gestured toward one of the benches. "Let's sit down."

Tenney led the way to the nearest bench, where Sam had dumped his blanket roll, and they both sat down. Tenney, blessedly, had sense enough not to chatter, nor could she have done so even if she had wanted to. Sam was on his feet again almost immediately and, fists jammed in his jacket pockets, he began pacing up and down the aisle between the two rows of benches. Tenney watched his head-down, measured stride, trying to guess what he was thinking.

Sam's thoughts, now that the first shock had worn off, were distorted with anger, and he had sense enough to know it. Where had Red Macandy got his story? Remembering Ben Harness in Primrose, he guessed that Red had a correspondent in Crater, but how had the correspondent got the story? Then he remembered the story had said Deputy Byron Packer had aided in the interrogation, which was a lie. That was it. Packer, to gain a measure of self-importance, had spilled the story to the Crater correspondent, who would have had to telegraph it in to make today's newspaper.

Then a thought came to him so abruptly that he halted in his pacing. Couldn't this game of revelation by newspaper be worked two ways? It was worth trying anyhow. He walked up to Tenney and stood before her. "Where are you staying, Tenney?"

"Mrs. Schell's rooming house. She's a friend of Mother's."

"I'll take you there," Sam said. "We'll see if she has room for me too."

They went out into the wind then and Sam steered Tenney toward the hack stand, where a pair of carriage lamps shone. The wind bucked them and Tenney stooped, Sam thought to catch her balance. She said, "Where are we going, Sam?"

"To take a hack to the rooming house."

"But it's only three houses down Main Street. We can see it from here. Let's walk it."

It was useless trying to talk in the gusty night wind as, arm in arm, they went down the street and Tenney indicated the house. She led the way into the big front parlor, where a lamp in the window was burning dimly.

"Mrs. Schell!" she called, and from the back of the house came a woman's voice, "Is it you, Tenney?"

Sam heard footsteps coming down the corridor, and then a pleasantly plump woman of forty stepped into the room.

"This is the friend I was meeting, Mrs. Schell. He's Sam Kennery. Sam, this is Mother's friend, Mrs. Schell."

Mrs. Schell gave him a swift appraising glance and, apparently liking what she saw, came up to him and held out her hand. Her black dress might be widow weeds, Sam guessed.

Tenney said, "Do you have a room for him tonight, Mrs. Schell?"

"Down the hall from yours, Tenney. Would you like to look at it, Mr. Kennery?"

"I'm sure if Tenney likes hers, then this one is all right too," Sam said, and smiled.

"Then she can show you the way, Mr. Kennery. Those steps are getting steeper every day for me." She said good night and added, "Breakfast is at six-thirty for the early morning train."

Alone with Sam, Tenney went over to the sofa and sat down. "You want to talk now, Sam?"

"No," Sam said quietly. "Either I'm a genius or a fool, but I've got an idea, Tenney. If it works I'll talk as long as you'll listen. But now I've got to go."

Tenney looked disappointed, but she stood up beside Sam. "I'll help Mrs. Schell with the morning stuff, Sam. Will you—" She halted, leaving her question unasked. "If I don't see you later, good night, Sam."

"I think you'll see me, Tenney, because I want you to. You see, you're a part of all this. You've paid for your ticket over and over, and you did again tonight."

Sam, moving toward the door, halted halfway, turned, and said gravely, "You're pretty, Tenney. Anybody ever tell you that?"

Tenney nodded, blushing. "Mostly people I don't want to hear it from."

"Like me?" Sam teased.

"Not like you," Tenney said.

Sam stepped out into the windy night and headed toward the business district, impatience riding him. He could see the distant lights in the capitol building on the river bluff and recalled his last meeting with Wilbarth. Would the marshal approve of what he was about to do? Sam didn't know, and there was no time to get the authority. Besides, now that they knew and respected each other, Wilbarth would probably tell him to use his own judgment.

Of a passer-by who looked like a townsman, Sam asked

directions to the *Capital Times*. He realized that the *Times* might be closed at this hour, but he had to start his search for Red Macandy somewhere. When he rounded the corner and turned off Main Street, he saw there was a light burning dimly in the *Times* building; probably the night light, he thought, but he went on. Moving up to the front window, he saw a lamp burning in the rear. Standing on tiptoe to look over the painted section of the window, he could see a man wearing an ink-stained apron fiddling with the press in the rear. Sam tried the door, found it unlocked, and walked into the big ink-smelling room. He saw the swing-gate in the railing and went back toward the gray-haired printer, who looked up at his approach. Sam halted and said, "I'm looking for Red Macandy."

"Try the saloons," the printer said curtly.

"Any special one?"

"The Prairie House or the Grandview."

Sam's glance dropped to the printer's grease-stained hands. "You got trouble?" he asked.

"You could call it that," the printer said sourly. "If I don't get this damned thing fixed by four o'clock, there'll be no *Times* tomorrow."

"What happens at four o'clock?"

"That's when I start the press-run."

"Why then?" Sam asked.

"To catch the early trains, is what Macandy says." He snorted. "What do those farmers and cowpunchers care if the paper's a day late? They can't read anyway."

Before Sam could say anything more, the man was attacking the press with a wrench.

Out on the windy street again, Sam retraced his steps to the Prairie Hotel. Its small saloon did not hold Red Macandy, and Sam wondered now if his five-second look through a keyhold at Red had been sufficient for him to recognize him again. He thought it had been.

A block further down Grant Street was the Grandview, and Sam headed for it. The wind was driving great banners of dust along the street, and Sam, head down, bucked it to the entrance of the Grandview saloon. Through the tall glassed doors he could see that the saloon was doing a thriving business. He went in and moved slowly past several card games, glancing at each player and spectator.

Achieving the crowded bar, he took up a position around its curve so that he could see the faces of the customers.

His glance traveled the line and stopped on one man. This had to be Red Macandy who, just as Sam had last seen him, was waving a thoroughly chewed cigar in the next man's face to emphasize a point.

Sam moved back down the bar and bellied up to it beside Macandy. Red's hat was pushed to the back of his head and his townsman's suit was rumpled and as dusty as if he had rolled in the street.

Sam heard him say, "You politicians are all alike. You stink."

The fat man he was addressing laughed. "Coming from a man who hasn't had a bath in two months, that's kind of funny, Red."

Sam did not miss the good-natured contempt in the fat man's tone.

The bartender came up as Sam was unbuttoning his jacket.

"Your best whiskey," Sam said. As he expected, Red turned at the sound of a new voice, and now Sam brushed his jacket open to put his hand in his pocket, a maneuver calculated to reveal the marshal's badge on his chest. He did not look at Red, but he knew that Red saw the badge.

Sam put a coin on the bar, and was silent as the bartender set a labeled bottle and a glass in front of him. He was pouring his drink when Red said, "That's a marshal's badge, ain't it?"

Sam turned his head and regarded him carefully. Red's drink-puffed face and bloodshot eyes held a sham belligerence that was part of the aggressiveness he liked to show the world.

Sam said quietly, "Deputy marshal's badge."

"You a new boy for Wilbarth?"

"No."

"Well, if you're looking for him, he ain't here."

Sam said quietly, "I know. I left him in Crater this morning."

Now Red turned to face him, and Sam could see the gray drift of cigar ashes on his coat front. Red was examining him carefully as Sam poured his drink.

"Sam Kennery! Is that it?" Red said.

"That's right."

Red's next question was a pounce. "Joe talked yet?"

Sam looked at him coldly. "Who are you?"

"You know damned well who I am," Red snarled. "That's why you came up beside me. Has he?"

"Of course," Sam lied.

"Who was it?"

Sam looked at him wonderingly. "You must think I'm simple."

"You were the man in Wilbarth's closet, weren't you?" At Sam's nod, Red said, "Come on. Who'd Joe name?"

"You'll know when the arrest is made," Sam said.

"You going to make it?"

"Tomorrow."

"Here? Where?" Red pushed.

Sam smiled faintly and shook his head.

"Where's Wilbarth? Still at Crater?" Red asked.

"I told you I left him there."

"What's he doing?"

Sam pretended to consider the bounds of discretion. Then he said, "There's the confession to take down, then the arraignment."

"Come on," Red wheedled. "Name the man. I won't print his name until you say so."

Sam had his drink under Red's watchful gaze. He set down his glass and said, "Nothing doing, Red."

"Why'd you hunt me up?" Red demanded.

"Wilbarth wanted you to know I was the man in the closet."

"So I'd get off his back? I don't believe it."

Sam only shrugged. He pushed away from the bar now, but Red asked quickly, "Where do you go tomorrow? Man, you can't get out of town without I know it."

"Good night, Red," Sam said.

Outside the saloon Sam headed directly across the street for the haven of a darkened store front and stepped into the bay of the entrance. Thanks to the darkness and the pluming dust, his hiding place wouldn't be visible from across the street. Watching the doors of the Grandview saloon, he saw them open and saw Red Macandy step out into the wind, holding his hat by its brim to keep it from being swept down the street. Red moved out to the edge of the plank walk and peered up and down the street and Sam knew that he was looking for him. Then Red turned down the street and Sam followed, keeping behind him on the opposite side of the street.

Red turned into the Prairie House. Sam backed into a doorway out of the wind and waited. In a few minutes Red came out and again headed downstreet, Sam trailing him.

When Red turned the next corner Sam crossed the street, a sudden hope within him. At the corner of the building, he looked down the cross street and saw Red angling across toward the *Times* building. Sam waited until Red had entered it before he turned and headed back up the street for Mrs. Schell's rooming house.

As he approached it he saw the lamp in the window burning dimly, and he felt disappointment. This looked like a night lamp, which meant that Tenney had given in against weariness and gone to bed. Letting himself into the house, he looked around the dimly lighted living room. There, in a big leather chair, Tenney was huddled, her knees drawn up, her skirt spread over her feet. She was sleeping.

Quietly Sam moved across the floor and turned up the lamp. The added light wakened Tenney and she sat up, smiling sleepily.

Sam took off his hat and jacket and tossed them on the sofa, then swung a straight-back chair in front of Tenney, its back to her. He straddled the chair, folded his arms on the back of it, and looked fondly at Tenney.

"Are you an idiot or are you a genius?" Tenney asked quietly.

Sam smiled. "I think a genius, Tenney, but it's too early to tell."

He told her then of his search for Red Macandy, beginning at the *Times* office. He said he hadn't found Red there but he did learn that the *Times* would not be printed until four tomorrow morning. This was a bit of blind luck, as Tenney would see later, he said. He went on to tell of hunting down Red, and a look of puzzlement came into Tenney's face.

Continuing, Sam told her of the flat-out lie he had told Red when he said that Joe had talked and confirmed his accomplice, who, still nameless, would be arrested tomorrow. And he went on to tell her of following Red to the *Times* office.

He finished by saying, "He was excited, Tenney. I think he went back to write up the story for the paper."

Tenney looked puzzled. "But none of what you told him is true, Sam. What does the lie get us?"

"I'm hoping it will force Carnes into running. If he does, there's the proof he's the man Joe named."

"But that isn't catching him."

"If he runs I'll catch him, Tenney. Tomorrow morning

I'll telegraph Morehead not to let Carnes out of his sight. If Red prints what I hope he does, copies of the *Times* will be on our train. I want to give Carnes time enough to read it before I hunt him up."

"It's a dangerous bluff, Sam. What if he calls it?"

"He can't afford to call it, Tenney. He can't help but think, 'What if the story is true?' "

Tenney said quietly, "He may shoot you, Sam."

"Yes. There's that," Sam agreed.

"That doesn't worry you?"

Sam grinned faintly. "Come, come, Tenney. Would I be in this business if it did?"

Tenney shivered. "But it worries *me*," she said.

"I'm sort of glad it does."

Tenney looked surprised. "Why would you be?"

"It makes me think I'm a little bit special."

Tenney said softly, "Oh, Sam, you are. That's just it."

"You want me to give up on Carnes, Tenney?"

"No. No."

Sam unfolded his arms, put out his hands, palms up. Willingly Tenney put her hands in his.

"Then take what comes, Tenney. Because we're both what we are, we don't change it."

Still holding her hands, he stood up, then drew her into his arms. When she looked up, expecting and wanting him to kiss her, he did. Gently then, he moved her away from him, his hands on her forearms. "This morning I said you were pretty, Tenney. Now you're beautiful."

"I feel beautiful," Tenney said.

Sam turned her around and said quietly from behind her, "Go up and dream we're lucky, Tenney. Good night."

Chapter 15

OTHER SCHAEFFER KILLER
TO BE NAMED AFTER ARREST

According to information received late last night, the Indian held in the Summit County jail at Crater has named
his accomplice in the June shotgun slaying of Morton
Schaeffer. Arrest of the accomplice, whose name was not
disclosed, will be made today. Place of arrest was not
given. While Deputy U.S. Marshal Sam Kennery is making
the arrest, Marshal Wes Wilbarth remains in Crater seek-
ing the arraignment on a murder charge of the Indian called
Joe. No motive has been given for the accused pair's
killing of Schaeffer, but it is known that Schaeffer was to be
the prime government witness in the much delayed trial of
Big Dad Herrington and Agent Con Brayton for criminal
fraud.

The name of the alleged accomplice will be given to
the *Times* after the arrest has been effected.

Sam, standing at a distance from Tenney, watched her
read the article, and then she lifted her glance and smiled.
Afterwards, she took her place in the ticket line two places
behind him. His own copy of the *Capital Times* was rammed
in his jacket pocket, and Red's story contained all he had
hoped for.

Sam and Tenney had agreed at breakfast this morning
that they should not appear to be traveling together. This
was at Sam's insistence. He did not want Tenney to seem involved in any way in this case before Brayton, Herrington,
and Carnes were behind bars.

When Sam moved up to buy his ticket, he paid for it and
then thrust a folded sheet of paper in front of the agent. It

read: "To Sheriff Morehead, Primrose: Keep the shotgun owner in sight at all times until I see you today. See today's Times. Kennery."

"Will that telegram beat me to Primrose?" Sam asked.

Perry, the station agent, looked at him and said tartly, "If you didn't think so, why are you sending it?"

"Fair question," Sam said agreeably, and paid for the telegram.

Stepping out of the line, Sam moved over, picked up his blanket roll, and headed for the train standing alongside the rain-drenched platform. He had made it almost to the door when he felt someone touch his arm. He turned and saw Red Macandy standing there, his black raincoat wet and glistening.

"Where to? Primrose?" Red asked.

Sam grinned. "Well, the train stops at West Haven, New Hope, and Primrose. Take your choice."

"I can find out from Perry quick enough. You sent a telegram too. Who to?"

"Can't you find that out from Perry too? Even the message?"

"For a little money, yes," Red said bluntly.

"Then spend it," Sam said, and shouldered past him.

"Wait a minute," Red called. Again Sam halted. "You walked in here with a pretty girl. Who is she?"

"Ask her," Sam said. "We stayed at the same rooming house last night and I walked her to the station with her umbrella."

"She bought a copy of the Times, read something in it, looked at you, and smiled."

"Some people look at me and laugh," Sam said coldly.

"You know her," Red said accusingly.

"No, but if you do, introduce me."

"Ah-h-h," Red said in a tone of disgust. He reached inside his raincoat, brought out a cigar, and wedged it in the corner of his mouth. "Come on. Name me Joe's friend, Kennery. I'll get it after you arrest him today anyway. Why not now?"

"Good-bye, Red," Sam said, and this time he achieved the door. Tramping across the platform in the rain, he marveled at the gall of this man who, seemingly, would ask anyone, any time, anywhere, questions whose answers were none of his business.

Sam took his seat on the train toward the rear of the car and minutes later he regretfully watched Tenney move down the aisle and take a seat at the front end. After last night, there were a thousand things he wanted to ask her. One of them was if she would marry him. Most of what he really knew of her through their few brief meetings he had learned from her mother. They simply hadn't had time to get to know each other. Yet he was glad they had decided to travel separately and the wisdom of his decision had been underlined by his meeting Red. He wanted desperately to protect Tenney and her mother until this whole affair was finished.

All through the morning the train drove through rain. Low clouds shrouded the distant Rafts and puddled the dusty plains into mud. The Raft River, now placid after its charge down the mountains and foothills, was pocked with raindrops and its usual green-black was turning into the color of mud.

When the train pulled in alongside the Primrose depot the rain was still holding. Sam let the car empty and then went outside and crossed through the rain to the protection of the depot's overhanging roof. He watched the baggage car unload under the impatient gaze of the hack drivers from the Primrose House and the Consolidated Mine. The Primrose driver settled for a trunk, which was hoisted onto his broad shoulders by the brakeman—and a bundle wrapped in old newspapers, which Sam was sure was the Primrose House's ration of today's *Capital Times.*

He turned his head and saw Tenney seated in the waiting hack with two others of the train's passengers. As the hack driver adjusted his burden someone on Sam's other side said, "Hello, Mr. Kennery."

It was Ben Harness, grinning at him, looking small but cheerful in an oversize raincoat that was obviously borrowed.

"So Red's been on the telegraph," Sam said wryly.

"That's right. It looks like today's the day I earn my money."

"How you going to earn it?"

"Follow you until you make an arrest."

"Don't follow too close," Sam said quietly.

"You expecting trouble?"

"I'm always expecting trouble. Just you keep out of the way."

The hack pulled out into River Street and headed for the bridge. Sam turned up the collar of his duck jacket and stepped out into the rain. Ben Harness, remembering Sam's admonition, waited until Sam reached the bridge before he followed.

When one of the depot loafers stopped by Sheriff Morehead's office in mid-morning, the sheriff was in another office down the corridor. The loafer, regretting the loss of the price of a couple of beers that Morehead would have given had he been there, left the open telegram on the desk. When Morehead returned some minutes later, he found the telegram and read it. The man with the shotgun referred to Carnes, of course, but why hadn't Kennery named him? Probably today's *Times* would answer that question.

Morehead folded the telegram and put it in his shirt pocket, then walked over to the coat rack and took down his cracked yellow slicker and put it on. His hat was still wet from his walk to the office in the rain and when he put it on it felt cold and heavy and uncomfortable enough to bring a small irritation to him. Strange how insignificant things were beginning to annoy him lately, he thought, and he put it down to his years, which were well over fifty. The wet hat, to be sure, was a little thing, but were the other irritations?

As he went down the corridor and let himself out into the rain he reviewed the incidents that nagged at him. Perhaps the gravest, the most hurtful, was the inescapable feeling that he was being ignored in this Herrington, Brayton, and Carnes business. It was left up to a slip of a girl to tell him that Brayton and Herrington had paid Kennery money to kill an Indian. Come to that, why hadn't he been asked to arrest them both for paying for a murder? And why hadn't Kennery asked him instead of little Tenney to check the hotel register to find out Carnes's room? That was his business, and Louis Selby would have cooperated with him and kept his mouth shut. Was Kennery in such a confounded hurry that he couldn't write him, telling him all the things he had to learn from Tenney? He was being treated like some country Reuben who couldn't be trusted with the chores of his office. He had to learn from the *Capital Times* and not from the marshal's office that Kennery had captured the Indian. And what was Tenney, missing from the dining room, doing in Junction City yesterday?

Then his common sense said to him, *Quit it. You're getting older, your hip aches, and it's raining, so you're feeling sorry for yourself.* Still, this feeling of neglect was with him as he mounted the veranda steps of the Primrose House, peeled off his slicker, and shook it and his hat free of water before entering the lobby.

He knew Brayton and Herrington and Carnes would be in the saloon because they always were. Come to think of it, this wasn't a bad time or a bad day to have a drink himself. As he passed the lobby sofa to the right of the barroom door, he threw his slicker on it and moved into the bar. When he crossed the threshold he heard the distant sound of the morning train whistle which, in the damp air, seemed closer and louder than usual.

The three polecats, as he called them to himself, were seated at their regular table, with Carnes, as usual, facing the entrances, his back to a wall. That was the mark of a hardcase or a hated law man, he thought, as Alec moved up behind the bar to serve him.

Alec was pouring his drink when Herrington called over, "We're still here, Sheriff," and gave his howl of a laugh.

Morehead half turned and regarded them sourly. "You better be," he said in his gravelly voice. As he turned back to his drink, Morehead spat in the cuspidor at his feet, a gesture of contempt he hoped would not go unnoticed. The sight of them reminded him of another grievance. If the Indian had talked, why hadn't Wilbarth telegraphed him to pick up these three blackbirds? Even if he hadn't talked, why was Wilbarth allowing them to run free? Why was he talking to a newspaper man instead of to a brother law officer? Why was Wilbarth sending Kennery down to make an arrest that he, as sheriff, could easily make? Did Wilbarth want the glory of their arrest to go to his marshal's office?

Then, for the first time since he was a young man, he poured himself a second morning drink, carefully and obstinately. This he sipped, killing time until the newspapers were brought in from the hotel hack. He had almost finished this second drink when, reflected in the bar mirror, he saw Tenney cross the lobby heading for the dining room. Two men, both strangers, angled off toward the desk, followed by the hack driver carrying the guests' baggage, which he placed beside the desk. He vanished, and in a few moments came in with the newspapers.

When Selby had finished registering the guests, he moved over to the bundle of newspapers and opened it.

Seeley Carnes, his attention attracted by the lobby talk

which meant the hack was in, got up, walked past Morehead, and headed across the lobby for the desk. Deliberately, Morehead finished his drink, turned, and walked out into the lobby. Carnes, he saw, had finished glancing at the first page of the *Times*. Lazily, he folded it, rammed it in his hip pocket, then went across the lobby toward the stairs, presumably to go to his room.

Morehead went over to the stack of newspapers on the desk, put down his money, then moved over to a lobby chair by one of the windows. Seating himself, he spread out the newspaper on his crossed legs and began to scan the columns.

The Schaeffer story caught his attention immediately. He read it hurriedly, then read it again, this time more thoroughly, and now its information fleshed out the bare bones of Kennery's telegram. Surely, Kennery was coming today to arrest Carnes, upon whom Morehead had been instructed to keep an eye. It came to him with slow shock that Carnes had already read the story and was now up in his room. Morehead rose and moved swiftly to the veranda doors and looked down the street. Where in the hell was Kennery? Why hadn't he come in the hotel hack? Had he missed the train, or had he changed his mind about coming?

The sense of urgency almost smothered Morehead's breathing. Carnes would be starting to run, and what was he doing about it except looking down street for the man who would make the arrest?

He came to a sudden decision. Turning, he hurried across the lobby to the stairs and mounted them swiftly, his boots thumping as he climbed. Reaching the corridor, he turned left, remembering that ten was the number of Herrington's and Carnes's room.

Drawing his gun, he approached the door. Should he knock? Hell, no. He'd surprise him if he could. It was only when he was reaching for the doorknob that he realized his footfalls on the hardwood floor had announced him. Recklessly then, he wrenched at the knob, found the door unlocked, swung it open, and stepped inside. Carnes, his slicker on, blanket roll on the bed beside him, was facing the door, his gun drawn.

Carnes shot, and Morehead felt something slam into his side, whirling him around and driving him off balance. He shot even as he was falling. The next instant he had crashed down on his back, his head hitting the floor with such violence that there was an explosion of light in his eyes before black oblivion took over.

Morehead's bullet knocked Carnes's left leg from under him and turned him so that he fell on the bed, face down. As he rolled over and lunged to his feet he could feel only a numbness in his leg, but pure panic was in him. The shots would draw people from below, and climbing the stairs they would block his way.

He stumbled for the door, skirting Morehead's sprawled body. Once in the corridor, he heard steps charging up the stairs.

Remembering now, Carnes turned to the left and hobbled past Brayton's room to the corridor window. Hanging from a hook buried in the window frame was the coiled rope that was the fire escape.

Carnes slashed at the window with his gun and in three swift blows the frame was clear of glass. He took the coiled rope and flung it out the window. Holstering his gun, he threw his good leg over the sill and then let himself slack out the window and down, dragging his hurt leg out last. The knots spaced at intervals in the rope made his descent swift and easy.

On the wet boardwalk Carnes looked about him. A team and wagon passed down Grant Street, but its driver, huddled against the rain, had apparently neither seen nor heard his escape. Hugging close to the side of the hotel, Carnes moved along it to the street. Across the way an alley's mouth gaped, and Carnes headed for it, trying not to limp, but failing. His left boot was full of blood, and he knew that he would soon have to stop and tend to the leg. The numbness was going and replacing it was a searing pain in his thigh that threatened at each step to buckle his leg.

Once in the alley and out of sight of his escape window, he leaned against the wall of a building. His original plan, conceived only moments ago in his room, had been to steal a horse, any horse, that could put distance between him and Kennery. Now he knew he could not make it to the street to steal a horse or, if necessary, commandeer one at gun point. Even if he had one, his leg would prevent him from riding it. No, there was only one thing to do, and that was to hide and stop the bleeding.

He hobbled down the alley in a mire of mud, his glance searching both sides of the alley for a hiding place. When the hunt for him got under way he knew these sheds he was passing would be the first places to be searched. He must look for something safer, a place where they wouldn't think to look.

When he was abreast the loading dock of Pollock's Emporium, the thought came to him that a store as big as this one must have a basement. If it had a basement, there must be a loading door into it from the dock, and it would be close to the back door.

He climbed the short ladder up onto the dock and headed for the big double doors opening into the store. Reaching them, he tried the latch and found the door unlocked. It opened into a small storeroom that held mostly kegs of nails and horseshoes, with harness and rope dangling from the wall. Beyond the big rear doors a short corridor opened into the store itself.

This room was empty, and Carnes stepped inside, looking about him. To his immediate right he saw a pair of double doors almost as big as the ones he had come through, and he moved over to them. They had a metal latch which he thumbed down, swinging out half the big door. He peered down into blackness. But there was just light enough to see a ramp that vanished into the darkness. He could see that it was cleated so that in the manhandling of barrel goods there would be foot braces.

Carnes stepped inside and pulled the door closed behind him. Painfully placing his good leg against the cleats, he went down slowly. Down on the floor he stumbled into a stack of crates and leaned against them. His leg was throbbing with every beat of his heart, but he hoped a kind of relief would soon be possible.

Somewhere close by, he thought, there surely must be a lantern, for no clerk or freighter could work in this darkness.

He pulled a match from his pocket, struck it on a crate, and looked about him. There, to one side of the ramp, was a lantern hanging on a nail and he hobbled over to it and lighted it. By its light he moved through a maze of barrels and crates until he came to a pile of tanned hides. He could lie down here, once he had checked his wound.

Shucking off his slicker and stripping down his trousers, he saw that Morehead's bullet had entered his thigh well above the knee and its exit had made a great tear in his flesh. Blood was still oozing from the wound. The bullet had missed the bone, he knew, or else he couldn't have walked this far.

Reaching up, he untied his neckerchief and bound it
around the wound. From his jacket pocket he took out his
knife, and then, seating himself on the hides, he reached
out for the top one and cut a six-inch-wide strip from it.
This strip of soft hide he used as a bandage, winding
it tightly over the neckerchief, and finally bound it by slitting
the end and knotting the two halves. He waited a minute
to see if the pressure of the bandage had stopped the flow
of blood. Apparently it had, for there was no blood seeping
out of the crude hide dressing.

He pulled on his trousers again, took off his hat, doused
the lantern. The pain was a constant ache now, but it would
keep him awake and alert to any surprise. He lay back on
the hides and took stock of his situation.

Joe had talked. That meant that at their trial for murder
Joe would testify that he, Carnes, had done the shotgunning
of Schaeffer through the passenger-coach window. It was a
cinch he would hang. Herrington and Brayton couldn't help
him, for they would be in jail too for hiring Kennery to kill
Joe. He'd been right all along in mistrusting Kennery, and he
thought of him now with quiet hatred. If he had had the
sense he was born with, he would have sneaked out of
Primrose the night of the day Kennery left to hunt down
Joe. Maybe he was born without any sense, he thought
wryly. If proof of that were needed, why had he let Brayton
send Joe along to help with Schaeffer? He knew that Big Dad
wanted Brayton to be equally involved with him in Schaeffer's
killing, but that was no excuse for accepting Joe as his accomplice.

He put aside these dismal thoughts now and tried to concentrate on his present predicament. He couldn't hide here
for long without food or water; he would have to move out
tonight under cover of darkness. But move to where? With
his leg the shape it was in, he couldn't ride a horse, and that
meant if he was to get away it would have to be in a stolen
or rented rig.

Who did he know here who would rent a rig for him? Nobody. He was the hunted, surrounded by strange hunters.
He swore then, bitterly, viciously.

Chapter 16

WHEN Sam stepped into the Primrose House lobby he was confronted with turmoil. Tenney, still in her traveling dress, her mother, Louise Selby, and Mary were gathered at the foot of the stairs, as were a handful of townsmen. They were all watching the stairs and talking excitedly among themselves.

A gray apprehension came to Sam, and he moved swiftly across the lobby to Tenney. "What's happened, Tenney?" he asked.

Tenney looked at him, and he saw the backwash of fright in her face. "Morehead and Carnes had a gun fight, Sam. Morehead was hit and Carnes is gone. That's all I know."

Sam knifed through the group and took the stairs two at a time. In the upper corridor he could see a cluster of men around the door of Carnes's room. Even as he watched, they parted, and four men carrying a body slung in a blanket moved into the hall.

He stood aside and as they passed he looked down at Morehead. The sheriff's square face was ashen and his eyes were closed. The group that had parted to make way for the bearers had fallen in behind them. Kennery put out a hand and touched the sleeve of a townsman, who halted.

"Tell me what happened," Sam said.

"Nobody really knows. I was down in the barroom when we heard two shots. Some of us ran up here and found Morehead on the floor shot in the side. Whoever it was shot him kicked out that window and went down the rope fire escape."

Sam nodded and walked to Carnes's room and looked inside. There was a smear of blood on the floor by the door. Carnes's blanket roll lay on the bed. Sam wheeled and passed the closed door of Brayton's room.

Right there he saw the spot of blood that somebody's boot sole had smeared on the floor. At the paneless window there was another big smear of blood that was slowly being dissolved by the driving rain. It could have come from a cut made by the jagged shards of glass still in the window, but Sam thought different. No, Carnes had been shot too, as the corridor blood bore witness.

Sam looked out onto the rain-drenched street trying to piece this together. His telegram, besides telling Morehead to watch Carnes, had told him to see today's *Times*. Had Morehead read Macandy's piece and concluded that Carnes was to be arrested, and then jumped the gun by trying to make the arrest himself? It must have been like that, for Carnes had been in his room, his blanket roll readied for travel.

But where were Herrington and Brayton? They hadn't been in the downstairs crowd or the one that trooped after the sheriff's body. Had they escaped in the turmoil that followed Morehead's shooting?

Sam wheeled and started down the corridor, and then halted abruptly, assessing his hunch. Retracing his steps to Brayton's room, he knocked on the door. There was no answer and he tried the knob and found the door locked. This made no sense, Sam thought. If Brayton and Herrington had followed their usual custom they would have been sitting in the bar downstairs, hatless and coatless when the shooting took place. If they'd run out into the rain heading for the livery and horses, they would have been stopped, since everybody in town knew who they were and why they were here.

Sam came to his decision then. He backed off a step from the door, drew his gun, raised his leg and crashed his foot against the door just below the knob.

The door burst open and Sam pivoted against the wall just as a shot boomed out from inside the room. Instantly he was in the doorway, crouched low, his gun raised. There by the dresser was a slickered Big Dad, his gun tilted up for his thumb to cock it. Sam heard the click of the hammer and saw the gun begin to come down.

He shot, and Herrington's breath was driven from him in one explosive cry as he took a step backwards. He swayed, and then cracked down on his back, his gun kiting out of his hand. Sam stepped back into the corridor.

"Con," he said flatly, "throw out your gun where I can see it and come out."

He heard a shuffle of feet inside, and then a gun arched out and fell with a clatter in the doorway.

It was followed by Con Brayton, his haggard face white with fear. He, like Herrington, was wearing a slicker and hat.

"You and Big Dad going somewhere, Con?" Sam taunted. "Get back in there and stand away."

Brayton backed off, and Sam, after kicking Brayton's gun out into the hall, came into the room. Circling around to Herrington's head then, his gun covering Brayton, he knelt and pulled open Herrington's slicker. His shot had caught Herrington high in the chest and Sam guessed he had died within seconds.

He rose now and looked at Brayton. "He's dead, Con. You ought to envy him. You'll be dead too, but it will be a little tougher."

"You damned traitor!" Brayton exploded.

"That's right, I am," Sam agreed. "Still, I saved you a hundred dollars, Con. You can take it to the gallows with you. You're under arrest."

There came the sound of men running in the corridor and Sam waited for the first man to show. It turned out to be Ben Harness, who halted abruptly in the doorway. He stared at Herrington and then raised his glance to Sam; saw the pointed gun and shifted his glance to Brayton, then back to Sam.

"Is he—dead?"

Sam nodded. Other men had moved up behind Harness, but Sam knew none of them. "Ben," he said, "I'm stuck for help. Can you give me some?"

"If I can," Ben said.

"I'm taking Brayton over to the jail. Carnes is loose somewhere in town, if he hasn't already ridden out. Can you go to the livery and tell them Carnes might make a try for one of their horses? After that, will you hunt up whoever's coroner to come up here for Herrington. Then come over to Morehead's office."

Harness turned and pushed through the group of watchers.

"All right, Con. Head for the lobby," Sam said.

Brayton moved to the door, and Sam, holstering his gun, fell in behind him. After closing the door on the curious watchers, Sam crossed the corridor, retrieved Brayton's gun, and rammed it in his waistband.

The lobby held even more people now, and Sam, seeing Tenney, said to Brayton, "Stop right here, Con."

Brayton halted and Sam moved the few feet to Tenney, who was standing beside her mother.

"Where'd they take Morehead, Tenney?" he asked.

"To Doctor Price's house. His spare room is the hospital." She hesitated a moment. "Sam, what was the shooting?"

"Herrington at me, and me at him. He's dead. I'm taking Brayton over to the jail. Can you come along with me, Tenney?" He looked at her mother. "I'm still asking for help, Mrs. Payne."

"Go along, Tenney," Mrs. Payne said.

Tenney went to get her coat from the row of hooks by the dining-room door and then she joined Sam. "All right, Con," Sam said. As the three of them moved through the crowd toward the veranda, Sam spotted the middle-aged hack driver among the watchers and beckoned to him. "Is your team still harnessed?" he asked.

The driver nodded. "Out front."

"Can you take us to the courthouse?"

The driver nodded and led the way down the steps.

"You sit with the driver, Con," Sam said.

Wordlessly, Brayton climbed up into the front seat. The horses were glistening wetly in the still falling rain. Sam and Tenney got into the second seat and the hack moved away from the crowd that had trailed them to the veranda.

At the courthouse they went directly to Morehead's office. Sam, acting on a hunch that Morehead would have the jail key handy, found it hanging on a nail behind the door. When he had locked Brayton in one of the basement cells, he returned to Tenney, who had seated herself in the straight chair behind the desk. Taking off his hat, Sam tossed Brayton's gun on the desk, then slacked into the swivel chair. "Tenney, tell me what I ought to know. What happened?"

"Mr. Selby said Carnes was the first to buy a paper. He read the front page right at the desk. Then he put it in his pocket and went upstairs. Only seconds later the sheriff bought a paper, and sat in one of the lobby chairs and read it. Then he moved over to the door and looked down the street—maybe looking for you. Afterwards he went upstairs and then we heard the shots." She paused. "Carnes is gone, isn't he?"

Sam nodded. "I think he's shot, Tenney—I don't know how badly. He was able to slide down that rope and disappear."

"You think he's still in town?"

"I don't know, Tenney, and won't unless somebody tells

me they saw him ride out. Until then, we assume he's here in Primrose."

"How do we find him?"

"That's why I asked you to come along, Tenney. Did Morehead have any deputies?"

"Two, of a sort. They patrol the River Street saloons and stop the miners' fights. They're really just hired toughs."

"Then who's sheriff now, Tenney?"

"Why can't you be?"

Sam shook his head. "Not without the county commissioners deputizing me. Who are the commissioners?"

"Mr. Pollock at the store is one. Hargreave is another—he's a rancher down south. And there's Kimbrough, he's a rancher too, but he lives in West Haven."

Sam heard footsteps in the corridor then and turned his head just as Ben Harness, his black slicker streaming water, stepped into the room. At the sight of Tenney he smiled and said, "Why, hello, Tenney. Are you under arrest?"

Sam answered for her. "Not yet," he said dryly. "Find the coroner, Ben?"

"That's Doc Price. He'll take care of it as soon as he's finished with Morehead. He took the bullet out of him, but he's mighty sick, Doc says."

"Is he conscious?"

"No, Doc said."

Sam went to the window and looked out on the gray noonday. Then he turned and said to Ben, "Tenney tells me your boss is a county commissioner, Ben."

"Yes, sir. He's chairman."

"Does he know what sort of a problem he's got?"

"I wouldn't know, Kennery. He gave me the morning off to follow you."

Sam said grimly, "This town has to be searched for Carnes, Ben. Who leads the search, and what men will do the searching? Can you and Tenney make up a list of responsible men who don't mind getting shot at?"

Harness looked at Tenney. "I think we could, couldn't we, Tenney?"

"They should all be men who can recognize Carnes. That's where you come in, Tenney. They'll be men who ate at the hotel and drank at the bar there. While you and Ben make up the list, I'll go to the livery and pick up my horse."

As Sam went down the courthouse steps he noted that the rain was slacking off a little. He considered now the events of the last hour. Red Macandy's *Times* story had worked all too well, he thought. It had forced Carnes to make his move, but it could cost Morehead his life. He wished bitterly that his telegram to Morehead had contained the admonition to leave Carnes's arrest to the marshal's office. It had not occurred to him that this was necessary, since Morehead knew the marshal's office was handling Carnes's case, just as they were handling the Brayton and Herrington case. So now they had a killer to catch, and Sam had no delusions that it would be easy. Carnes wouldn't stop at killing anyone who tried to capture him, since he believed he would be tried for murder in any event.

At the livery stable Sam picked up the horse he had rented his first day in town. Inquiring of the hostler if Carnes was boarding a horse there, the horse was pointed out to him. Kennery asked the hostler to bring the horse into the stable where he could be guarded, and afterwards he rode back to the courthouse. Leaving his horse in the open shed behind the courthouse, alongside Morehead's gelding, he went across the muddy road and entered the side door of the courthouse.

Tenney and Ben Harness, between them, had come up with the names of a dozen men, none of whom Sam knew. He pocketed the list, saying, "Let's go see your boss, Ben."

They walked back to Main Street together and parted from Tenney at the Primrose House corner. At Pollock's Emporium Ben took over, leading the way back to the stairs that went up to a balcony overlooking the store.

Pollock, in shirt sleeves, had seen them coming and was standing when they reached his big flat-top desk. He was a small man with a thin, scholarly face, and under a thatch of white hair he wore heavy, iron-rimmed glasses, which were now pushed up on his forehead.

Ben introduced them to each other and a look of relief came into Pollock's face. He gestured toward a lone straight-back chair and Sam waited until Pollock sat down before he slacked into the chair.

"That was a tragic business with Morehead, Kennery. I understand he may not live."

"I'm sorry about that," Sam said. "Still, his office goes on, Mr. Pollock, and at the moment it's vacant."

Pollock nodded and said reluctantly, "He had a couple

of deputies, but both of them together couldn't do the sheriff's job."

"Would you consider deputizing me?" Sam asked. "I think Carnes is hiding here in Primrose, and there'll have to be a search for him."

He explained the necessity of someone leading the search and he showed Pollock the list Ben and Tenney had drawn up of men who would recognize Carnes.

The rest was routine. Pollock swore him in and even gave him his own deputy's badge, which, along with his Bible, was stored in a drawer of his desk. It was agreed that Ben would get in touch with six men on the list during the noon hour, giving each of them the name of another man to speak to. After the noon meal all of them, well armed, would meet in the empty second-story courtroom in the courthouse. There the search plan would be decided on and warrants distributed.

Chapter 17

IN the darkness of Pollock's Emporium cellar, Seeley Carnes lay listening, and thinking hard. An hour had gone by since he had shot Morehead, and still no hue and cry seemed to be raised for him. He had heard, dimly, two gunshots, but it was senseless trying to read any meaning in them. Why hadn't Kennery started a search for him? Did he think Carnes had succeeded in leaving town?

He knew now a fierce longing for somebody to talk to, someone who knew what was going on, who could warn him of danger. In less than an hour's time this dark cellar had turned from a haven of safety into a torture chamber. He would have to get out of here, he knew, and quickly; but where would he go? He thought of the sporting houses, but rejected the thought of hiding in one of them. Any of those girls would turn him over to the law simply as a way of currying favor. What about the back rooms of the River Street saloons? They, too, would be risky, he reflected. All

bartenders would be warned to be on the lookout for him.
Then what about the boarding houses and rooming houses
that catered to the miners? That was a possibility, but he
had heard most of them were run by women, and women
talked. What he needed was a place where he could be
anonymous, where he could bribe somebody to get him food
and provide shelter until his leg healed enough so that he
could ride.

He had a feeling that on the other side of River Street
someone might hide him. In the nights of drinking with
Brayton and Herrington in the sporting houses and the
River Street saloons, he had learned that Primrose was two
distinct communities. On the other side of the river were
the miners, the muckers, and the timbermen of the Consolidated and other mines—Germans, Irish, Canadians,
Austrians, cousin-jacks, and Italians. They lived in their
own rough world, which had no connection or contact with
the world of ranching, horse-trading, and business that lay
on this side of the river. If he could make it to River
Street he could be absorbed among that incurious, foreign,
work-drugged, and drink-sodden world.

But could he ever make it as far as River Street? Carnes
thought of Kennery now with an objective hatred. Looking
back on it all, he was certain that Kennery getting the
drop on Morehead at the Primrose House that first night
was as rehearsed as any theatre play. Brayton was a fool,
but Big Dad had a head, if he bothered to use it. The
trouble was Big Dad had a weakness for the bad boys, and
Kennery had shrewdly played on it. Kennery had trapped
them into admitting they were responsible for Schaeffer's
death, and only Carnes's own stubborn insistence that he not
be named as Joe's accomplice had saved him up till now. In
fact, Kennery had pretty much had his own way, but that
was only temporary. If he could make River Street and let
his leg heal, then he, Carnes, would become the hunter, not
the hunted.

"It's time to move, Carnes thought. He reached out for
the lantern and, grasping its bail, struggled to his feet. After
lighting the lantern he took a few tentative steps, testing
his leg. It hurt to put his weight on it, but he could manage
to walk. What if he did limp? Who knew he'd been hit—
so who would suspect him because of his limp?

Walking slowly, Carnes began to range the basement,
sizing up what was stored here. It seemed to him that this

storeroom held all the hard goods on one side—stoves, tubs, crocks, axes, pitchforks, and the like cluttered one side of the room. The other side held men's and women's clothes, including coats and hats, boots and shoes.

It was this side that Carnes prowled now. From the racks of stored clothing he chose a miner's round black hat that fitted him, a pair of miner's high boots, and a heavy mackinaw. In a few minutes he had exchanged his cowman's boots, his Stetson, and his bloody trousers for thick-soled boots, miner's hat and corduroy trousers. He added a red bandanna neckerchief and a heavy wool mackinaw with pockets big enough to hold his gun on the right side and his rolled-up shell belt on the left. He made sure he had transferred his tobacco pouch and cigarette papers. His own clothes he rolled in a bundle which he hid in a barrel only half filled with children's shoes. On his way to the ramp, he picked up from the hardware side a round dinner pail such as every miner carried on shift. Pausing by one of the bigger crates that was covered with dust, he rubbed his hands in the dust and then smeared his face with it. Then he blew out the lantern and labored up the ramp.

At the top he listened with his ear to the door. At least two men were in the storeroom, for he could hear a pair of voices but he couldn't hear clearly what they were saying. Presently he heard receding footsteps. Lifting the latch, he opened the door, and stepped out into the room, where he moved toward the rear door. It was still unlocked, and he went out onto the loading platform, closing the door behind him.

The rain still was falling and Carnes turned up the collar of his mackinaw and, dinner pail in hand, went down the ladder. He started down the alley, heading toward River Street. To anyone observing him, he appeared to be only another lanky, dirty miner with muddy boots, carrying his dinner pail. When he left the alley he turned toward Grant Street and, reaching it, went slowly toward the river. His hobbling gait attracted little attention as he moved along. Half the miners one met on the street had been crippled in mine accidents and the townspeople were so used to their disabilities that they attracted no attention.

It was slow going, but Carnes reached the bridge without being intercepted and even paused on the bridge, staring down to the rushing torrent below while he rested his throbbing leg.

Once on River Street, he went into the nearest saloon, ordered whiskey, and asked an off-shift miner where a man could live here.

"The big tent. The cheapest. Out by the Consolidated dumps, it is," the man answered.

Carnes made his way past the Miners' Rest saloon and turned toward the towering dumps of the Consolidated Mine. Across a couple of vacant lots he could see the huge gray tent dormitory sagging in the rain. Carnes had heard about this and he remembered seeing its big kerosene flare at night. It had been mentioned to him once as a place where rootless drifting miners could sleep off a drunk in the vermin-ridden blankets of a cot. It was a place for the sick, the almost broke, the out-of-work, and the homeless. It was, Carnes thought, exactly what he wanted.

There were two horses standing out of the rain under a canvas fly over the entrance flap. Before Carnes was half-way across the road, two men came out and mounted. They were wearing yellow slickers against the rain, and one of them Carnes recognized, even at that distance, as a man who was a regular patron of the Primrose House dining room. The pair headed for the big main gates of the Consolidated.

Inside the tent, immediately to the right of the door, a surly old man took Carnes's quarter, and Carnes moved into the dimly lighted interior. There were perhaps a hundred cots in the tent, less than half of them occupied by off-shift miners. The stench of sweaty, dirty clothes and blankets was so overpowering that Carnes breathed through his mouth. Moving down the aisle, he took a cot as far from the door as possible and lay down on it. It wasn't exactly elegant, he thought grimly, but it would serve until he could hunt down Kennery.

The afternoon's search had been a thorough one, Kennery thought, but there was just too much ground to cover and too many people to look at. Besides that, when the day shift at the mines made way for the night shift, there would be another thousand faces to scan. The building search had been tedious and time-consuming. By dark, all of the wet and discouraged deputies had reported in to Sam and Ben Harness at Morehead's office. To a man, they stated that there were too many places and too many shifting people to make the search effective. They were willing to try tomorrow, but with a whole night before him, Carnes could either flee

Primrose or hide himself in some building already searched. When the last deputy left, Ben Harness looked at his list. "Counting me, that's the lot of them, Kennery."

From the straight chair by the desk he watched Kennery slowly pace about the office, his head down. Presently Ben said, "Can I go now, Kennery? I've got this story to telegraph Red tonight, and it'll be a long one."

"Sure, go on," Kennery said. "And thanks, Ben, for all you've done."

Harness said good night and left, but Sam continued his pacing. He had hoped, but hadn't really believed, that a search started only an hour after Carnes's escape would turn up his man, but luck had been against him. What was there left to do now? Carnes had successfully made it to nightfall and, depending on how badly he'd been hurt, he was almost sure to put many miles between himself and Primrose before tomorrow's dawn, heading for Texas and freedom. Once there, no Texas sheriff would bother to hunt down Carnes, a Texan who had killed a northern sheriff in a fair fight.

I've really ripped it, Sam thought bitterly. Wilbarth would be angry at his failure to corner Carnes, his failure to ward off Morehead's attempted arrest of him, his presumption in planting a lie with Red Macandy, and his failure to capture Carnes after his escape. Maybe this was the time to turn in his badge and get back to the ranch that was waiting for him.

But the idea of quitting in the face of defeat was intolerable to him. And what about Tenney? She had been an intimate witness to his failure. Although she would never call it by that name, it was what she would think.

These gray thoughts were interrupted by the sound of footsteps in the corridor. When they came past the adjacent office, Sam looked at the door, wondering who was coming at this hour. A tall, middle-aged man in a black rubber raincoat entered the room, and Sam noticed that underneath the unbuttoned coat he was wearing a townsman's suit. He was a lean man with a quietly vindictive face. Halting just inside the door, he looked stonily at Sam and said, "You have a client of mine locked up. This is the fifth time I've called at this office this afternoon and found it locked."

Sam made a guess. "That's right. I was hunting another of your clients."

"What are the charges against Con Brayton?"

"Brand new ones, Mr.—Phelan, is it?"

"Thurston," the man said coldly.

"The charges are complicity in murder and complicity in attempted murder. Two counts, Mr. Thurston."

Shock showed in Thurston's face. "You can't mean it. Whose murder?"

"Morton Schaeffer's murder, and paying for the murder of an Indian called Joe Potatoes. You can see your client, Mr. Thurston. The judge will have to decide if you can free him by bond."

Thurston thought this over a long moment and then he said, "Come to think of it, I don't believe I have a client locked up. Fraud is one thing, but murder is another." He paused. "What happened betwen you and Herrington today, Kennery?"

"He shot at me. I shot back. He missed. I didn't. It's about that simple," Sam said. He waited a moment, then added, "You want to see Brayton?"

"Not ever," Thurston said flatly. "If he asks for me, don't bother to send for me. Good night, Mr. Kennery."

Thurston turned and walked out. Watching him go, Kennery felt a faint stirring of satisfaction, the first he had felt today. With Herrington dead and Carnes escaped, Brayton had to face the music all alone.

Well, the law would have to keep Brayton alive, and that meant that Sam better get the prisoner some supper before he got some supper for himself. But first he should inform Wilbarth of the day's events before the marshal read of them in tomorrow morning's *Times*.

Outside, the rain had slacked off and the weather was turning colder. In the darkness of the shed Sam cinched up the saddle of his livery horse, then sought Grant Street and the depot, wondering if the agent would still be on duty.

Approaching the depot, he saw a lamp was lighted in the agent's office and as he passed the window to go to the tie-rail, he saw the agent hunched over his telegraph.

Inside, Kennery picked up a telegraph blank and, standing at the counter, composed his message to Wilbarth. In as few words as possible he wrote of Morehead's attempted arrest of Carnes, of Morehead being shot, and of Carnes's probable wound and his escape. He stated that a search for Carnes

was unsuccessful, and that Herrington had been killed by
him after attacking him, and Brayton was being held in
jail pending orders from the marshal. He said he had been
deputized by the county commissioner and was temporarily
acting sheriff. Finally, that he was awaiting Wilbarth's
orders. As he turned the telegram over to the agent, he reflected bitterly on how few words it had taken to relay this
mass of bad news.

From the harried agent he got directions to the home of
Doctor Price. At the big frame house in the residential district a couple of blocks east of Grant Street, his knock
on the door was answered by Mrs. Price. The doctor was out
on a call but had left orders that under no conditions were
visitors allowed to see Morehead. Yes, he was alive, but had
lost much blood, and was in delirium.

Afterwards, Sam dismounted in front of a Grant Street
café, went inside and ordered two steaks, one of which he
would eat himself and the other he would take out. The
dining room at the Primrose House, where he would rather
have eaten, would be closed at this hour, he knew.

Once back in the courthouse with a plate of food wrapped
in a clean dishtowel, Kennery got the cell key from his
office and went downstairs to the basement jail. Brayton had
been pacing his cell, but when Sam appeared he came to the
door.

Sam put the food on the floor and said curtly, "Back off,
Brayton."

The agent did so and Sam opened the cell door, set the
plate inside, and relocked the cell.

"Is there any whiskey there?" Brayton asked hoarsely.

"Just food."

"You couldn't find me a drink, could you? I'm a sick
man, Kennery."

He looked a sick man, Sam thought, and for a moment he
considered Brayton's request. Whiskey wouldn't do him any
harm and it just might make him cooperate.

"I'll look. Maybe Morehead had some in his office."

Upstairs in the sheriff's office Kennery searched the desk
and, sure enough, in the lower right-hand drawer was a
half-full bottle of whiskey.

Downstairs again, Sam turned up the wick of the corridor wall lamp, then let himself into Brayton's cell and
handed him the whiskey. The food he had brought was

still where he had put it. When he extended the bottle to Brayton, the latter, his yellow-toothed smile trembling in anticipation, took the bottle with both hands.

Sam sat on the cot opposite Brayton and watched him, still standing, wrench the cork from the bottle, tilt it up to his mouth, and take three huge gulps of the whiskey. The sigh that came from Brayton then was one of pure bliss, and Sam wondered how long it had been since Brayton had had six waking hours without a drink.

Now Brayton sat down on his cot cradling the bottle between his knees and regarded Sam. "You're a good lad even if you are a traitorous bastard," he said.

Sam gestured toward the food. "That'll get cold. Better eat it."

"Let it get cold," Brayton said scornfully. He patted the bottle. "This has got enough heat in it for me."

Sam watched him as he took another long drink, and he observed that some color had crept into Brayton's ravaged face.

Abruptly Brayton said reflectively, "So Joe talked."

Since it was a statement rather than a question, Sam said only, "Kind of changes things for you, doesn't it, Con?"

A sly expression came into Brayton's face. "Oh, no, you don't, Sam. I won't talk to anybody about this unless my lawyer's with me."

"Would that be Thurston?" Sam asked innocently.

"Him or Phelan."

"Thurston came in for permission to see you. When I told him you'd be charged for complicity in murder, he said he didn't mind defending you for fraud, but murder was another thing. He doesn't want to see you, and he won't come if you send for him."

"You're lying, Sam. Again. For about the thousandth time."

"I don't have to lie to you any more, Con. I've got you where I want you. Herrington's dead. Carnes will make a trade with us for a life sentence instead of a hanging."

"You haven't got him."

"No. But when we catch him, he'll trade."

"What will he trade you to beat the hangin'?" Brayton asked skeptically.

"He'll testify that you and Herrington paid him to kill Schaeffer. Joe will testify that you paid him, too, to kill Schaeffer."

Brayton smiled cynically. "What are you trying to get out of me, Sam? A signed confession?"

"I hadn't thought about it, but now that you mention it, a confession would help us both."

"How would it help me?" Brayton challenged.

"Well, look at it this way, Con. You're due for a jury trial. There isn't a man in the state who hasn't read or heard about your indictment for fraud. Even if every prospective juror swears he won't be influenced by your indictment, you know and I know that just isn't true. You know what it's like? It's like a lawyer saying something before a jury that the judge orders struck from the record. He orders the jury to ignore what they just heard. Do you really think it's possible for a man to wipe from his memory words that he's just heard?"

"No," Brayton said. "That bit of court business always seemed crazy to me."

"All right. Let's go back to you, Con. You'll walk into court with that skunk in your pocket—your indictment for fraud. Carnes's testimony, Joe's testimony, and my testimony won't be pretty, Con. The jurors will already think you're a crook. Then when you're proven an accessory to a murder and when it's proven you tried to buy a second murder, you won't have any place to hide from that jury. You'll wish you'd never been born."

Brayton, who had been watching Sam intently, now let his glance slide away. "You think a signed confession will prevent all that?"

"Hell, I'm not a lawyer and I'm not a mind reader. I know if you signed a confession and threw yourself on the mercy of the court, there wouldn't be a jury trial. It would be up to the judge to sentence you."

"One fool instead of twelve, is that it?" Brayton said sourly.

"Let's say a better educated fool than the other twelve."

Brayton thought about that a moment and then lifted the bottle and drank from it. He wiped his mouth on his sleeve and then grinned crookedly at Sam. Rather than a smile of confidence, it was a sorry effort to hide despair, Sam thought.

"Oh, no, Sam," Brayton said. "I'm not worried about a thing. Big Dad is dead and Carnes is loose. Joe has already told you Carnes killed Schaeffer. I'll prove that Carnes was Herrington's man and the killing was Herrington's idea. I only loaned Joe to Herrington so he could point out Schaeffer for Carnes. That makes my part in all of it mighty small."

"What about paying me to kill Joe?" Sam asked.

Brayton's reply was bland. "Why, Sam, I did no such thing. It would take Carnes's and Big Dad's word to hang that on me. Like I said, Big Dad's gone to the Other Shore, and Carnes is gone like smoke. No, I didn't pay you to kill Joe and you can't prove I did."

Sam shrugged and said indifferently, "Well, I'm going to find out if I can, that's damn sure." He stood up and made a loose gesture in Brayton's direction. "Drink it up, Con, or leave it, but either way give me the bottle."

"Can't I keep it for after I eat?" Brayton protested.

"No. If I left it with you, you could get to thinking about what's going to happen to you. You could break it, cut your wrists, and bleed to death before I found you." He smiled faintly. "Of course, that would save us trying you, but it wouldn't look good, would it?"

Brayton glared at him with quiet hatred. The bottle was only a drink from the finish, and he tilted it and drained it.

After taking the bottle from Brayton, Sam let himself out, relocked the cell, and said, "Good night, Con." He went upstairs, thinking as he shut the stair doors and crossed the corridor that he would probably have to sleep tonight on the sofa in the sheriff's office. Possibly, just possibly, Carnes might still be hanging around town. It would be like him to try and break out Brayton.

He stepped into the office and saw Tenney sitting on the straight chair beside the desk, her coat still on. He halted and for a moment they looked at each other. Then Tenney came over to him, stood on tiptoe, and kissed him.

"That was for what?" Sam asked gently.

"That was because I like to do it," Tenney said. "Come sit down and tell me about today." She led him back to the desk, removed her coat, and sat down again while Sam slacked into the swivel chair by the desk.

"Well, the best part of my day happened ten seconds ago." He said then that she already knew what the planted story in the *Capital Times* had triggered off at the Primrose House that morning. Then he told of the fruitless search for Carnes. Seeley could have been wounded by Sheriff Morehead, he said. He told her, too, of his talk with Brayton, and all through his flat-toned monologue Tenney could see the discouragement in him.

He finished by saying, "The plain hell of it is, Tenney, Brayton might walk away from Primrose a free man. If Joe Potatoes keeps his mouth shut, where are we? Joe can claim, and likely will, that he only pointed Schaeffer out to Carnes. That's a provable lie, because Carnes already knew Schaeffer from having delivered beef to the agency, but Joe will stick to that story, and maybe spend a short time in prison. If Brayton gets to him, promises him money and whiskey for not involving him in the Schaeffer killing, then where are we? Herrington's dead and Carnes is gone. So do we bargain with evidence that will convict Brayton?"

He ran a hand through his hair in a gesture which Tenney interpreted as quiet despair, and his eyes were somber as he said, "I blew it, Tenney. All by myself, I blew it."

Seeley Carnes and the dormitory tent were wakened early by miners rising for the day shift mingling with men just off the night shift. The latter were in no hurry to get in their blankets, for this was the end of their working day and the time for relaxation.

Carnes, fully dressed, threw off his blankets and, to test his leg, mingled with the men roving the aisle. His wound was achingly sore to the touch but, surprisingly, it took his weight and he knew he could walk.

Back at his cot, he sat down and considered the day that lay ahead of him. It would be foolhardy to leave the tent and risk being recognized. The search for him had probably ended, for Kennery would have reckoned that he had managed to get a horse during the night and was headed out of the state. Still, he couldn't be sure. Then there was the problem now of food and drink.

Carnes looked about him in the dimly lit tent and spotted a face that looked honest, and spoke to the man. He was answered in German. The next honest face he saw belonged to a middle-aged, stoop-backed Irishman who had the cot across the aisle from him. Carnes got up and hobbled over to him. The man was changing into dry boots, which indicated he was going out.

"My friend," Carnes began, "how would you like to earn a pint of whiskey?"

The Irishman looked up at him and said pleasantly,

"That's why I've been workin' all night, lad. I would like to earn another, though. What is it you want?"

"I hurt my leg and I'd like to rest it. Could you go to one of the saloons and get me a sandwich and a pail of beer? Buy yourself a pint of whiskey and me one too, and bring them back here."

"I can do all that, but let us see your money first."

Carnes went back to the cot, took out the lunch pail from under it, came back, set it on the Irishman's cot. Then he reached in his pocket and drew out an eagle. There was a chance, of course, that as soon as the Irishman left the tent he would throw the bucket off in the weeds and proceed to get roaring drunk on Carnes's money, but that chance had to be taken. The Irishman finished tying his boots, stood up, gave Carnes a grin, and walked out.

Carnes lay back on the cot. Once the food and drink problem was settled, there was some thinking to be done about the matter of cornering Kennery. The wise thing to do, of course, would be to forget Kennery, wait until night, steal a horse, and clear out of the country. Well, he could leave the country and head back to Chain Link, but not before he had evened the score with that traitor of a deputy marshal. It had taken him a good three days to recover from that beating Kennery had given him—three days during which Big Dad and Brayton, while sympathizing with him, were also laughing at him.

He'd been right about Kennery all along. The story of the beating would get back to Texas, of course, but he'd see to it that the story would end with a statement that Seeley Carnes killed the man who beat him up. Nobody would ever be able to accuse him of accepting a beating without retaliating. When you came down to it, Carnes thought, a man wasn't even half a man if he had no pride. He did.

If Joe Potatoes had talked, that meant that Big Dad and Brayton had been arrested and were very likely in the jail across the river right now. He wondered if his shot had killed Morehead; and if it had, who was sheriff now? Kennery, of course, would stay close to Big Dad and Con, at least for a few days. With the sheriff dead or badly hurt, the prisoners would be Kennery's responsibility. Would he take them to Junction City? It really didn't matter, Carnes thought. Wherever Kennery was—Junction City, Primrose, or somewhere else—he would find him and kill him.

The Irishman came back sooner than Carnes could have

hoped for. He had a free drink with Carnes out of his bottle, then left Carnes to his beer and sandwich, his whiskey and foul cigarettes.

As Carnes munched on his sandwich he thought of all the questions he was unable to answer. He couldn't send somebody like the Irishman across the river to find out what had happened to Brayton and Herrington and where Kennery was, without risking betrayal. Somehow in the long day that lay ahead of him he would think of some way of learning what the situation was across the river.

Chapter 18

WHEN Kennery heard the knock on the door, he woke up and for the briefest part of a second did not know where he was. Then, when the knock was repeated, he called, "Coming," and threw the blanket off him. The sofa at the sheriff's office had made such an excellent bed that his sleep had been deep and dreamless. Crossing to the door in his socks, he opened it and found a twelve-year-old standing in the corridor holding out a paper to him. When Sam saw it was a telegram he reached in his pocket for a coin for the boy, and then went over to the window, which looked out on a gray but rainless day. Unfolding the telegram, he read its brief message: "Meet me at Primrose depot this morning. Wilbarth."

Moving over to the sofa, Sam folded his blanket, then sat down and began pulling on his boots. *Well, it had to come sooner or later,* he thought. Wilbarth was coming to Primrose to salvage what he could out of the mess Sam had mostly created. There probably could be no criminal action against Brayton if Joe Potatoes had kept his silence. There would be no action either on the criminal-fraud indictment, since Herrington and Carnes—one dead, the other vanished —had got Schaeffer out of the way, leaving no proof Brayton had a part in killing him. All he himself had contributed, Sam thought, was the useless death of Herrington and the inexcusable escape of Carnes. Getting up, he concluded sourly that this would be one of the less pleasant days in his life.

He put on his jacket and hat and went out into the corridor, locking the door behind him. Last night, before sleep came to him, he had realized that the presence of Brayton downstairs in the jail was a hindrance to any free movement on his part, and he aimed to take care of that right now.

He found Commissioner Pollock in his store, which he had just opened and which was empty. Pollock was heading for his balcony office, his coat still on, when Sam hailed him. There in the aisle they both decided that Sam must have a deputy. Pollock knew a man who would be willing to sleep in the sheriff's office—a guard at the Consolidated Mining & Milling. Sam gave the key to the office to Pollock, who in turn would give it to the guard, whose first duty would be to hustle food for the prisoner.

After that, Sam went up the street, turned in at the Primrose House, and went into the dining room for breakfast. Tenney, her tray loaded with other breakfasts, saw him and detoured past his table to give him a soft and warm "Good morning" before she went on to the other customers.

Returning a minute later, she halted to take his order and Sam drew out Wilbarth's telegram and handed it to her. She read it and looked at Sam with a question in her dark eyes. "Trouble, Sam?"

"What else could it be?"

"Breakfast will help," Tenney said. "The same?" At Sam's nod, she left.

A very practical woman, Sam thought fondly. *Feed the beast first and then comfort him.* Well, that had worked for women all through history, so why wouldn't it work this morning with him?

Tenney brought his breakfast and had to hurry away to wait on other customers. Sam ate Mrs. Payne's eggs, steak, and potatoes with an almost wolfish hunger. Yesterday, he remembered, he had mostly forgotten to eat.

He was thinking of what he should do this morning before Wilbarth's train arrived when Tenney returned to fill his coffee cup.

"Tenney," he said, "could you do something for me this morning while you're upstairs making the beds?" At Tenney's nod, he continued, "Check with Mr. Selby first to see if it's all right. If he says yes, will you move me into Con Brayton's room?"

"It's not as nice, Sam. Yours is a front room and his is a back one." She frowned. "What's behind it, Sam?"

Sam grimaced. "I've missed too many chances, Tenney, and I don't want to miss another. If Carnes is hurt and is still here in town, or if he's not hurt and has ridden out, the chances are he'll try to get in touch with Brayton. Maybe he hasn't heard that Herrington is dead and Brayton's in jail. He just might want to send some word to them. I want to be in Brayton's room if a messenger comes."

"That makes sense," Tenney conceded.

"Tell Mr. Selby not to change my number or Brayton's number in the register. Just leave everything as it is, only move me into Brayton's room."

Tenney nodded and started for the kitchen, then halted and looked searchingly at Sam. "Nothing's your fault, Sam. Just keep believing that."

Kennery smiled crookedly. "I wish that would fix things, but it won't, Tenney."

He finished his coffee, left the Primrose House, and went up the street to the livery, where he checked to see if anyone had come in late in the day or after dark yesterday to rent a horse or a rig. Getting no for an answer, he headed for Dr. Price's house. There he was told by Mrs. Price that Morehead's condition had worsened, and that the doctor, who had been called over to the scene of a mine accident, thought it was touch and go with the sheriff. Afterwards he went back through the chill morning to the courthouse.

He found Matt Fisher, the Consolidated guard, waiting for him. Fisher was a big man; he was young and looked as if he could handle himself. He had already fed Brayton, and now Sam told him to return the dishes to the café. He himself would be here until train time.

After Fisher left, Sam sat down at Morehead's desk and, finding paper, pen, and ink, he set himself to writing. It was a detailed account of Brayton's involvement in the death of Morton Schaeffer and in the paid-for-murder of Joe Potatoes. It was, as far as Sam knew, the whole truth, and it was written in the form of a confession, using the personal 'I' as if Brayton had either written it or dictated it. There was the finishing statement that it was the whole truth and nothing but the truth. Place was left for the signature of a witness and for Brayton's signature. He would never sign this confession, of course, Sam knew, but he wanted it ready. Beyond that, the confession would serve as a summation of events for Wilbarth to read.

Fisher was back a little before train time and sat in silence while Sam finished writing. Then Sam put on his jacket, put the confession in his pocket, and told Fisher to bar anyone from seeing Brayton until he returned.

Sam was climbing the platform steps as the train whistled for the bridge crossing; a minute later it ground to a halt alongside the platform.

Marshal Wilbarth was the first passenger off the train and Sam gloomily interpreted this fact as the measure of Wilbarth's anxiety to take over the situation here. For all the big marshal's recent traveling, his face still held the pallor of a man bound indoors against his will. His townsman's suit and overcoat were rumpled, and unless a man was careful to note the calm in his pale eyes, he appeared to be only another uncared-for and probably lazy old man.

They shook hands and Sam asked, "Did Joe talk, Marshal?"

"Not a word. We had to give up on him, Sam."

Sam took his valise and steered him to the Primrose House hack. Only after he had registered did Sam say, "Too early for a drink, Marshal?"

Wilbarth grimaced. "I've had enough of that stuff in the last ten days to float a frigate, but the answer is yes."

In the bar, which held only a handful of customers, Sam chose the card table nearest the front window. He got a bottle and two glasses and some cigars from Alec, and when he turned back to the table he saw that Wilbarth was rubbing closed eyelids with thumb and index finger in a gesture of weariness. His hat was on the table and his white hair seemed over long, as if he had not time for a barber recently.

Sam sat down, took the confession from his jacket pocket, and handed it to Wilbarth. "That's a confession I wrote out for Brayton to sign. He won't sign it, of course, but it will bring you up to date on Brayton's connivings here."

Wilbarth laid the paper aside for the moment and said, "Now tell me how you got that piece in the *Capital Times* about arresting Joe Potatoes."

It took Sam until dinnertime to bring Wilbarth up to date. He told of Tenney's visit to Junction City to head him off from almost certain death. His plantings of wrongful information with Red Macandy was intended to accomplish just what it did—flush Carnes out. The rest of it was distasteful, but Sam went through it doggedly. Carnes, probably hurt, had escaped, and without him and with Herrington dead, the case against Brayton was weak, he said. If Joe remained silent, it was no case at all. To all this Wilbarth listened with neither censure nor approval on his face.

At dinnertime Wilbarth was introduced to Louise Selby and her father, and only moments later to Tenney. Standing by the table and shaking Tenney's hand, Wilbarth said, "So you're the little lady we're indebted to?"

Tenney flushed, but before she could say anything Wilbarth continued, "I'd like to meet your mother, too, Miss Payne, but this wouldn't be the time, would it?"

"No, I don't think so," Tenney agreed.

"Later then," Wilbarth said.

They had the usual good meal, and afterwards they went back to the courthouse for an afternoon session with Brayton. Sam took the precaution of buying a quart of whiskey from Alec. As he put it in his jacket pocket under the puzzled gaze of Wilbarth, he said, "Without this, I don't think Con Brayton can even talk."

Chapter 19

SOMETIME in the middle of that gray afternoon it came abruptly to Seeley Carnes lying in his filthy cot that he had a way to get at Sam Kennery. It was there all the time, but he'd been too thick-headed to see it. At peace now, he turned over and went to sleep immediately.

The night shift left and the miners from the day shift began to flee the tent for the saloons. Again Carnes tried to find an honest face to buy him food and liquor. He made a wrong guess; this time the miner to whom he gave the money showed up an hour afterwards, drunk and with no food. He tried with another of the tent inmates, and was

brought his sandwich and another pint of whiskey. After that
he let the evening drift into deep night before he stirred.

Putting on his boots, he got up, took his gun and shell
belt from his mackinaw, and strapped it on. A big kerosene
flare burned beyond the entrance of the tent, a beacon for
the late reveling miners. Seeley walked slowly, trying out his
leg. On this side of the driver he knew he would not be recognized and he made his way up River Street to the bridge,
ignoring the drunken miners who crowded him off the boardwalk. He skirted one street flight and then paused on the
bridge to rest. So far, so good.

Minutes later he moved on toward deserted Grant Street.
There were a few store lights burning, but at this hour the
town this side of the river was asleep. The only noise came
from the river itself and from the whiskey festivities on
the other side of it.

When Carnes, his pace slow but steady, came up to the
Primrose House veranda, he paused and saw that it was deserted. There was a night light by the bell on the lobby desk
and the doors would be open to accommodate late travelers,
he knew. As he passed the saloon he saw that it was dark,
and only then did he realize how late it really was. At the
corner of the Primrose House he turned right and headed
down the alley, passing the loading bay, and halted at the
corner of the building beyond it. Yes, the rain barrel was
there, a symbol of the humiliation he was about to revenge.

Now, from his left-hand mackinaw pocket, he took out
a couple of matches. Most of the day he had debated what
he was going to do next. From his quick search of the
women's rooms before Kennery had charged in to start the
fight that night, he knew that the door to the right in the
bedroom was the entrance to the kitchen. He knew this because he had opened it, just as he had opened the door to
the closet in the opposite wall. That night the door to the
kitchen had been locked with a key left in the lock and he
supposed it would be locked tonight. Once he was inside
he must beat them to that door.

He moved forward, halting at the alley door, and knocked
softly. He was remembering Sam Kennery's words that he
had overheard the night of the fight, and now when the girl's
voice came from inside asking, "Who is it?" Carnes said,
"It's me, Sam. Open up, Tenney." He counted on the door's
thickness to blur his voice just as it blurred hers.

He heard the key in the lock turn and waited until the

door started to swing open. Then he moved against it with his shoulder and it bumped the girl, placing her location for him. With a single sweep of his arm, he moved in and grasped her around the waist, and then kicked the door shut behind him just as she cried out.

Lifting her, he hobbled as fast as he could into the bedroom. He was through the door as Mrs. Payne called, "Tenney! Tenney! What is it?"

Carnes set the kicking, struggling girl down and with his left hand he struck a match against the wall. In the sudden flare he saw Tenney standing there in her nightgown, terror in her face. Mrs. Payne had thrown the covers off and was standing between the two beds, a look of fear and anger in her face.

"Light that lamp and be quick about it," Carnes said. He watched Mrs. Payne turn, take a match from the dish beside the lamp on the table between the two beds, strike it, lift the chimney, and light the lamp. When it was lighted, Carnes took his gun from its holster.

"What do you want with us, Mr. Carnes?" Tenney said.

Seeley didn't answer immediately. He looked around the room, and his glance fell on the bed where Tenney's gray wrapper lay at the foot. "Put that on," he said.

"What are you going to do?" Tenney demanded.

"It's not me that'll do anything, it's you. Put it on."

Tenney looked at her mother, who said, "Do it, Tenney."

Tenney moved over, slipped into the wrapper, and tied the belt.

Now Carnes moved to the kitchen door, felt for the key and lifted it out. "Now you, lady," he said to Mrs. Payne, "climb over that bed, get in the closet, and close the door."

"Not until I know what you're going to do," Mrs. Payne said flatly.

"I'm taking Tenney on a trip."

"Kidnap her, you mean?"

"For ten minutes maybe," Carnes said quietly. "She'll be back and let you out."

"I won't go with you!" Tenney said.

Carnes looked at her and said unsmilingly, "Is Morehead dead?"

"Dying," Tenney said.

"I shot him," Carnes said. "I killed Mort Schaeffer. If they catch me, I'll hang. I won't hang any higher if I kill you."

"What is it you want exactly?" Tenney said.

Carnes ignored her, and looked at her mother. He gestured with his gun. "In the closet, lady."

Helpless and furious, Mrs. Payne climbed over Tenney's bed, opened the closet and stepped into it, closing the door behind her.

Carnes gestured again with his gun, saying to Tenney, "Get over there."

Tenney backed over to the kitchen door and watched helplessly as Carnes, gun still in hand, manhandled the heavy dresser up against the closet door. Then he came back to Tenney. "Go into the dining room, through it and upstairs," Carnes said. "Don't make any noise. Now move. I'll be behind you."

"What do I do up there?" Tenney asked.

"Go to Kennery's room. Knock on his door and call him. I know his room. It's the front corner one. Don't try and pick an empty room and hammer on the door till you wake the whole hotel. I'll be right behind you all the time."

"Kennery's gone," Tenney said.

For answer Carnes gave her a stinging backhanded clout across the cheek. "You're lying. I saw him." He raised his hand again. "Now do you say he's gone?" Tenney shook her head and put her hand to her cheek. "Then get going."

Tenney led the way out of the kitchen, through the dining room only faintly lit by the lobby lamp, and through the glass doors, where she turned. Without halting, she started to climb the stairs. She could hear Carnes's labored breathing as they went up. He was hurt, she knew, but she didn't know where.

She had accepted Carnes's blow in the kitchen after failure to make him believe Kennery had left. She had admitted lying, and she knew that now she was nearing the last chance for saving Sam. Sam was not in the room Carnes had named, and when Carnes discovered it what would she do? What could she do?

At the landing she turned left and walked quietly down the corridor, Carnes following. The wall lamp at that end of the corridor was nearest to Sam's old room and lit the corridor faintly but clearly. At the door of the room she stopped so abruptly that Carnes bumped into her, his pistol jabbing her in the back.

"What do I say?" she whispered.

Carnes whispered back, "Say 'Sam, let me in. Something's happened.'"

"Do I knock?"

"I do," Carnes said.

Reaching around her, he knocked firmly on the door. Then he looked at Tenney and nodded. Tenney called out as loud as she dared, "Sam, let me in! Something's happened!"

They waited, but no sound came from the room. Carnes leaned across her to knock again on the door.

Tenney looked over his shoulder at the door of Brayton's room, the one that Sam was occupying. It was closed.

Carnes drew back and nodded to her again. This time, risking everything, Tenney called loudly, "Sam! Sam! Let me in! Something's happened!"

Carnes gave her a ferocious scowl and she felt the gun move into her back.

And then Kennery's voice came from behind, saying sharply, "Drop, Tenney!"

As Carnes wheeled at the sound of Kennery's voice, Tenney dropped to the floor. A shot, followed immediately by another, blasted out in deafening twin explosions and Tenney felt Carnes's boots drive against her huddled body. She heard him slam against the wall above her and then, with a gagging sigh, slide sideways and hit the floor with a heavy thud.

Fearfully, Tenney looked up and saw that Sam, stripped to the waist, was unmarked by blood; he started to stride toward her and a torrent of relief swept over her. If he had been hit he couldn't come to her. She struggled to her feet and was engulfed in Sam's arms. She held him tightly to her, fighting back the hysteria that made her want to cry with relief. "Tenney, Tenney," Sam murmured. "Thank God he didn't kill you."

The doors along the corridor began to open. Wilbarth, pants pulled over his nightshirt, came out of Herrington's old room, gun in hand. He saw Kennery holding Tenney, and then his glance shuttled to the figure on the floor that was turned facing the wall.

"That's Carnes, Marshal. He came to the wrong room with Tenney as a shield and tried to make her call me to the door."

Now men came up from other rooms and they were all in various stages of undress. Sam said to Tenney, "Steady now. We've got to make sure he's dead." He left her to join Wilbarth, who had rolled Carnes on his back.

Sam's shot had caught him, angling across the chest and smashing into his heart. Carnes's shot, which had ripped into the floor at Sam's feet, must have been pure reflex, for Carnes must have died instantly. Wilbarth stood up and told the half-dozen men gathered around, "This is a hunted killer you're looking at. He's dead, but take a look at him if you want. Then please go back to your rooms."

Sam went back to Tenney, led her into his dark room, where he lighted the lamp, and had her sit down. He picked up his shirt and while he was putting it on he said, "Tell me about it, Tenney."

Tenney told him almost incoherently of Carnes's break-in, the locking up of her mother, and his forcing her to lead him to the room Carnes remembered as Kennery's. She had hoped almost beyond hope that her call to him would be loud enough to waken him, and it had.

Sam listened, wondering if either of them would ever realize how close to death they had been. If a precautionary whim had not made him decide this morning to change his room, if Tenney had been frightened enough to take Carnes to Brayton's room, he instead of Carnes would be lying dead out in the hall.

Sam swept the blanket from his bed, then held out a hand to Tenney and eased her to her feet. "Let's go to your mother," he said.

Out in the hall he threw the blanket over Carnes and was turning away when Tenney said, "The key's in his pocket, Sam."

Sam knelt beside the body, pulled out Carnes's doeskin pouch of stinking tobacco, felt below it, and found the key. As he rose he heard footsteps on the stairs and looked down the hall. Mr. Selby and Louise came into the corridor, and at the same moment Wilbarth, dressed in his townsman's suit, came out of his room. Taking Tenney by the arm, Sam said to Wilbarth, "Tell the Selbys what happened, Marshal, then come down into the kitchen."

As they approached the Selbys, Sam said, "The marshal will tell you about it, Mr. Selby. We've got to hurry."

Tenney went ahead of him and he was on the stairs before he realized that he still held Carnes's doeskin tobacco pouch. He would have thrown it away if there was any place to throw it, but there wasn't, so he rammed it in his jacket pocket.

Tenney hurried through the kitchen swing doors, pausing

only long enough to turn up the lamp so that Sam had light enough to put in the key. Unlocking the door, Sam moved swiftly across the bedroom to the closet, wrestled the dresser away from the door, and opened it. Mrs. Payne rushed past him into Tenney's arms. She had been crying, Sam saw. He moved past them into the kitchen, swinging the door partially shut behind him.

Sam thought, *This cleans it all up—except for Brayton.* Without Carnes to bargain with if he gave evidence against Brayton, the agent would very likely go free. Neither the purchase of one murder nor the attempted purchase of another, nor criminal fraud could be proven against him. All the witnesses except the silent Joe Potatoes were dead.

Then abruptly Sam stopped his pacing. He remembered that Brayton in their first conversation in the jail had momentarily been tempted to sign a confession. Only the fact that Brayton was sure Carnes couldn't be caught to testify against him had led him to brazen it out.

At that moment, Louise Selby, followed by Wilbarth and Mr. Selby, came into the kitchen. Sam caught Wilbarth's attention and beckoned to him as the Selbys went into the bedroom.

Wilbarth moved over to him. "That cleans us up, Sam," the marshal said wearily. "There are questions you'll have to answer, but this cleans us up."

"Not quite," Sam reminded him. "There's Brayton."

"If he misses conviction, he'll be ruined anyway."

"Maybe he won't miss it," Sam said. "Do you have that confession with you?"

Wilbarth slapped his side pockets and then his upper coat pockets. Hearing the crackle of paper, he reached into an inside coat pocket and brought out the confession Sam had drafted that morning.

"Would we be proper witnesses to this confession, Marshal?" Sam asked.

"Yes. But as a matter of course his lawyers will claim he was forced to sign it."

"Would a third witness help?" Sam pursued.

"I'd judge so. But you won't get him to sign it anyway, Sam. You've talked with him, I've talked with him, until we're both hoarse. What good's it done?"

"Things are different now, maybe," Sam said quietly. "Wait here a minute." Sam moved over to the door of the bedroom, where Mrs. Payne was seated on the bed telling the Selbys of Carnes's break-in.

Tenney was listening, but when Sam came into the doorway she looked at him and smiled. Beckoning her to him, Sam stepped back into the kitchen and when she halted before him, he said, "Tenney, can you get dressed now? We're paying Brayton a visit. We need you again."

"Of course. It's almost daylight, anyway."

Sam and Wilbarth waited in the kitchen until Tenney, having dressed in the living room, came to join them, her coat over her arm. Sam led the way out through the dining room and lobby to the street and their walk to the courthouse was a silent one. In the courthouse corridor, while Tenney and Wilbarth waited, Sam roused Matt Fisher to let him in. When the door was opened for him, Sam said, "Go back to bed, Matt. I'm only after pen and ink and the cell key."

He crossed to the desk for the pen and ink, and after getting the cell key from the nail behind the door, he joined Wilbarth and Tenney in the hall. At the head of the cell-block stairs, Sam hesitated. "Remember, let me do the talking—all the talking. Either of you might spoil it with one word."

They nodded, and Sam swung open the door and led the way down the steps into the cell block. Brayton was awakened by the noise of their descent and was sitting up under the blankets looking at them when Sam turned up the wick of the lamp.

"You again," Brayton said sourly.

Sam moved over to unlock the cell door, the keys in one hand, the confession, pen and ink in the other hand. He stepped inside, leaving the door open. "Yes, me again, Con," he said. "Not everybody gets a last chance like you're getting."

"Last chance of what?"

"To sign this confession."

"I told you I wouldn't sign it!" Brayton said. "I told you a hundred times!"

"Well, you've got one more chance, Con." He paused to emphasize what he was about to say. "We've got Carnes. They're bringing him in."

"I don't believe it!" Brayton said.

Sam reached in his pocket and brought out Carnes's tobacco pouch. "We found that when we searched him. Recognize it?"

Brayton picked up the pouch, smelled it, made a face, and tossed it on his blanket. He said nothing.

"Remember the afternoon I locked you up? We had a talk, Con. I told you if we caught Carnes, we'd offer him a trade. We'd ask for a life sentence instead of hanging, if he'd give evidence against you. Well, we've got him."

"Is he talking?"

"No."

"He never will," Brayton said.

"Want to bet an extra five years in prison he won't, Con?"

Brayton was silent a long moment, studying the hump his feet made in the blankets. "Got a drink?" he asked.

"Not this time, Con. Nobody can claim we got you drunk enough to sign it. This has got to be your dead-sober choice."

"I haven't even got a lawyer!" Brayton protested.

"By the time you get one, they'll have brought Carnes in."

"Too late, you mean."

"I would judge, but I leave it up to you."

"I never trusted that damn Texan!" Brayton said viciously. "He'll make this all my idea from start to finish. It wasn't."

"Last chance, Con," Sam said almost idly. "We've got to take care of Carnes. You read the confession this afternoon. Sign it or don't sign it. Don't sign and face your twelve fools; sign and face your one educated fool, the judge." When Brayton was silent, Sam said, "Good night, Con."

He turned and started for the cell door.

"Come back here!" Brayton snarled. "Let me read the damn thing again!" Sam handed him the confession, then went out into the hall, took down the lamp from its bracket, and came into the cell with it. He did not look at Wilbarth or Tenney, who were watching this in mute wonder.

While Brayton read the document by the light of the lamp held by Sam, the room was so quiet they could hear the distant mill sounds. When he had finished reading it, Brayton gave a shuddering sigh. Then he said in a weary voice, "All right, I'll sign it."

Sam extended the pen and uncorked the bottle of ink. He lifted the pile of the *Capital Times* beside Con's cot, folded them until they made a stiff enough support to write on and handed them to Brayton.

"Come in, Tenney, Marshal," Sam called. The slender girl and the big man filed into the cell and watched as Brayton signed the confession. Sam dated the confession, noted the approximate hour of signing; then, in turn, he signed, Tenney signed, and Wilbarth signed as witnesses. After that Sam said to Wilbarth, "You keep that, Marshal."

He turned now, and picked up the lamp from the floor. "I think you'll sleep better now, Con."

The three of them filed out of the cell block and while Wilbarth returned the lamp to its bracket and turned down the wick, Sam locked the cell.

"Good night, Con."

Brayton grunted.

Tenney started up the steps and Sam waited for Wilbarth to precede him. Then Brayton called from the cell, "Sam, wait! Will they put Carnes in my cell when they bring him in?"

Tenney and Wilbarth halted, looking down at Sam.

Sam turned and looked back at Brayton. "No, Con. They'll bury him. He's dead, you see."

ABOUT THE AUTHOR

LUKE SHORT, whose real name was Frederick D. Glidden, was born in Illinois in 1907 and died in 1975. He wrote nearly fifty books about the West and was a winner of the special Western Heritage Trustee Award. Before devoting himself to writing westerns, he was a trapper in the Canadian Subarctic, worked as an assistant to an archeologist and was a newsman. Luke Short believed an author could write best about the places he knows most intimately, so he usually located his westerns on familiar ground. He lived with his wife in Aspen, Colorado.

To my fellow romance author Kandy Shepherd,
thanks for helping work out the tricky timelines!

Praise for
Scarlet Wilson

"Charming and oh so passionate, *Cinderella and
the Surgeon* was everything I love about Harlequin
Medicals. Author Scarlet Wilson created a flowing
story rich with flawed but likable characters and...
will be sure to delight readers and have them
sighing happily with that sweet ending."
—*Harlequin Junkie*

**Scarlet Wilson won the 2017 RoNA Rose Award
for her book *Christmas in the Boss's Castle*.**

Scarlet Wilson wrote her first story aged eight and has never stopped. She's worked in the health service for more than thirty years, having trained as a nurse and a health visitor. Scarlet now works in public health and lives on the West Coast of Scotland with her fiancé and their two sons. Writing medical romances and contemporary romances is a dream come true for her.

Books by Scarlet Wilson

Harlequin Romance

Cinderella's Costa Rican Adventure
Slow Dance with the Italian

Harlequin Medical Romance

California Nurses

Nurse with a Billion Dollar Secret

Christmas North and South

Melting Dr. Grumpy's Frozen Heart

Honolulu Medics

Hawaiian Kiss with the Brooding Doc

Night Shift in Barcelona

The Night They Never Forgot

Cinderella's Kiss with the ER Doc
Her Summer with the Brooding Vet
Nurse's Dubai Temptation

Visit the Author Profile page
at Harlequin.com for more titles.

CHRISTMAS SURPRISE
FOR HER BOSS

SCARLET WILSON

H Harlequin
ROMANCE

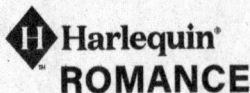

H Harlequin®
ROMANCE

ISBN-13: 978-1-335-47062-1

Christmas Surprise for Her Boss

Copyright © 2025 by Scarlet Wilson

Recycling programs for this product may not exist in your area.

Harlequin Enterprises ULC
22 Adelaide St. West, 41st Floor
Toronto, Ontario M5H 4E3, Canada
www.Harlequin.com

HarperCollins Publishers
Macken House, 39/40 Mayor Street Upper,
Dublin 1, D01 C9W8, Ireland
www.HarperCollins.com

Printed in U.S.A.

PROLOGUE

CLEMENTINE GRAYSON SHIVERED. It didn't matter that the sun was shining, or the temperature fine. This day would make anyone shiver.

She watched as the large group of people slowly streamed back through the gates of the cemetery. The tears flowed freely down her cheeks—and had done ever since she'd heard about Tyler's death in a road accident. Wrong place. Wrong time. A life with such potential gone, in an instant.

Her mother, Natalie, wrapped her arm around Clem's shoulders as they watched the rest of Tyler's family climb back into the funeral cars. Clem had been offered a seat, but had told them she wanted to travel with her mother.

'I'm so sorry, honey,' whispered Natalie. 'I would do anything to make this better for you.'

Clem's voice broke. 'But you can't, Mum—no one can. And it's worse than you think.'

'How can it be any worse?'

Her mother's face was confused. Clem shook her head and sighed, lifting her face up to the sky as if Tyler would be able to hear her.

'We'd come to a decision, Tyler and I.'

Natalie frowned. 'What do you mean?'

Clem ran her fingers through her dark red hair. 'You know we'd been on and off for the last few years?'

Natalie nodded and gave a sad sigh. 'I never could really understand your "friends with benefits" thing.'

Clem took a deep breath. 'Well, during our last holiday in Greece—'

It had been only a month ago but now felt like a million years.

'We'd decided we were better off as just friends—no benefits. It was like—one last fling for us—a farewell.' The tears started to flow even more as the words kind of choked her. 'It wasn't going anywhere and I didn't want to do that any more, so I told Tyler that we owed it to ourselves to find more meaningful connections.' She took a shaky breath. 'And he agreed, but…then he looked at me as though he wanted to have that more meaningful connection with me.' She put her hand to her chest and sobbed. 'But I didn't feel the same about him, not in a long-term way.

'But... I never thought... I never imagined...something like this would happen.' She threw up her hands. 'Tyler was the guy I expected still to be friends with in thirty years. When we'd found true love and were both married, with families, but all spent time together because we treated each other like family.' She let out a sob. 'I never imagined him dying.'

Natalie put her hands on Clem's shoulders, pulling her around towards her and cupping her daughter's face in her hands. 'None of us did. I'm so sorry, Clem. And you're right. Tyler was like family. I was so used to seeing him around I almost thought of him as a son.' She wiped Clem's tears and took a breath. Clem could see her mum was struggling just as much as she was. 'I'll miss him too. Stealing the bacon. Lying on the sofa. Looking for the hidden chocolate.' She shook her head. 'Tyler Kennedy was a wonderful person.' Then she gave Clem a small smile. 'But I understand what you're saying. I did wonder sometimes if the two of you would be better off as friends. Don't ever be sorry about being honest with him, honey.'

'But I am,' sobbed Clem. 'I couldn't give him what he wanted because I didn't love him that way.'

Natalie pushed a piece of hair back behind Clem's ear. 'Don't say that. You couldn't help how you felt. Be thankful you got that last holiday together. A chance to say goodbye, and to decide what your future should be.'

Clem gave a nod and then closed a hand over the one her mother had put on her shoulder. 'It's like a part of my family is gone,' she said steadily. 'We already lost Hugo. And now we've lost Tyler. It feels like it's just you and me now, Mum.'

She knew that wasn't strictly true. Her mother's family still existed, but they weren't close. They hadn't been particularly nice to Natalie when she'd fallen pregnant with Clem as a teenager. They'd liked Hugo—her stepdad—because his family was wealthy and money was never an issue.

Natalie gave her a hug. 'I'll always be here for you—you know that.'

Clem revelled in the heat and embrace. Nothing could beat a warm hug from her mum. No matter how bad things were around her.

She took a deep breath and squared her

shoulders. She and Tyler had also talked about what they would both do next—they'd been excited for their futures, even though they'd have been apart. She wanted to keep hold of that little feeling that was lingering deep down inside her. She knew her best friend would have wanted her to go on with her plans.

'I have three interviews in London over the next two weeks,' she announced. 'I've checked with Aunt Audrey, and she says I'm welcome to stay at the house in London.'

Natalie blinked for a moment. 'By yourself?'

Clem couldn't help but smile. Her mum still worried about her. 'Yes,' she said steadily. 'By myself.' She gave a little sigh. 'You've been in the house. You know the security system and you know it's in one of the best parts of London. I'll be perfectly safe there. Aunt Audrey didn't even blink when I asked. Just told me to keep an eye on the place since she's in Spain right now.'

Aunt Audrey wasn't really Clem's aunt. She was her godmother. An older friend of the family—and a very wealthy one—who hadn't taken kindly to how Natalie had been treated years ago. She'd delighted in being Clem's godmother and always invited them to stay at her town house in London whenever they wished.

Natalie took a deep breath and nodded slowly. 'I know you'll be safe there. I just worry about you being alone in London.'

Clem shook her head as her mother put her arm around her shoulder again and they started to walk back to the car. 'Haven't you heard, Mum? There's a population of over eight million—I won't be lonely.'

Natalie smiled and squeezed her shoulder. 'Let's get today over with first. Let's go and be with Tyler's family.'

Clem gave a slow nod, taking in another deep breath. This was truly the hardest thing she'd ever done. Tyler's family were loving and caring and had always welcomed her with open arms. She knew their hearts were breaking right now—even more than her own.

Her stomach gave a little flip as she opened the door and nodded at Natalie. 'Let's do this.'

CHAPTER ONE

THE FIRST INTERVIEW had been a bust—the job clearly marked for someone else—the second had been okay. Clem had answered all the questions with no problems, and solved the IT security issues she'd been asked to look at as part of the practical test. But the company was one of the bigger banks, and it had felt soulless.

Staff had nodded and walked past, but Clem wondered if any of these people actually knew each other's names. The open-plan office had been full of people with their heads down, and talking quietly on the phones or in virtual meetings with others. There was no zest, no spirit, and she'd have to think carefully if she was offered the job there.

Number three? Was already looking interesting. Clem pulled her suit jacket straight as she walked through the black-and-gold glass doors.

A comfortable wave of warmth hit her, along with a fresh floral and pine scent. A woman with her hair swept back in a sleek ponytail and bright red lipstick spoke to her from behind the nearby desk. 'Welcome to Artullo's bank, how can I help you today?'

Her manner was pleasant. 'Clementine Grayson, I'm here for an interview.'

The smile broadened. 'Welcome, Ms Grayson.' The woman glanced down and checked a list before walking out from behind the desk and gesturing towards a wall of elevators. 'Come this way, please.'

Clem turned her head to the inside of the bank. She could hear some quiet chatter, and some laughter. Black marble flooring, chandelier overhead lighting, and carved individual wooden desks with comfortable leather chairs reminded her of a bank she'd once seen in a film based on a children's book. She wanted to run over and try one of the chairs to see if they were as comfortable as they looked.

'Impressive, isn't it?' said the quiet voice next to her. 'Is this your first time visiting Artullo's?'

Clem nodded as she took a breath and smiled gratefully at the woman, following her into the elevator. She scanned a card before pressing a button to a higher floor and the journey was smooth and over in seconds.

She showed Clem to a waiting area. 'Mr Constello will be with you shortly.' Then gave her a little wink. 'Good luck.'

Clem's eyes glanced at a clipboard with a piece of paper lying on the desk. It was a list. Of over twenty names. Hers was somewhere in the middle and the top names all had little squiggles next to them—as if someone was marking them off after each interview. Every job in the city had competition. At least she had some idea of the numbers. Another quick scan told her she didn't recognise any of the names. Was that good, or bad? She took a few steps away, a little fearful of being caught reading something she shouldn't.

She felt a sudden wave of nausea. She wanted this job. She really did. She put her hand to her mouth and willed the nausea away. It was just nerves. She had to concentrate.

Clem moved over to the glass walls in the waiting room, which looked over the city. In the distance she could see the winding Thames and Tower Bridge, if she turned her head the other way, she could see the Shard against the clear blue sky. The bank really had a wonderful spot, right in the heart of the city.

She was still getting used to being in London. She loved the buzz of people and the rattle of the underground trains as they raced through the tunnels. She loved her godmother's house. It was something she would never be able to afford in a million years. White on the outside, with all period features maintained inside, the house had large windows, high ceilings and tasteful décor that ran through the whole lower floor. Original parquet flooring, cream walls and pale green furnishings. The upstairs bedrooms had thick carpets and luxurious bedding, the bathrooms were updated but retained the elegant Victorian themes.

The house was far too big for one person, but Clem felt remarkably comfortable there and, with its modern alarm system, also completely safe.

A door opened behind her and she spun around. She'd never been a girl that had been easily impressed. But the man in front of her stole the breath from her throat.

Dark-haired, tall, with a lithe frame, skin that caught the sun easily, and deep, deep brown eyes. Even before he spoke, she'd noticed his well-cut suit, his expensive designer shoes and the aroma of his aftershave that drifted towards her.

If she'd been a different kind of woman, she might have felt a bit weak at the knees, but that had never been on Clementine's bingo card. Instead her mouth was instantly dry and her brain decided to jumble up all the pre-prepared introductions and answers to potential inter-view questions. In her head she could practically see an imaginary bowling ball getting a full strike at the calm demeanour and professional manner that she'd wanted to impart.

He strode across the room with his hand extended towards her. 'Clementine Grayson? I'm Leonardo Constello.'

There were at least two seconds of relief as she realised she could get away with an action instead of speaking, so she slid her hand into his, using her best firm grasp. Nobody liked a floppy handshake.

He was younger than she'd expected. In his mid to late twenties, maybe? She'd thought someone in his position would be at least ten years older.

'Pleasure.' She managed to find a single word in her brain.

It was all she could do not to say the word 'zing' out loud. Because the shot that pulsed up her arm at his touch was aimed straight at her heart. Could her mouth be any drier?

He gave her a wide smile, showing perfect teeth, released her hand and gestured towards what was clearly his office. She smiled back, but wondered if she'd stepped into some kind of reality TV show. This guy was way too hot. Too perfect. Too Italian. Too well-dressed. Too much like a movie star.

Her stomach clenched and then rolled again. As soon as she'd walked through the doors downstairs, she'd known she wanted this job. Now? How on earth could she work with a guy that looked like that every day?

She took a few deep breaths to calm her stomach and settled into a chair opposite his desk. One wall in the office was the same as outside, glass from floor to ceiling, giving more spectacular views over London.

She turned to face him and gave a tiny jerk. He was studying her closely with those velvet dark eyes. It was a little unnerving.

'Clementine Grayson,' he repeated.

'Yes.' She nodded, wondering why he was checking again.

He glanced at papers in front of him. 'You did a joint degree in Accounting and Cyber Security at Edinburgh University.' His eyes were still fixed on her. 'Why did you decide on that combination?'

Clem felt her shoulders relax a little. She could answer standard interview questions until the cows came home. 'I always found numbers easy, so accounting was natural for me, but, in a modern-day world, particularly in banking, background knowledge in cyber security is essential. I decided combining the two would make me a better candidate for employment.'

'Banking, in particular. You always knew you wanted to work in banking?'

His voice was smooth, those eyes hypnotic. She thought about another of her well-rehearsed answers. She considered the other twenty unknown candidates on that list. Wouldn't they all have rehearsed their answers just as she had? It was likely some had more experience than her. How did she make herself stand out as a prospective employee?

'Since I was five,' she replied.

He raised his eyebrows. 'What attracted a five-year-old to banking?'

She gave a nod. 'The tellers. I thought they were the most glamorous people I'd ever seen. I loved their uniform. The fact they were in charge of money. I even loved the glass screens in front of them.' She took a breath then held out her hands. 'And the thing you can't really describe. The hum.'

His eyebrows went even higher and he had a hint of amusement on his face. 'The hum?'

'You know exactly what I mean,' she said with a smile. 'You feel it.' She put her hand up over her heart. 'You sense it. That quiet sensation you only get when you walk into a well-run establishment such as a bank.'

She wondered if she was truly talking about the bank or the sensation she'd just experienced when he'd shaken her hand. It didn't really matter which, though. If she did get this job, places like this would have rules. There would be no way she'd be allowed to date her boss.

A tiny part of her gave a sharp pang— wouldn't that be a pity?

His eyes narrowed for a second, but there was something she couldn't read on his face.

'So many things are online these days, and I admit to finding it very convenient. But that first time? As a child, entering the bank with my mother to open an account and getting my own little bank book. It was…' She tried to find a word, then leaned back in her chair and smiled at him. 'Magical.'

He was smiling, and she couldn't decide if

he liked her, or if he thought she was completely on another planet.

For a second she was blinking and Leo was dressed as Prince Charming on an inordinately white horse. Magical. Funny what that word conjured up. She licked her lips. Darn, she really was losing her mind. She had an interview to ace, here.

She straightened her shoulders and let herself focus as he spoke.

'Most people think online is the way forward.'

'And most people would be right—because it suits their circumstances.' She pointed her finger at the floor. 'But for others—and not just the richest clients—that face-to-face service downstairs is still what they need.'

Leo was trying not to show his amusement. This interview wasn't turning out like all the rest. He'd been struck by Clementine Grayson as soon as he'd seen her. But that wasn't something he would admit to anyone.

Her dark red hair and cool green eyes were striking. Her dark suit, which showed off her shapely figure, and the pale green shirt that emphasised those stunning eyes were the epitome of the modern-day bank employee. Smart, well turned out, with a hint of sophistication.

She was the only person on his list today that had done a joint degree. Her application had been impeccable—like many of the others. But interviewing in person was always different. There was the art of gelling with an individual and knowing you could work alongside them. He could sense a hint of orange and jasmine drifting towards him—clearly her perfume. It suited her.

She was younger than many of the other applicants. But, at twenty-eight, he was younger than most of the other employees too. His sister had already hinted that he should hire a candidate that had many previous years' experience in the banking field. And yet Clementine had only six months.

He couldn't afford to make a mistake here. He was still proving himself in the company and needed his project manager to be his right-hand man, or woman. His family had worked in Artullo's bank for years and were major shareholders. His grandfather had been the manager of the branch in Florence, his grandfather's two brothers managers in Rome and Milan. When Artullo's had expanded internationally, Leonardo's uncle had originally managed the branch in London and his own father the branch in Madrid. Banking really was in the family.

He took a breath and fixed his gaze on the woman in front of him. 'Wouldn't most people find that view old-fashioned nowadays?'

She licked her lips. They were dark red, and complemented her hair colour and skin tone. 'I'm happy to be the most old-fashioned twenty-four-year-old that you know.' She kept smiling but her eyebrows arched a little at him. 'And you don't really believe that—do you?'

He thought for a second he might get a chance to answer, but Clementine Grayson kept going. She had an air of confidence around her. Not arrogant at all. But just a surety in what she was saying.

'We all know that the most exclusive clientele always like an in-person service at the bank that holds their funds. If you take away all front-line counter services, you can disservice your older customers and those who need assistance. While all banking should be modern, and safe, there's nothing wrong with maintaining the personal touch.'

Leo tried to keep the smile from his face. The world had moved to mainly online everything, but he was pleased to hear from someone who shared his thoughts about the value of the human touch.

He didn't get a chance to ask his next question because it seemed as if Clementine was on a roll.

'As soon as you walk through the doors downstairs, there's just something about it. That hum I spoke about. That feel of the personal touch. That welcoming air.'

He didn't want to interrupt and tell her how much that welcoming air had cost them. Aromas were apparently very important—even in banking.

'That feeling that spreads through your stomach.' She made a little gesture with her hand. 'The way your shoulders relax when you come into a place, because you want to be there, and it makes you feel welcome.'

She wasn't looking at him. She was staring off into space as if she were in a world of her own.

But he liked her. He liked her enthusiasm for banking. The way she was so invested in things.

Nope, he didn't just like her. He *really* liked her.

Leo wasn't dating right now, which was an issue for his mother, who seemed determined to marry him off to an Italian girl from a good family. He wasn't entirely averse in theory, but in practice he knew he absolutely wasn't ready to commit to one woman. And the more his mother pushed, the more determined he was not to do her bidding.

He'd rarely dated anyone for longer than a month or two, and his last girlfriend had been a supermodel. It wasn't hard to find dates when for the last few years you'd been included in a list of the most eligible bachelors in London.

But the more he watched Clementine Grayson, the more intrigued he became. The way she tucked her hair behind her right ear. Her straight gaze. Her determination.

He gave himself a shake. He was interviewing her, not sizing her up as his next fling. He had to get the right person for this job. He couldn't employ someone with the sole purpose of potentially dating them. Clem was bright and articulate. That was what he should be concentrating on—not the fact he'd like to take her to dinner. She spoke again, and it jolted him back to the present.

'Is there a plan for the future?' she asked. 'To ensure that front-counter banking remains in place for customers that need it?'

He settled back into his chair. 'Are you interviewing me now?'

Her eyes widened as she realised how it might have sounded. But, instead of retreating or apologising, she gave a nod. 'My stepdad, Hugo, always told me that interviews are a two-way street.' She gestured towards Leo. 'The bank needs to decide if the interviewee is the right fit for their job and ethos, and—' she pointed back at herself '—the interviewee needs to understand if they are a good fit for the company and how it plans to proceed.'

Leo nodded slowly. 'Sounds like a wise man. What kind of business is your stepdad in?'

He could instantly tell it was the wrong question. Her face fell, and the healthy colour in her cheeks faded a little.

'Was,' she said steadily. 'He was a good businessman, but he died last year. Eighteen months ago actually. Pancreatic cancer. Hard to diagnose. Worse to treat.'

Those words spoke volumes and Leo had an overwhelming urge to walk around the desk and take her hands in his to comfort her. But that was ridiculous. And likely a type of sex discrimination he absolutely did not intend. She just looked so vulnerable right now.

He let the silence hang there, not wishing to push, and after a few seconds, she took a deep breath, put a smile on her face, and met his gaze.

'Sorry, did you want to ask me something else?'

A thought flitted into Leo's head. *Are you single?* No! He couldn't ask that, he shouldn't even be thinking that! It had workplace disaster written all over it.

He straightened himself in his chair. 'Yes, Ms Grayson. I want to do as your stepfather suggested and see if you are a good fit for the job. Do you understand the role of the project manager at Artullo's? I get a lot of reports, about a variety of subject areas. None of us can be an expert in all those fields. But I need someone to read these reports and ask questions. Are the numbers correct? Are we missing something that we should ask to be included in the future?'

'Who reads those reports right now?' asked Clem, apparently instantly interested.

'My PA collates them, from a purely administrative sense. But she doesn't have the time or expertise to pick them apart and scrutinise them.'

'I guess we would need to agree what our definition of scrutinise is,' she said.

'What do you mean?'

Clem looked him straight in the eye. 'What powers would I have if I don't get realistic and honest answers to the questions I ask?'

It honestly felt as if something settled across Leo's shoulders. Like a cloak, an arm, a reassuring weight. It was a comfort.

Here was someone on his wavelength. Someone who was already asking all the right questions.

'We'd need to explore that. Try a few different methods until you had a feel for the role, and the expectations I have.' He gave the slightest raise of his eyebrow. 'I can be difficult at times.'

'I don't doubt that.' She answered quickly, and he wasn't sure whether to be offended or not.

What struck him was how differently this interview was going from the ten he'd had before now. A few candidates had been better than others. Most had been suitably qualified and sufficiently demonstrated their experience and depth of knowledge.

All had been entirely traditional. None had spoken with heart.

Clementine Grayson was the youngest person he was interviewing today. The odds had probably been stacked against her. But she was the one person so far that he genuinely felt as if he could work well with—form a partnership with that would make his business life a bit easier.

He regarded her carefully. 'There's a skills test I need you to complete.'

'Shouldn't I have done that before the interview?'

'Call me old-fashioned,' he said with a glint in his eye, 'but there's too much online fraud. If you complete it here, in our building, I know it's all your own work.'

'No problem.' She picked up her bag and stood, moving to the door. 'Take me to your skills test.'

Leo wanted to laugh out loud. But he showed Ms Grayson along to another office that had only one desk and chair, the skills test and some pencils. She extended her hand, holding out her bag. 'I take it you want me to leave this outside, in case I have any secret weapons?' She was smiling now, as if she were auditioning for a TV show and there were hidden cameras around.

His fingers brushed hers as he took her bag

and set it in the small cubicle next to the door. He tried very hard to ignore the warmth, and the little zing that shot up his arm. He swallowed, his mouth feeling dry. 'When you complete the exercise, just leave your paper on the desk, and you're free to go.'

She gave him an amused glance. 'Cold, but I kind of like it. It was nice meeting you, Mr Constello.' She gave a little nod of her head.

'And you, Ms Grayson.'

He tried not to stare as she settled herself at the table and lifted the testing sheet. This interview had taken longer than it should, and he had several others he still needed to run through the process with.

But as he walked back to his office, he knew it was pointless. He'd already decided who he wanted to employ.

His PA, Anne, brought in the pile of tests just before seven in the evening. She gave a nod. 'I've ranked them in order of how they did. No one did badly, you'll be pleased to know. There's only a few points between them all.' She gave a half-smile. 'But at least one candidate enjoyed this a little more than the others.'

She turned and left before he could ask more. He picked up the tests. Candidate name was the first question, and he was immediately drawn to the slanted writing, *Clementine Grayson*. He couldn't wipe the smile from his face as he flicked through the skills test. There were two sheets of accounts, one with an error that most people could spot, and one with a minor error that most people missed. She'd circled both and noted next to the second—*Too easy*.

The next was a work-based problem-solving exercise that depended entirely on the mindset of the candidate. There were no real wrong answers.

But Clementine had written on both the left-hand and right-hand side of the paper. Next to that were the words *I like lists*. It was clear she was considering both sides as if she were some kind of criminal investigator who was representing each side's case.

Below, she'd written a short note.

This is a complete no-win situation. These two parties will never work well together, and will cause disruption throughout the company. Pay one off and give them a good reference.

He was surprised. As he flicked through the other candidates' papers, he saw they had all gone for one side or the other, listing their reasons. None of those reasons had been missed in the summary Clementine had made on each side of the page.

The final exercise was on four start-up companies, and asked which one the bank should invest in. She'd numbered them one to four in priority—another list—but also asked how each company's values aligned with Artullo's bank, and if any of them had a ten-year plan showing reinvestment in the local area they intended to work in.

He laughed. He laughed out loud at this one. Smart. Cheeky. And to the point.

He needed someone he could trust to pay attention to details and ask questions. It looked as if he'd found her. The fact that Anne had agreed gave him a little assurance that he wasn't being biased. He wasn't thinking about the dark red hair, the smattering of pale freckles across her nose, or those green eyes.

He was thinking about her capabilities and how he could trust her to read reports and just give him the relevant overview.

He knew that, in a matter of weeks, his sister would appear to check out his latest employee. He also knew if he'd picked a candidate that was twenty years older than Clementine, his sister might not be quite so interested.

He left instructions for his PA to contact Clementine's referees, and once he'd checked the references, they could confirm a start date.

As he gathered the papers into a pile, his eyes caught sight of Clementine's address. It made him stop. It was one of the most prestigious addresses in London. Kensington, just off Hyde Park.

Leo had spent the last eight years in London, surrounded by London's so-called elite. Clementine didn't strike him as that way at all.

She was grounded and down to earth. She had a good education and, if her CV was to be believed, had worked ever since she'd left university. She'd mentioned a stepfather. Was the house that cost millions his?

Leo shook his head. This was none of his business. He'd found a suitable candidate for his post. That was all that mattered.

As he packed up and left the office, he didn't doubt who would be in his mind for most of the evening. But if he was going to employ her, he was also going to have to work hard to suppress any attraction to her. The last thing he needed was workplace drama.

CHAPTER TWO

THE TUBE WAS chaotic that morning—just like every weekday morning—and Clementine prayed for no delays. When she exited at the Strand she took a few moments to ensure her new suit was pristine, and she had not a hair out of place.

This time, when she walked through the dark doors of Artullo's she felt a sense of pride. She worked here. She belonged.

If she blinked, she could imagine a small child being brought in to open their first account with their parent. She could feel the firmness of the little bank book in her hand. Something struck her. Would a bank as prestigious as this one open children's accounts? She made a mental note to ask Leo later.

She'd done a quick Internet search of Leonardo Constello. He was incredibly hot. In every picture she found. Did the guy even take a bad photo?

It seemed he'd worked at the London branch since graduating from university in Italy, and his whole family worked across a variety of the Artullo's branches. His family had been involved in the international set-up of the numerous Artullo's branches across the world. They were impressive—and a little bit terrifying.

She greeted the woman at the front desk. 'Clementine Grayson, I start working here today.' Her stomach gave a little flip and she tried to ignore it. She had no time for nausea or nerves today!

The woman gave a wonderful smile. 'Welcome.' She escorted Clementine to get her bank ID, showed her how to use it and then walked her back to the elevators. 'Top floor,' she said with a smile, leaving Clem to ride up to the glass office she'd been interviewed in.

This time when she arrived there was a desk in the corner that had clearly been set up for her. Leo was nowhere in sight, which disappointed her a little, but his PA, Anne, arrived and ran through a number of things that Clem would be expected to do. It all seemed perfectly reasonable and she settled at her computer and got started.

She set up her calendar noting when she should receive reports, and sent out an email to all the contacts, introducing herself and her new role at the bank. She then took some time to read through all the previous reports, making notes on bits she didn't quite understand, and getting a feel for the best way to summarise them in future.

She was so caught up in her work that she didn't notice Leo until he was standing straight in front of her. 'Welcome, Ms Grayson.'

Her head shot upwards, and she couldn't help but smile. She stood up and extended her hand. 'Thank you, Mr Constello, but you should call me Clem, that's what I prefer.'

He grasped her hand firmly, and a little tingle ran from her palm straight up to her shoulder. 'How are you settling in?'

She glanced around the room. 'Good, I think. I mean, I have an office with one of the best views of London.'

He nodded in agreement. 'Call me Leo. Is there anything you need?'

She wondered if she should say anything. She didn't want to seem difficult in any way, especially not on her first day.

'Clem?' He could clearly tell she was thinking about something.

'Do you have a specific induction package I should complete?'

He frowned. The first time she'd seen his brow creased. 'What do you mean? Didn't Anne show you how to get started?'

She pressed her lips together and decided to just go for it. 'What I'd like is a chance to work on the shop floor.'

His frown deepened, and, although his English was impeccable, she wondered if he might not be so familiar with some of the English phrases.

She handed over a piece of paper. 'I wrote you a list. I mean working down with the bank tellers, the advisors, and other parts of the bank. I would like a chance to meet them all—shadow them for a few hours if I'm allowed.'

'Ahh.' He stared at the paper in his hand. 'You wrote me a list.' He was clearly trying not to smile as he nodded in recognition. 'I think I can arrange that. After all, you should be familiar with all the places that might send in reports.'

She grinned at him. 'In that case, I notice one of your reports is from the Solomon Islands. Do I get to go there too?'

He laughed. 'Nice try. And don't think I've forgotten that your childhood dream was to be a bank teller. This is all just a chance to get behind one of those desks, isn't it?'

She could feel herself start to relax a little. She'd been nervous this morning, and wondered if Leo would be as good a boss as she suspected he might. 'Talking of childhood dreams, I'd like to know the bank's position on children's accounts.'

He straightened up and looked at her in surprise. 'We're an exclusive bank; children's accounts aren't how we do business.'

She licked her lips. 'Think of the fine example you could be setting. Introducing children to saving and trusting their bank.' She waved a hand. 'But we can talk about that another time.'

He looked at her suspiciously and gestured to her. 'Follow me,' he instructed, walking through to his office and pulling a list of contacts from his top drawer. 'This is information on everyone based in this building, including their speciality. Why don't you start here, and tell them I've asked for you to spend a few hours with each team.'

She blinked as she looked at the list. She'd spent the last few weeks reading everything she could about Artullo's bank but it seemed as if she'd barely scratched the surface. There were more people and departments than she'd imagined.

She could sense he was still looking at her, so lifted her head and met his gaze. He was amused. Playing her at her own game. She smiled. 'Perfect, thank you. As you know, I like a list. Mind if I start on the ground floor? I can't wait to sit behind one of those desks.'

Leo was starting to wonder if he might have made a mistake. He'd always been a hard worker, putting in more hours than others. And he'd always been entirely focused on his work.

Until now. Until Clementine Grayson. Or Clem, as she'd reminded him.

He'd known it from the first glance, but he couldn't help but find her attractive. But Clem was also fulfilling the role of project manager perfectly.

She was enthusiastic. He'd had mainly positive feedback from all the departments that she'd worked her way around. One older colleague didn't like the idea of sending any report to a 'youngster', as he'd put it, but Leo would deal with that later.

Clem had loved working her way around the bank. It seemed to have answered lots of the questions she had, created a whole host of others, but mainly had got her familiar with most of the people and processes in a time-efficient way.

While her fulfilling her role perfectly was wonderful, what wasn't wonderful was how big a distraction she was proving to Leo.

He liked chatting with her. He liked spending time with her. Probably a bit more than a boss should. And she hadn't been joking when she'd said she liked lists. He'd seen more than a few of them.

She'd been here two weeks already and he could sense the moment she appeared in her office. It wasn't only the aroma of her perfume and the timbre of her voice and her contagious laughter. It was just an odd presence. And one that he found strangely unsettling. It wasn't as though Leo had no history with women. He dated, frequently. No one had lasted very long, but that surely wasn't unusual. And he usually ended things on good terms. There had only been one individual who'd picked up a vase of flowers and crashed it off his penthouse wall. But 'drama' had literally been her middle name.

So, he couldn't quite put his finger on what was different about Clem—as he'd got used to calling her. There had been some mild flirtation at the interview, but he'd made sure to keep things in check since then. Dating an employee would be unwise—particularly one he worked closely with.

It was ridiculous to think his body was in tune with hers. Of course it was. But he got this weird sense whenever she was around. Before her voice reached his ears. Before he inhaled the scent of her perfume. Maybe he was being taken over by some clairvoyant spirit and he was actually in some cheesy movie right now, or maybe, and far more likely, he was having an almost-thirty crisis.

His sister and mother were still pushing— good-humouredly—the 'settling down' mantra. Mamma had, of course, a list of suitable Italian women, from suitable Italian families. Leo was quite sure that none of the women on that list had been consulted. So he avoided all of these conversations at all times.

But he still couldn't understand the strange connection to Clem. It didn't help that, inevitably, she would soon be introduced to the family. Maybe he should let her in on that part of the plan soon?

Leo stood up and walked through to the office. Clem was on the phone to someone, her dark red hair obscuring her face. He could tell by her tone that she was charming her way through this conversation. Her dynamics of changing her manner and language when she was on the phone with different people had him intrigued.

Anne had already mentioned she thought that Clem could charm honey from bees. That she was good at reading people, and how to get the best reaction out of them.

He waited until she replaced the receiver and tossed her hair back over her shoulder. She blinked in surprise to see him waiting. 'Who was that?' he asked.

The edges of her lips hinted upwards. 'Tony, in Trading. He doesn't like me, but I'm working on it.'

'So I can see,' said Leo with amusement. He wasn't even the slightest bit jealous. Tony was argumentative, angry and entitled. 'Good luck with that one.'

She tapped the side of her nose. 'I have a plan, leave it with me.'

He gave her a half-smile. 'I have a plan too, and it involves you, and some travel.'

Now that got her attention. She turned her face up towards his. 'What?' He could tell she was instantly interested.

'We're going to visit another branch of the

bank. In two weeks, we'll be flying to Florence. We'll be there until Friday so bring some suitable work clothes.'

Her brow creased. 'What, is there a list of approved clothes? Or do you think I'll travel with a onesie or a thong bikini?'

He laughed out loud. 'That's not what I meant.'

She stood up. 'Be careful how you treat your favourite employee, Leo. I might start making demands.'

'What, like trips to Florence?' he teased.

Her gaze met his. 'Where are we staying?'

'The family home. Don't worry, you'll be perfectly comfortable. It's about an hour away.'

'*Your* family home?'

He laughed. 'Yes, we do have one.'

'Will your family be there?' Her voice was rising slightly.

'They might be. My mother is usually always there. My sister will likely visit.' He paused for a second. 'My father is probably in Rome. But I guess we'll just see.'

She looked a little pale. 'I thought you were joking to begin with.'

He shook his head. 'Why would I joke about something like this? My whole family is in the business. We meet regularly. Depending on the skill set of who is working for us, we sometimes move reports around. And if clients move base, they often want a bank that is nearer to home. This is everyday work for us.'

He watched as she gulped. 'Is meeting my family really so scary?' he asked curiously. A picture of his mother and sister sitting at the main dining room table came into his head—and the way they'd been teasing him about settling down. They were his family. He didn't hesitate to tell them to back off. But, all of a sudden, he wondered how intimidated Clem might be. He hadn't even considered it—not for a second.

He'd need to be careful. His sister was astute. If she picked up on the fact that he was attracted to Clem, she would be on him like a shot. That was the last thing he wanted.

Clem took a breath. 'I guess I'd just like to have been in the job a bit longer before I met them. I get that this is literally a family business, but I don't want them to think I'm a fool. I haven't really had time to remember every single detail about the company yet.'

He raised his eyebrows and put a hand on her shoulder. 'I've seen your spreadsheets—and your lists. You're doing fine. It's more likely they'll give us more work, not quiz us about the business we currently have.'

He was trying to be helpful, hoping to allay her fears. But he wasn't entirely sure it was working. 'You still have time. Don't worry, things will be fine.'

Things will be fine. That was what he'd said, and those words reverberated around her head as she wheeled her suitcase behind her at the airport. There had been an offer of a car to pick her up, which she'd refused. It was just as easy to jump on the Tube.

She made her way to the airline check-in, and saw Leo at the business desk. As if by magic, he turned around, fixed his gaze on her and gave her a wave. She moved beside him, ignoring the check-in girl, who clearly already had her admiring eyes on him. 'We're flying business class?' she asked.

'Of course.' He nodded.

'I've never flown business class,' she admitted. 'This could be nice.'

And it was. Even though both she and Leo worked on their laptops on the flight, and she refused any alcoholic drinks, the lunch and service were delightful. She half wished that the journey to Italy were much longer so she could have enjoyed it more.

A black stretch limousine was waiting for them at the airport and Clem watched as the Italian landscape streamed past for almost an hour. She thought they might head straight to the family home, but they pulled up instead at the Artullo's bank in Pisa.

She was half disappointed that the leaning tower, baptistry and cathedral weren't immediately in her line of sight. But she straightened her suit and followed Leo into the branch.

The Italian language flowed freely around her, but the staff in the branch were multilingual and also spoke to her in English. She suddenly felt a touch light-headed and excused herself for the moment to freshen up, and to press her overheated cheek against the wall of cold tiles for a second. She'd forgotten about the temperatures, that was all. It was July. High summer in Italy and not ideal for her suit jacket. She slipped it off, washed her hands and face and took another few moments to try and cool down.

Then she needed to use the toilet. Her skirt felt a little snugger as she refastened the zip and she hoped that they didn't just serve pasta at the family home. She was clearly going to have to start paying attention to what she was eating. The temptation for takeaways when she was living alone was strong, and she was going to have to make some changes.

She reapplied some lipstick and went back outside to join Leo.

He moved quickly next to her, resting one hand on her arm. 'Are you okay?'

The touch of his palm on her bare arm was more than a little distracting. She gave a sigh and admitted honestly, 'It's a bit hotter than I expected. I'll be fine.'

He glanced around them. 'The air conditioning is on. And I can turn it up further in the next meeting room we're going into. I'll get you some water. Or would you prefer something else to drink?'

'Water is fine,' she said quickly, before adding, 'Is there any ice?'

He gave her a smile and a nod of his head. 'Of course. Come and take a seat in the meeting room, and I'll sort things out.'

Clem was slightly embarrassed. The blissful chill of the air conditioning was starting to kick in and she could finally feel herself cooling down. Leo brought her in the iced water and sat next to her as others came in and settled around the table. She sipped the water slowly as they made introductions and everyone opened their laptops.

It was still overwhelming. Clem had been in this job for one month and now she'd been flown to Florence, and taken to Pisa for international meetings. In her head, she'd thought she would take things in her stride, but she was actually feeling a bit stressed. No one in the room had introduced themselves as being a member of Leo's family as yet, and her stomach was doing flip-flops at whether they might like her or not.

It shouldn't matter. She was in a professional position, but she was also a stranger, and this was a family-run bank. Being Leo's right-hand woman would put her under the spotlight and she would have preferred to meet people six months down the line when she'd learned everything she could. It would have given her a better footing. She went into her bag and pulled out the list of notes that she'd made ahead of time.

The meeting went well, and they were briefed on an Italian watchmaker and goldsmith who was opening a large branch of their store in London and would be managed out of the London bank.

Clem paid attention to the reports, the layouts and the relevant issues discussed. She ignored the fact she'd developed a pounding headache, or that she was feeling a bit queasy. What she really wanted to do right now was lie down.

Maybe it was the five a.m. start? Travelling had never made her feel ill before. But she just didn't feel quite right. As she sipped her water, she stared down at her stomach. Her mind drifted for a moment and she contemplated the tighter zip on her skirt. She was definitely a bit bloated. Maybe she had developed some sort of allergy or intolerance. That had happened to a few of her friends in the past.

And then, as she recalled all the times she'd felt nauseous over the last few weeks, a crashing wave blasted over her. No. Oh no. Not that. She couldn't possibly be? Could she?

A rich Italian voice filled the room and she started to attention. Leo was talking and once he finished speaking, he turned to her and added in English, 'That's us finished for today. Come, Clem. Come and meet my family.'

She gave her best smile. It was absolutely the last thing she wanted to do right now. Her brain was screaming at her. Her thoughts spinning like a tumble dryer. She was in Italy. She didn't speak the language. How on earth could she get her hands on a pregnancy test? She'd never had a pregnancy scare. Never. She and Tyler had always been so careful.

She was on the mini pill, so rarely had a proper period now. Occasionally one day of spotting, but when was the last time that had happened? And because she took her tablet faithfully every day, and had done for six years, the possibility of pregnancy hadn't entered her head. Her stomach rolled again, and she took a breath, trying to convince herself this was all psychosomatic.

Leo lowered his head next to hers. 'Clem? Are you okay?' There was a gentle hand between her shoulders and a look of concern on his handsome face. The smell of his aftershave enveloped her as he bent down. But for some reason it didn't make her stomach roll.

'Yes.' Her voice came out almost as a squeak.

'Come on,' he said. 'It isn't far to my parents' house and you'll get a chance to rest before dinner.'

Her mouth was dry. 'I need to find a pharmacy first,' she blurted out.

His brow creased. And she knew she was creating a whole issue for herself. But now the thought had entered her head, she didn't want to wait another four days until she was back in London to find out.

'Are you sick? If you're unwell we have a family doctor I can take you to.'

'No!' She held up one hand and the reaction came out a little more forcefully than she meant it to. She licked her dry lips. 'Just some female necessities,' she heard herself say.

She wanted to cringe. Of course she didn't need to reveal what was wrong.

But Leo straightened up and gave her a nod. 'I'll get our driver to stop on the way back to the house. There are a number of pharmacies. Let me know if you don't find what you need and we can stop somewhere else.'

Some men might have been embarrassed at her excuse, but Leo didn't seem bothered in the slightest. She wondered if Italian men were just more relaxed than British men about that sort of thing.

She allowed herself to be escorted to the car. Jumping out when the driver gestured they were at a pharmacy, and, once she was inside, stammering to explain what she needed.

The Italian pharmacy assistant picked up a test, and explained in halting English to wait two minutes for the result, which would show a plus or a minus sign. Clem nodded gratefully. She could manage that, she thought, before stuffing the test deep into her bag and jumping back into the car.

Leo smiled at her, and then talked about the rest of the city and surrounding countryside as they moved towards the family estate. 'If you feel up to it tomorrow, I'll of course take you to see all the tourists' sites. You can't leave Pisa without a photo next to the tower.'

She gave a small smile. An hour ago, she would have been delighted at this suggestion, but now? She had too much to think about.

However, as the long sweeping tree-lined driveway of the family home appeared, she was brought back to the present-day world.

A pale pink extensive luxury villa emerged, revealing a fountain at the front doors and immaculate gardens.

'It was originally built in the fifteenth century,' said Leo, not hiding the pride in his voice. 'Of course, there have been lots of renovations since that time.'

'It's gorgeous,' Clem breathed as she pressed her face nearer to the window. This was their regular house? 'You grew up here?'

He nodded and smiled. She leaned back. 'Wow. It's like a fairy tale.'

He gave her a sideways glance. 'Your address would be a fairy tale to some people too.'

She blinked, momentarily confused, then laughed. 'Ah-h-h,' she said slowly, shaking her head. 'The address in London, you mean? The house belongs to my godmother, who very kindly lets me stay there. She lives in Spain part of the year. It suits her to have someone staying so it's not empty.' She shook her head. 'I grew up in Surrey, and we didn't stay anywhere even close to posh until my mum met my stepfather. Up until then, grand houses were only in my dreams.'

Leo shot her another smile. 'Well, I hope our home lives up to your dreams.'

She sat back in the chair again and swallowed. Dreams? What even were they? Because the only thing filling her head right now was panic.

The whirlwind that was Leo's mother and sister took over the next two hours of his life. It started from the moment he and Clem set foot over the threshold and were hustled into the large family kitchen where preparations for dinner had already started.

Leo's family always ate a little earlier than most, but he assumed that would suit Clem since most people in the UK had their evening meal earlier too.

They barely had time to wash their hands before chopping boards, knives and graters were set in front of them along with some instructions.

He could sense Clem's discomfort. It wasn't entirely obvious, but he had the overwhelming feeling she wanted to go and lie down somewhere. It was what he'd hoped she'd be able to do when they'd arrived. But he hadn't reckoned on his family waiting excitedly for them.

He also wondered if Clem's family wasn't quite like his own. He knew she was an only child. Both his mother and his sister, Juliette, were loud, flamboyant, and took a bit of getting used to. In twenty-eight years, he'd rarely invited a woman home to meet them. But they knew that Clem was a work colleague, so at least they weren't prodding her with the usual family heritage questions.

Juliette opened a bottle of white wine and passed around glasses as they finished preparing the food. It didn't take him long to notice that Clem hadn't taken so much as a sip.

'Do you want some water?' he asked, remembering she hadn't been feeling well earlier.

She shot him a grateful smile. 'I'm sure the

wine is wonderful,' she said, 'but I'm just a little queasy.'

His mother shot a look over his shoulder at him that he couldn't decipher. 'Will we eat in the kitchen?' she asked.

Leo nodded. He preferred the kitchen to the long and formal dining room table they had. Particularly when it would be only the four of them.

'Almost ready,' said Juliette as she finished setting the large oak table to the side of them all.

He pulled out a seat for Clem and gestured for her to sit down. She still looked a little pale and anxious. Hopefully she would realise soon that his family were just typical Italians. Loud, passionate, and very interfering.

His family had prepared a typical family recipe of sea bass that was one of his favourites. He loved it—from the scent of the fish, the oregano, paprika, garlic and chilli flakes, it truly reminded him he was home.

Juliette put the plates down at everyone's places and he heard a little noise at his side, then Clem bolted from the table.

There were a few startled glances, and then Leo ran after her. She was pulling open doors, clearly desperately looking for a rest room with her hand over her mouth.

'Here!' he said quickly, opening a downstairs cloakroom with toilet and sink and closing the door behind her as she dashed inside.

He heard exactly what he suspected he might hear.

He walked back through to the kitchen. 'Clem appears to be unwell. Let me get her bags, and I'll take her upstairs and let her rest.'

His mother stood immediately. 'The guest room is ready, and towels are in the bathroom. I'll get Juliette to take up some chilled bottles of water for her.'

Juliette's eyebrows were arched but she moved quickly to open the giant family refrigerator and put some bottles on a tray, along with glasses and an ice bucket.

She waved her hand at Leo. 'Look after your employee and let's hope it's not infectious.'

Leo took a deep breath and watched as his sister made her way up the stairs while he gently knocked on the cloakroom door. 'Clem? Are you okay? Do you want to go upstairs and lie down?'

After the sound of running water the door clicked open and her tear-stained face appeared. 'I am so, so sorry. I'm not sure what came over me.' Her hand was resting against the wall.

'Are you feeling light-headed?'

She grimaced and nodded. 'This is not like me at all. I normally travel well.'

He nodded towards the stairs. 'Let me help you upstairs, get you settled and you can tell me what you need.'

Her body gave an involuntary shudder as she nodded. He took her slowly up the stairs and to the rooms that had been designated her guest quarters.

He nodded at the open shutters. 'Would you like me to close them?'

She gave a nod as she sat on the edge of the bed and kicked her shoes off. He closed the shutters, dimming the room instantly, then picked up her luggage and sat it next to her.

He brought over the water, and opened a bottle, pouring it into a glass for her and sitting it on the bedside table. It was then that he noticed her hands were shaking.

He couldn't help it. He knelt down in front of her. 'Clem, is there something else wrong? Do you need me to phone a doctor for you?'

She dissolved into sobs, and he didn't quite know what to do, but eventually sat on the bed beside her and wrapped an arm around her shoulders.

'I don't know what is wrong, but if I can help you, I will,' he said steadily.

Her tear-filled green eyes turned to his. 'I think you might live to regret saying that.' Her voice barely a whisper.

Something prickled down his spine. He'd known this woman only a month. He liked her. He knew that already. There had been a few moments of flirtation. Half of him wondered where things might actually go between them if he broached the issue. But besides all that, what he absolutely knew was, if he was in a position to help Clem, he would. The overwhelming urge to keep her wrapped in his arms right now felt almost primal. He'd never seen himself as a protector of women. All the women he'd met in life were sure of themselves, and didn't need, or want, his protection. But right now? He'd move mountains to protect Clem Grayson.

She took a deep breath and everything came pouring out. Her ex, their relationship, his accident, the funeral. And now her overwhelming fear that she might be pregnant.

Was he ready to hear any of that? Absolutely not.

And that was the thing about Leo. His face could betray him at times. His sister regularly told him that, and had made him vow to never take up poker.

While his head tried to compute everything he'd just heard, he didn't want to contemplate the fact his heart had sunk a little. She thought she was pregnant. Of course, he couldn't date her now—all that would have to be pushed far away. From everything Clem had told him, she was grieving a terrible loss and would also likely be a single mum in a few months' time.

Trying to tread carefully, he took a breath. 'Why don't you do the test, Clem? You could be panicking over nothing.'

She gave a nod of her head, and dug into her bag, pulling out the test. She gave him a half-hearted smile. 'At least I have someone who can read the instructions now if I do something wrong.'

She disappeared for a moment and he heard the toilet flushing and sink running. Then... he waited. She didn't come back out.

And...he kept waiting.

Eventually he made his way over to the bathroom door and knocked quietly. 'Clem, is everything okay?'

He heard the strangled sob from inside and

his stomach flipped. He pushed the door open. Clem was sitting on the floor between the washbasin and the bath, the test in her hand.

Her eyes were even more waterlogged than before. 'It's positive,' she said.

She tucked her head onto her knees that were pulled up in front of her and he joined her on the floor.

He patted her back, wondering what on earth women said to each other in situations like this. What would he say to Juliette if this were her?

'Clem, do you have any idea how far along you might be?' He bit his lip and said the next words. 'You don't have to have this baby if you don't want to.'

Her head lifted and she shook it fiercely. 'I couldn't do that. I just couldn't. It's the last surviving part of Tyler. And he was an only child. This baby will be his parents' only chance of a grandchild. I love those people, I could never do that to them.'

Leo gave a slow nod. There was so much here that he couldn't even begin to understand. 'You're giving up at least the next eighteen years of your life, Clem, so you have to be sure about this. Can you do it on your own?'

Her bottom lip trembled. 'Are you going to

sack me? I've just started. I don't even know if I'll be entitled to pregnancy leave.' He could hear the panic start to creep into her voice.

He held up one hand. 'I'm not going to sack you. You'll get all the leave you should. I just think you should take a few days to think about things. This has clearly been a surprise. Do you have a friend or family member you can talk to?'

Her shoulders deflated a little. 'My mum,' she said, her voice tinged with sadness.

'Will she support you?'

Clem blinked and looked up at him. 'To the moon and back,' she said straight away, then paused. 'It's…it's just that Mum had me when she was even younger than I am now. Things didn't work out too well, and I think she'll be disappointed when I tell her.'

He couldn't remember the last time he'd ever seen anyone look so sad. He reached his hand over to her. Her hair was plastered to the side of her face and he gently pushed it back, untangling it with his fingers and letting his palm rest on her cheek.

'This is entirely your decision, and I'm sorry you found out like this. You have a lot to think about. If you want to see a doctor, I'm sure we can find someone for you. If you want to go home immediately, I can arrange that, too.'

She licked her lips and took a deep breath, lifting her hand to cover his. She closed her eyes for a second, letting their hands rest together, and he could tell she was taking comfort from that.

But his heart was somewhere down next to his stomach. He'd watched her the last month. Had he misread their flirtations? Was there actually no spark to speak of, when he'd thought that sparks were exploding all around them?

She'd said Tyler had died in a car accident. Was it wrong that he felt a surge of jealousy right now, over a guy who was dead? What kind of human did that make him? And if he'd been worried about the potential of dating an employee before—could he even imagine the furore if he dated an employee who was pregnant with someone else's child? His mother would likely have a heart attack.

After a few moments Clem's green eyes blinked open. 'I'm here for work. I'm here to do a job. Let me lie down for a few hours, and then I'm sure I'll be fine. I've not actually been sick before this; just felt a bit nauseous now and then. I think it might be the heat, the travel, the spices—a bit of everything.' Her hand moved away from his and covered her mouth.

'I have to go down and apologise to your mum and sister. They made me a beautiful meal and I ran away.'

He shook his head, sorry that she'd moved her hand away. The logical part of his brain was telling him it was a good thing. He shouldn't be making any promises or thinking anything personal at all about this woman who was his employee.

And it was almost as if he could sense her pulling away, or pulling back at least. What did that mean? Was she still in love with the father of her baby? Maybe this pregnancy was making her realise that?

He should probably be cursing the fact she was pregnant and would need time off, and that he would have a vacant post again, just as he was getting used to working with Clem. But he didn't actually feel like that at all. He felt a little sad.

Sad that this now very complicated situation would likely end any chance of a future relationship before it had even begun.

And, as long-term had never been in his vocabulary, that was a sensation Leonardo Constello was generally unfamiliar with.

He pulled his own hand back. 'Let me worry about my mother and sister. Can I bring you up anything to eat? Some fruit? Some cookies? Some ice cream?'

Her eyes shone with gratefulness. 'Fruit would be good. Melon or grapes if you have any. I'll lie down for a few hours, and I'm sure this sickness will pass. Thank you for being so understanding, Leo.'

He held out a hand and pulled her up from the bathroom floor. She padded straight through and lay down on the bed, closing her eyes as soon as her head touched the pillow.

He walked over to the door, turning for one last look before he left. She looked peaceful. Even though he could imagine how fast her brain was spinning right now.

He wasn't entirely sure how any of this would turn out. But if he could help, he already knew he would.

CHAPTER THREE

ONCE ALL THE initial shock was over—and her dismay over what she'd told her boss—Clem was logical. She made a list.

She booked in to see an obstetrician. She had bloods taken, a scan, a few tests, and was given plenty of antenatal advice.

In all honesty, she was swamped with emotions and it all seemed like too much. But she tried to compartmentalise it for herself—it was the only way she could do things.

No matter that this baby had never been planned, she could never think about not having it. Yes, her life would change for ever. Yes, she would be on her own. But her mother had coped and so would she. The one thing she was sure of was that she wasn't about to be sacked. That gave her more comfort than most things, because she wanted to be sure she could look after this baby.

The truth was hard though. If Tyler was

still here, would she be having this baby? Maybe not. But now that they'd all lost him, the thought of destroying this final, precious part of him could never be a decision she'd be comfortable making.

There was a seed of sadness deep inside. The fun, albeit small flirtations she'd been having with Leo would have to stop. He wouldn't be interested in her at all now. She was pregnant with another man's child—it must be the ultimate turn-off for a man who could have any woman he wanted. But he'd been kind, and he'd been supportive, and that was more than she could ask for right now.

When she had all the information she needed, she picked up the phone to her mother.

'Hi, darling, how was the work trip?'

Clem took a deep breath. 'Not good, Mum. I found out I'm pregnant.'

She heard Natalie suck in a huge breath. 'Clem?' It was the question. The one her mum didn't want to ask.

'It's Tyler's, Mum. I'm twelve weeks and I'm due on 30 January.' She didn't add the part about how she was definitely having the baby, because she knew she didn't need to.

'Oh, honey,' Natalie sighed. 'Do you need

help? Do you want me to come to London? Are you sick?'

Clem shook her head even though her mother couldn't see her. 'I'm fine. I think it was the heat in Italy and the travel that made me unwell and even then I was only sick a couple of times.'

'Does…does your boss know?'

Clem gulped. She didn't exactly want to tell her mum that Leo had picked her off the bathroom floor.

'He knows and has been surprisingly supportive. I half expected him to fire me on the spot. But he says it's fine.'

'And you feel okay to keep working?'

'I do.' She took another breath, hoping to get the words out quickly. 'I'm going to phone Aunt Audrey and let her know since I'm staying at her house. I'd hate for her to come back unexpectedly and be met with me and a giant belly.' She kept going. 'And I'm going to phone Dad.'

There was a silence. It probably wasn't that long, but in Clem's head it lasted for ever. She couldn't help but fill the gap. 'My doctor asked me lots of questions about my family history of medical conditions and, while I know everything about our side of the family, I've never asked Dad those kinds of questions.'

'Hmmm…' The silence continued for a bit before there was a sigh. 'I'm not sure I remember anything significant.'

'It's fine. I'll contact him and ask.'

'Are you sure you don't need anything? Because you know I'm only a train journey away.'

'I know that, Mum.' Clem smiled. She'd known her mother would have her back. She was sure at some point she would get all the worried questions when Natalie thought back to her own circumstances and lack of family support.

'What about Tyler's parents?'

Clem swallowed the huge lump that instantly appeared in her throat. 'I'm going to wait a couple of weeks and then I might go and see them. I'm not sure I can give them this news over the phone.'

'Do you want me to come with you?'

'I don't know yet. I'll think about it, and let you know.'

'Okay, darling. But you know I love you.' Then there was something resembling a little squeak. 'Did you get a picture, a scan? Can I see a photo of my new grandchild?'

Clem beamed. 'Yes, wait and I'll send it to you.'

She waited until she heard the buzz of her mother's phone. Then, there it was, the sniffs and sounds of her crying. 'You know Fiona and I will be fighting over this little one,' she said in a broken voice.

Clem felt herself go too. Once they were over the initial shock she knew Fiona and Gary, Tyler's parents, would be overjoyed to still have part of him to love and spoil. 'And I'll gladly take all the help that is offered.' She took a breath. 'And I will happily share. I know what this baby means to everyone.'

'Love you, darling.'

'You too, Mum. I'll phone if I have any updates.'

Clem put the phone down. Then picked it straight back up and phoned Aunt Audrey. Whose reaction took her by surprise. 'Ooooh, is it that hunky new Italian you're working for? I looked him up online.'

Once Clem explained that the baby was Tyler's, Audrey became a bit more subdued. 'You can stay for ever in the town house. There is plenty of room for us all. Know that you, and baby, will always be welcome. Put my vases away though, please.'

Clem smiled as she put the phone down.

She'd done it. She'd started telling people. There was still her dad, and Tyler's parents, but she would get to that.

She wondered how her father would react. They'd been estranged since she'd been around thirteen. He lived in Australia, and he'd seen her once a year, initially. But when Natalie had married Hugo, she'd felt awkward about the arrangement. Seeing her father had somehow felt disloyal to Hugo. So, she'd made excuses to stop him visiting. It had seemed such a waste for him to come all that way just to see her. At least, that was what she'd told herself. But she'd secretly missed him. He'd kept in touch by phone, and they talked occasionally, and she wondered if the news of the pregnancy might help them re-establish their now adult relationship.

She needed a little time. Time to get used to the idea of being a mum. Time to figure out all the family stuff. But it was only mid-July. There was plenty of time for all that.

The weeks flew past. For some reason, she was completely relaxed at work. Likely because Leo knew. The guy had literally seen her at her worst moment and still wanted her to work for him.

And the work was great; exciting, fulfilling and capable of distracting her from her problems.

The new gold company in particular was taking up a major amount of her time. She'd spent hours on Bond Street where the exclusive store was opening soon with a red-carpet event. She'd seen the names of the guests in the appointment book. It was a cross between a London Who's Who and a real celebrity guest list.

So, it was no surprise when Leo stuck his head out of his office. 'Bond Street again,' he said. 'Can you join me?'

'Sure,' was her immediate reaction.

He glanced at her. 'Do you want me to get a car?'

She smiled as she picked up her bag. 'Rather than the crowded, slightly smelly Tube on an August day?' She laughed and shook her head. 'How about we walk? I'd like some fresh air.'

If he was surprised he didn't say so, and they walked out into the warm, clammy London air.

The streets were busy with residents and tourists. As they walked along, Leo gave her a sideways glance. 'Want to stop for coffee, or decaf along the way?'

'I'd love an iced tea,' she said. 'So if you know somewhere good, that would be great.'

After a few minutes he gestured to a side street and stopped at a café with large fans and lots of plants.

As he set her iced peach tea in front of her Clem leaned forward to whisper, 'Do you think the plants are actually real?'

Leo laughed. 'I know they are. The owner is the sister of someone I went to uni with.'

Clem shook her head and frowned as she sipped her tea. 'Thirty days. That's how long anything that's green lasts around me.'

'So you don't have a touch for horticulture?'

She raised her eyebrows. 'Let's just say I like to admire gardens from afar. Very, very far.'

He smiled as he sipped his coffee. 'What do you think about our new clients?'

She gave a knowing smile. 'The demanding ones, you mean?'

'Oof!' he laughed as he leaned back in his chair and waved a hand in front of his face. When he was done laughing he leaned across the table towards her. 'So, even though you know they are family friends and have done business with Artullo's for years, you still call them demanding?'

Clem was unruffled. 'I call them demanding, because they are. They are opening a new branch of their store, in a city that's unfamiliar to them. The shop fittings haven't gone well because of late deliveries and supplier issues, which is adding to the stress. But—' she took a deep breath '—they have a wonderful reputation for their jewellery and gold work. We know this shop will be queued out of the door. They are well prepared. They have one of the most enhanced security systems I've ever seen. This is all last-minute nerves and in two weeks' time, it will all be forgotten about.' She gave a little sigh. 'I would just like to visit when the jewellery is actually there, in the cabinets, with the fancy lights that show all the jewels refracting and sparkling like something out of a fairy tale.'

He gave her an amused smile. Something inside her tingled. At times, when Leo looked at her like that, it gave her the feeling of butterfly wings against her skin. There was nothing in it, she told herself. He knew exactly how ineligible she was right now. But, deep down, it gave her hope that somewhere, out there, someone might make her feel like that in the future.

It was almost as if he could read her mind. 'How have things been?'

'With what?'

'With everything. You said you were going to tell some people about the baby last week.'

Clem nodded and sipped her tea again. 'I went to see Tyler's family and gave them a scan picture.' She took a deep breath, and blinked back the tears that instantly came to her eyes. 'It was hard. It was really hard.'

'Are they happy?'

She let her shoulders slump a little. 'So, so happy. It's their last piece of their son. And I guess once I have this baby I'll understand a bit better how that feels. But…' she paused, trying to find the right words '…now I feel a bit panicky. They've texted me constantly. They want to be involved. And that's fine, I want them to be…'

'But?' he prompted.

She sighed. 'They've been so sweet, but they've also become a bit overwhelming.' She shook her head.

Leo looked thoughtful. He pointed to her stomach. 'All the hopes and dreams they had invested in their son are now invested in you and this baby. That's a hard role to take on. Could your mum talk to them, maybe?'

She shook her head. 'They were friends while we were dating. But I don't want to cause an argument between them. I can't tell Mum how they're stressing me out a bit right now.'

Leo reached over and took her hand. 'Clem Grayson, this is your baby. Tyler isn't here. And while it's good that you have people to support you, all the decisions about this baby should be yours, not anyone else's.'

She gave him a weak smile. 'I know that in theory, but—' she let out her breath through her lips '—I'm hardly a baby expert. What I know about a baby I could write on the back of a postage stamp—' she gave a short laugh '—and still have room for you to write something too.'

He held up both hands, shaking his head with a smile on his face.

She leaned towards him. 'You never told me. Have your mother and sister forgiven me yet for rushing off from their dinner table and being sick in their guest bathroom?'

He didn't quite meet her eyes. 'They were fine. You saw that. As soon as they knew why you were feeling under the weather they understood completely.' He waggled a hand. 'My mother might have been a bit put out that you didn't want to see her hundred-and-three-year-old, extremely retired obstetrician, but apart from that? They just wanted to make sure you were all right.'

He was saying all the right words, but the atmosphere in the house had been…telling. Yes, his mother and sister had been polite, courteous, and had offered whatever help they had available. But she could tell they weren't really impressed that Leo's brand-new project manager had just found out she was pregnant. And Clem had the distinct feeling they'd been even less impressed when he'd told them there was no husband or father in the picture. The disapproval had been a palpable sensation she was sure she hadn't imagined.

But that was how things were, and thankfully, she'd had no reason to see them since the trip to Italy.

She drummed her fingers on the table. 'There's someone else I've been talking to.'

Leo must have sensed something big from her words. 'Who?'

'My dad.'

'Your dad?' He looked confused. 'Didn't you say he was dead?'

'No, that was Hugo, my stepfather. But my real dad, he's living in Australia.'

'How long has he been over there?'

'Since I was tiny. I saw him once a year up until I was thirteen. I kind of stopped seeing him once Mum married Hugo—it felt disloyal.'

'And now?'

'And now I needed to know my dad's family medical history to see if it would have any potential impact on my baby. So, I got back in touch to let him know I was pregnant.'

'How did that go down?'

'It turned into an immediate video call. He wanted to know if I was hurt, upset, if something had happened...'

'He basically panicked, then?' Leo asked knowingly.

She half smiled. 'He might have—just a little. He told me everything I needed to know, but...'

'But, what?'

She ran her fingers through her hair. 'I think I've missed having a dad. He asked if he can come and visit, and I kind of want him to.'

'So, what's the problem?'

She blinked at him. 'Mum, of course.'

Leo put his elbow on the table and leaned

his chin in his hand. 'Your life is a soap opera. Tell me more.'

'They got together when they were young. Split acrimoniously, after some family interference. She *won't* be happy if I tell her he's potentially coming over.' She winked. 'And don't think I missed that reference.'

'But you're all adults, surely you can make this work?'

'Maybe, maybe not. I'll speak to him in a few weeks. And I hate to break it to you, but if my life is a soap opera, you're in it too.'

'Touché,' he laughed, leaning back and finishing his coffee.

He gave her a few moments and then said, 'Clem, are you regretting your decision to have this baby?'

She lifted her hand to her chest. 'No, not really. Only when I haven't slept in hours, there's no one in the house with me, and I'm wondering if I'm really good enough to take all this on. Or when I have dreams that my baby is actually an alien and erupts from my stomach. Or I start looking at the list of everything I need to buy. Or when I wonder if I'll cope with even more sleepless nights because I really don't have a clue what I'm doing. Apart from that? Never.'

He was quiet for a few moments, as if he was taking in all the words that had just spilled out of her mouth without a filter. Then he looked up with his serious dark eyes. He asked the obvious question.

'When you're lying there worrying, you don't phone your mum, or your aunt that owns the house? Or your dad in Australia, as he'd probably be awake anyhow?'

For a moment, she was hooked by those eyes. Such a velvet-dark brown, so soulful, so full of empathy that she found it hard to speak. She wanted to reach out and touch him. But that wouldn't be appropriate. They were at work. This was only a pit stop for the day. He was only trying to be kind and, by now, he must be sorry he'd brought this conversation up. She'd be lucky if he ever wanted to talk to her again.

She shook her head. 'I don't want them to know. I want them all to think I'm doing fine. Because I am. Really, I am.'

And as she said those words, she wasn't entirely sure who she was trying to convince—him or herself.

Leo was trying to put himself in someone else's shoes. But his brain wouldn't fulfil the requirement. Maybe it was a male/female brain thing. Maybe his mind wouldn't allow him to pretend to be a woman, four years younger, with her whole life ahead of her, finding out her boyfriend had died, and now she was pregnant with his child. Having expectations of her, like an elephant planted between her shoulder blades. Staying in someone else's home, in a barely started job.

The trouble with this was only one word came to mind. Terrifying.

Every now and then, it was almost as if he saw that emotion flash across her face. It had certainly been there on the guest bathroom floor at his mother's house. But the terror had been mixed with a whole host of other emotions that he could bet right now Clem Grayson wouldn't normally let anyone see.

But he had been there that day, and he had seen it. Which meant he was in a privileged position.

He'd tried not to cringe when she'd asked about his mother's and sister's reactions to her pregnancy news. Thankfully, because Clem had been exhausted and upstairs, she hadn't heard the deluge of Italian voices asking one hundred questions at a time.

His mother's first reaction had been that Leo

was the baby's father. That had sent her off on a rant about Italian families, bloodlines, taking time to get to know someone, before she'd finally heard his sixth attempt to tell her this was not his child.

By that point, he'd been beyond annoyed. And when his mother had started a new rant about the inadvisability of being pregnant when starting a new job, he'd been just as colourful with his response to his mother about moving into the correct century, about there being laws to protect women, and the fact that Clem's lover had died in a horrible accident and that this was an unexpected outcome.

His sister had tried to join in, but he'd silenced them both, telling them sternly that he expected them to go out of their way to be nice to Clem while she got over the shock of the discovery, and to help her with anything she might need. To be fair to them, from that point onwards, they had been fine.

But his sister had winked and had told him he would have been better to say it was his baby, because his mother still had a reason to plot weddings with other Italian families.

Looking back, he thought Juliette might have been right.

But now, as he made his way towards the

jeweller's with Clem, he felt oddly comfortable with her by his side. Her dark red hair was
shining as they threaded their way through the
crowded streets. He could see the glances that
were thrown in her direction. It wasn't overly
obvious she was pregnant, as her suit jacket
was open and hanging loosely. She chattered
away, smiling and glancing at him, and he did
his best to push his feelings away.

He couldn't help but notice how good she
looked right now. That word that was used to
describe pregnant women—glowing, was it?
Absolutely applied to Clem right now. She was
gorgeous and he was doing his best to ignore
his ongoing attraction to her. She had enough
to contend with. The last thing she needed was
a boss who considered himself as anything
other than her boss. Theirs would remain a
purely professional relationship.

He shook his head. They had work to focus
on. Clem was incredibly astute. And Leo
agreed with her summary of the situation.
The team at Pellegrini's Jewellers were having a last-minute attack of nerves. There was
a great amount of pressure on the team. Their
investment in the building in central London
was huge, and they'd paid a ridiculous price
for the site. Their exclusive store came with

exclusive fittings. If anything was less than perfect, some eagle-eyed journalist or celebrity was sure to comment.

One brand-new staff member had dropped out at the last minute for a similar job in Dubai, and another staff member had failed at the final security hurdle due to something not having been declared. Tempers were getting frayed.

Leo knocked on the still-covered door—the trademark gold glass inlay wouldn't be seen by the public until the official opening. After a few moments it was partly opened and they were ushered inside.

While the final finishes were still being completed, and electric wiring was visible in the black-velvet-lined cabinets, the majority of the work in the store had been done.

Clem trailed her finger along the glass-topped cabinet as they walked through to the offices at the back. A strong smell of metal and the noise of grinding split the air around them. Both Clem and Leo winced.

Ricardo, the man who was going to be the manager of this branch, appeared. From his wizened face it was difficult to put an age on him. 'This way,' he said, waving his hand at the noise, adding, 'Final adjustments to the safe.'

Leo saw Clem's eyes widen in interest for a second, and he could sense the hundred questions that were circulating. He bent down and whispered in her ear. 'These jewellers use the same safe installers that Artullo's use. We can get a guided tour back at the bank.'

'Oh, don't worry,' she whispered back. 'I've already had the tour of the safe at the bank. How could I plan my perfect heist without one?' She winked at him. 'I planned to audition for the next *Mission Impossible* movie.'

They sat down with Ricardo and went over a number of further transactions needed to complete all the contracts with the bank and the insurance company. Ricardo complained about delays, shipments, tradesmen, working hours, the weather and the plumbing. It seemed he had a lot to get off his chest. But Leo and Clem listened politely in an attempt to placate their client's worries. There was a pile of glossy brochures next to them, and Ricardo couldn't help but notice that Clem's gaze kept being drawn to them.

When they had finished their business, he pulled one towards him and flipped it over. 'Are you interested in gold work, or signature gemstones?' Ricardo's eyes brightened. It was clear that this was where his true love was—the actual business of making beautiful jewellery.

Leo smiled as he watched a little colour stain Clem's cheeks. She gave a huge smile. 'To be honest, I'm interested in everything, but I fear it will all be out of my price range.'

Ricardo flicked through the brochure. 'Remember that our most exquisite pieces are all custom-made to order. Designed with the customer for an individual experience. But these are the items we carry in stock. We can also source gems for customers and then design their piece around the gem they've custom-ordered.'

'Like Magdalena Amora's blue diamond?' she asked. The popular movie star was widely rumoured to have got her latest engagement ring from the branch in LA. To be fair, it was her fourth engagement ring, but who was counting?

Ricardo tapped the side of his nose. 'We never reveal who our clientele are, but I do believe Ms Amora has an *extraordinary* ring.'

Leo couldn't help but watch the exchange. Clem was in her element, describing a piece her godmother had once shown her with intricate, delicate gold work, and Ricardo finding similar items, and telling her, in great detail, about the hours of craftsmanship involved, and that only a few goldsmiths in the world had that level of skill.

She really did put people completely at their ease, he realised. She wondered at some of the sample gemstones in the brochure and didn't even blink when Ricardo told her the price— seven times her current salary. As Leo continued to watch, he could see all the tension that had been in Ricardo's face and shoulders when they'd first arrived gradually dissipate.

It was hard to qualify that gift in words. How would someone describe that in a job advert as a quality they wanted in their staff?

By the time they were finished, Ricardo was laughing and joking, inviting them back for the opening night in a fortnight.

As she stood, Clem straightened her skirt. 'In a fortnight, I'll likely need a new wardrobe,' she joked. 'I don't think I'll fit into much any more.'

Ricardo blinked as she smiled and pointed directly to her belly. 'I'm expecting and, at the moment, seem to be getting bigger every day.'

The reaction from Ricardo was instantaneous. Ricardo jumped to his feet and threw

his arms around her. 'Wonderful, congratulations, *bella*! What a gift, what a blessing,' he
crooned as he leaned back and gave the slightest touch to her cheek. 'And I can already tell
you will be a wonderful *mamma.*'

Leo could tell that Clem was a little stunned.
But she smiled gratefully and assured Ricardo
that she would see him again in two weeks.

Once they got outside, it took Leo a few
steps to realise that Clem wasn't walking next
to him.

He turned. She was standing outside the
jeweller's as if she was trying to catch her
breath. He took a few strides back to her.
'Clem? You okay?'

Her hand moved, wiping a tear he hadn't
noticed from her face. She gave a nod, her
lips pressed together for a second. 'Yes,' she
gulped. 'It's just…' she took another breath
and smiled sadly at Leo '…that's the first time
I've had a reaction like that to my pregnancy.
Unadulterated joy.' The tears started flowing
again. 'Everyone else has had questions, or
giant pauses, or worry written all over their
faces.'

She sighed as she wiped away more tears.
'I'm being silly. But if I'd ever imagined being
pregnant, then that's what I thought the reac-

tions around me would have been like. Like
Ricardo's.'

A part of him squirmed. He remembered
his own reaction. His own questions. And
now he wished he hadn't done that. He wished
he'd simply picked her off the bathroom floor,
swung her around and congratulated her.

Only that wasn't his job. That wasn't his
role in her life.

But he could tell by her face how it must
feel to have everyone question every part of
her life before they found the time to use the
word 'Congratulations'.

How horrible. How hard.

Something swelled deep down inside him.
A wave of protectiveness towards her. It didn't
matter that he'd known her only two months.

He liked her. She was nice. She was good
at her job. She'd had a rough last few weeks
and she deserved to be happy.

And if Leo Constello could help with the
happiness part of her life? Then he certainly
would.

CHAPTER FOUR

LEO PUSHED THE box across the desk towards her. 'Now,' he said carefully, 'I don't want you to take this the wrong way, but…'

'Good things don't usually start with those words,' said Clem automatically, her brows rising. The flat box on her desk had a designer logo on it. She absolutely wanted to open it.

He lifted his hands. 'You've been kind of quiet these last two weeks and I remembered what you said when we left Pellegrini's.'

He swallowed, wondering if he was about to make an absolute mess of this. 'You agreed to come to the opening, and you mentioned you'd probably need new clothes, and as this is a work event I thought we should supply you with something.'

He pointed to the box.

'You picked me something to wear?' He could tell from her tone she was totally surprised.

'Yes, and no,' he admitted. 'I asked my sister to deal with the sizing. I just picked the dress and checked it would be suitable for someone who was pregnant.'

Her hands froze about the box. 'Juliette helped with this? Are you sure there isn't a secret hex doll buried in here?'

'Stop that.' He paused, then added, 'She likes you.'

'When you tell her to,' said Clem, with no hint of irony.

She opened the box and stared in. Her hand brushed over the pale blue satin. She lifted the dress, shaking it so it opened out for her. Sleeveless but with thick straps, a V in the front, some ruching around the waist going to one side with a silver clasp, and reaching her knees, with a hint of a split in the front.

She tilted her head and looked at the design around the waistline. 'That will virtually disguise my bump,' she said, nodding her head in critical approval.

'Do you like it?' He was waiting for her to say she hated the design, or it was her least favourite colour.

'It's beautiful, Leo. But way out of my price range.' She laid the dress back on the tissue paper. 'I'm just…not sure you should be giving me presents. It might give people ideas.'

'What ideas? And anyway, you're accompanying me to a business event. I should cover the cost of what you wear.'

She rolled her eyes at him. 'Because I couldn't possibly have any dresses at home that might work.'

'You said that you were going to need to buy a new wardrobe soon.'

She patted her tummy. 'I do, actually. Some things just won't zip up any more. But this was clearly very expensive.'

He shrugged. 'If you like it, that's all that matters, isn't it?'

She kept looking at the dress. Then, after a few seconds, she whipped it back up and walked to the doorway. 'Well, let's see if your sister got the sizing right,' she said over her shoulder.

Leo crossed his fingers that his sister hadn't sabotaged him as he waited for Clem to reappear. She came back in a few moments later.

Leo couldn't help but smile. She was stunning. The V in the dress was low enough to complement her figure without being revealing, and the pale colour made her dark red hair stand out even more.

He could see just the hint of her stomach. It wasn't obvious she was pregnant, but if she chose to tell people, they would be able to admire the start of her curving abdomen.

Yes, he'd told her he'd supplied the dress because it was a work event. But the truth was, he knew she'd had a lot to cope with recently, and he'd wanted to take this one thing off her shoulders. To see her smile in pleasure.

He said the words, just as he'd thought them. 'You look stunning.' He couldn't help it.

Her lips moved to a gentle smile. And he'd never been so grateful that no one else was in the room. It was just them. This was solely *their* moment.

There was silence. He could hear her breathing. He could hear his own breaths too, and feel the thud of his heart against his chest wall. He was sure he shouldn't be feeling like this about Clem. But he did. It was a fact. And he could almost reach out and grab what was twinkling in the air between them.

Something about this moment was ignoring the red caution flags waving in his brain.

He liked Clem Grayson. He liked being around her. Wasn't it time to stop fighting it?

No. He still wasn't sure how she really felt about Tyler. Why would he deliberately hurt himself by potentially pitching himself against a man who was dead, but still doubtless held a lot of happy memories for Clem? He should start dating again. For some reason he hadn't bothered, ever since he'd met Clem.

Dating had never been difficult for him; women usually scrambled over themselves to get to him, but he realised now that his head had been so full of Clem recently that he hadn't even contemplated it. Maybe it was time to distract himself and get back out there?

The silence broke between them.

'Well, it's a perfect fit; Juliette knocked it out of the park,' Clem admitted, glancing downwards to her painted toenails. It was as if she'd had to say something. As if the moment had got too fraught, and she'd urgently needed to break the tension.

He took an easy breath, focusing on those very nice toes. 'Shoes,' he said, running his fingers through his hair. 'I have shoes for you, too.'

'You do?'

She followed him through to his office where two shoeboxes were sitting on a chair. 'These were more difficult,' he said a little gruffly. 'Wasn't sure what height you'd prefer.'

She opened the boxes and looked at the two

similar-sized sparkling sandals with different sizes of heels.

'How far do I need to walk?' she asked critically.

'Just around Pellegrini's. I've ordered a car to take us there, and one will take you home.'

Her eyes met his at the mention of her home. There had been no reason for Leo to ever visit her home so far, although he knew where it was. It was as though something froze somewhere in the universe, leaving Leo in his work suit and Clem in her new satin dress stuck staring at each other. It likely didn't last long. But it seemed as if it lasted for ever, because Leo didn't want to look away.

Her green eyes were totally fixed on him. He could swear he felt tremors going down his spine.

Leo Constello had dated a substantial number of women. Only one had lasted a bit longer than the others, but that had been a set-up between both families. Caroline had eventually admitted that, although she liked Leo and could easily fall in love with him, she was worried about both their families pushing them into an engagement and marriage before they were ready. It had been the wake-up call he'd needed. Because she'd been entirely right. They'd parted ways on the best of terms, and even had a joke agreement that they might get back together in future years, if they were both still single.

But he'd never felt like this about her, or anyone else. Not the sensations currently running through his spine. Was Clem the most beautiful woman he'd ever seen? Maybe not to other people, but somewhere in Leo's brain, all the right things were firing. All in extremely good ways.

Her pink tongue appeared, tentatively licking her lips, and he almost let out a groan, before tearing his gaze away. 'Happy with the shoes?' he murmured.

'Sure,' she said, not helping things at all by slipping her foot into one and extending her leg so she could admire it. He started to laugh and shook his head at himself. He should probably start dating again. Soon.

'What?' she asked, still staring at the shoe and clearly having no awareness of the fact his brain and body were busy sending messages like fireworks that lit up his entire nervous system.

'Nothing,' he said hoarsely. 'I need to get changed. I'll call the car for us.'

He moved swiftly through to his office,

which had a large accompanying bathroom. Leo had brought a suit from home for the event this evening and it took him only a few minutes to get changed.

'Aren't we going to be a bit early?' asked Clem, glancing at her watch.

'Ricardo asked if we could go early,' he replied. 'I think he wants to make sure everything is perfect before he opens the doors to the press.'

'I'm not surprised; there are lots of celebs coming,' Clem said.

Leo shrugged his shoulders, unimpressed. 'I'm sure there are. I usually avoid these kinds of things, but since Pellegrini's are a valued customer of ours, avoidance is not an option.'

'Are you like the Christmas grinch?' Clem asked, with a glint in her eye.

'It's only the beginning of September, and you're asking me if I'm the Christmas grinch?'

'It's never too early for Christmas.' She winked at him and he groaned.

'Oh no, don't tell me you're one of those people that celebrate Christmas for around six months a year?'

'Three.' She held up her fingers. 'I definitely start in October; November is when it begins to get serious and December is go time.' She looked at him sternly. 'You'd better have some Christmas jumpers.'

He closed his eyes for a second. 'I have no Christmas jumpers because I have no need for Christmas jumpers. I have perfectly good clothes that I can wear all year round.'

'Knew it.' She snapped her fingers. 'You are a secret Christmas grinch.'

'Again, it's September, so why are we talking about Christmas?'

'Why don't you like Christmas?' she asked, hands on her hips, ignoring what he'd just said.

He sighed and threw up his hands. 'Christmas is too big these days. Too commercial. Christmas in Italy is incredibly…busy. Our families are large and loud, and, mainly, I can't hear myself think. There are always demands to do things with others, play games, join in. Is it wrong that I just want things to be quiet, to have time to myself?'

She gave him a careful look. 'And that's part of what I love about Christmas. The buzz. The atmosphere. Being around other people that are happy. Making memories. Feeling good.'

He raised his eyebrows and said a few words. 'Noise. Chaos. Headaches.'

She picked up her jacket and slung it around her shoulders. 'Don't worry, I have plenty of time to work on you. You might even be my Christmas resolution this year.'

'Aren't resolutions supposed to be a New Year's thing?'

'When you're a Christmas girl, you make all things around that time of year about Christmas.'

Leo sighed mournfully. 'I can see I have unleashed the Christmas beast.' He looked around the office. 'Absolutely no Christmas decorations in here, please. I have to draw the line somewhere.'

Clem stuck her fingers in her ears and started walking. 'La, la, la, la, la.'

He pressed the button for the elevator and shook his head. 'Focus, Ms Grayson. We are going to pat our client on the back, tell him everything looks wonderful and help ensure his grand opening goes without a hitch.'

She pulled her fingers away from her ears and nodded. 'I think this will be a dream. Ricardo already has the gift. You can see when he talks about jewellery what a passion he has for his job.'

'If only I could say the same about you.' It was a quip, but Clem gave a little start and straightened.

'You think I don't like my job?'

He held up a hand. 'Joking, Clem. I'm just joking. Promise me you won't fall in those shoes and twist an ankle.'

She gave something that sounded like a snort. 'I could run a mile in these shoes. Amateur.'

The expression on her face was almost a challenge. But he didn't have time for that. As the elevator doors slid open, he walked towards the central doors and the waiting car outside.

It was past the time for rush-hour traffic in London, so they glided through the streets and waited in a queue of vehicles outside Pellegrini's. There was an actual red carpet outside. 'I thought we were arriving early,' said Clem.

'We are,' agreed Leo. 'Looks like Pellegrini's is the hottest place in town tonight.'

They waited for their turn and Leo walked around to take her hand as she exited the car. He resisted the temptation to look at her legs, and kept his eyes focused on her face.

This was work. This was a job. And what he wouldn't concentrate on was the fact that he already knew Clem would be the most beautiful woman in the place tonight.

Ricardo practically combusted as they

walked through the door. 'Everyone is early!' he exclaimed.

Clem looked around. There were several staff with silver trays handing out canapés and champagne. She made her way over to the side and whispered in someone's ear.

'What are you up to?' asked Leo as he moved alongside her.

She smiled. 'It's a secret.' Clem took a deep breath. 'Now, you've brought me to Aladdin's cave, let me have a look around and dream.'

Clem moved from glass case to glass case, now full to bursting, admiring the sapphires, diamonds, rubies and emeralds. They had some of their signature designs from the catalogues, with tiny gold filigree earrings and rings. The shop was very busy. Leo recognised a few people that were also customers of the bank. They nodded at him.

'Uh oh,' whispered Clem as she looked discreetly over her shoulder.

'What is it?'

'That couple behind us—her in the white trouser suit, and him in the black? They won that huge reality TV show last year. They've been everywhere.' She gave Leo a nudge. 'What if we're going to witness them looking for an engagement ring?'

'Looks more likely that we're going to witness them having a spat,' he said under his breath. Then his brow furrowed. 'Who did you say they were? I don't recognise them at all.'

'Do you watch any reality TV?'

He shook his head.

'Well then, you just need to rely on me to be your celebrity Z spotter.'

He rolled his eyes as he put his hand gently on her back. His skin immediately prickled as his hand came into contact with her bare skin. There it was again. That sensation that he constantly tried to push down and ignore. That zing. He told his brain it wasn't really there. He was at a work event, with a work colleague. Nothing more, nothing less. 'I'm not even going to ask what that means.'

'Here you are, madam.' A uniformed man appeared with a glass for Clem, she smiled, thanked him and took a sip.

Leo frowned. 'What's that?'

'Soda water with a tiny hint of lime. It looks sparkly and will stop any questions I don't want to answer.'

'You don't want anyone to know that you're pregnant? Well, apart from Ricardo, of course.'

She shook her head. 'I don't know anyone here. I don't imagine anyone will ask. This looks almost the same as the sparkling wine that they are serving. It'll help me fade into the background.'

Leo burst out laughing. 'Clem, there's no way you can fade into the background, especially not in that dress. You're the prettiest woman in the room.'

Her head tilted up towards him and she shot him the most genuine smile. 'Thank you,' she said in a quiet voice. 'But I don't think that footballer over there, with his model wife, would agree with you.'

'Well, we're not going to ask them, are we?' he said, as if they spoke to the celebrity couple every day.

She snorted.

'Oh, I recognise her.' He gestured with his head to the TV presenter currently talking with Ricardo.

Clem watched carefully. 'She's got a reputation for being nice. Let's hope it's true. I don't want Ricardo stressed this evening.'

Leo glanced down at her. He liked that. She was protective of their client. Even strangely maternal towards a man who was likely several decades older than her.

But Ricardo had a vulnerability about him. He did stress over things, and Leo was glad that Clem recognised this and wanted to look out for him. Artullo's bank didn't just look after businesses, they looked after people.

Leo could say that, over the years, his family members had been part counsellors, cheerleaders, therapists, and medical advisors. On more than one occasion Leo, his father, uncle or sister had urged a client to make contact with their doctor after complaining about mild, yet persistent symptoms.

As they moved along to the pristine cases, Clem started to name who she thought would wear certain pieces. 'This one is Jackie O, and this one—so elegant, it reminds me of Grace Kelly.' She let out a little gasp, 'This? It's like from the film *Pretty Woman*. You know, when Richard Gere shows Julia Roberts the diamond necklace and catches her fingers with the box?'

Leo leaned forward for a better look at the necklace. 'I guess it is a bit similar.'

'And this ring is for Zendaya—she had something similar on in a press article the other day. Isn't it stunning?'

He watched her for a few moments, her eyes bright. Occasionally, her hand rested on her belly, for only a few seconds, and he only noticed because he was right beside her.

'So, what do you actually like?'

'Hmmm.' She glanced all around the store. People were crowded in front of some of the cases and it wasn't easy to see everything. She pointed to the other side. 'I could write you a list,' she joked, 'but I don't need to. I liked a stunning emerald and diamond ring over there.' She rolled her eyes. 'Totally in my price range…not.'

'You could always sell the town house.'

She laughed. 'Told you, it's not mine.' Her face became a bit more serious. 'But Aunt Audrey told me that me and the baby are welcome to stay as long as we want to, so that's a relief.'

Leo could feel little hairs pricking at the back of his neck. She was definitely going to stay? 'I wondered if you might have wanted to go back to Surrey and live with your mum after you had the baby.'

Clem looked at him in surprise. 'Why?'

He shrugged. 'I thought you might want a hand.'

Clem started to catch on. 'You thought I might want to move back home permanently?'

'Yes.'

'You thought I might not want to come back to work?'

'I didn't like to ask,' he admitted.

She lifted her hand and placed it on his arm. 'Leo, I'll take maternity leave and then come back to work. I might ask my mum to come and help me for the first few weeks. But Surrey isn't five minutes away. And she has her own life to live.' She bit her bottom lip for a moment and gave a sigh. 'If I asked my mum, she would do anything for me.' She put her hand on her chest. 'But I want to do this myself. I want to be able to manage.' She shot him a beaming smile. 'And I have a wonderful job that I'm just starting to get my teeth into, so why would I want to give that up?'

'You're not worried about childcare?'

'I'll start looking into options soon. One of the other women in the bank told me her childminder is likely to have an opening some time next year.'

It was the oddest sensation. As if an elephant that he didn't even know had been there had stepped off his shoulders. He felt instantly lighter in his steps now he'd heard Clem say she wanted to come back to work and would continue to stay in London. He wasn't a fool. He knew that a whole variety of things could impact on those choices, but if this was how Clem was feeling right now? He couldn't help but be glad and secretly relieved.

She pointed a finger at him. 'Now, don't think I've finished choosing all the imaginary jewellery I could wish for in here. If I have a small lottery win, I would go for the gold filigree necklace, the one that looks like a tree.'

They'd moved several cabinets over. The delicate gold tree design was small, and inside a gold hoop. It was one of the least expensive items in the shop, but still substantial. He watched her reflection in the glass as she grinned at it, and lifted her finger, as if she wanted to touch.

'Why this one?' he asked curiously.

She turned her head up to him, holding his gaze with those green eyes. 'I have absolutely no idea,' she admitted. 'I'm just drawn to it. Sometimes there's no explanation for things. Sometimes things just are.'

Clem was trying to keep her voice steady. But something was building between her and Leo. She'd seen the visible shift in his demeanour when she'd told him she was staying in London and definitely coming back to work after the baby was born. She'd felt the zing when he'd touched her back earlier. It was all she could do not to lean into his hand.

She hadn't considered for one second that

Leo would have worried about anything like that. Surely he would just replace her once she left? For her maternity leave, and maybe for ever?

But all these little skittering moments and growing feelings were starting to add up. She was beginning to forget she was pregnant with someone else's child.

He'd presented her with this gorgeous designer dress and shoes this evening. Why would a boss do that? She knew that he'd made an excuse about it being for a work function and that he'd said his sister had helped source it. But, somewhere, deep down inside her, things kept nudging at Clem.

The glances, the jokes, the teasing, the looks between them that were held just a few moments longer than they needed to be.

When he'd told her she looked stunning tonight, she swore she could have floated away on an imaginary pink cloud, her unicorn right beside her.

Was she making all this up in her head? It didn't seem like it. She could sense it. The twinkle in the air between them. It had been there since they'd first met. And even though most men would have run a thousand miles when Clem had found out she was carrying another man's baby, strangely, Leo hadn't given her those vibes at all.

He'd been caring. Considerate. Was it too much to hope that this connection between them could be something else?

Maybe her pregnancy hormones were playing havoc with her brain and the sizzle she sensed was in her imagination. Now that *would* be embarrassing.

But the way that Leo had looked at her hand when she'd placed it on his arm? No. That was something. It was.

'Sometimes things just are,' he repeated back in a voice that was barely above a whisper. Just for her to hear.

This was like a Cinderella moment. The designer dress and shoes. The celebrities of all alphabet letters around her. The millions of pounds' worth of jewellery. This was a night not to be repeated, and she wanted to live every second of it.

It was hard to keep all the balls juggling in the air that her brain seemed to lob there. Could she be a single parent? Would she be good enough to bring up a child on her own? Would she ever have a chance to meet someone for herself? What if her concentration at work was ruined, and she didn't perform at her job? What if her body decided to keep the shape of a nine-month-pregnant woman for ever? How would she cut her toenails in the final month?

She was reading too much into this thing with Leo. She had to be realistic. He was her boss. And he was a good boss. That was all. She was having someone else's baby. Of course he wasn't interested in her in a personal way.

As another glass of soda water and lime was pressed into her hand she nudged Leo. 'Follow me.' She smiled. 'I just spotted chocolate.'

He let out a laugh that he turned into a cough when several heads turned and she slipped through the crowd to where a waiter was holding a silver tray adorned with fine-smelling chocolates.

Leo pointed to the sign and grinned. 'Italian chocolatier.' He leaned and whispered in her ear. 'I might know all these by sight. What do you like? Cherry? Truffle? Caramel? Dark chocolate? Mousse?'

'Orange, lime, blackcurrant and nuts. You didn't mention any of those. Please tell me they make them.'

His eyebrows rose in amusement. 'That's

very specific.' The amusement deepened. 'Are you having cravings already?'

Her hand went to her stomach automatically. 'I didn't think so. But I swear, I could smell that chocolate from across the room.'

He handed her a plate and pointed. 'That one, that one and that one. I can buy you some of these if you want.'

'Yes please,' she said without hesitation. Then wondered how much they might cost. Never mind.

Ricardo appeared next to them. Kissing her on both cheeks. 'You are having a good time? You think all the other guests are happy?' He looked anxiously from side to side.

'How many appointments have people made for the custom jewellery?' Clem prompted.

Ricardo looked thoughtful. 'Another thirty this evening. Three hundred overall. The waiting list is growing.'

Leo clapped his shoulder. 'That's wonderful. Just what you want.'

And while Ricardo seemed happy he kept his focus on Clem. He didn't touch her stomach but gave it a courteous nod. 'Your baby. You find out soon what you're having?'

Clem was happy he'd remembered, and thought how nice it was for him to ask. 'Thirteenth of September,' she said. 'I have my detailed scan then, but I've decided not to ask what I'm having. Call me old-fashioned, but I want it to be a surprise.'

'Bravo!' exclaimed Ricardo. 'And I have something for you.'

He pulled open a drawer and lifted out a fine gold bracelet, with a tiny charm. The charm was a tiny baby. He held it up and let it glisten in the light. Clem caught her breath.

'Oh, my goodness. That's beautiful.' She could feel a wave of anxiety. 'Ricardo, I can't possibly accept a gift like this.'

His face beamed. 'Thank your boss. I told him we wanted to give you a gift for all your hard work but weren't sure what to give you. He said a gift might compromise the principles of the bank. He commissioned it and covered the cost.'

Ricardo had already fastened the fine chain around her wrist as he spoke. 'A beautiful gift, for a beautiful lady.'

Clem's heart seemed to swell in her chest. Leo had commissioned this just for her? She kissed Ricardo on both cheeks and thanked him profusely. The workmanship was exquisite. And it was only a few seconds before someone was pulling him away again.

She tried to remain rational. Leo would probably have done this for any staff member he valued who'd done a particularly good job. It didn't necessarily mean anything else.

She turned to face Leo. Space was tight now, as even more people had arrived, so now they were chest to chest, with only a few inches between them. She put both of her hands on his upper arms. 'I'm getting a little warm,' she whispered.

'Ready for some fresh air?'

She nodded, and he slid his hand into hers and weaved through the bustling crowd. It took a few moments to get through the throng of people at the door and Leo gestured for their car to pull up to the front.

As they waited for the car, he slid his jacket around her shoulders, opening the door for her as it drew up.

She looked up at him. 'Thank you,' she said before sliding into the back of the car.

Leo walked around the other side and climbed in the back next to her. She nodded at her own jacket lying on the seat. 'Silly not to take it in with me.'

'Are you warm enough now?' he asked.

She pulled his suit jacket further around her. It felt good. She could smell his aftershave from it, and the satin lining was smooth on her skin.

'Perfect,' she said, and meant it. She held up her arm and gently shook the bracelet. 'This is too much. Thank you. Ricardo said you paid for it.'

He gave a casual smile. 'It stopped any complications. You like it?'

His words seemed so matter-of-fact. As she'd suspected, she'd been reading too much into things. 'I do,' she said, trying not to be disappointed. 'It's a beautiful gift. Thank you.'

He gave her a sideways glance as the car pulled into the London traffic. It was surprisingly light and they moved quickly. 'You never said it was so soon until your next scan.'

'You never asked,' she replied promptly, her heartbeat quickening. She fixed on those brown eyes. It felt as if they were dancing around each other, not saying what they really meant.

'Is your mother going with you to the scan?'

Clem gulped. 'I haven't asked her to.'

He gave her a curious glance. 'Do you want to go by yourself? Or maybe you want to ask someone from Tyler's family?'

Tyler's family. He said the words easily,

with no hesitation, no disapproval in his tone. She shook her head. 'I want to be sure that everything is fine first. I'd hate to invite them along and then find out there's anything wrong with the baby. They were devastated enough by what happened to Tyler. I'm not sure they could take anything else.'

'Are you nervous about that?'

She gave a laugh, although she wasn't quite sure where it came from. 'Of course I am. Any woman would be. All anyone wants is for their baby to be healthy.'

He looked thoughtful. 'And you don't care what you have? You don't want to decorate a nursery or buy clothes?'

She breathed out slowly. 'I can decorate and buy clothes in neutral colours for whatever comes.'

He was looking at her with such intensity and understanding that she felt a little over-whelmed. 'Do you want company at the scan?'

Her breath caught in her throat. She'd wanted him to ask, but hadn't thought that he would. Did she really want to go to that ap-pointment, and look around the waiting room at all the other happy couples, and be sitting there herself? No, not really.

She licked her dry lips. 'That would be nice,' she said, trying to keep her voice steady.

'Then put a note in my diary. I'll take you,' he said without hesitation.

She thought about her swelling stomach and how it might not be the most attractive sight in the world. But Leo wasn't a little boy. He knew exactly what he'd see if he came to that appointment with her.

His hand squeezed over hers and she shot him a smile. 'Thank you.'

The car slowed and Clem realised they'd pulled up outside Audrey's town house. The driver got out automatically to walk around and open her door.

She lifted her head as Leo leaned over to kiss her on the cheek, as Ricardo had done earlier.

She'd turned her face to his, about to say something else. But the timing was all wrong. So, just as his lips were about to touch her cheek, they touched her lips instead.

The kiss was light, but he opened his eyes, clearly realising something had changed.

And it had. Even though the kiss had been soft, gentle and fleeting.

She pulled back, her eyes fixed on his. His were slightly widened, clearly caught out with the surprise. She could only hope his heart was racing just as hers was.

'Thank you for the lovely evening, Leo,' she said in a low voice as the car door opened and she stepped out into the warm London air, already knowing she wouldn't sleep a single wink tonight.

CHAPTER FIVE

IT HAD BEEN two weeks since the accidental kiss and Leo was slowly but surely going out of his mind. Should he make a move on a pregnant woman—someone who was likely vulnerable and possibly still in love with the baby's father?

All sensible words shouted no. But all the cells in his body shouted yes!

Clem hadn't said a word to him about it since, but she'd floated around the office with a huge smile on her face, getting through her work as if she were being chased in a marathon.

He might have made an error in asking his sister to help with the dress. There had been a number of messages and calls in recent days, all about Italian friends in London, and very, very distant relatives he might consider dating.

Leo could find his own women; he definitely didn't need anyone else to interfere.

But his mind wasn't on anyone right now that wasn't Clem, so he was ignoring all communication from his family.

Clem had mentioned she'd been speaking to her father more. She'd also mentioned that her father might come over from Australia, and he wondered what he would think about his pregnant daughter dating someone else.

This was the trouble, really. When he sat down and considered everything, it felt as if the whole world were telling him to walk away.

But the whole world wasn't in a room with him and Clem. When it was just them? They could tease, have fun, and flirt with each other, and it felt entirely right. Trouble was, his brain kept going back to his underlying concern—what if Clem wasn't over Tyler?

Today was the day for the scan, and he'd promised to go with her. His phone started ringing again as he was due to walk out of the door.

He signalled to his secretary. 'I'm out of the office for the next few hours with Clem. I'll pick up anything when I come back later.'

Clem was waiting in a bright green raincoat as he walked through to pick her up. She was jostling from one foot to the other. 'Nervous?' he asked.

Her fingers grabbed for a lock of bright red hair and started twisting and twirling it. 'No,' she said, looking him in the eye. 'I mean, it's only a routine scan. Everything should be fine.'

The way she said the words he could tell she was trying to convince herself.

As she knotted her hands together in the elevator he decided some distraction was in order.

'You know how we handle the banking and accounts for Hansons?' It was a large independent department store in the heart of London.

She nodded, half listening, half thinking about something else.

'If you feel up to it, you can help them with their Christmas campaign.'

'What?' Her head shot around.

He smiled. 'You said you like Christmas. They always decorate the store and have a huge campaign. They've been let down by a supplier. So, the plan they had for this year had to be scrapped. Over the next two weeks they'll be working on another—and they've asked if we could help with the costings.'

Clem had her hand on her hip now. 'Hansons, the place that had the whole department store as Santa's Grotto one year, the Grinch's house the next and the Polar Express another year?'

He nodded. A smile started to spread across her face. 'I think I could manage to help with that.' There was a gleam in her eyes. 'I'd probably get the chance to make lots of lists.'

He raised his eyebrows. 'Because they've been let down last minute, there's a chance their normal costs could soar. Keeping an eye on the budget will be your main concern.'

The doors slid open and they walked outside to where the car was waiting.

Clem turned and put a hand on Leo's chest. 'My main concern will be making sure the children of the world see the magic of Christmas before them. Their hopes and dreams will be met, and they'll still believe in Santa.' She winked at him. 'That, and the costings.'

He couldn't help but laugh as he climbed in the car next to her and they headed to the hospital. She kept her hands on her lap and he could see them twisting together.

After a few minutes, he couldn't stand it any more and put his hand on top of hers. 'Stop worrying, Clem. Everything is going to be fine.'

Her eyes were wide as she turned to him.

'But this is the stage where they can find things wrong. With the heart, the kidneys and brain. The bones. All sorts of things.'

'You've had your first round of tests and scans?'

'Yes.'

'And there was nothing to worry about?'

She nodded.

'So, take a deep breath. In an hour's time this will all be over, and you'll likely have another picture of your baby.'

Her lips were pressed together but she nodded again. He could feel the tension emanating from her. He felt helpless, all of a sudden. He was so clueless about babies and yet he was trying to reassure her? What did he actually know?

Part of him wanted to back out of going with her. But he would never do that to Clem. And some part of him, he realised, wanted to know that this baby was okay. It struck him how strange that was, but he pushed it aside.

When they arrived at the hospital she sat in silence until they were called. Leo wasn't entirely sure of his role here. He didn't want to overstep, so he waited until Clem gestured with her head that he was to join her.

As the sonographer closed the door behind

them and issued some instructions to Clem, she climbed up onto the examination couch.

She took a breath. 'This is my friend Leo,' she said in a shaky voice. 'And I don't want to know what I'm having. I just want to know if everything is okay.'

Leo could tell from the sonographer's expression that she'd dealt with anxious patients before. She talked in a reassuring, calm voice and explained exactly what she'd be doing, and what she'd be looking at. 'Let's decide what to call your baby before we start—just in case you think I've slipped up and told you the gender.'

Clem took a breath. 'Just refer to the baby as he.'

'No problem,' said the sonographer. She lifted a large tube. 'I'm just going to put a little gel on your stomach.'

She flicked the lights off and started putting her transducer on Clem's stomach and pointing out everything she was looking at. Leo had seen scans on TV before, but he'd never been in the room. He felt like some kind of biology student as the sonographer pointed out the stomach, brain, spine, bones, heart, kidneys and face. At every step of the way she gave reassurance to Clem.

He watched as Clem's face started off tight, with frown lines across her forehead, becoming more relaxed and finally smiling. The sonographer explained that the earlier scan photos were usually better, before printing out a few for Clem anyway.

As they made their way outside he could almost see the weight shedding off her with every step.

Her footsteps got quicker and when they reached the outside air she turned around and flung her arms around his neck. 'What a relief!'

Leo was bamboozled for a second. His arms and hands having a two-second panic before settling at her waist.

'Feel better now?' he asked as the aroma of her light floral scent drifted up to his nose.

'I couldn't do that inside. You never know what news people are getting, so I didn't want to seem too happy. But thank goodness. Thank goodness that's done and everything is okay.'

She seemed to have a little jolt and she laughed awkwardly. 'Oh, sorry.' She stepped backwards, out of his embrace.

'It's fine,' he said. 'Thanks for letting me be there. I've honestly never seen anything so detailed.'

She narrowed her gaze suspiciously. 'Did you spot any bits?'

'What?'

She waggled her fingers. 'Down there. Did you spot any bits?'

'I thought you didn't want to know what you're having?'

'I don't. But I just wondered if you noticed anything.'

He shook his head. 'Let me assure you my inexpert eye noticed nothing.' He led her back over to the car, which was waiting for them. 'Anything else you need to do before we go back to the office?'

She took a little mis-step and looked at him, licking her lips. 'Well,' she said slowly. 'There isn't anything I *need* to do. But there is something I *want* to do.'

Leo was intrigued. 'Well, let's do it.'

She gave a little shriek and whispered something to the driver before she settled back into the car. A little while later they pulled up outside a very famous store in London with dark green canopies and gold writing.

Leo looked amused. 'You do know this is a direct competitor of one of our clients?'

She leaned over to him, her eyes gleaming.

'You do know that the Christmas shop in this store opened last week?'

He threw up his hands. 'Clem, it's still only September.'

'I know, they start early,' she said, already climbing out of the car.

The store was busy, crowded with tourists, and Clem reached and grabbed for his hand, knowing exactly whereabouts the Christmas store was inside. As they exited the elevator, he almost caught his breath. Trees everywhere. Santa. Christmas baubles. And lots and lots of bears.

She pointed at him. 'Now, this feeling is what we need to capture in Hansons. That wow moment.' She gave a nod of her own head as she looked around. 'Leave it with me,' she said over her shoulder as they headed in a specific direction.

He watched as she stopped in front of one display. It had, like many others, multicoloured Christmas baubles with the year on them. But these ones were a little different. They also said *Baby's First Christmas*.

Clem's hand poised first above the purple, then the silver, then the red, then the gold. She lifted a gold one and clutched it to her chest. 'This one, this is what I came in for.'

'A Christmas bauble?' He was more than a little surprised.

She nodded. 'Of course. I've already told you I'm a Christmas girl, and I knew I wanted one of these. I just didn't want to buy it too soon.'

And then he understood. She'd wanted to know everything was okay before she bought her first gift for her baby. He knew that people could be superstitious about things like that, and he understood that too.

'But your baby's not due till January.'

She waved her hand. 'I know that, silly, but—' she looked downwards '—we both know that my baby is here. I don't mind that they're still inside.'

He reached over and took the bauble from her hand. 'Well, let the grinch buy your baby their first bauble.' He nodded over her shoulder to what looked like a temporary Christmas café. 'And why don't we go the whole way and have a hot chocolate too?'

Clem's smile widened and they sat down at the café, ordering hot chocolate with marshmallows and cream.

'I can't believe we're doing this in September,' he sighed as the waitress set down their order. 'It is actually still warm in London, you know.'

Clem was still smiling. She looked so relieved and he was glad. He'd had no idea exactly how anxious she'd been, and he was so pleased he'd offered to come with her.

'Think of this as work. We're just here to see how our rivals capture the Christmas spirit. It will help me focus on helping Hansons.'

'So, that's what we'll tell anyone who asks?'

'Absolutely.' Clem grinned, taking a sip of her hot chocolate and ending up with cream on her nose. She spluttered and he laughed, trying to remember the last time he'd spent part of his day having fun instead of working.

Because that was what this was. Fun.

He felt good about today.

He had to admit to himself how personal it was to have gone to Clem's scan with her— although neither of them had admitted it to each other. As he'd sat in that darkened room and wondered at everything the sonographer had pointed out to them, he'd asked himself a million questions.

Why was he there? It wasn't exactly typical to support a member of staff like this.

But wasn't the world wonderful? Wasn't the human body spectacular to be able to create a whole little person like this? Why had he never wondered more about this process—and why had he never been interested?

So many questions circulating in his brain, as he'd been paying absolute attention to everything the sonographer had shown them. Because Clem hadn't been the only one panicking. And he hadn't even realised, until he'd sat down, how ill-equipped he was to know how to comfort Clem if she got bad news.

That two-second thought had almost swamped him.

Something prickled at the back of his brain. If he wanted to be interested in this woman and her baby, then he had to find out more. He could practically hear his Italian family roar in the background. The objections if he showed any more interest in Clem. He could hear the voices of some of his friends in his head too. But the truth was, he was sitting here with Clem across the table from him, her dark red hair falling about her pale face. Those green sparkling eyes fixed on his. And he knew the huge gamut of emotions she was clearly going through right now, but he also knew he wanted to think this through.

They might be a poor match. They might have no similar interests, and vastly different values. But Leo didn't think so. Didn't he know enough about her already?

He took a breath. 'Is there anything else you want company for?'

For a moment, there was silence as he watched her eyes widen, her brain clearly trying to compute what that question actually meant.

'I might need a hand with putting up the crib my father's bought for the baby.'

'You've already bought the crib?'

She pulled a face. 'Well, I've picked it. I didn't want to order it until…'

'Until today.'

She gave him a soft smile.

'Tyler's parents have bought the rest of the bedroom furniture for the baby, and my mum and I are going pram shopping soon.'

He gave a shrug. 'I can help with the bedroom furniture too. Just tell me when it all arrives. Do you need the room painted first?'

She shifted in her seat then met his gaze. This time it was different. It was almost as though she sensed the resolve in him. Her voice was very low. 'What are you doing, Leo?'

He met her gaze head-on. 'I'm letting you know that I'm here for you, and happy to help.' He held up both his hands. 'This…this is weird, I know. I appreciate you're Miss Independence. But I also know that sometimes you need a friend. Let me be your friend.'

The edges of her lips tilted upwards. The look she gave him was almost shy. 'Leo, I'd love it if we could be friends.'

Clementine Grayson's life was a roller coaster. She was pretty sure that pregnancy hormones played a part in all this, but she was also sure there were a whole lot of other hormones currently wreaking havoc with her thought processes and emotions that were nothing to do with pregnancy.

They'd danced around each other since that accidental kiss. Was she sorry? Not even a little. Maybe pregnancy gave her some super powers? Or maybe it just made her care less about things she would previously have obsessed over.

If Leo Constello hadn't wanted to kiss her, then he wouldn't have.

She'd replayed that kiss over in her head approximately a million times. All of them sending shivers through her body.

And now? Now he'd said he wanted them to be friends.

She even liked the way the word 'friends' rolled about her tongue. Because she knew what he meant. She knew he'd been testing the water. And she liked that, too.

If someone had told her a year ago she would be in this position, she would have laughed in their face.

But life had a funny old way of showing you who was boss.

Since her scan, she'd let her parents and Tyler's parents know everything was good, and then she'd put her head down at work to help Hansons with their very new, very late Christmas plan.

First thoughts had been to stick to the original theme but source the items from elsewhere. That thought had lasted only around ten minutes. The theme had been animals, domestic and wild, at Christmas. Trying to source those kinds of products at very short notice was proving impossible.

So, they'd brainstormed more traditional themes. Then gone back to some of the themes that had been around films. Clem had been involved in a very fun argument about whether *Die Hard* was a Christmas film or not. She'd won, of course—it was—but it wasn't the most suitable for children.

Finally, she'd been walking past a theatre in London when she'd stopped dead at the promo poster with a background setting of a very grand house. The play was coming to a close, getting ready for a pantomime to take over.

She snapped a photo and sent it both to Leo and to the general manager of Hansons. She accompanied the photo with a text.

Just going to negotiate with the theatre for their background settings. House remind you of anything?

The replies were instant.

Home Alone.

And then another two weeks passed in an instant. The creative team at Hansons were true artists. They'd transformed the various sets into scenes from the famous Christmas movie. She was sure that the paint-can scene was going to be a big hit. They also took scenes from the second film in the series, with plans to transform a whole floor into Central Park complete with its own bird lady.

The sense of excitement around the work was infectious. Most of the work would be done in the evenings and overnight, with all the preparations continuing behind the scenes. The deadline was mid-October, just as Clem was due to hit twenty-five weeks.

Her abdomen was growing slowly but steadily. There were trousers she couldn't zip up any more, and skirts that required a very large safety pin hidden under a loose top. Clem still wanted to look smart at work, and one of the other members of staff had given her an online website that stocked smart wear for work, most with not obvious elasticated waists and reasonable prices.

London was starting to transform around her. She'd even spotted her first Christmas tree in a window and it had made her smile. Now she and her work colleagues were taking bets on how many Christmas trees they could spot on the way to work in the morning. Photographic evidence was required, and Leo walked in as she was showing someone an upstairs flat in Notting Hill she'd passed at the weekend.

'Tell me you didn't start this?'

She turned around and gave him a beaming smile. 'Well, hello, Mr Grinch. Of course I started it. Would you like to join in?'

Before she could blink he whipped out his phone and showed her a picture. She squinted at the house, not recognising the neighbour-hood. 'Where's that?'

'Madrid,' he admitted. 'It's my uncle's house. My mother is not impressed.'

Clem paused for a moment. 'I'm going to have to find Aunt Audrey's decorations. I imagine they are up in her loft.'

'Don't you dare.' Leo's voice was low.

'What?'

'Don't you dare climb up a ladder into the loft.'

Clem looked down at her swelling belly. 'Yeah, maybe not.'

'Tell me when you want them and I'll come and bring them down for you.'

'Well…' she paused, clearly wondering how he would take the next piece of information '…I'll need them down for 30 October, be-cause my Christmas tree needs to be up by 1 November.'

'You mean 1 December?' said Leo without a blink.

She gave him a sideways smile. 'No, defi-nitely, 1 November.'

He looked at her, a bit aghast. 'Really?'

'Got to get into the flow with the season.' She looked around the internal offices. 'In fact, shouldn't we really support our clients and co-ordinate our office decorations along-side the unveiling at Hansons?'

'Please tell me you're joking.'

'I'm absolutely not.' Clem was delighted. Teasing him was more than a little fun. 'We do have decorations for the bank, don't we?'

He nodded. 'There's a fresh tree delivered at the start of December every year. It's deco-rated by a firm, but we also do a wish list of gifts for different charities that customers can donate to.'

She glanced at her watch. 'Okay, want to go play at being *Home Alone*?'

'Are things almost ready?'

'Some of the final touches are being made tonight. I said I would go along.'

He looked at her. 'What time?'

'Store closes at seven, so any time after eight.'

'Want to grab dinner first?'

'Sure.'

Clem thought he might take her to an Ital-ian, but instead he took her to an Indian restau-rant near Borough Market. 'It's my favourite,' he said with a grin. 'Just don't tell my mother.'

The waiter quickly seated them and Leo rec-ommended his favourite things on the menu.

Clem brought out her over-the-counter indigestion tablets and set them on the table.

'What are they for?'

She laughed as she sipped her water. 'All of a sudden, I'm getting indigestion no matter what I eat. The midwife advised it's a part of pregnancy and told me what I could take to help.'

He pulled a face. 'You should have said. I could have taken you somewhere the food isn't so spicy.'

She held the menu against her chest. 'I swear, an apple, a glass of milk or a plain biscuit can give me indigestion right now. I want to enjoy what I eat.' She set the menu down and pointed at the text. 'And I want that cauliflower and sweet potato chaat.'

He nodded and placed the order. 'You're looking forward to tonight?'

'At Hansons? Of course, things seem to be going well and I can't wait to see the final pieces.'

He gave her an admiring look. 'So, you're enjoying your job.'

'Apart from my boss?' she said as quick as the wind. 'I'm enjoying my job.'

His fingers ran along the cutlery in front of him. He knew Clem liked to tease, but he wanted to take this conversation to another place.

The waiter appeared, setting down their plates then vanishing again. The restaurant was warm, with a pleasant buzz of voices chatting, glasses clinking and people enjoying themselves.

She picked up her knife and fork and sampled her food. 'Aahh, just as perfect as I thought it would be.'

Leo looked at her for a moment, trying to get a sense of her feelings. 'So, you're happy with us being friends? Me helping you get things sorted for the baby? I don't want to overstep.'

'Why on earth would you think you were overstepping?'

He raised his eyebrows. 'Because I'm your boss. People might not understand or appreciate us being friends.'

'And why would it be anyone else's business but ours?'

'True.' He tried not to imagine what his family might say.

She took a sip of her water. 'As long as you understand that, as a friend, I'm likely going to get ve-e-ry big over the next few months. I might be tired and short-tempered. And everything will probably be your fault. But as long as you know that—then we'll be fine.'

She held up her glass of water to him. 'To friendship?'

He clinked his bottle of beer against it. 'To friendship.'

The evening had passed in a blur. It was the oddest thing, but she hadn't expected the conversation to go quite like that.

They stepped out of the car at Hansons. The temperature in London had dropped suddenly. Clem had purchased a new grey wool coat the other day, two sizes bigger than normal, that she hoped would see her through this pregnancy.

She pulled it around her and looked up at the dark sky. 'Do you think there could be snow?' she asked.

He was right beside her. 'Warn me now, exactly how many times will you ask that question between now and Christmas?'

She gave him her most sincere look. 'Every day.'

He nodded in acceptance and led her to the main door of Hansons. The creative director let them in, excitedly filling them in on how the final preparations were going. 'Four days,' he said, clapping his hands together, 'and I think this will be our finest Christmas theme yet.' He leaned over and put his hand on Clem's shoulder. 'All thanks to you, Ms Grayson.'

Clem gave a gracious nod. 'What's an idea without a fabulous team to deliver it?'

The man swept his hand outwards in a little bow. 'Well, take a look around, and let me know any more ideas you have, or anything you think doesn't look quite right.'

They started on the ground floor, walking through the fake entrance of the McCallister home. It led to other rooms in the house, including the famous staircase where the paint-can incident took place. Large cinema screens were set up throughout the store. Clem pointed to them. 'They have a licence to play the movies all day, every day.' She gave a shrug. 'Just in case there's anyone on the entire planet that hasn't seen *Home Alone*.'

They moved up the heavily decorated escalator and onto the first floor that resembled the Central Park theme. The bird-lady figurine was there, surrounded by birds, but also looking as if she were standing on a glistening lake.

A technician saw them, gave them a nod and flicked a switch. The second movie started playing on the screens around them. Special effects came into play, the ice beneath their feet glistened even more, there was the gentle noise of birds, and after a few moments, and a cold blast, some fake snow started to gently float down around them.

Clem lifted her hand to the sky. 'Isn't it magical? Isn't this just perfect?'

Leo's arm gently rested behind her back as they both stared at the magical setting. This night had been…almost perfect. She'd wished that their dinner together had actually been a date. She was delighted they were friends and he'd told her he wanted to help her out, but did that also mean he was making sure she knew he wouldn't consider anything other than friendship developing between them?

The accidental kiss lingered in her brain. All she really wanted him to do right now was to lean down and kiss her for real.

But instead, Leo was looking at the snow falling around them, dusting their hair and shoulders, with a wide smile on his face.

'Well done, Clem, you've definitely captured a bit of Christmas magic in here.' He looked down at her, the broad smile still in place.

For a second, she held her breath, wondering…

But the kiss never came. A part of her was

sad, longing. But at least Leo was her friend. That was good. And was probably exactly what she needed right now.

CHAPTER SIX

THE LAUNCH AT Hansons was a huge success and people were starting to take notice of Clem's contributions. In the meantime, staff had started to notice the growing friendship between Leo and Clem.

Leo smiled as his secretary put a call through from his sister. 'I need you to entertain a family friend,' said Juliette. 'You've been quiet on the social scene lately—a date will be good for you.'

He sat a bit more upright and scowled. 'I don't need you to find a date for me, Juliette. I am perfectly capable of doing that for myself.'

'She's in London. She's the daughter of Enrico Embella. You remember him? He's in oil. Anyhow, I've booked you a table at Claridge's. She's staying there. You just need to meet her at eight.'

There was movement in his peripheral vision, and he saw Clem in her grey wool coat, leaning just outside his door.

'I can't meet her at eight. I have other plans.' He was going to get Clem's Christmas decorations down from her loft.

'Well, you'll need to cancel them,' said Juliette. 'You can't let her down now.'

'I won't be letting her down,' said Leo swiftly, trying to keep his temper in check, 'because I didn't make any arrangements to meet her. And I told you, I'm busy.'

'Well, just cancel whatever it is,' Juliette snapped back.

'I will not. I told you, I can find my own dates and I already have plans tonight.'

He looked up. Clem's face was pale, and there was a deep frown line across her face. But her expression? It was obvious she could hear the entire conversation. Even on the telephone, Juliette wasn't quiet.

'But she's exactly your type,' continued Juliette. 'A beautiful model, from a good Italian family. She's clever, and fun.'

Leo looked up, in time to see Clem walking casually away from the door—obviously not wanting to hear any more. He lowered his voice. 'Drop it, Juliette. I'm not interested. There's someone else…'

'Who?'

The silence extended, and he knew it wouldn't take his sister long to make the connection. 'It's that project manager of yours, isn't it? You know that can only end in disaster, Leo. Or do you plan on ignoring a potential scandal? One, she's an employee, and two, she's pregnant by someone else. Both of those are good enough reasons not to date her.'

Leo put the phone down, not even bothering to argue with her. He knew from experience that kind of conversation could go on for hours, and he wasn't prepared to have it out with his sister. Not right now, anyway.

He rested back in his chair. He knew the next call would be his mother.

Was it anyone's business but his? No.

Family was very important to Leo. Most decisions in his life had been based around what was best for the family. But, as much as he loved and respected them, and he did love being part of the family business, they weren't in charge of his private life.

As if by magic, his mobile started to ring. His mother. He rejected the call and slipped on his jacket.

He walked out to where Clem was waiting

for him. She looked a little pensive, as if something was on her mind.

She looked at his suit. 'You might want to change before you climb into the loft.'

He looked down and nodded. 'Why don't we stop by my place and I'll grab something?'

She gave a nod. 'Let's go.'

Clem had always thought that Leo likely stayed somewhere grand, but she hadn't thought closely about the details. When they pulled up to the glass-fronted building in Canary Wharf, she stepped out quickly.

Two minutes later, the doorman had let them in, greeted them both warmly and showed them to a private elevator. There was a quiet hiss, and the doors opened straight into the penthouse, with views all down the Thames from the floor-to-ceiling windows. Clem let out a little gasp. 'Wow.'

Leo shot her a smile. 'Take a look around while I get changed. Then you can tell me off for my housekeeping skills.'

Clem didn't need to be told twice. She crossed the dark wooden floor of the main room and slid open the doors to stand on the balcony. The view from here was even more magnificent and she imagined waking up to it every day.

The kitchen was sleek and modern, and she couldn't resist a peek into some of the cupboards. Most were neat, but the cupboard where she found the biscuits met her approval. Randomly half-opened packets of a wide range of chocolate biscuits. This was more like it.

She strode quickly through the two other bedrooms, bathrooms, study and home gym, and one thing stood out to her. There were family snaps everywhere. Of course, she didn't know who everyone was. But she could make out Leo as a child, his sister, his mother and father, and other relatives. He had such a wide family it made something pang deep inside her. It would only be her for this baby. Her mum, and maybe even her dad would be around occasionally. Tyler's parents would hopefully be present sometimes, too. But Clem didn't have a huge family.

These pictures made her a little sad. Sure, she had a few photos of her as a baby with her mum and dad before they'd split up, and some later in life with Hugo featuring in them. But that was basically it. She touched her stomach. What did she want for this baby? She was doing this on her own. She'd known that from the start. But as she trailed her finger across one of the large family pics filled with love and laughter, was it so wrong that she wanted that for her baby, too?

Clem shook her head, unsure of where all of this had come from. It must have been hearing part of that call between Leo and Juliette. She was acutely aware she was nothing like the type of woman that Leo normally dated. She hated the way that made her feel so...lacking. It was enough that her body was changing in ways that she was frightened would never go back to the way they were, but to have to hear about Leo's family cajoling him into going on dates with gorgeous models made her feel fat and dowdy.

As she turned around, she noticed he'd changed into comfortable clothes, a T-shirt and joggers, things she'd never seen Leo wearing before.

He must have noted her expression as he looked down with his hands open and started laughing. 'What? Did you think I was born in a suit?'

She shook her head. 'Just never seen you so casual before.'

It was the laugh that did it. The fact he was so at ease right now, when she felt absolutely the opposite. If she hadn't overheard that phone call, she would have been fine. But now, her head was swirling.

She was doubting everything. Leo wanted them to be friends. He'd offered to help her wherever he could. But was she just some poor colleague to him? Was this all because he felt sorry for her?

She was vulnerable. Definitely hormonal. A little angry. And a lot frustrated. She wasn't a model. She hadn't even wanted to be one, had always been happy in her own skin. So why, she thought as she caught sight of herself in the glass in Leo's apartment, did she suddenly hate everything about herself?

'Stop,' she said quickly, raising her hand. 'I'm sorry. This is a mistake. I still have work to finish. We should reschedule. I'll just go on home.'

Leo's forehead creased and he looked momentarily confused. 'What?'

She shook her head and moved towards the door. But before she could reach the handle his hand was on her shoulders. 'It's after hours, Clem. You definitely don't need to be working. Anything outstanding can wait until tomorrow.'

She blinked, frozen in place. Not sure what to say next.

He stepped in front of her. 'What's going on?' His voice was low and steady.

Something flared inside her. 'I could ask you the same thing. Don't you have somewhere better to be tonight?' Her voice cracked a bit and she hated herself.

'What?'

He bent his knees so his face was right in front of hers. 'Clem, we made plans, and I'm exactly where I want to be.'

She shook her head as angry tears threatened to fall. 'Are you sure about that?'

Something clicked in his brain and he gave a big sigh, standing up and taking a few steps away. 'Is this about what Juliette said?'

Clem gave a shrug. 'She clearly thinks you should be spending time with someone more suitable.'

'Who I spend my time with is up to me.' He put his hand on his chest. 'I promised you that I was going to help with your tree. I don't go back on my promises.'

She tried to keep her voice steady. 'That's really nice of you, and I know we agreed you'd help me. But—' she took a breath, not meaning a word of what she was about to say '—if you've had a better offer, I won't be offended if you want to change those plans.'

She looked at him, keeping herself together as best she could.

Leo looked her straight in the eye as he lifted his jacket. 'I don't want to change our plans. I have no interest in going on a date tonight—and I told my sister that. What I do have an interest in though—' he gave her a half-smile as he opened the door '—is making sure my friend doesn't try and harm herself climbing up a ladder and getting her—and her baby—wedged in a tiny loft-hatch opening. So, come on. Let's get this tree down.'

Clem licked her dry lips. She wasn't sure why she was being so emotional about this, but the words from Leo were exactly what she wanted to hear.

And her heart gave a little flutter in relief.

As they arrived at the house there was a large cardboard box outside, clearly left by a delivery company. Clem frowned and checked the label. 'It's bedroom furniture for the baby. I wasn't expecting it yet.' She opened the front door and switched off the alarm, watching as Leo hoisted the heavy box, his biceps flexing. 'Want me to help?'

'Don't you dare,' he mumbled, bringing it in.

He looked at the wide staircase in front of him. 'Where's the baby's room?'

She pulled a face. 'Upstairs.'

'Of course it is,' he said with a rueful smile. 'Show me the way.'

He took the furniture up the stairs and into the large room that Clem was designating for the baby. He sighed as he set the box down in the room. It was bare for now.

'I moved the rest of the things to other rooms,' she explained. 'I haven't started in here yet.'

He touched the walls. 'What do you need? Are you painting?'

'I'd like to. I think I want a pale yellow.' She pointed at the packed furniture. 'And then I'll likely need a hand assembling all this.'

He nodded and put his hands on his hips, taking in the whole room and moving over to the window, which looked out onto the street. His hand touched one of the curtains. 'Are you changing these?'

Clem paused. 'I hadn't thought about it. Maybe.'

He gave her a stern glance. 'If you want to, let me do it. You'd need to climb a ladder to change them.' He stretched out his back and it made a loud click.

'Leo!' she said, putting her hand to her mouth. 'Have you hurt your back lifting that box?'

'Not any more than I do at the gym. They laugh at me there when my back cracks.' He moved back over and turned the light switch off in the room. 'Now, don't we have a tree to put up?'

In the end it took two phone calls to Aunt Audrey to finally locate the artificial tree and the rest of the Christmas decorations in the cavernous loft.

'There's no way I could have got this out myself,' said Clem as she stared at the dismantled tree on the floor of the main room. 'It's huge.'

Leo laughed. 'It's apparently eight feet, once I get it set up.' He looked upwards. 'Thank goodness for town houses with high ceilings.'

Clem made an excited little sound. 'But think how beautiful it will look in the window as people go by.' He looked over at her and saw the joy on her face.

'You really are a Christmas girl, aren't you?'

'Of course, I told you that.'

One hour later, Leo had got the towering,

heavy tree in place, trimmed with golden lights, and positioned at the window.

Clem was digging through boxes, trying to decide on a colour theme. Aunt Audrey had Christmas baubles dating back for years—a huge mismatch of styles.

'Don't you want to just put them all up?' asked Leo, staring into the box and not really able to tell one from the other.

'No!' She looked shocked. 'I want it all to tie in together.' She tugged some tinsel from another box. 'Look, we have gold and rose-gold tinsel here. I can pick out all the baubles that match and we can put these up together.'

Leo lifted the garlands of tinsel and positioned the stepladder. 'Stay back,' he warned her. 'Don't try and climb this ladder and adjust anything.'

He laughed as he listened to her instructions, telling him to tweak this and that, to move something to another branch, and when he finally climbed down he put his hands on his hips. 'Kind of bossy, aren't you?'

Clem stepped forward, her red hair all mussy and her earlier lipstick a bit smudged. She wrapped her hands around his neck. 'But look what we've created. Isn't it wonderful?

And doesn't it just put you in the mood for Christmas?'

'We're not quite finished yet though, are we?'

She wrinkled her nose. 'What do you mean?'

He walked over to one of sideboards and lifted a box from it, opening the tissue-wrapped bauble. 'Shouldn't this one have pride of place?'

She let out a little gasp and held up the bauble. The one that had been bought specially. *Baby's First Christmas.*

He pointed out, 'Isn't it funny that it matches your theme? I wonder why you picked gold and rose gold?' He was teasing but couldn't help it.

She gave a little shake of her head as she hung the bauble on one of the middle branches. 'I hadn't even thought about the colour.'

He slid an arm around her shoulder so they could both look at it. 'I believe you, millions wouldn't.'

'The magic of Christmas.' She looked up at him. 'Is it working on you yet?'

Leo gave a sigh and relented a little. 'It is a gorgeous tree. But tomorrow is only 1 November. It still seems too soon.'

'What am I going to do with you?' Clem laughed. 'I've brought you *Home Alone* in London, and New York's Central Park. Now, I bring you a Christmas tree, and you're still a bit bah humbug.'

He pretended to scowl at her.

She smiled then gave him a hesitant look. 'I was thinking earlier about how I don't have the size of family you have. There's only a few of us, and we're spread so far apart. I was thinking of asking both my mum and dad if they would come to mine this Christmas.'

He blinked. 'But your dad is in Australia.'

'I know. But I've been talking to him a lot, and I feel as if there's a lot of missed time here. Him and Mum—I just don't know how they'll get on. But I'd like them to be in the same place for once, for my and the baby's sake.' She met Leo's gaze. 'My dad, he has already offered. He's told me he wants to come to London and meet me. He wants to see the baby when it's born. He said if I need help, he would be there for me.'

She put her hand on her chest and said, 'Am I being selfish, wanting my grown-up parents to be with me at Christmas?'

Leo was thoughtful. 'What do you normally do?'

'I would have spent it in Surrey with Mum and Hugo. But he's not here now. And I'd like to invite them here, to Aunt Audrey's. Kind of neutral ground.'

'Don't you think that's a lot to take on when you'll be more pregnant?'

She looked down, smiled, and stroked her belly. 'More pregnant,' she murmured. 'Well, I'm not due until the end of January. So, on Christmas Day, I'll still have about five or so weeks to go. I think I should be okay.'

'What about your cooking skills?'

She gave him a determined look. 'I can put roast potatoes in the oven. The turkey needs to cook for hours, I think, so it can start off in the morning. I'll buy ready-made gravy and just get some carrots and Brussel sprouts. Surely even I can't ruin those?'

'How are you going to break it to your mum? Will she take some persuading?'

'She might.' Clem looked at him. 'What are you doing at Christmas? Are you going back to Pisa?'

He shook his head. 'I don't have plans yet.'

He watched as she took a nervous breath. 'Would you like to spend Christmas here?'

He gave her a knowing smile. 'Am I your back-up plan, or your referee?'

'Both,' she admitted.

He squeezed her hand. 'I'm very happy to accept your offer. Let me take care of dessert.'

Her mouth fell open. 'I hadn't even thought about dessert.'

'And now, you don't need to.'

They settled on the sofa for a bit to watch some TV, and even though it was the end of October Clem still managed to find a Christmas movie to watch. It didn't take long before they were relaxed next to each other, and he had his arm gently resting around her shoulders. After around an hour she gave a little shudder. Leo half squinted at her, trying to see her properly in the dimming light. 'Clem, what is it?'

She bit her bottom lip. 'My midwife asked me today who my birth partner will be, and I didn't know what to say.'

Leo was surprised, and he couldn't hide it. 'Aren't you going to ask your mum?'

She swallowed and he could see her blink back tears. 'Of course I can ask her. But there are classes every week. And I don't want her driving at night in the winter. All the other women at the class seemed so put together. They all knew what they were doing, and had everything already planned out.' A tear started to trickle down her cheek.

'Clem, do you want me to come to your antenatal classes with you? Do you want me to be your birth partner?'

She blinked again, her eyes full. 'But is it even fair of me to ask that of you?' She put her hand on his arm. 'I hate that this is so awkward. I hate that I'm putting you in the position of even asking. But I saw all the other women this week and it brought everything home to me. How little time I've got left. I know that we're relatively new friends, and me asking something like this might just push you a million miles away.'

He shook his head. He could feel her panicking. And wondered if he should be panicking himself. But all he wanted to do was reassure her. To tell her that he cared about her. He wanted to help her. 'Clem, if you want me to come to your antenatal classes with you, I will. I'm happy to. And—' he took a breath before he said the rest '—if you want me to be your birth partner, I'll do that too.' He gave her a smile. 'But I can't promise you that I won't faint.'

He could feel it. The tension. Slowly, but surely, releasing from her body. The relaxation around her jaw and shoulders. She gave a sigh and stood up, holding out her hand towards him.

He could feel the buzz in the air. He could sense the electricity between them again. It didn't matter how much he tried to dampen things down, ignore it. It was still there.

Clem moved back over to the Christmas tree, touching its branches and admiring their work. 'Christmas, don't you just love it?' She threw her arms up, with a gleam in her eyes.

Leo stepped back. 'Oh no, I know what's coming next and it's *definitely* too soon for that. Don't do it, Clem.'

She pressed a button on her phone and 'Last Christmas' from Wham started playing in the room.

He shook his head and his finger. 'Oh no. No way.'

But Clem started singing along, her voice rising as she danced around the room. 'It's my favourite!' she declared, with her arms in the air.

He watched her for a few moments. She was wearing a baggy white shirt and black leggings. Her hair was loose and her feet were bare. The room was warm, and even though

Leo didn't consider himself a keen dancer—he could move if he wanted to.

So, he joined her, dancing alongside her and singing along with her. He was watching her belly. Although it protruded, it was firm. She was almost twenty-eight weeks. If Clem had her baby now, it might be premature but should still have a reasonable chance of survival.

The thought was slightly terrifying.

He enjoyed being around her. She was smart and she was fun. But she was also vulnerable. He imagined that every woman likely questioned if she would be a good mother when they were pregnant for the first time. But he'd never experienced that. He'd not really had those kinds of conversations with Clem, so he wasn't entirely sure he was doing or saying what he should.

And was it crazy that he found her so attractive? Because he did. He liked the fact her stomach was starting to swell, and her face was filling out a little. Clem looked good, she wore this pregnancy well, even though she probably didn't know it.

He wondered if that made him a bit odd. Pregnant women usually had some kind of 'don't touch' sign around them. But with Clem, he'd been there from the beginning, and he just wanted to keep seeing where this might go. Despite the barriers between them.

As they danced and laughed around the main room, he pushed all the thoughts of his family from his head. The voicemails from his sister, followed by a few from his mother. All saying the same thing. Did he realise having an attraction to an employee, and someone who was pregnant, would all end in disaster?

But none of those thoughts or questions belonged here, in this happy moment.

It was inevitable, he supposed. As the song progressed, they moved closer. She wound her arms around his neck again, and he slid his arms around her waist as they moved in time to the music. Her stomach was pressing against him.

It was as if she was finally relaxing around him. He was aware he still had guards in place, as he didn't really know how she felt about him beyond friendship. But right now? He didn't care about any of that.

Her warm skin was next to his. Those green eyes were hypnotising, and they were only for him. He wasn't bothered by what anyone else might think about this.

'Clem,' he said huskily, 'can I kiss you?'

Her pupils dilated. 'If you don't,' she replied instantly, 'I might just kill you.'

It was all he needed. He dropped a kiss on one eyelid, and then the other, trailing his kisses slowly down the side of one cheek until finally he got to her lips.

They'd had the briefest of kisses before, but this was completely different. This was no accident.

He meant every second of this.

Her lips were soft, malleable, and waiting for him. She met the kiss head-on, returning it with as much pent-up fire and sensation as he'd spent months hiding.

He ran his fingers through her dark red hair as they continued kissing. His hand moved under her loose shirt and skirted over her skin. She sucked in a breath and let out a little laugh. And then pulled him closer.

CHAPTER SEVEN

CLEM WAS LIVING in some kind of dream world. In one world, the most handsome man in the world had kissed her. But in the other world, he'd gone home shortly afterwards and now it was business as usual back at work.

Occasionally, he would do something unexpected. He'd asked one of the staff to do a health and safety risk assessment on her due to her pregnancy and she now had a new work chair that stopped her back from aching. But apart from that, there had been no talk of spending more time together. No secret looks or glances. And definitely no more kisses. She couldn't help but feel disappointed even though it was probably for the best.

Although everyone told her she was neat in her pregnancy, as she approached the middle of November, she felt ginormous at around thirty weeks.

'I'm a cross between a whale and dinosaur,'

she said to Lisa, her work colleague, as she sampled some cookies Lisa had made.

Lisa laughed. 'I can bring you some more maternity clothes. There's no point buying any.' After three children, Lisa had vowed never to be pregnant again. 'And it's getting cold. I've got some bigger jumpers and trousers that will keep you warm.' She gave Clem a critical gaze. 'Though they still might be a little big on you.'

'That's fine,' said Clem easily. 'Let's face it, I'll grow into them. Thank you.'

She put her feet up on another chair, glancing over her shoulder to see if anyone was watching. 'My ankles have been swelling so much by the end of the day. What do you call that? Cankles? Or something like that. If I put my feet up for a bit, they seem to go down.'

Her workmate looked at her with a small frown. 'Are you still being checked by your midwife?'

'Yes, I saw her last week and she said everything is fine.'

Her workmate pointed at her ankles. 'Well, make sure you mention it to her next time you see her. It's all part of pregnancy, but let the experts do their job.'

Clem pulled one foot up and gave it a rub.

'I've got another appointment soon, so I'll make sure to do that.'

She grimaced. 'I keep wondering if my belly can really stretch much further. It already feels at full capacity.'

Lisa's smile was wry. 'Oh, don't worry, your belly will stretch. It's going back the other way that's the problem.'

'I'm trying not to think about that,' Clem admitted. 'I've told myself just to wait and see what happens.'

'Good attitude,' said Lisa, 'Now come on, you've got that conference call with Hanson's soon.'

Clem settled into her office chair for the on-line meeting—she had her list ready. It was sharp and to the point. The executive team at Hansons were delighted with their Christmas opening in mid-October and had reported a significant rise in sales. There was also good media coverage, and lots of reviews online reporting that Hansons had the best theme and Christmas decorations in all of London. Clem was delighted things had gone so well and were deemed a success. The chairman asked for a few moments alone with Leo, and she signed off with the rest of the group and moved on to her next task.

She had a new project to oversee for the next few weeks and had two more reports to review before they could be submitted to Leo with feedback. The longer she was here, the more her workload grew. She finally felt people around the bank were hearing about her and beginning to trust her. Those that had proved reluctant to begin with were starting to be won around. Clem was going to have to stop being so nice to everyone, as she was working longer and longer hours. It wasn't that she minded. She wanted to do a good job. She wanted her name to be on people's lips connecting her with the work she did. Her work would prove her reliance and capability, and that was what she wanted to focus on right now.

Because anything to do with Leo was messing with her head. He hadn't made any attempt to kiss her again, and as she looked down at her growing stomach, she had to ask herself if he just wasn't as attracted to her as she was to him.

It wasn't that he hadn't touched her. As he'd promised, he'd come along to the antenatal classes, where she regularly sat on the floor between his legs and leaned back into him. He wasn't shy about following the instructions and rubbing her shoulders and back.

His touch drove her crazy, and she thought he might know that due to the gleam she sometimes saw in his eyes. There was warmth and affection there too, and all she did was yearn for him to touch her more. Other women in the class had commented on their chemistry. But Leo still hadn't made any attempt to kiss her again.

Having someone by her side had made it all so much easier to navigate. Having someone to laugh with on the way home—whether it was recalling a joke the midwife had made, or something another attendee had said—made the whole thing seem so much more normal to her. She was going to do something that other women had done for thousands of years. Finish a pregnancy and have a baby.

And she was doing it with someone by her side. She should be elated, and inside she was. But there was still a tiny part of her that wondered if she and Leo knew what they were letting themselves in for. Clem wasn't stupid. She knew if there was a problem, birth plans were flung out of the window and the priority was to keep mum and baby safe.

What if her baby did get stuck? What if she was left with lots of problems? What if she became one of those women who peed when she laughed? She was only twenty-four. That was the trouble with antenatal classes: they were remarkably unsexy.

It wasn't surprising Leo was keeping her at arm's length. Clem's trouble was that, ever since that kiss, she'd been waiting for him to whisk her into his arms again. Now she was thinking about what he was seeing and hearing at the antenatal classes, was it any wonder he hadn't made any kind of move on her?

She let out a groan and patted her stomach and counted what blessings she could. She had a healthy baby. She had a wonderful friend. And maybe, when this was all over, they could be more than friends.

Leo's meeting with Hansons had gone better than he'd ever imagined. The chairman had asked to speak to him at the end to compliment Artullo's bank on the role that they'd played in the Christmas campaign. He'd reminded Leo of something that he already knew: that not all banks were as invested in their customers and went—as he'd called it—above and beyond.

He'd then joked that in ten years' time, once Clem had a bit more business experience, he might be tempted to poach her for his own board. And while in principle Leo didn't like that, it also made him immensely proud that someone else was recognising exactly what Clem brought to the table.

Things were going well between them. He liked every second he spent with Clem. He was enjoying watching her change before his eyes, and how her thoughts seemed to jumble around in her head. Christmas had brought out the chaotic side of Clem, jumping from one festive idea to the next. She had even pinned a list of Christmas to-do activities to the office fridge.

Occasionally he had the briefest moment where he wondered if he was good enough for her. If he would have what it took to support her the way she would need.

But his biggest issue was Tyler.

Although he'd been mentioned in passing, they'd never had a detailed conversation about Tyler. Leo was determined not to progress things further between them until he was completely clear about Clem's feelings for Tyler. There was no point trying to form a relationship with Clem if she was still in love with her baby's father. It didn't matter that he had died. Sometimes partners could never get over the loss of a loved one. They didn't ever feel able to move on and really love someone else. He knew he was filling in gaps in Clem's life, and he was trying hard to keep his feelings suppressed, but falling for someone who was still potentially in love with someone else would only result in disaster. And it was a disaster that Leo didn't want to contemplate.

Was it even a question he should be asking her? Would it upset her too badly? He didn't entirely know. But he knew he'd have to, if he wanted this relationship to progress.

Clem climbed out of the taxi and stretched. It was eight o'clock. Pitch black in London and she'd had a long day. The warm glow from the windows of the town house was already welcoming her. As she slid the key into her lock she had a strange feeling. One of something being not quite right. She moved to punch the numbers into the alarm and noticed a strange flashing light. One she hadn't seen flashing before.

She stood frozen for a few seconds. There was an instruction manual somewhere. Clem had just been used to entering the code when she left, and putting it back in when she got home. Nothing else out of the ordinary had happened.

She dug around in the cupboard that housed

the alarm and pulled out the slightly crumpled instruction booklet. As she stepped through to the front room, she froze again.

The air was slightly cooler than normal and Clem could instantly see why. One of the tiny panes of glass in the old-fashioned patio doors was broken. Cracked, with a chunk of glass missing. Her body reacted viscerally, almost making her vomit on the spot.

But more than anything, she listened. Listened for every creak and groan of the old house. It made noises constantly. Sometimes it seemed as if it were talking to her. But she wasn't listening for house noises now. She was listening for human noises, and nothing had ever terrified her so much.

She pulled out her phone. It was Leo she called. He answered in a low voice. 'Everything okay? I'm still on a call.'

'No,' she whispered as quietly as she could. 'I think someone has broken in, and I don't know if they are still in the house.' Her throat was dry. She was waiting for a movement, or a shadow, and she truly didn't know what to do if she saw one.

She heard the screech of a chair at the end of the phone, and Leo cutting himself off from his meeting. 'Have you phoned the police?'

She shook her head, then realised he couldn't see her. 'No,' she whispered again.

'I'll phone them. And I'm coming straight over. Get out of the house, Clem. Don't put yourself in danger. If people want to steal something, let them. Just get you and the baby out of there.'

She could hear the steely panic in his voice. He was trying to be calm. But she knew him. She knew his brain was racing just as much as hers.

Why hadn't the alarm sounded? Surely whoever, or whatever, had caused the glass to break should have set off the alarm in full.

She looked at the crumpled instructions in her hand and knew she didn't have the mind-set to read them right now. She moved quietly back to the front door, still listening for any-one inside.

She turned the handle of the main door. The click seemed to echo around her and made her hold her breath. Was that a noise upstairs?

Before she gave herself a chance to think any further, she flung open the front door and raced down the steps, standing out in the mid-dle of the street, breath panting.

Around her was quiet, with an occasional

noise of a car, or the rustle of the trees in the road in front of her.

Her hands rested on her stomach. Was she safe? Was her baby safe? She glanced at the houses on either side, tempted to go and knock on their doors. But she didn't know any of Aunt Audrey's neighbours, and she wasn't sure she would make much sense right now.

Staring up at the house was intimidating. Someone could be in there right now, violating her privacy, stealing from her aunt, and making her feel insecure in the place she was currently calling home. It was so unfair. What made someone do something like this?

Then she had a moment of madness. Maybe something ridiculous like a kid's tennis ball had hit the window, or a bird had flown into it. She hadn't even taken the time to check. She could be causing a whole fuss about nothing.

Her eyes caught the cornicing around the front windows and door. CCTV. There was CCTV around the main and back entrance. Would there be something on that?

She knew she could view it on a monitor in the house, and on her laptop. But she didn't have access to either right now. Her heart continued to race in her chest, and then, of course, she had to cross her legs, since her body had decided it needed to pee.

She shivered in the cold December air. Was it the cold, or was it just terror?

It seemed like for ever before she heard the familiar noise of police sirens and the simultaneous noise of Leo's engine.

He pulled up almost at the same time as the police, taking her in his arms straight away. 'Are you okay? Did you see anyone? Do you need to see a doctor?'

The questions came out one after the other without pause, as if he didn't even have time to breathe. 'I'm fine. I still don't know if anyone is in the house.' She couldn't stop shaking.

The police came over to speak to them for a few moments, before telling them to stay where they were, and three officers went to go through the house.

The wait seemed endless, and a number of curtains were twitching in the street due to the flashing blue police lights.

Eventually one of the officers came out and gave them a nod. 'Come inside, the house is clear. You're safe. But we have to show you something.'

Clem walked back up the steps, anxious to go to the bathroom and then to sit down.

They waited for her, speaking to Leo in low voices. She glanced up the stairs as she exited the bathroom. 'There's definitely no one inside?' she asked again.

One of the policemen checked in with her. 'Ms Grayson, I can see you're expecting. Is there someone you'd like us to call for you?'

She reached out for Leo, still not feeling warm enough to take off her coat. 'No, I've got who I need,' she said.

The policeman gestured for her to sit. 'I understand you have CCTV?'

She nodded.

'We'll need to see the view of your back garden.'

'Leo, can you hand me over my laptop?'

He slid it towards her and she fired it up and opened the app with the feed from the back garden.

The policeman pointed to the cracked and partly missing pane. 'We can tell by the marks on the door frame that someone tried to break in. Whether they were disturbed, or just couldn't get through the door frame—the glass panels are tiny, too small to fit a hand through—we know you've been lucky. This likely happened much earlier. Your neighbour, four doors down, was broken into early this afternoon. We suspect this was the same person, or people.'

Clem let out a gasp. 'Are the neighbours okay?'

The policeman nodded. 'Like yourself, they were out at the time.'

Leo spun the computer round to face him and scrolled to the footage from the afternoon. Sure enough, a man in dark clothes with a baseball hat partly obscuring his face could be seen at the back door. He looked unaccompanied but they couldn't be sure.

Leo took one look at Clem, and flicked the kettle on. 'Can I get the window fixed tonight, or at least boarded up?'

The policeman gave Leo some contact details as he sent the footage from the CCTV to the police. 'The alarm system, it didn't go off. I take it that it needs updating?'

One of policemen pulled a face. 'It is, or was a good system, five or six years ago. Things are so sophisticated now that if you're thinking of your family's safety it might be time to revisit.'

It was clear that the police thought Leo lived with her, and Clem had no thoughts of correcting them. They stayed a while longer, told them to expect someone tomorrow to fingerprint the outside glass and wished them well. The words 'This could have been much more serious' from one of the policemen as he left did little to comfort Clem.

She sat with her coat on, sipping at the tea Leo had made for her, as he spent some time on the phone, arranging a joiner, a glazier and a visit from a new security-system team the next day. 'Can you give me Audrey's number?' he asked.

'What for?'

'I need to let her know about her house, and that we will be making some changes to it, to make it more secure,' he said.

She handed over Audrey's number and let him make the call. Of course, she should tell Aunt Audrey herself what had happened to her home, but she just couldn't find the energy right now.

'What if they'd got in?' she murmured with a shiver. 'What if he'd been in the house when I got back?'

Leo sat down next to her and wrapped his arm around her, pulling her in towards him. 'We can get all this sorted. Do you want to come and stay with me in the meantime?'

Clem looked around. Someone being in the place where she lived felt like a violation.

Everything seemed unclean. She wanted to scrub the place, even though she knew he hadn't actually got inside. But she didn't want the potential intruder to win.

She shook her head firmly. 'No, thank you. I want to stay here. We have plans for Christmas. This is the place I want to invite, and cook for, my mum and dad. I don't want to be driven out of this place. And I want to keep it safe for Aunt Audrey.' She bit her bottom lip and looked up at him, wondering if this was a step too far.

'Will you come and stay here, instead?'

Leo blinked and then nodded. 'Of course, we can get the new security system in and make sure you feel safe.'

She gulped. 'I don't just mean for a few days. I mean…for…for as long as we both want.' It was the best way to say it. She couldn't quite bring herself to say for ever.

He gave her a long look, and then smiled. 'I'll stay with you until you can't stand me leaving my clothes lying around the place any more.'

She laughed and shook her head. 'Oh no, you won't. I'll have you trained in days. You just won't know it.'

Was this the right thing to do? She didn't

want to stay here by herself right now, and she wasn't sure when she would get that sense of safety back. But was she taking advantage of Leo's kindness, asking him to move in for an unspecified amount of time? And if their friendship turned into something else, could it put a lot of pressure on them? She'd dated Tyler on and off for six years. Imagine if she'd been pregnant right at the beginning and this sort of timeline had been pushed on them? Would they have coped? She didn't imagine so.

She'd known Leo for a small fraction of the time she'd known Tyler. Maybe her fear was making her jump into things without proper consideration? But every minute with Leo made her heart beat quicker, made her feel entirely connected to him. Nothing about being around Leo felt wrong. So why was she so nervous about this?

'Are you sure?'

He nodded. 'Absolutely. Come with me while I pick up some things from my place, and then we'll get settled back in here.'

Leo was livid. He was doing his absolute best not to appear so. From the second he'd heard Clem's voice on the phone and thought she was in danger, the whole world had turned to red around him.

He hadn't been able to think about anything other than getting to her. He didn't even remember what he'd said to the police on the phone.

But when his car headlights had shown her standing on the side of the road in her grey coat with her arms wrapped around herself, the wave of relief had been like nothing he'd ever experienced before.

She was safe, and her baby was safe.

In a way he'd have preferred her to stay with him. The penthouse had exclusive access and a security system downstairs that ensured no one could get up. While it was spacious enough, it didn't have a garden, it didn't have the same character as the house in Kensington, and, for Clem, it wouldn't have the same family connection.

He got that. He respected that. But he just wanted to keep her safe. Her Aunt Audrey had been very concerned when she got the call, but Clem had been too upset to talk to her. Leo had reassured Audrey he was looking after Clem, and would look after the house too. When he'd mentioned the state-of-the-art system he wanted to put in, Audrey had agreed instantly.

They were quiet as they got out at the penthouse. Clem stood looking over Canary Wharf and the glittering lights on the Thames. He packed as much as he could into a case and lifted out a pile of suits and shirts on their hangers to save time. His toiletries were flung in a bag, along with a few other things.

'Ready?' she asked.

He nodded. 'Let's head back. I'll go in first and check around.'

She gave him a small smile. 'Can we take all your food?'

He'd forgotten about the contents of the fridge and let out a short laugh. 'Of course, give me a sec.'

He called down to the foyer and the security guard helped them carry everything out to Leo's car.

Then he drove back through the dark streets of London with his hand on Clem's knee. When he parked outside the house she pulled a parking permit from her bag.

'Didn't even think of that,' he said, noticing the bag jostling in her lap.

'Give me the key and I'll come back out and get you once I've checked the place over.' He didn't truly expect anyone to try and break in again in their short absence, but he didn't want Clem to be nervous walking back into the house.

He did a quick sweep of the house to check everything was fine, and then he went back to get Clem and carry his things indoors.

By the time he'd heaved his suitcase up to the first floor Clem was looking a lot more relaxed. She stood at the edge of the room she'd made up for him. 'I've created room in the wardrobe for you to hang up your clothes, too.'

He paused, with all his suits and shirts over his arm. 'Thanks.'

He was conscious of her watching him for a few moments as he hung up his clothes.

She bit her lip. 'Can I ask you something?'

He nodded.

'Why haven't you kissed me again?'

The question seemed to hang in the air between them for a few seconds. Leo gave a small smile. Then he sat down on the bed and patted the space beside him.

'Am I too pregnant, too big? I thought we had chemistry, but you don't seem to want to act on it.'

She looked so sad, and he could tell it was time for some honesty—for them both.

He took her hand. 'Clem, I think you're gorgeous. I've always thought you were gorgeous, and nothing has changed. What I don't know, and what I need to know before this goes any further, is exactly how you feel about Tyler.'

She wrinkled her nose and honestly looked confused. 'Tyler?'

He nodded. 'Are you still in love with him, Clem?'

She made a tiny strangled noise at the back of her throat, her eyes widening. 'Is that why you've been holding back?' Her voice sounded incredulous.

He nodded. 'There's no point in starting something if you're still in love with someone else. I can't and won't compete with a ghost.'

She leaned forward as best she could and put her head in her hands, still shaking it. He wasn't sure what was going on, but when she pushed her hair back and looked at him, she gave him a half-smile and the biggest sigh.

'Leo, the biggest issue between me and Tyler was that I *didn't* love him. Not like that. He was my friend—well, my friend with benefits for too long. We never really had a proper relationship. Our last holiday was a goodbye. At least it was for me. I told Tyler it was time we had to stop our arrangement and go out and

find more meaningful connections. And...'
She paused and swallowed. 'And I did wonder at that moment if he'd hoped that we could
have been more meaningful.' She shook her
head. 'He didn't say anything out loud, I just
caught a look on his face that made me think
that. But we had definitely split up by the time
we came back from our holiday.'

She put her hand on her chest. 'I never loved
him the way you should when you want to be
with someone for ever. I never had the kind
of chemistry with him that I do with you.'
She looked up to the ceiling. 'I admit, I wish
he were still here. But I have no idea what
would have happened with our baby then.'
She looked regretful. 'I might not even have
gone ahead with the pregnancy, because Tyler
would likely have got married to someone else.
Started a family of his own.'

She held up her hands. 'But he didn't get
to make any of those decisions. And, as I've
told you before, I couldn't kill the last part of
him that existed.' She turned to face Leo with
those green eyes. 'I promise you that I don't
still love him like that because I never did. He
will always have a piece of my heart as my
friend, but that's it.'

The relief that flooded through Leo was

game-changing. This was it. This was what he'd wanted to hear.

He reached his hand up and touched the side of her face, tucking a long dark red strand behind her ear. 'You have no idea how happy I am to hear that.'

She put her hand over his, holding it on her face. 'Does that mean you might kiss me now?'

'Oh, I think so,' he said, leaning towards her and putting his lips on hers. The kiss was tender, delicate. One of relief and connection and new beginnings.

When they pulled apart, he rested his forehead against hers. 'And, Clem, just know that I love how you're growing into this pregnancy. I find it—and you—extremely attractive.'

He let out a low laugh and she joined in. 'Let's see how attractive you find me when I can't get my shoes on.'

'Now, that will be interesting,' he agreed. He still couldn't admit how relieved he was regarding her confession about Tyler, but he could tell that she was picking up on all his signals.

But he could also tell how tired she still was. This had been a long day for her, and a horrible one. 'How about you tell me where the bathroom is, and I'll run you a bath?' He reached over and touched her cheek again. 'You need to get some sleep tonight.'

Clem let out the biggest sigh he'd ever heard. She looked thoroughly exhausted. And he felt instantly guilty she'd worked so long today.

'What about tomorrow?' she asked. 'You spoke to so many people tonight.'

'Let me worry about tomorrow. I'll work from here, so I can speak to the police and the tradesmen when they come.'

For a second he thought she might object but instead she relaxed her shoulders and leaned into him.

'Thank you, Leo,' she whispered into his neck. 'Thank you for being here.'

'Any time,' he replied, and meant it.

CHAPTER EIGHT

CLEM STARED AT her ankles. Were they bigger? They felt bigger. Her legs felt heavier, but then so did her entire body.

Leo had made sure they were finishing sharp tonight. Even early—four o-clock since they were booked to see the Christmas lights at Kew Gardens.

The car dropped them off at the entrance and she pulled her coat around her. The buttons were barely fastening these days. It was as if she'd reached thirty-two weeks of pregnancy and her baby had gone on a sudden and exhausting growth spurt.

Part of her wondered if it was stress since the break-in. But that seemed ridiculous. The town house now had a brand-new state-of-the-art security system and new cameras around the house. Both of their phones would ping if any disturbance was noted and they could view any part of the house instantly. The po-

lice had taken some fingerprints and matched
them to the house a few doors down that had
also been burgled. The pane of glass had been
replaced, and the door frames repaired and
strengthened.

The house felt safe now, but she was sure
the fact that Leo was there was the main con-
tributor to that feeling of security.

As she looked at the entrance to Kew Gardens her heart gave a little leap. It was dark
already and as they filed through she could
see the brightly coloured lights laid out before
them. 'It's wonderful,' she whispered.

'Tell me if you want to sit down at any
point,' he said to her as they were handed a
map.

She stared down at her feet. She'd changed
out of her normal work wear into a jumper,
maternity jeans and trainers before they'd left
the office. She wanted to be comfortable.

'I will,' she said as she slid her hand into his.
They walked slowly, first through a dazzling
tunnel of tiny white lights that took them part
way around the gardens. Then to look at the
front of the building, where a multicoloured
display was ongoing.

Different parts of the building lit up at different intervals. With all the paths in the gar-

dens lit up in a timed manner that made them look as if they streamed off the building like a flood of water.

Then the lights changed again and they seemed like flashing fireworks instead of streaming water and Clem could hear the gasps of the crowd around her. She leaned into Leo, happy to watch the display in all its glory.

There was a carnival with an old-fashioned merry-go-round with horses bobbing up and down. There was a helter-skelter that neither one of them was willing to try.

The trail through the event was just over three kilometres and took them two hours to walk slowly around. There were lots of pit stops. Food trucks for hot chocolate and snacks, entertainers for children and adults with areas to sit and watch, and lots of guides to tell the visitors more about the gardens and their purpose.

The night seemed magical. She could see the occasional glance in their direction, mainly from women gazing admiringly, enviously, at Leo. She understood completely. With his dark wool coat and striped scarf around his neck he would definitely have caught her eye if she hadn't already been with him.

And the best part of it all was how she felt

around him. Leo never glanced at anyone else, or looked in any person's direction but hers. He focused his full attention on her comfort and happiness.

This relationship was still brand new. Neither one of them had mentioned any possibility of Leo moving out, now the secure system was in place, and she was glad. She wanted him to stay. She liked him being around her.

She still wondered how committed he might be as she reached the final stages of pregnancy. Leo—although they hadn't ever really discussed it—had been a player in the past. His relationships with a succession of beautiful, glamorous women had rarely lasted more than a month or so. He could, quite literally, have any woman he wanted. What would happen to them once a baby was in the mix?

She tried to push her doubts away.

'Feeling the magic of Christmas yet?' she asked.

'You're beginning to wear me down,' he admitted.

'At last,' she said, just as his phone buzzed. He took it out of his pocket, stared at it, and slid it back in.

'Who was that?'

'My mother.' He looked slightly annoyed.

'Does she know you're staying with me yet? Will I feel the pins going into my voodoo doll any time soon?' Clem was doing her best to joke about it. But she knew his family were unlikely to approve of them dating. Could she blame them? Her hand rested on her stomach. If this child was a boy and she jumped years into the future—would she want her son to tell her he was seeing someone who was already pregnant with another man's baby? Truth was…probably not. But she hated the way that must make Leo feel.

'No one in my family has any say in the matter,' he said firmly.

She reached up and touched his face. 'Family matters, Leo. I know that. Please don't fight with them about me.'

Leo closed his eyes for a few seconds and let out a big sigh as he hugged her closer. 'Let me deal with them,' he said.

Clem was struggling to find the right words. People always said that when a woman was pregnant, hormones could change things for her. So, she hadn't been sure if she could rely on how she was feeling about Leo. The attraction and flirtation had been there since day one. But right now? She didn't want to expose herself to potential heartbreak if he decided he wanted to walk away.

Had she been an absolute fool to invite him to be her birth partner? She'd seen some of the social media posts about men never looking at their partners in the same way after they'd given birth. Had she put them on course to destroy their relationship just as it was beginning?

'I'm just scared your family will think I'm taking advantage of you—and that's the last thing I want to do.'

He let out a deep laugh. 'Clem, I'm nearly twenty-nine. I'm not stupid. I've been around the block a few times. What my family wants for me and what I want are two very different things.' He looked at her again, and she could see the affection in his eyes. 'And now we've discussed where we stand, I know what we want.' He took a breath. 'What we've had from the beginning has just been…different. In a good way.'

He paused for a second. 'Is it the storybook way for a relationship to start? Probably not. But that doesn't mean that it's wrong.'

She could feel the heat of affection flooding through her body. This was what she'd wanted to hear, wasn't it? This was different. And she hoped he meant different from all his previous relationships. But something was still holding her in place. Part of her wanted to say this was fate. That they were meant to meet. They were meant to get together. But a tiny part of her, deep down, still felt fear.

Fear that Leo didn't really want to commit long-term to this relationship, no matter what he said right now, and fear that she and her baby would eventually end up alone.

'You're right, we might not be traditional, but that doesn't mean we are wrong.' She stood on her tiptoes to initiate the kiss, wrapping her arms around his neck and holding on tight.

She wanted to stay in this moment. Just her and Leo, in a beautiful place, wrapped up in their own little world.

She didn't want to think about everything that came next, she wanted to enjoy the remaining weeks of her pregnancy and her life before the baby arrived.

'I just want to have fun these next few weeks,' she whispered in his ear.

'Don't worry,' he replied. 'Leave it all to me.'

'You good with this?' Leo asked a few days later as Clem raised her head to look at the structure above her.

She rested her hands on her stomach. He'd noticed she'd started to do this more and more. 'I've never been on the London Eye before,' she admitted.

'Well, tonight is your night,' he replied, 'and don't worry. I've organised seats and treats for us.'

The attraction itself had a whole array of lights that zipped around the wheel. Multicoloured to begin with, and then white lights like shooting stars, followed by a mixture of gold, green and red for Christmas.

They filed on when it was their turn and settled themselves in the chairs that had been included in the pods for the night-time view of London. Leo poured them some alcohol-free champagne to sip as the pod door closed and they started to move.

As the pod climbed slowly upwards, all of London was spread out before them. The rest of the South Bank was lit up in time with the lights in the wheel, showing more red, green and gold.

The white lights of the Houses of Parliament and Big Ben were visible, alongside the glimmering Shard, which had its own dazzling display going on.

Further down the Thames river they could

see the illuminated Tower Bridge in white and blue, looking quite spectacular.

'This is fantastic,' breathed Clem as she looked around, then she gave him a wink. 'Do you know what would make it even more spectacular?' she asked.

Leo smiled at her. 'Why do I instantly know I might not like this?'

'Because you can read my mind.' She laughed, then stood up and twisted her chair a little. 'There, now I can put up my feet.'

He knew, without her even saying it, as she slipped off her shoes and lifted her feet onto his lap. 'Who says the last few months of pregnancy aren't sexy?' he teased.

'Oh, I do,' she replied quickly as she took a deep breath. 'Ah, that's better.'

Leo reached down and touched her ankle that was covered in thick black tights. 'Are your feet sore?'

'No, well, yes, a little. My ankles and my feet are a bit puffier than normal, which makes my shoes feel a bit tight.'

He frowned. 'Do you want to stop and get some new shoes?'

She shook her head. 'They get worse during the day, so night-time is the puffiest. I'm sure this is entirely normal in pregnancy. I knew buying a new wardrobe would be on the cards, but didn't realise that included new shoes, too.' She looked down at her ankles and twisted them in his lap. 'Doesn't really make sense to buy shoes I'll only wear for a few weeks.'

He looked down. To be honest, because she had thick black tights on, he couldn't really notice any difference in her feet or ankles. 'We can get you shoes if you need them. There's no point being uncomfortable.'

She gave a shrug. 'It's fine. I'm seeing the midwife next week. I'll ask her if it's normal then.'

'Do you want to change our plans for Saturday? We were going to go to the Christmas markets but could stay home instead?'

She looked a bit offended. 'Leo, I'm only at thirty-three weeks. I'm not going to spend the next seven weeks sitting about doing nothing. I'm staying on at work until Christmas, and then I will have a few weeks off until the baby comes.'

She pulled her feet down and sat forward, giving a groan. 'Imagine if my baby decides to hold out until the full forty-two weeks and doesn't actually come until Valentine's Day. Now, that would make me seriously cranky.'

He lifted his glass to her. 'You mean you're not cranky now?'

She swatted his arm. 'I'm sure this is the point you're supposed to be nice to me. In fact, from here on in, I'm pretty sure you should just agree with everything I say.' Her gaze flicked sideways and she pointed. 'Look, isn't that Buckingham Palace? It's lit up too.' She screwed up her eyes and moved closer to the glass for a better look. 'Maybe I'm going to need glasses in the future too. That seems so far away.'

'Because it is,' he said simply. 'You don't need glasses. It's more than a mile away.'

She leaned back and sighed. 'I'm glad we've done this. I've always wondered what it would be like.'

He gave her a wink and kissed her cheek. 'How much more can we fit in across the next few weeks?'

'Let's find out.' She grinned back.

'What do you mean you missed the midwife appointment?' Leo asked with a frown.

'I haven't missed it, I just changed it to next week instead.'

'Are you allowed to do that?'

Clem's brow wrinkled. 'Of course, I am.

She just wants to routinely check my blood pressure and urine. When I phoned the surgery to change it, they said as long as I book another appointment within the next week that would be fine. If my midwife was concerned, she would phone me.'

Leo leant one hand on the desk. 'But don't you need to tell her about your puffy ankles?'

'You heard what they said at the antenatal classes—everyone can get tired at the end and have puffy ankles. Haven't you noticed I'm turning into a whale?'

'You are not,' he said quickly, kneeling alongside her. 'But please don't change your appointments because of work. You have to look after yourself and the baby.'

She rolled her eyes. 'It's one appointment. That client could only do the video call at that day and time.'

He sighed. 'You just need to be firmer and tell them it doesn't suit you.'

'Are you telling me how to do my job?' she asked, tilting her head to the side in a way that Leo knew would be dangerous for him.

'I'm telling you that I'm very grateful for all the work that you do, but, at this stage, I want you to put your needs first.'

She put her hands on her belly. 'Leo, I'm

fine. We're fine. I'll see the midwife next week. Don't worry.' Then she waved a hand. 'I won't be here in a few weeks, so let me finish up what I can.'

He bent down and kissed her cheek. 'If you insist.'

Saturday appeared all too quickly and Clem bundled up in her warm clothes. The temperature in London had dropped rapidly resulting in a few days of snow. 'We're going to have a white Christmas,' she said excitedly. 'I should have put a bet on it. They won't take one now—not when it's already snowed.'

'You'd put a bet on?' he asked, clearly amused.

'Not serious betting,' she said. 'But silly betting. Like it being a white Christmas, or who the next James Bond might be.'

Leo shook his head. 'Every day I learn something new about you.'

'I like to keep a bit of mystery,' she teased, heading to the front door. She turned just as they went to leave. 'You do understand that the whole purpose of visiting a Christmas market is to buy Christmas tat?'

'Christmas what?' asked Leo in horror.

'Tat,' she replied, heading down the steps

while he turned on the new alarm. 'Some people might call it rubbish, but I believe anything connected to Christmas can be found a place in our home.'

'*Our home?*' He smiled.

She climbed into the car. 'You know what I mean.'

The words should make him feel warm and fuzzy inside, but they both knew that the town house wasn't really their home. Would it have unsettled him if she'd moved into his penthouse? Maybe not so much. But he was aware the penthouse wasn't the most suitable place to bring up a child.

Then his head started spinning. Should he have asked Clem if she wanted to look for a place of their own? Maybe. But was that also rushing things? It was all still very new.

It did make him uncomfortable staying rent-free in a home that neither of them owned. He hadn't even met Audrey, and yet he felt as if he was taking advantage of the older woman. She might come back from Spain, decide she hated Leo, and throw him out. Yes, his brain was working overtime.

He started the car and they drove through London to the Christmas market where they parked a few streets away. The market was in full flow, it was crowded and busy, and seemed to have attracted a lot of visitors.

There were numerous stalls with Christmas foods from around the world to sample, around two hundred craft stalls selling things that Clem declared could be considered Christmas tat but she liked it all.

She picked up a few more ornaments for the tree—despite them not being part of her colour scheme. They watched a show put on by entertainers and based on Christmas traditions from Norway. They found a book stall, with beautifully wrapped books—all Christmas themed—and learned that in Iceland it was a tradition to give a book on Christmas Eve.

'Don't you love that? I think I want to start doing that,' said Clem as she dug through a huge pile of books.

Leo leaned over to join her as his phone sounded. It was his mother, and this time he answered. 'Everything okay?'

'I came by your place and you're not home.'

Leo froze. 'You're in London, Mamma? Why didn't you tell me?'

He hadn't actually broken it to his mother that he'd moved in with Clem. 'I'm only here for a few days, and I wanted to see you.'

He knew exactly how this was going to go.

He looked at Clem's face. She was still looking through all the books—thoroughly happy. He wasn't going to spoil that. 'Sorry, I'm at the Christmas market with Clem and I have something else planned this afternoon. I can meet you tomorrow.'

'Tomorrow?' His mother sounded annoyed.

'Well, you should have told me you were coming and I would have made plans with you. Showing up unannounced isn't really a thing in the adult world, Mamma.'

He heard her suck in an outraged breath, but he wasn't going to be guilted into rushing over there. His mother was an expert in emotional manipulation.

'I'm a twenty-eight-year-old man who could have all sorts of plans. Juliette is exactly the same. If I'd been sitting at home twiddling my thumbs, you would want to know why.'

'Is something going on? Your place is extremely tidy.'

'You're inside my penthouse?' His voice rose and Clem turned to stare at him. He tried to keep calm.

'Of course, I'm inside,' she said. 'Your very nice doorman let me in.'

'Aren't you staying in a hotel?'

The family didn't own property in London

and his mother usually stayed in her favourite boutique hotel when she was visiting.

'Well, of course. But just where are you staying, as it doesn't look like it's here?'

He shifted on his feet. This wasn't the place he wanted to have this conversation, and it was clear now that Clem was listening.

'I'm staying in Kensington with Clem.'

'You are?' This time it was his mother's pitch that rose.

'I am,' he said, refusing to go into any explanation that might make it look as if he were justifying himself.

'And when were you going to tell me that?' Her voice was clipped.

'When it was appropriate.'

'Everything okay?' Clem appeared at his shoulder, holding two books in her hands. He could tell from her face she knew who he was talking to.

'Everything's fine,' he reassured her. 'Mamma, I have to go. I'll call you tomorrow.'

His mother went off then, speaking in rapid Italian about the plans she had on Sunday and how she'd expected to see him today. He gave a short apology. 'Sorry, you should have called ahead of time. I'll see you next week, then.'

'Trouble in Italian paradise?' asked Clem.

He frowned, not quite understanding the phrase. She waved her hand. 'Don't worry, it would take too long to explain. Do you need to go and see your mother?'

He shook his head and wrapped his arm around her waist. 'I do not. She's shown up unexpectedly, and will just need to wait until I'm free.'

Clem swallowed and bit her bottom lip. 'I sense another black mark for me.'

He kissed her cheek. 'That's nothing for you to worry about. Trust me.'

He paid for her books and they continued through the market, stopping to eat cream cakes and drink hot chocolate in a café at the market, and then moving off to watch some of the activities that had been set up for families. There were children's rides, a few entertainers and a Christmas choir.

It was still cold, and Clem leaned in next to him as they listened to the choir, made up of people of all ages and nationalities singing a variety of Christmas songs, some carols, some pop songs, and most of the crowd joined in.

He forgot about the time until he sensed a little sway from Clem. It brought him to his senses quickly. 'Are you okay?'

'Bit tired,' she admitted. 'I'd like to sit down.'

He gave a nod, cursing himself for not keeping a closer eye on her. 'I have the perfect place,' he told her as he led her back to the car.

Clem's eyes widened as they drew up to the Ritz. 'We're going here?' She looked down at her clothes. 'I don't think I'm dressed for it.'

'It's afternoon tea,' Leo said easily. 'And what you are wearing is fine.'

A uniformed valet appeared to take their car, opening the door for Clem first, and then Leo. The car disappeared as the concierge showed them inside.

They were shown through to a beautiful room with a wide array of tables covered in white linen tablecloths. They were handed a menu with a wide range of teas, which the waiter was happy to explain further and give recommendations on, and, after they had ordered, he brought plates of different varieties of delicious sandwiches. Clem sighed as she took her first sip of tea and leaned back into her chair. 'This is lovely,' she whispered.

Then a tiny pang of guilt hit her. 'Maybe I should have gone back home for a lie-down and let you bring your mum here instead.'

Leo shook his head. 'I would never live it down if I brought my mum here. My sister would…' he looked up as if searching for the right word '…eviscerate me.'

Clem laughed. 'Okay, then.' She leaned forward and whispered, 'I do recognise a few faces in here.'

He glanced around, clearly recognising nobody. 'The same kind of people who were at the jewellery opening.'

She shook her head. 'There's an author in the corner. I think she's doing a book signing somewhere in London tomorrow. And there's an English actor over there with, I think, his daughter?'

Leo tried to discreetly look and nodded. 'Ah, I remember him being in a few films.' He raised his eyebrows. 'So, what you're telling me is we have a better class of celebrity in here.'

'I think so,' she agreed, reaching for one of the sandwiches.

The setting really was gorgeous. There was quiet music in the background and a real ambience around them. Their waiter was attentive without being too much, and there was a beautiful aroma from the fresh flowers sitting on all the tables.

Once they'd finished the sandwiches, scones

appeared with jam and cream and another plate with pastries and mini cakes.

'Thank you,' she said to Leo in a low voice.

'You're welcome. I just wanted you to have some quiet time before things go crazy.'

'With Christmas, or with the baby?'

'Both,' he said simply. 'How are things going with your parents?'

Clem pulled a face. 'I'm glad that Dad is here. It's given me a chance to get to know him again. But I can't help feeling that the old attraction is still there between my parents.' She sighed and shrugged her shoulders. 'But then I feel like a five-year-old fool. Doesn't every child with split-up parents want them to get back together?'

'Probably,' he agreed. 'Isn't it a bit quick for your mum?'

Clem raised her eyebrows and pointed at her stomach. 'Isn't it a bit quick for us, too?'

There was a crease in his brow. 'Probably, but you said that you and Tyler had already split up, that it was time to say goodbye. And if that's the way you felt deep down, it likely makes you more ready to move on.'

Clem nodded for a second. 'And I wonder if that's true for my mum as well. Don't get me wrong, Hugo was a wonderful stepdad and I loved him and don't doubt that he loved my mum or me. But I never really saw much of a spark.' She gave Leo a bashful grin. 'You know, that thing that we had, right from the beginning?'

She took another sip of tea. 'From the way she and my dad talk about each other, I think it's still there between them, though.'

'I'm still stuck on the spark.' Leo was grinning at her across the table, making her feel like the only person in the room.

That made her skin tingle. Those deep brown eyes were hypnotic. She didn't even care that other people in the room were probably looking at the handsome Italian who looked like some kind of model, wondering why he was currently sitting across from a heavy-lidded, half-asleep woman who resembled a beached whale. She just wanted to happily wallow in his attention.

There were too many things to fret about. His mother's phone calls. The fact he'd just told his mum they were living together. How easily things seemed to annoy her these days. How tired she was. Her ugly swollen cankles. The pieces of work she wanted to get finished in the next three weeks so she could finally breathe, and start to enjoy her maternity leave.

Her fear she was taking maternity leave too early, and her baby might decide to hang on in there until February. The simple thing that most of her maternity wear couldn't possibly stretch much more. The list seemed endless.

So, to sit in these beautiful surroundings, with the most gorgeous man she knew, and sip piping-hot tea and eat delicious cakes wasn't exactly a hardship.

Except, she still wasn't quite sure about Leo, either. What if he changed his mind? What if, after the allotted one or two months he usually spent with a woman, he grew bored of her and the thought of being around a new baby? That actually made her stomach ache. Then there was the fact he hadn't told his mother yet they were pretty much already living together. Was it because he knew she would object? Or was it because he didn't see this as serious enough to tell his family? Yes, she had far too many thoughts spinning around in her brain.

She didn't want to focus on any of that—not today. She wanted to think about their chemistry. The way his smile could make her skin tingle.

She took a breath. 'I like the spark too,' she said to Leo, sitting a little more forward and leaning towards him. 'What are our plans for the rest of the day?'

'Whatever you want,' he said easily.

'Really?'

He nodded. 'Of course.'

She smiled. 'Well, since it's freezing outside, I'd like to pick up some vegetables on the way home and some crusty bread, so we can make soup.'

Leo couldn't hide the surprised expression on his face. He gave a slow nod, but she had a glint in her eye and waggled her finger back and forth between them. 'See how I said we?'

He gave a little laugh. He knew exactly where this was going.

He pointed to his chest. 'Did the "we" actually mean me?'

'That's what I like about you best,' she said. 'You get all the hidden messages.'

She settled back a little, trying to push any doubts about Leo away. He still had to go through the Christmas Day hurdle of meeting her parents. Most men would want to run very fast the other way. But Leo hadn't been like that at all. Maybe he was relieved not to be spending Christmas Day with his own family, in case they started pushing introductions with someone else more suitable on him.

She could only pray that both her mum and her dad would approve of him. She hadn't exactly given them much detail. Just that he was her boss, they liked each other a lot and were living together now.

Oh, of course they'd asked questions. But Clem wanted to wait for them both to see her and Leo together. Hopefully that would reassure them and make everything good. Life would be difficult if they didn't like him, but she couldn't think of one reason for them not to like her choice.

Leo called the waiter over, settling the bill and leaving a generous tip. By the time they reached the front door, the valet had their car waiting for them.

Clem sank into the front seat as Leo drove through the streets of London. 'It's been a wonderful day,' she breathed, closing her eyes for a moment.

'It's only going to get better,' he said. 'Wait until you taste my minestrone soup. You'll want it for the rest of your life.'

Just like you, she thought as she decided it might be time for a little nap. 'Can't wait,' she sighed in pleasure, and she kept her eyes closed for the rest of the journey.

CHAPTER NINE

CLEM SIGHED. She felt like a lumbering giant.
Thirty-four and a bit weeks. Six or maybe even
eight still to go. Her flat shoes were pinch-
ing and she didn't like it. She liked even less
the fact that the buttons on her blouse were
pulling. Unprofessional at best. She'd need to
nip out at lunch time and buy another size up
again.

She organised her desk, putting her proj-
ects in piles and prioritising them accordingly. Then she stretched her back and made
a coffee. Her head was twinging a little so she
grabbed some paracetamol and started to get
to work.

Her phone rang a few hours later and when
she answered it was her midwife.

'You moved your appointment last week.'

'I know, but I've made one for Thursday.'

'Yes, I've seen that. Last time I saw you,

your ankles were a bit swollen. Are they still the same, or are they worse?'

Clem paused and decided to be truthful. 'Maybe a bit worse.'

'Okay, in here today at two o'clock. I want to check you over.'

'It can't wait until Thursday?'

'No, Clem, it can't. It's probably nothing, but I like to keep an eye on my mums, particularly towards the end of their pregnancy.'

Clem nodded. 'Okay, see you then.'

She looked at her desk. She could get part of the first project finished today and tomorrow. She could even take some work home with her tonight. That would make up for the time she'd need to take for her midwife appointment today.

A cup of tea landed on her desk and she looked up to see Lisa looking at her with her arms folded. 'You okay?'

Clem frowned. 'What is it? Do I give off a homing signal or something?'

Lisa raised her eyebrows and Clem shook her head. 'I'm tired, that's all. The midwife just phoned to bring forward my next appointment. I'm seeing her at two.'

'Good,' said Lisa. 'I'll get your lunch for

you. I want to make sure you eat before you go across London for your appointment.'

'You are such a fusspot,' Clem said with a smile, but absolutely grateful.

Leo had been on a call since seven a.m., and she hadn't had a chance to tell him yet. But it would be fine. He would offer to come with her but she preferred to attend the midwife appointments on her own as it gave her a chance to ask personal questions that she really didn't want to share. He'd already heard enough unsexy stuff at the antenatal classes.

She finished as much work as she could, ate the lunch that Lisa had bought for her, and packed up her laptop to take home after her appointment.

Leo's office door was ajar, which meant he must have got out of his meeting. But as she went to push it fully open, she heard his phone ring. Normally, that wouldn't have stopped her, but as the first words out of his mouth were 'Hello, Mamma', she paused.

And it was immediately clear she was the main topic of conversation. It would have been so much easier to walk away if Leo hadn't flicked his phone onto speakerphone.

'Why are you still dating this girl? And

what are you doing moving in with someone who is pregnant with some other man's baby?'

'This girl has a name. You know it, you've met her. Clementine. And I've moved in with her because I wanted to.'

'You hardly know her. It's been no time at all. You're a young man. You should be thinking of having a family of your own, not looking after someone else's.'

Leo didn't even get a chance to speak before his mother continued. 'And what if she doesn't really love you? What if her big attraction is your money and the security that represents?'

Leo sighed. 'Mamma, like I said, you know nothing about her.'

'Neither do you.'

'Yes, yes, I do. I get that it's a bit unusual to have a girlfriend who's pregnant. But you know the story. You know that the father isn't in the picture and isn't ever going to be. I like Clem. If only you would spend more time with her, you would see how good we are together.'

'But what about when this baby comes? How are you going to feel then? A new mum, they want to spend all their time with their new baby. It's entirely natural. She'll be tired, she won't sleep, the baby will cry. You'll have sleepless nights, many of them. All the romance, all the glamour will be gone. You'll both come to earth with a bump.'

'Isn't that what happens to every couple when a baby comes along? And Clem's tired already and not sleeping well. I can help her with the baby. We can take turns. Her mum and dad might help too.'

Her mother made a clicking sound, which Clem presumed was a sound of dissatisfaction. 'But what about her family? She hasn't exactly had the best example in that respect, has she? They split up when she was young, didn't they? Her father doesn't even stay here. He lives on the other side of the world. What if she decides she wants to take her baby to Australia to be with her father?'

'Mamma? Where is all this coming from? She's not going to move to Australia. She has a job here, with me. That's where she's going to stay.'

'You have blinkers on,' said his mother sharply. 'You seem to think you're some kind of knight in shining armour for this girl. What happens if you change your mind after the baby is here? You walk away and just carry on with your life? You haven't thought this through properly. You could actually really hurt her. Better to rethink things now, before you reach that stage.'

'I don't need to rethink things.' His voice was stiff, and even though Clem couldn't see him, she could tell his jaw was clenched. 'I'm not going to change my mind.'

Clem gripped the wall. She was feeling a little dizzy. This woman seemed to absolutely hate her.

'What about Caroline?' asked his mother. 'You know that she's just split up from her latest boyfriend? You were such a perfect couple. Maybe a little too young to commit, that's all. Now? With a few years behind you both, this could be exactly the right time. You're both from good Italian families. You could have such beautiful babies together. It would be a perfect union. Why don't you give her a call?'

Who the hell was Caroline? And why on earth was his mother bringing her up now?

Leo sounded weary. 'No, I hadn't heard about Caroline, and yes, she's a perfectly nice girl. But I'm not going to marry her. We weren't in love with each other then, and I doubt we would be now, either.'

'Really?' asked his mother. 'You don't have a single doubt in your head about this Clementine? Because that wouldn't be normal. You must have.'

There was a small silence. Clem's stomach did an unpleasant flip, and it was nothing to do with the baby.

It was the pause.

His mother seized the advantage. 'Leo, you are my only son. I want you to be happy. I don't want you to make any mistakes. This girl? If you tell me that she's it for you, then I will be happy for you, and I will treat her like family. But when this baby comes—are you completely sure you're going to love it like you should? What if the baby looks like their father? What if the baby has lots of their father's traits, and as they grow, that's all you can see—a reminder that they are not actually yours. And what if, a few years down the track, you marry Clem and have children of your own? Have you thought it through? What if you love your own natural child more than you love the child that Clem has had?'

His mother's voice took on a pleading tone. 'Because you can't do that, Leo. It would be wrong, it would be so wrong. All children in a family deserve equal love. You've seen what happens in some families. It destroys them. You have to be sure. You have to be completely sure that you can love that child as if it were your own. Have you thought about that? Have you really thought about that?'

Clem's skin was cold. She suspected Leo hadn't thought about it, because she hadn't thought about it either, and now she was terrified. Terrified he wouldn't love her child.

She'd just assumed when her baby popped out, they'd both love it. And that would be it.

But it looked as though Leo's mother had thought about this a whole lot more than they had. She couldn't believe that, with the list of worries she already had, this one hadn't found its way onto that list. Or at least before now.

But the worst part was, Leo still wasn't speaking.

She leaned against the wall, willing the ache in her head and the horrible feeling in her chest to disappear.

The pause continued, each second of it breaking Clem's heart.

Deep down, had she always known that Leo was too good to be true? That Prince Charming didn't exist in real life and she'd just been a fool for a handsome face?

Her hands started to shake and she willed herself to pull it together. She heard Leo stand up, grabbing the phone and beginning to pace the room.

She wasn't going to hear anything else, but she didn't need to.

She pushed open the door fully and stared at him.

He froze. Instantly realising she must have heard all, or at least part of, the conversation.

'Clem,' he started, but she raised her hand.

'I'm going to see the midwife, and I'm taking my laptop to finish some work at home later.' She didn't need to say any more, and wouldn't have been able to find the words. He was her boss, and as her boss he needed only the briefest of personal details.

'Wait,' he said. 'I'll take you—'

She cut him off dead. 'That is the last thing I want you to do.' Her voice was ice cold; she just couldn't help it. 'And I'd be obliged if you could stay at your own place tonight.'

He frowned and his mouth opened again, ready to start with a whole host of words she didn't feel equipped to deal with. She held up her hand again, 'Leave it,' was all she could say as she walked out of his office.

She picked up her bag and walked straight to the elevator, which was waiting with open doors.

She kept herself upright and steely as the doors slid shut in front of her face. It was only when the elevator began the quiet hum of descent that she finally let go.

Leo was shell-shocked. Not really by his mother. More by himself.

He hated it. He hated it that when she'd asked those questions about the baby he'd stopped to think, even for a second. And of course, he hadn't known that Clem was listening, but that shouldn't have mattered.

Clem. He couldn't imagine how she was feeling right now. But he hadn't really had a chance to explain things to her, or to talk things through. If he was totally honest, there had been a few doubts in his mind at times.

Would it be easier if Clem weren't having another man's baby? Of course it would be. Had he supported her from the beginning? Yes. Had he still been attracted to her? Yes.

Did that make him the bad guy? Maybe, but he was only human.

Should he have waited until after she'd had the baby and she'd returned to work, to see how things might be between them—if the spark was still there?

But being around Clem without reacting

to her was hard. He couldn't have pretended he wasn't interested in her. He was. He loved being with her. But that didn't mean that he expected things to be plain sailing under the circumstances.

In one way, he'd honestly thought that when the baby came, he would naturally love it. But was that idealistic? Maybe he was a fool who hadn't thought it through carefully enough. It could be that his mother was entirely correct. Not about being with Clem, but about taking the time to think things through properly.

He hated that. The last thing he wanted was his mother to think she was right.

He stopped pacing and tried to be rational. Wait. Clem's appointment with the midwife was on Thursday. Why was she going today?

He walked through to the general office. Lisa was scowling at him. It was likely she'd heard part of the conversation between him and Clem.

'What happened? Why did Clem change her midwife appointment?'

Lisa folded her arms and he could almost swear she was going to tell him to ask Clem herself, but instead she glared at him. 'The midwife phoned because she'd rescheduled.

She asked her a few questions and said she wanted to see her today.'

'Is Clem not well? She hasn't said anything.'

Now he got the giant eye-roll. 'You were on a call all morning.'

'What's wrong with her?'

More eye-rolling. 'You live with her. Haven't you noticed how tired she looks? The ankle swelling? I even thought she sounded a bit breathless this morning.'

Leo felt sick. He had noticed some of it, but had thought it was all normal towards the end of pregnancy, and he said so.

Lisa shrugged. 'Well, her midwife was wise enough to call her today. That's why she's gone.'

'Do you think something's wrong?'

Lisa paused for a moment. There wasn't anyone else he could ask, and Lisa had three children of her own.

'I'm not sure,' she admitted.

'Should I go?'

Another glare. 'I'm pretty sure she told you to stay away. You don't want to cause her any more stress—that's the last thing she needs.'

Leo strode back through to his office while his mind spun in circles. He didn't want to stay away, but would he make things worse for her if he went?

He took a few deep breaths. He thought about what his mother had said about walking away at a later date. About the damage that would do. He thought about the years ahead and if there was a possibility he could love any potential biological children that he and Clem might have more than any child that could be born now.

That made him cringe. It was horrible to even consider it. But he knew for some families it was a reality. He'd witnessed it amongst some of his friends whose mothers had remarried. Was he really that kind of person? He hoped not. He didn't imagine for one second that he would be, but could he guarantee it? Could anyone in the world guarantee anything?

But over and above everything he had to hold true to who he was. He had been brought up with a strong family experience and belief. She had that too. Clem had experienced a good life with her mum and Hugo and was looking to rebuild her relationship with her own father. She had just as much a core belief in solid family connections as he did.

Sure, families had problems. But as much

as he loved his family—would he be prepared to walk away from them if his mother didn't accept Clem and her baby? Yes, he decided, he absolutely would.

Because he loved Clem. Every part of her. And he wanted to spend the rest of his life with her.

And, as part of her, he was convinced that he would love this baby just as much as he loved her. It was as if someone had flicked a switch in his head to clear the fog, and how he felt was now front and central, and clearer than ever.

They would create their own family, together, and it would be as strong as any other. He could feel that, deep down inside.

Would things always be perfect? No, he wasn't delusional. But love mattered. And he loved Clem. Every single part of her, including this baby.

What if Tyler's parents didn't like him or the fact that Clem had moved on? He was an adult. He could navigate that situation. These were parents that had lost a child, after all. But they still had a grandchild on the way, and he could imagine they would want those links to remain strong.

He had thought everything through. He was

as prepared as he could be for the long haul. Leo sighed and ran his fingers through his hair. He pressed the button on his desk. 'I'm leaving early. I don't want any work calls. Anything that crops up will just have to wait until tomorrow.'

There was a noise of acknowledgement.

He grabbed his jacket and headed to the elevator. He knew exactly what he wanted to do. He had to convince Clem that they had the ability to create this life together and spend the next fifty years working at it, surrounded by love.

But first, he had one little stop to make.

Clem sat down in the hospital waiting room, sweat running down her back from the Tube journey, with the little bottle of pee in her hand after squeezing it out. Her headache was getting steadily worse and she just wanted to lie down and go to sleep. Her heart was pounding in her chest and she undid her jacket, hoping to cool down and breathe a bit easier.

She felt funny. And she wasn't sure why. Oh, sure, she might burst into tears as soon as she saw her midwife, but that wasn't just about Leo. Actually, she could push the Leo stuff aside and worry about all that later, because right now…she just didn't feel…right.

'Clementine Grayson, room 5,' said the electronic voice in the outpatient department.

Clem shrugged off her coat and walked through, pushing open the door to room 5. Rose, her midwife, was finishing off on the computer.

She turned to Clem, gave her what could only be described as a suspicious glance and said, 'Take a seat.'

Clem set the little bottle of pee down and sagged into the chair.

Rose's gaze narrowed. 'I can hear a bit of a wheeze. You sound a bit breathless. Do you have asthma?'

Clem shook her head. Rose lifted the bottle. 'Give me a second.' She put on some gloves and put a little dipstick in the urine, closing the lid and balancing the stick on top of the lid.

'On second thoughts, Clem, why don't you lie up on the couch? I want to have a feel of baby.'

Clem groaned; having to get up again was a pain.

She moved up onto the couch, pulling up her legs and letting them thump down.

Rose was over in moments. She moved

swiftly, checking her blood pressure, taking bloods, getting her to slip off her tights so she could examine her ankles, all while asking a barrage of questions and then recording a few things on the computer.

She moved back over to glance at the strip again, then washed her hands and asked Clem to pull up her jumper so she could feel baby.

Clem was slightly uncomfortable and flinched even though Rose's hands were gentle.

Rose let her hear the baby's heart rate and that made her feel a bit more relaxed. But two seconds later, Clem sat upright and vomited everywhere.

Rose pressed a buzzer and grabbed some towels to clean her up. Another midwife rushed into the room and Rose nodded towards the urine and the notes on the computer. The other midwife started to take over some of the tasks while Rose held Clem's hand. 'Clem, do you have anyone here with you today?'

Clem shook her head then wished she hadn't. 'No, I just came myself.' Her sense of calm started to disappear. 'Is something wrong?'

Rose looked her in the eye while still holding her hand. 'Your blood pressure is much higher than it should be. You have some albumin in your urine. Do you have a headache?'

Clem nodded.

'How long have you had it?'

Clem pulled a face. 'On and off for a few days. But it's much worse today.'

'And tiredness?'

Clem nodded. 'Much worse in the last few days.'

The other midwife came over and examined Clem's ankles and asked to look at her fingers. 'Was that the first time you've been sick?'

Clem nodded and gave a sigh. 'Do you mind if I lie back down again?'

'Give me two seconds until I listen to your heart and lungs,' said Rose, removing her stethoscope from around her neck, and placing the chest piece on Clem's back, and then her front. Once she'd finished, she went around to the other side of the bed and took her blood pressure from her other arm. 'Any problems with your vision?'

'I don't think so.' Clem was starting to panic. 'What's wrong?'

Rose sat on the edge of the couch. 'Clem, Liv is going to go and get our obstetrician who's on call today,' she said as Liv exited the room. 'You have all the signs of pre-eclampsia. They will come and assess you and decide if you need to deliver this baby sooner than expected.'

Clem's hands went to her stomach automatically. 'But it's too soon.'

Rose nodded. 'Your baby is between thirty-four and thirty-five weeks. Lots of babies are born at this time and are absolutely fine. We can give you a steroid injection to try and bring the baby's lungs on, to help them breathe on their own.'

'Isn't it dangerous? How long does it take to work?'

Rose put her hand on Clem's stomach. 'Let me phone someone to be with you, and then I'll answer all your questions. Do you have a bag with you?'

That simple question floored her. This wasn't a maybe. This was for real. When they asked if you had a bag—it meant you were staying. They weren't going to let you go home. She was going to have this baby early, whether she was ready or not.

There was so much about today to unpick. There hadn't even been a real chance for her to process the sense of betrayal she felt after overhearing Leo's phone call. He'd paused when his mother had asked him about the baby.

It hadn't even *occurred* to her that would be an issue. What kind of a mother would she be if she hadn't taken that into consideration? Maybe she didn't even deserve to be a mother, and this was the world's way of telling her that.

She folded her hands across her stomach and started to cry. 'Am I going to lose the baby?'

Rose put both hands over hers. 'You've heard the baby's heartbeat. Things are okay right now. It's what we do from this point onwards that's important. Who do you want me to phone?'

'My mum,' she said straight away. 'Please phone my mum.'

Her phone buzzed and Rose handed her up her bag. She pulled the phone out.

Can I call you?

It was Leo. She shook her head and stuffed the phone back into her bag. 'It wasn't my mum,' she said.

Liv, who'd come back in, lifted her set of notes. 'I'll go and call her now.'

Clem felt as if she couldn't breathe. She retched again, but didn't have anything left to bring up. Just at that moment, the obstetrician walked into the room. A tall woman, with grey hair. Clem had never met her before, but the woman joined Rose, scanned all the information and touched Clem gently on the shoulder.

'We're going to start by giving you an injection to try and mature your baby's lungs. We will move you around to one of the wards, and monitor you for the next few hours before we make a decision on what comes next.'

She gave Clem a reassuring smile. 'Don't worry, Ms Grayson, we've got this.'

But all Clem could do was cry. She was scared now; she was truly scared. Had she done something wrong to put the baby at risk?

It didn't matter how many times they answered her questions, she'd reached the stage where she couldn't really process the answers. The injection stung, but that was nothing to how every other part of her felt.

Leo was spinning around in her mind. She loved him with everything that was in her. She knew that now. That was why today's betrayal had hurt so much. She'd loved him for far longer than she'd admitted to herself. And while, at times, it had seemed too good to be true, there had also been other times when it had felt just perfect.

Was she a complete and utter fool? She loved a man who had doubts about her, about them, and about her baby. She wrapped her arms around her belly again, holding onto the baby she'd decided to have. There was no going back now. And despite how she'd got here, she wanted this baby more than ever.

Her head felt a little swimmy, and her eyes blurred.

'Your parents are on their way, and they said they've phoned the other grandparents,' said one of the midwives at her side. 'And your partner phoned; he's on his way, too.'

Clem opened her mouth to speak, and it was the last thing she remembered.

Leo would never forget the look on the midwife's face when he said who he was.

'Clementine Grayson's partner?' she confirmed. He nodded as she pointed to another part of the waiting room.

'Clem's parents are over there. And the other grandparents.' He could see her casting him a sideways glance as if she could tell he wasn't related to Tyler's parents. 'You can wait with them.'

'I can't get in to see her?' He was waiting for the midwife to tell him that Clem didn't want to see him, that she never wanted to see him again.

But the midwife didn't say anything of the sort. 'You haven't heard?'

It was a question, but her tone was that of someone who was resigned to telling bad news.

He shook his head and tried to quell the panic in his chest.

'Clem had pre-eclampsia, which rapidly developed into eclampsia. The obstetrician had just transferred her to the ward when she had her first seizure. They took her straight to Theatre to deliver the baby. We are waiting to hear back from them.'

Leo's legs decided to turn to jelly as he held onto the desk. 'Will Clem be okay? Will the baby be okay?'

The woman gave him a sympathetic look. 'I'd like to say yes to both, but we don't actually know right now.' She touched his hand. 'Just be assured that Clem was in exactly the right place when she became unwell. She and the baby will have the best chance possible.'

His heart froze in his chest as the realisation hit him. They could die. Clem and the baby could die. The possibility hadn't even entered his head before this moment and he had to forcibly stop himself from vomiting all over the floor.

He must have looked ill because she nodded over her shoulder. 'There's a room around the corner if you need a few minutes,' she said sympathetically.

His feet moved on automatic pilot. He pushed the door open. The room had pale colours and a dimmer than normal light. Was this the bad news room? Was this where they came to tell you things had gone terribly, horribly wrong?

His breath caught in his throat as he shut the door behind him and whipped out his phone to search for pre-eclampsia, eclampsia and all the possible outcomes.

There was a reason health professionals told you never to search for health conditions online, and it was simple. Because everything immediately became a worst-case scenario.

His heart twisted in his chest as he thought of Clem's parents. What on earth must they be thinking? They must be worried sick. Tyler's parents too. They'd already lost a son; losing a grandchild too would be unimaginable.

He was meant to meet Clem's parents at Christmas. Not like this. Not in a hospital waiting room where they waited to hear of Clem's fate.

Clem and this baby were his future. His

whole future. He didn't want to consider any other options. He knew exactly where he wanted to be, and exactly who he wanted to be with.

He didn't care about all the 'what if' questions that came alongside. His hand went into his pocket, fingering the ring from Pelligrini's that he'd remembered Clem mentioning at the opening. Ricardo had taken him straight to the glittering emerald and diamond engagement ring and told Leo that Clem had spent quite some time admiring it. Leo had already taken it out of the box and was now turning it over and over with his fingers.

All he wanted to do was tell her he loved her, and ask her the most important question.

She could say no, of course she could. Leo knew that. But he could only hope against hope she would hear him out. That she would let him show her, and the baby, just how much he could love them.

Family was important. It would always be important. But now Clem and this baby *were* his family. He took out his phone and made a call. 'Mamma? I'm at the hospital. Clem is very unwell. They've taken her straight to Theatre.'

'What's wrong?' She sounded genuinely concerned.

'Pre-eclampsia, then eclampsia. The baby needs to be delivered today.' He took a breath. 'And the next time I see her, I'm going to ask her to marry me. You asked me today if I'm absolutely sure. I'm telling you that I am. And the next time we speak I expect you to welcome Clem and the baby into the family with open arms.'

He knew his voice was shaking a little with the strength of his emotions. And he knew his mother would hear it. But he was drawing a line in the sand right now. Clem and the baby would be his family going forward, and his mother would simply have to accept that.

There was a noise at the end of the phone and he knew she was crying. 'Is she all right?' his mother asked. 'Is the baby going to be all right?'

'I don't know. I'm waiting to find out.'

'Oh, Leo.' It was a sob of worry and concern. 'Are you going to be all right?'

'I'll be all right as soon as I can see my girl and our baby,' he replied, then hung up.

He took a steadying breath and walked out to the waiting room to see Clem's parents, both with tear-filled eyes, holding hands together. Tyler's parents were right next to them.

These were the people he needed to support. These people were part of his new family.

He straightened up as he walked over and extended his hand. 'Jon? Natalie? I'm Leo Constello, Clem's partner. I'm the man who hopes to marry your daughter.'

CHAPTER TEN

CLEM WOKE FEELING FUZZY. There were unfamiliar noises around her. Beeps. Murmurs. And a quiet voice talking softly.

Her eyelids flickered open. She rubbed them, even that simple act of lifting her arms making her realise something had changed in her body. Parts of her seemed a bit numb.

Her mouth was dry and she gave a little cough. Her hands settled on her stomach. Still big, but not *as* big.

Just as she might have started to panic, she realised who was sitting next to her.

Leo was in a chair, with a little bundle resting on the bare skin of his chest. He was talking and singing. Some of it was in Italian and she couldn't understand a word.

But what she could understand was the look on his face. Pure and utter wonder and adoration.

She felt a pain in her chest. This was her

baby. He was holding her baby, and talking and whispering to it lovingly, as if he were the father.

A whole host of emotions flooded her. What had happened? The last thing she remembered was getting admitted to the ward and being given an injection. Everything after that was a total blank. But from the sight in front of her, she'd missed the most important part.

'Leo?' Her voice came out as a croak and his eyes widened instantly. He looked to the other side of the room and pressed the buzzer next to her bed.

'Clem.' He leaned forward, the baby still tucked against his naked chest. 'You're awake, that's fantastic.'

She watched as tears brimmed in his eyes and trickled down his cheeks.

'What happened?' she croaked as a midwife hurried over and started talking to her. 'Clem, you're awake. That's good news.' The midwife nodded at Leo. 'You gave us a bit of a scare and we had to do an emergency caesarean section after you had a seizure.' She rested her hand on Clem's arm. 'You are fine, and baby is fine. Sometimes things don't go to plan. Baby was looked after in NICU, the neonatal intensive care unit, for a few hours but has managed to feed, and we'll take care of you both now at your bedside until you've fully recovered.'

She hovered her hand over Clem's abdomen. 'So, you have a scar. Are you in any pain right now? We gave you some painkillers earlier.'

Was she in pain? She didn't think so, but she hadn't attempted to move. She shook her head.

'How about a drink of water, and I'll sit you up a bit? You must be dying to see this baby.'

Clem felt tears flood into her eyes and she nodded as the midwife propped her up with pillows and gave her some water to sip.

As the midwife moved away, Leo stood up and moved closer. 'Do you want to see our girl? How beautiful she is?'

'It's a girl?' Clem could hardly get the words out, and she started to sob.

He looked worried, but his voice was calm. 'Do you want to put her skin to skin? That's what they advised me to do earlier.'

She nodded as Leo let her adjust her clothing, and then let the little warm body press against hers. For a few minutes there was no noise. Just Clem taking in her tiny daughter. She had a hint of red in her hair. Perfect fingers and fingernails. And perfect toes. Her cord was clamped and she was dressed in a little white vest and pink woolly hat. 'What happened?' Clem said again.

Leo spoke slowly, repeating what the midwife had said. Then he added, 'The little pink hat came from NICU. Your mum said she'll go and get some tiny clothes once you're awake and she and your dad have seen you.'

'They're both here?'

'Oh yes, and Tyler's parents.' He smiled. 'They've been here the whole time. They saw the baby briefly, but none of them will leave until they've seen you as well.'

She took a breath. 'How long have I been out?'

He paused. 'About eight hours. They said you needed some recovery time and would wake up when you were ready.'

Eight hours. She'd missed the first eight hours of her baby daughter's life. She started to cry again.

'Who called you?' she asked as her brain came back into focus and she remembered that they'd fallen out.

'No one,' he answered easily. 'I just came here after you'd left. I met your mum and dad and Tyler's mum and dad in the waiting room, but as I was still named as your next of kin, I went with our baby to the neonatal unit.'

'So, she wasn't by herself?'

'Absolutely not. I didn't leave her for a second.'

He looked her in the eye. 'Clem, you might have been unhappy with me. But I know you, and I know what matters to you most—whether you're unhappy with me or not. I knew you wouldn't want her to be alone. So, I stayed with her. I love you, Clem. I'm so sorry I didn't tell you before now. I'm a fool, and that's on me. And to answer what you wondered before? I loved this baby too, before she even got here, and even more from the second I saw her. I'd do anything for you both.'

Clem closed her eyes and just breathed, taking in the new scent of her baby. The blanket she was wrapped in smelt a little of Leo too. Was that good, or bad?

A realisation swept over her. His words over the last few minutes. He'd called her *our* girl, *our* baby.

That was a huge jump for a guy who'd paused at a question earlier that day. Then another sensation came over her like a tidal wave. The sense of responsibility. She was a mum now. This little baby was hers to take care of. Hers to protect from the world.

'How can I trust you, Leo? Only a few hours ago your mother had you doubting yourself.'

He shook his head. 'We have to be honest with each other here, Clem, because I don't really think we have been.'

If her heart could stop beating now, it would have.

'I love you and I've been strongly attracted to you from the start. Is this relationship unusual? Of course it is. You were pregnant and your lover had died. But, before I knew that, and before you knew that, there was still an attraction between us. It was there. Right from the beginning. Nothing can change that. Did I have a few moments along the way where I doubted? Yes, I did. But not about you, Clem. Never how I felt about you or the baby.'

He put his hand to his chest. 'About me. Was I good enough to do this? Was I prepared? Could I give you, and our daughter, everything you both needed? I know nothing about babies. What if I made a mistake? What if I got something wrong? But then I realised—doesn't every set of new parents feel like this? Doesn't every couple who plans for a baby have a moment at some point thinking, what have I let myself in for? It's natural. At least, I think it is. Can you honestly tell me that at no point in this pregnancy have you asked your-self if you've been doing the right thing?'

Before she could answer, he pulled a face. 'I'm already questioning decisions I've had to make. Please, don't kill me. But, because you weren't awake, they asked me how our daughter was to be fed. I asked them to give her some donated breast milk. I didn't want to make a decision to give her some kind of formula—'

She held up her hand and looked down at her daughter, who was resting peacefully against her skin. 'That's fine.' Clem took a deep breath and gave a whole-hearted sigh. 'My whole birth plan went out of the win-dow, and everything isn't ready at home. Not to mention I still have work that's unfinished.' She glanced around the room. 'I literally don't have a single thing with me.' She stopped be-fore she let herself be overwhelmed.

'I can get you anything you need. And as for all the rest? Forget about it. All that's im-portant is that you are here, and our baby is fine. I should have noticed. I should have paid more attention to how tired you were. The fact you had swollen ankles.'

She shook her head. 'The person who should have paid more attention to that is me, not you.

I shouldn't have delayed my last midwife appointment.' She stroked her daughter's head. 'I can't believe what I risked.'

She started crying again then, and Leo shifted his position so he was perched on the edge of the bed with his arm around her.

'Maybe we aren't perfect,' he said steadily. 'Maybe we will make lots of mistakes in the future. But the one thing I know is that I want to make them with you.'

She looked up at him. 'I love you too, Leo. And I'm also sorry I wasn't brave enough to tell you that before. But what about the future? What if ten years from now we have another baby, and you feel just like your mother said you might?'

He ran one finger down the baby's face. 'That's never going to happen, Clem. How could it? She stole my heart the first second I saw her. When people ask any parent, how do you know you're going to love your child? The answer is, you don't. It just happens. And, I know, for some people it's different. That they take time to bond with their child, to feel that connection. But for me?' He put his hand on his chest. 'It's there already.' He set his jaw and looked at her. 'And I also know I want to make it official. I want us to be a family. I want us to be for ever.'

She blinked and looked up at him. 'What do you mean?'

He pulled the ring from his pocket. 'A very good friend helped me pick this. He said that the green matches your eyes.'

She let out a gasp. 'Ricardo? You didn't.'

'Of course I did.'

Clem took another breath and waited. 'If you want honesty, then that time is now. I fell in love with you within a few weeks of meeting you. When I discovered I was pregnant I didn't imagine you would want to have a relationship with me. And when you did, it all just seemed so unreal. Like make believe. Like I was actually stuck in some kind of fantastic dream that I would wake up from at any moment.'

She stared into his eyes. 'Things have been rushed between us, and I feel like my pregnancy put extra pressure on us both to commit. Because committing was what I wanted. But I wasn't sure if it was just because my hormones were in flux or if you were always going to be the man I fell in love with, the man I was supposed to meet.'

She took another breath. 'You asked if I

ever doubted myself during this pregnancy. Of course, I did. I just didn't ever want to admit that, because it felt like a betrayal of Tyler, of the baby. I wondered if I'd be strong enough to do this, be a good enough mother to do this. And while you were behind me, I always felt better prepared. But we have to be together because *we* want to be together, Leo. It can't be because we feel pushed into it, or because I was pregnant. I have to know that you are with me for the sole reason that you love me.'

'I do love you,' he insisted. 'But you're wrong. You're part of a package deal, at least for the next eighteen years and more. I love you both. With no doubt, and no hesitation. And I've already told my family, and yours and Tyler's, my intentions. My mother knows that she has to accept you and our daughter with open arms. She knows I won't accept anything less for my wife and daughter.'

'You keep calling her that,' whispered Clem. 'Our daughter.'

He touched the baby's head. 'Because that's how I feel. We are a family. We belong together.' He held up the glittering diamond and emerald ring. 'Clem, will you marry me? Will you let us be the family we deserve to be?'

Another tear slid down her cheek. 'I'd love

to be your wife,' she said, tilting her face up so he could kiss her.

It was a gentle kiss, a tender kiss and one with one hundred per cent intent.

He let out a laugh. 'So, what are we going to call our daughter?'

She smiled. 'Well, you caught me a bit early, but I have a list.'

And now his laughter turned into a roar. 'Of course you have!'

CHAPTER ELEVEN

IN THE END, they were lucky to get home on Christmas Eve. Belle was feeding a treat by then, and even though she was only five and a half pounds, there were no issues.

Natalie and Jon had picked up all the pre-ordered food and taken over the kitchen in the town house as they insisted on cooking dinner. Clem and Leo sat on the sofa together, admiring Belle's every breath and burp.

Leo's family had sent a whole host of flowers, exclusive Italian baby clothes, and Juliette had pulled together a special package of pyjamas, candles and scented toiletries for the new mum. Clem was grateful, but remained a little cautious. She would have to wait and see how things developed.

But what had certainly already developed was the relationship between her mum and dad. Even watching them for the few moments she'd been in the kitchen, she'd seen how they finished each other's sentences and worked in complete synch together.

What lifted her heart most was the spark she could see between them. It was as obvious as the one that existed between her and Leo. It felt like proof that love could last for ever.

Leo sat down beside her and put his arm around her shoulder as she admired her ring yet again. 'Now, Ricardo assured me that, even though you said it was your favourite, he would change it for something else if you preferred.'

She turned her face to her new fiancé. 'Nope, it's perfect.' She stared through to the kitchen at her parents, with the smell of delicious food drifting towards them, then back to her daughter, who was sleeping peacefully in a Christmas romper in the Moses basket. 'In fact,' she said, with a big smile on her face, 'everything is just perfect. So kiss me, and make it even more so.'

And he did.

* * * * *

*If you missed the previous story in the
Family Reunion in London duet,
then check out*

Second Chance Under the Mistletoe
by Kandy Shepherd

*And if you enjoyed this story, check out
these other great reads from Scarlet Wilson*

Hawaiian Kiss with the Brooding Doc
Nurse's Dubai Temptation
Melting Dr. Grumpy's Frozen Heart

All available now!

Get up to 4 Free Books!

We'll send you 2 free books from each series you try PLUS a free Mystery Gift.

FREE Value Over **$25**

Both the **Harlequin® Historical** and **Harlequin® Romance** series feature compelling novels filled with emotion and simmering romance.

YES! Please send me 2 FREE novels from the Harlequin Historical or Harlequin Romance series and my FREE Mystery Gift (gift is worth about $10 retail). After receiving them, if I don't wish to receive any more books, I can return the shipping statement marked "cancel." If I don't cancel, I will receive 5 brand-new Harlequin Historical books every month and be billed just $6.39 each in the U.S. or $7.19 each in Canada, or 4 brand-new Harlequin Romance Larger-Print books every month and be billed just $7.19 each in the U.S. or $7.99 each in Canada, a savings of 20% off the cover price. It's quite a bargain! Shipping and handling is just 50¢ per book in the U.S. and $1.25 per book in Canada.* I understand that accepting the 2 free books and gift places me under no obligation to buy anything. I can always return a shipment and cancel at any time by calling the number below. The free books and gift are mine to keep no matter what I decide.

Choose one: ☐ **Harlequin Historical** (246/349 BPA G36Y)   ☐ **Harlequin Romance Larger-Print** (119/319 BPA G36Y)   ☐ **Or Try Both!** (246/349 & 119/319 BPA G36Z)

Name (please print)

Address   Apt. #

City   State/Province   Zip/Postal Code

Email: Please check this box ☐ if you would like to receive newsletters and promotional emails from Harlequin Enterprises ULC and its affiliates. You can unsubscribe anytime.

> **Mail to the Harlequin Reader Service:**
> **IN U.S.A.:** P.O. Box 1341, Buffalo, NY 14240-8531
> **IN CANADA:** P.O. Box 603, Fort Erie, Ontario L2A 5X3

Want to explore our other series or interested in ebooks? Visit www.ReaderService.com or call 1-800-873-8635.

---

*Terms and prices subject to change without notice. Prices do not include sales taxes, which will be charged (if applicable) based on your state or country of residence. Canadian residents will be charged applicable taxes. Offer not valid in Quebec. This offer is limited to one order per household. Books received may not be as shown. Not valid for current subscribers to the Harlequin Historical or Harlequin Romance series. All orders subject to approval. Credit or debit balances in a customer's account(s) may be offset by any other outstanding balance owed by or to the customer. Please allow 4 to 6 weeks for delivery. Offer available while quantities last.

Your Privacy—Your information is being collected by Harlequin Enterprises ULC, operating as Harlequin Reader Service. For a complete summary of the information we collect, how we use this information and to whom it is disclosed, please visit our privacy notice located at https://corporate.harlequin.com/privacy-notice. Notice to California Residents – Under California law, you have specific rights to control and access your data. For more information on these rights and how to exercise them, visit https://corporate.harlequin.com/california-privacy. For additional information for residents of other U.S. states that provide their residents with certain rights with respect to personal data, visit https://corporate.harlequin.com/other-state-residents-privacy-rights/.

HHHRLP25